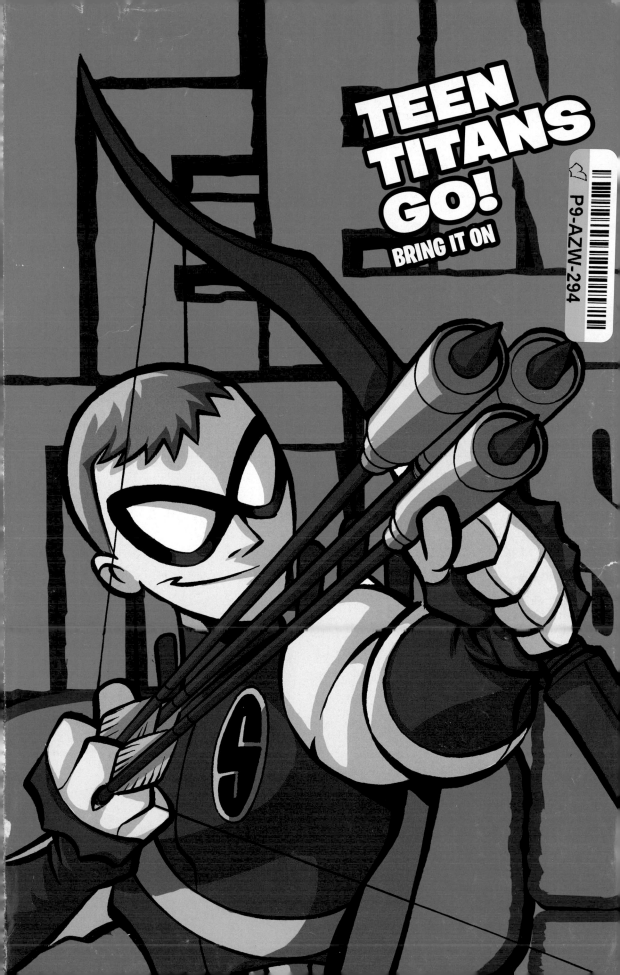

TEEN TITANS GO!
BRING IT ON

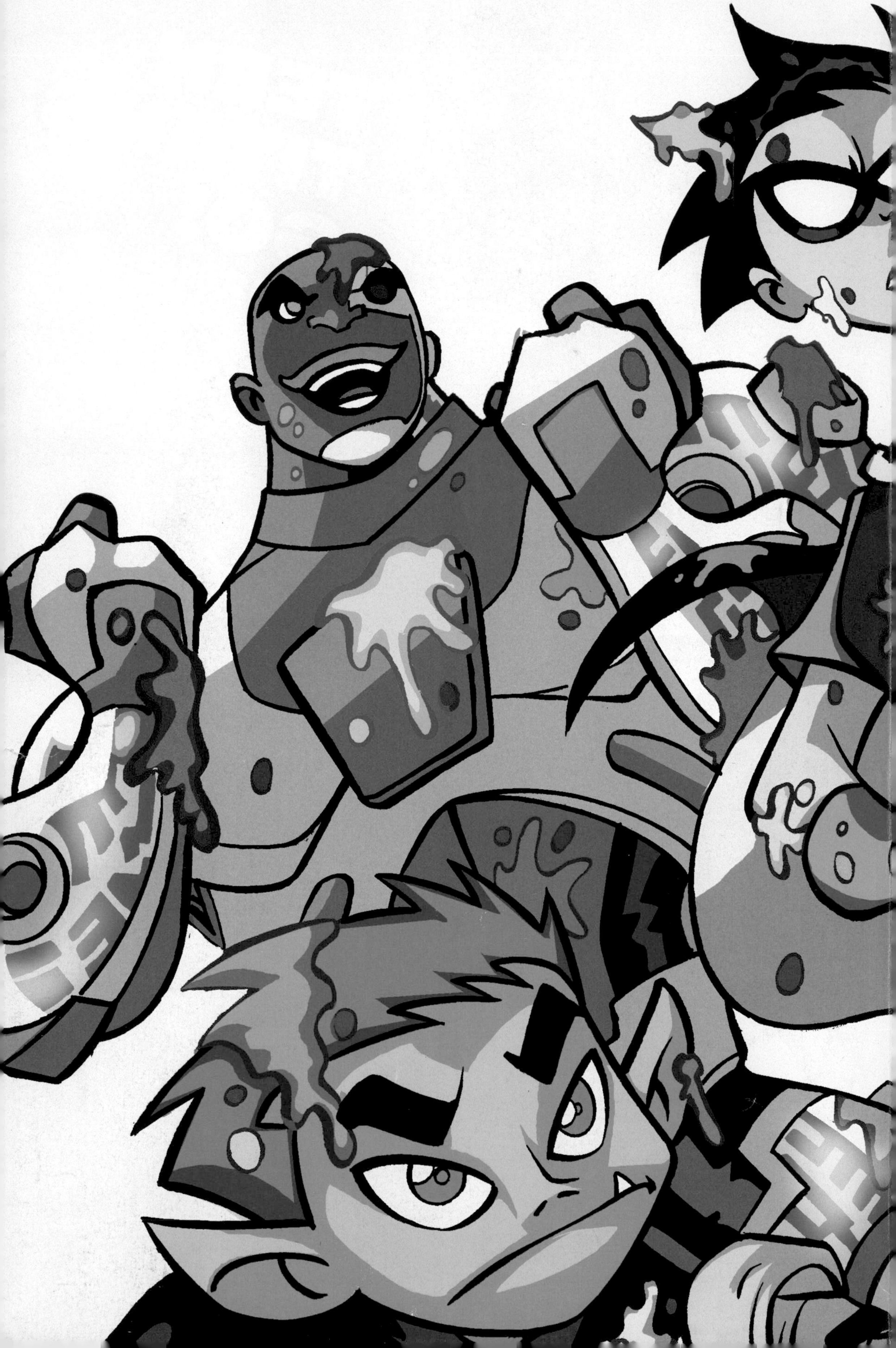

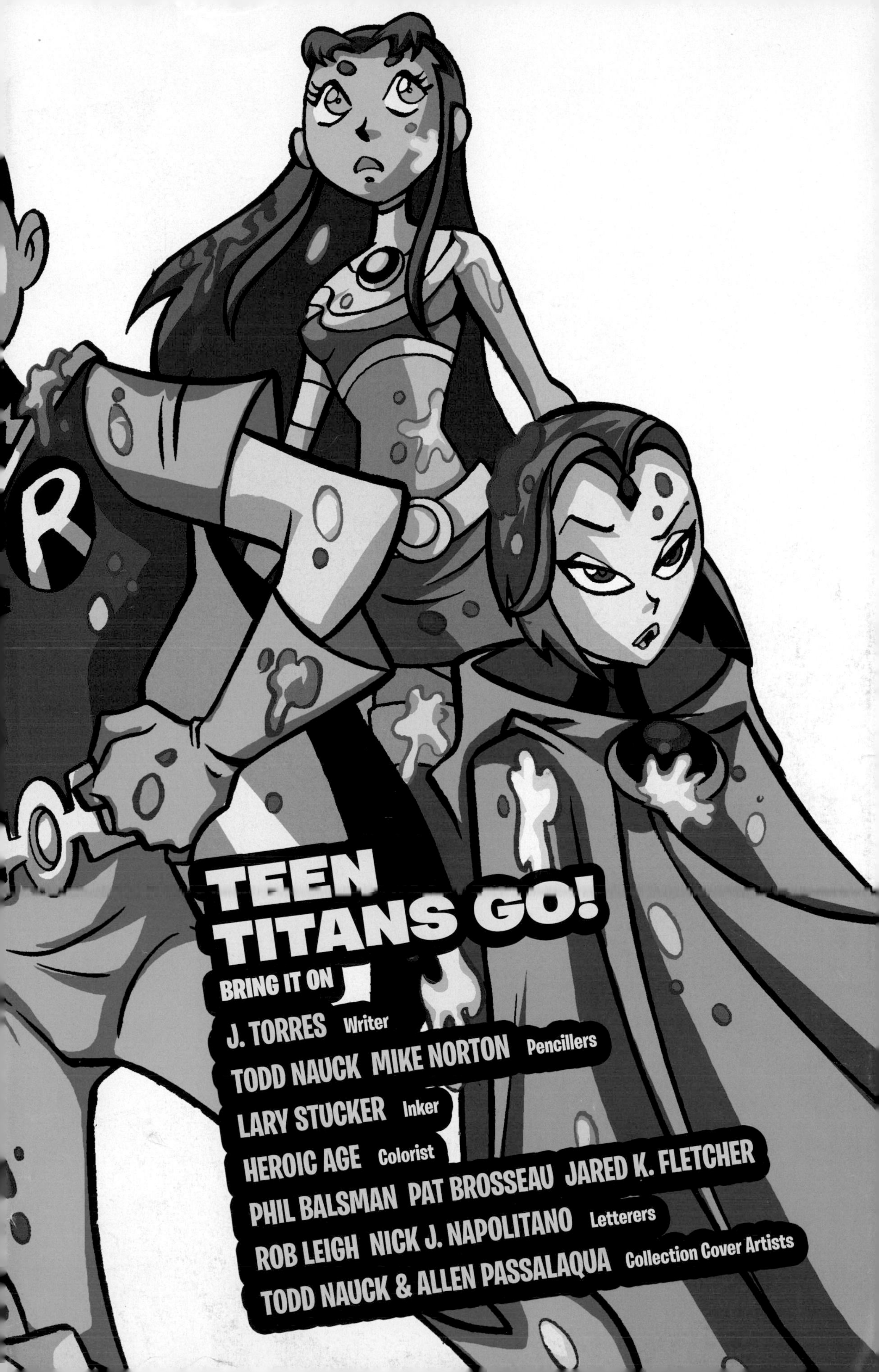

TEEN TITANS GO!

BRING IT ON

J. TORRES Writer

TODD NAUCK MIKE NORTON Pencillers

LARY STUCKER Inker

HEROIC AGE Colorist

PHIL BALSMAN PAT BROSSEAU JARED K. FLETCHER ROB LEIGH NICK J. NAPOLITANO Letterers

TODD NAUCK & ALLEN PASSALAQUA Collection Cover Artists

Tom Palmer Jr. Editor – Original Series
Jeanine Schaefer Assistant Editor – Original Series
Jeb Woodard Group Editor – Collected Editions
Steve Cook Design Director – Books
Louis Prandi Publication Design

Bob Harras Senior VP – Editor-in-Chief, DC Comics

Diane Nelson President
Dan DiDio and Jim Lee Co-Publishers
Geoff Johns Chief Creative Officer
Amit Desai Senior VP – Marketing & Global Franchise Management
Nairi Gardiner Senior VP – Finance
Sam Ades VP – Digital Marketing
Bobbie Chase VP – Talent Development
Mark Chiarello Senior VP – Art, Design & Collected Editions
John Cunningham VP – Content Strategy
Anne DePies VP – Strategy Planning & Reporting
Don Falletti VP – Manufacturing Operations
Lawrence Ganem VP – Editorial Administration & Talent Relations
Alison Gill Senior VP – Manufacturing & Operations
Hank Kanalz Senior VP – Editorial Strategy & Administration
Jay Kogan VP – Legal Affairs
Derek Maddalena Senior VP – Sales & Business Development
Jack Mahan VP – Business Affairs
Dan Miron VP – Sales Planning & Trade Development
Nick Napolitano VP – Manufacturing Administration
Carol Roeder VP – Marketing
Eddie Scannell VP – Mass Account & Digital Sales
Courtney Simmons Senior VP – Publicity & Communications
Jim (Ski) Sokolowski VP – Comic Book Specialty & Newsstand Sales
Sandy Yi Senior VP – Global Franchise Management

TEEN TITANS GO!: BRING IT ON

Published by DC Comics. Compilation and all new material Copyright © 2016 DC Comics. All Rights Reserved.
Originally published in single magazine form in TEEN TITANS GO! 13-18. Copyright © 2005 DC Comics. All Rights
Reserved. All characters, their distinctive likenesses and related elements featured in this publication are
trademarks of DC Comics. The stories, characters and incidents featured in this publication are entirely fictional.
DC Comics does not read or accept unsolicited submissions of ideas, stories or artwork.

DC Comics, 2900 West Alameda Ave., Burbank, CA 91505
Printed by RR Donnelley, Salem, VA, USA. 9/16/16. First Printing.
ISBN: 978-1-4012-6468-0

Library of Congress Cataloging-in-Publication Data is available.

PEFC Certified

Printed on paper from
sustainably managed
forests and controlled
sources

PEFC/29-31-75   www.pefc.org

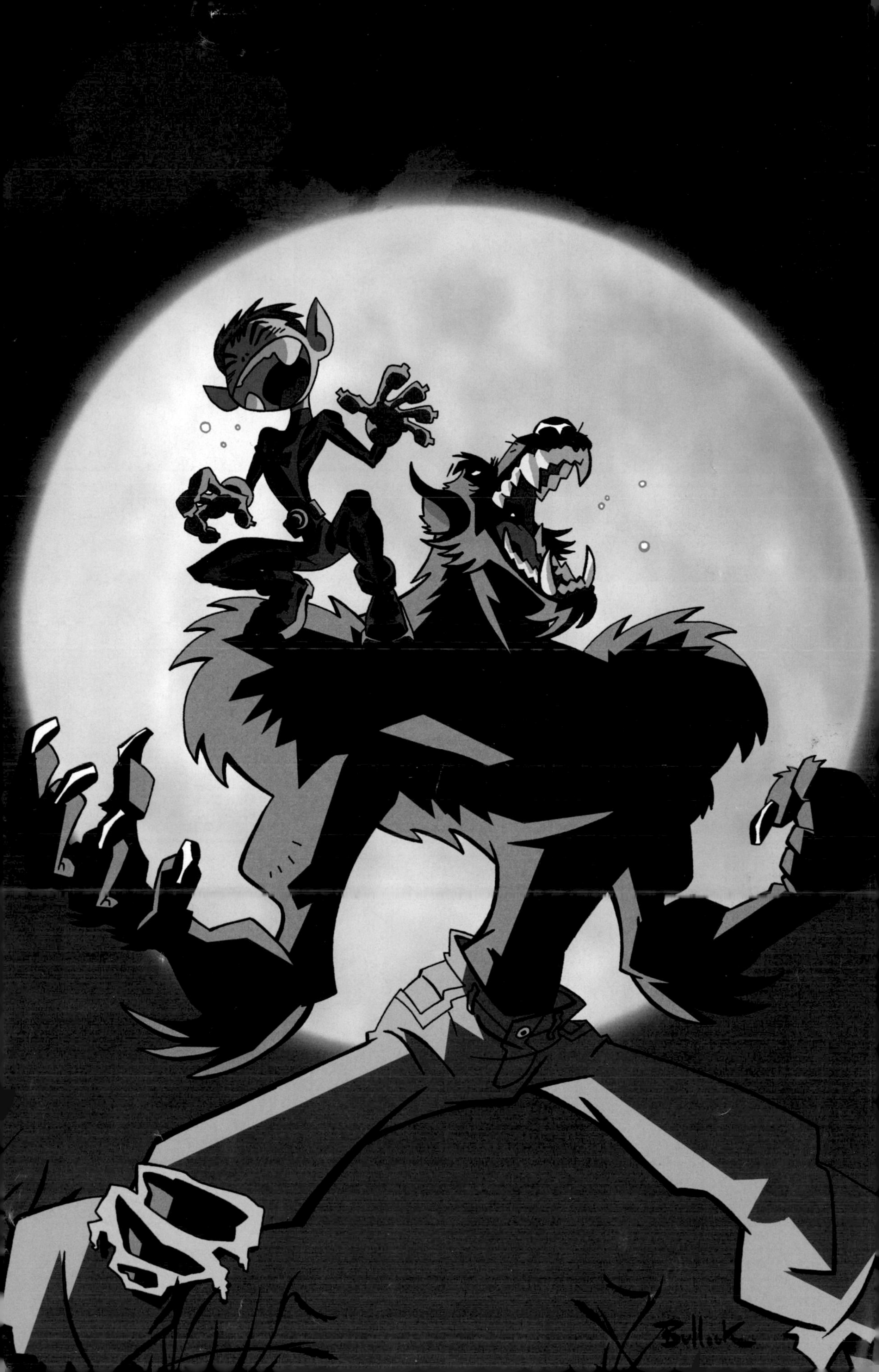
Bullock

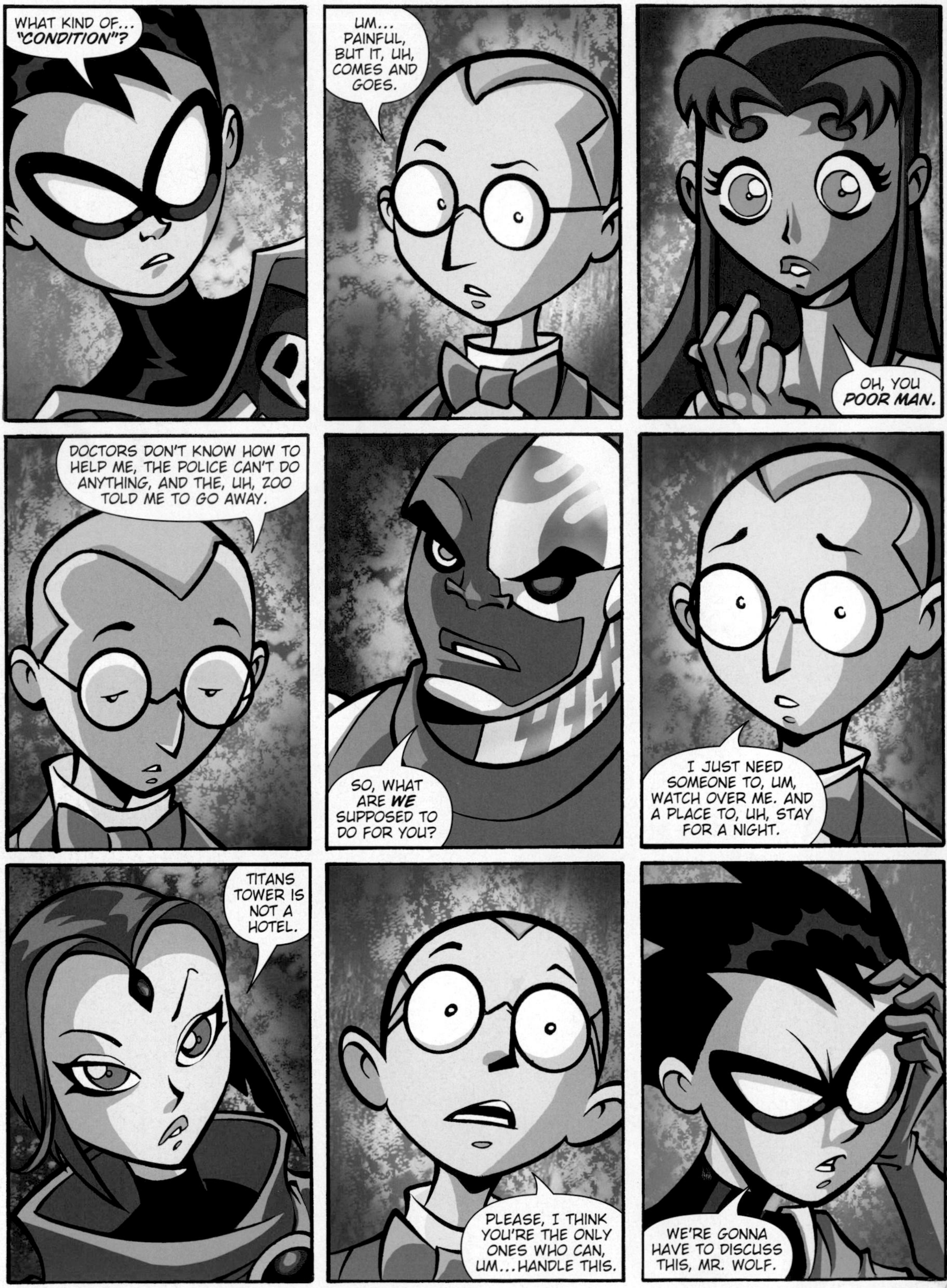
WHAT KIND OF... "CONDITION"?
UM... PAINFUL, BUT IT, UH, COMES AND GOES.
OH, YOU POOR MAN.
DOCTORS DON'T KNOW HOW TO HELP ME, THE POLICE CAN'T DO ANYTHING, AND THE, UH, ZOO TOLD ME TO GO AWAY.
SO, WHAT ARE WE SUPPOSED TO DO FOR YOU?
I JUST NEED SOMEONE TO, UM, WATCH OVER ME. AND A PLACE TO, UH, STAY FOR A NIGHT.
TITANS TOWER IS NOT A HOTEL.
PLEASE, I THINK YOU'RE THE ONLY ONES WHO CAN, UM... HANDLE THIS.
WE'RE GONNA HAVE TO DISCUSS THIS, MR. WOLF.

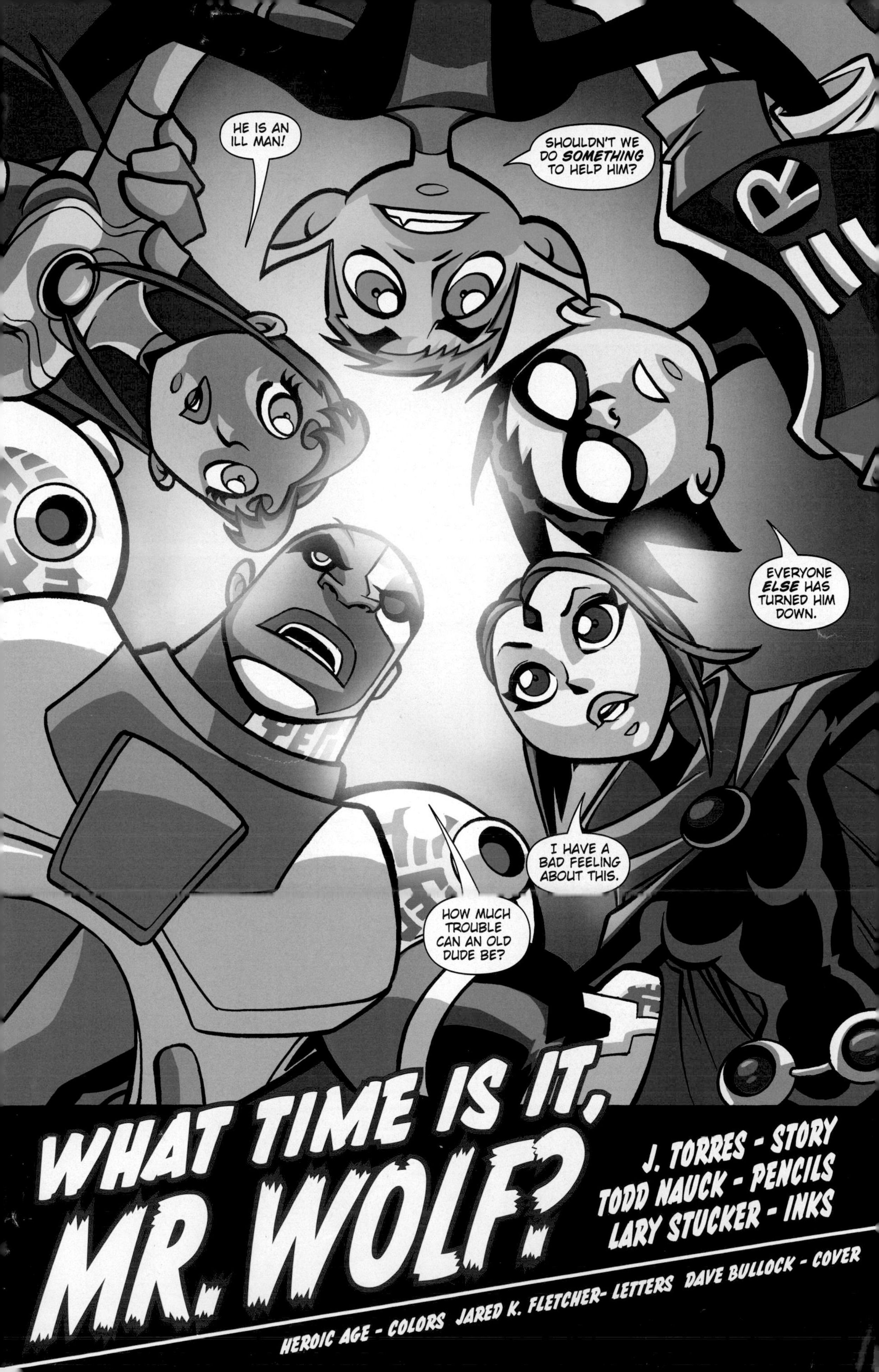
HE IS AN ILL MAN!
SHOULDN'T WE DO SOMETHING TO HELP HIM?
EVERYONE ELSE HAS TURNED HIM DOWN.
I HAVE A BAD FEELING ABOUT THIS.
HOW MUCH TROUBLE CAN AN OLD DUDE BE?
WHAT TIME IS IT, MR. WOLF?
J. TORRES - STORY
TODD NAUCK - PENCILS
LARY STUCKER - INKS
HEROIC AGE - COLORS JARED K. FLETCHER- LETTERS DAVE BULLOCK - COVER

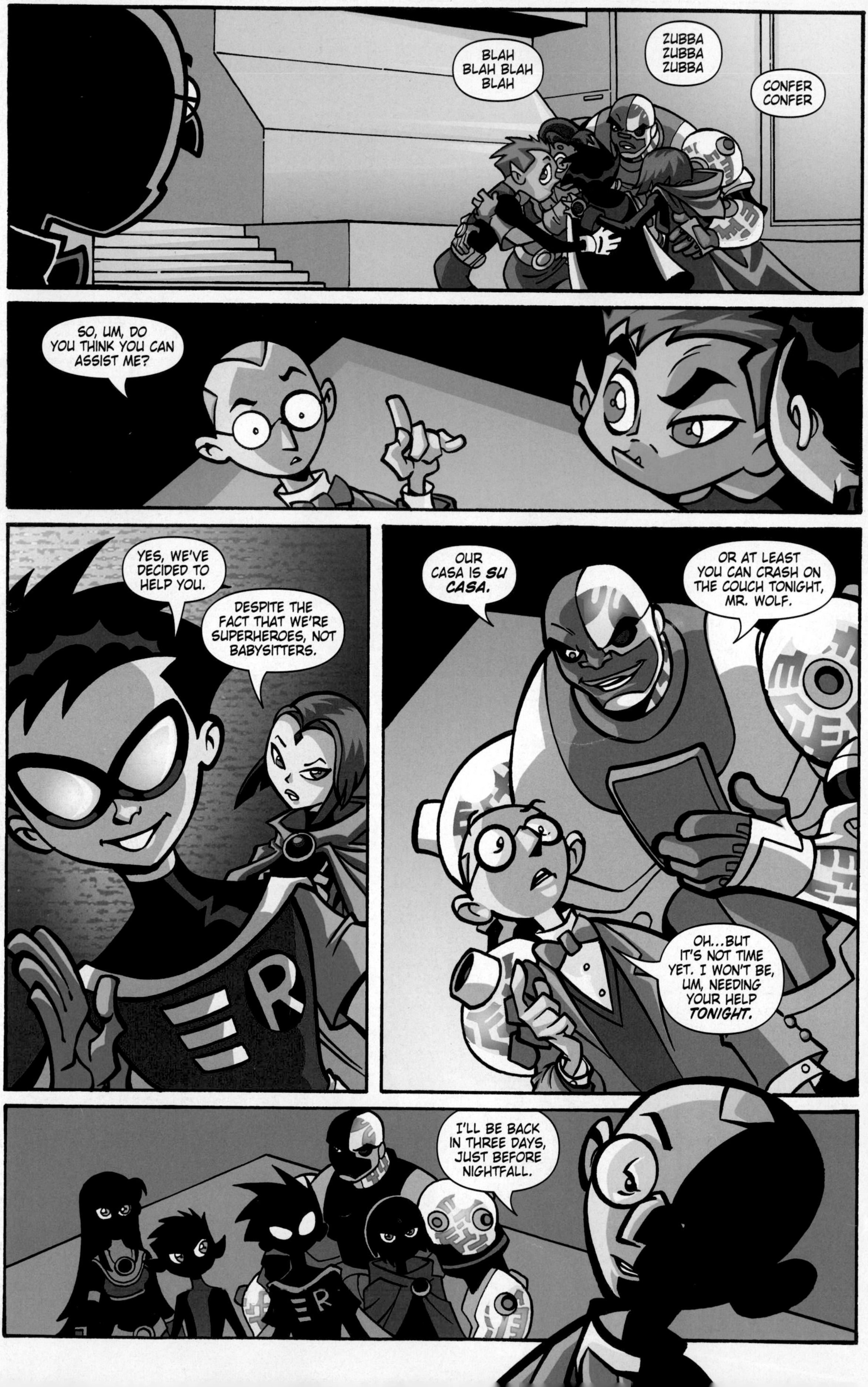
BLAH BLAH BLAH BLAH
ZUBBA ZUBBA ZUBBA
CONFER CONFER
SO, UM, DO YOU THINK YOU CAN ASSIST ME?
YES, WE'VE DECIDED TO HELP YOU.
DESPITE THE FACT THAT WE'RE SUPERHEROES, NOT BABYSITTERS.
OUR CASA IS SU CASA.
OR AT LEAST YOU CAN CRASH ON THE COUCH TONIGHT, MR. WOLF.
OH...BUT IT'S NOT TIME YET. I WON'T BE, UM, NEEDING YOUR HELP TONIGHT.
I'LL BE BACK IN THREE DAYS, JUST BEFORE NIGHTFALL.

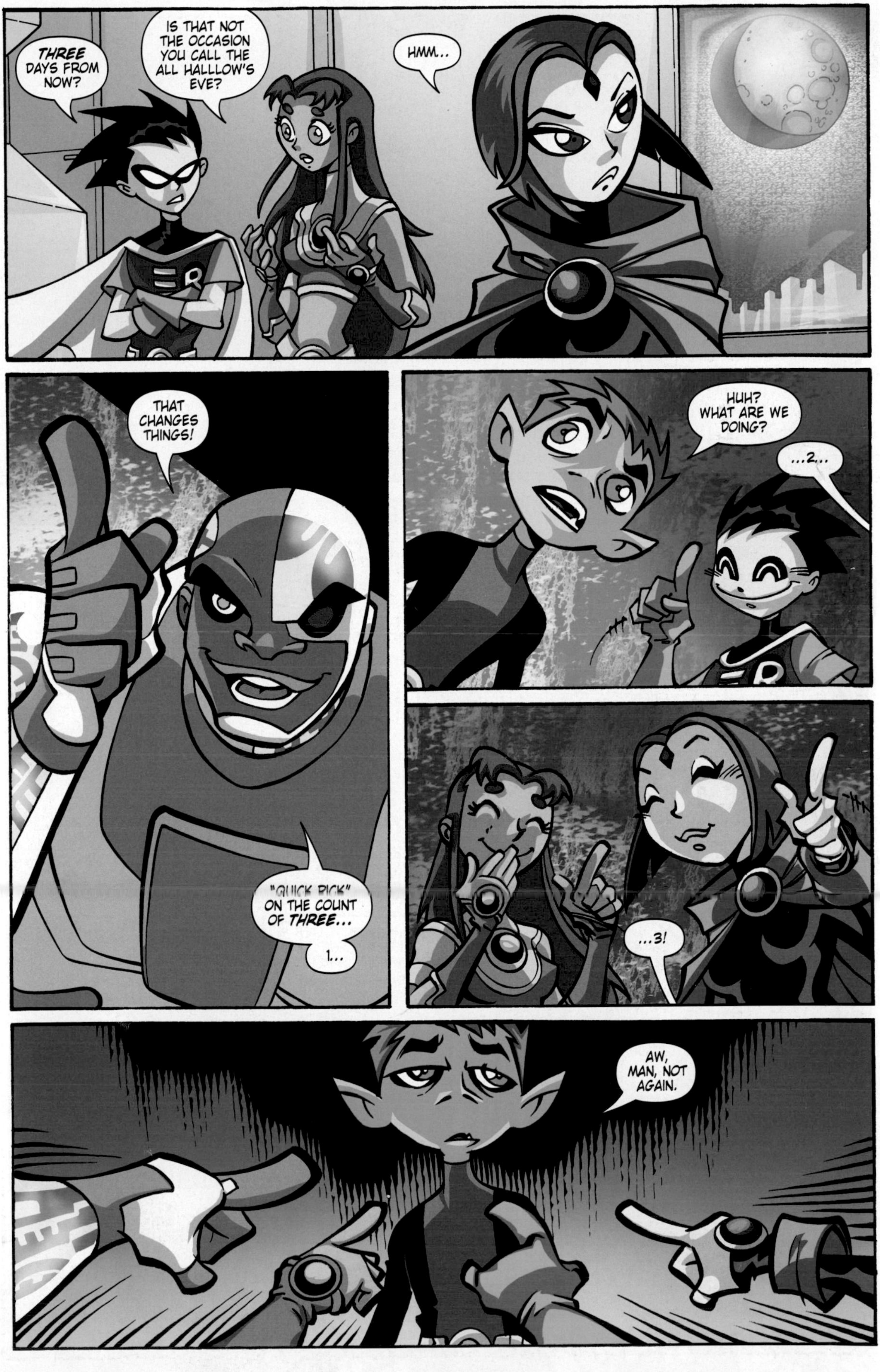
THREE DAYS FROM NOW?
IS THAT NOT THE OCCASION YOU CALL THE ALL HALLLOW'S EVE?
HMM...
THAT CHANGES THINGS!
"QUICK PICK" ON THE COUNT OF THREE...
1...
HUH? WHAT ARE WE DOING?
...2...
...3!
AW, MAN, NOT AGAIN.

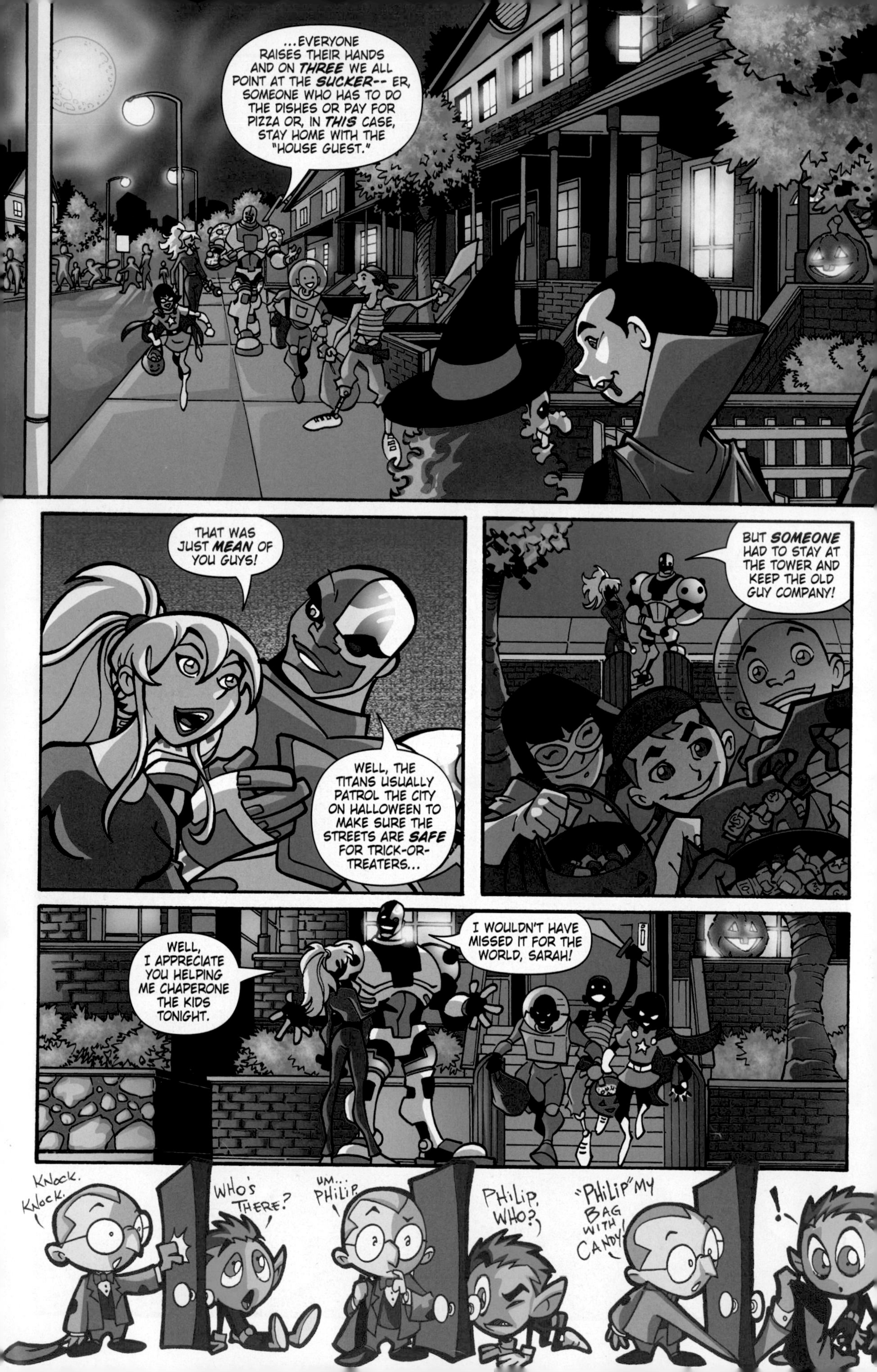
...EVERYONE RAISES THEIR HANDS AND ON THREE WE ALL POINT AT THE SUCKER-- ER, SOMEONE WHO HAS TO DO THE DISHES OR PAY FOR PIZZA OR, IN THIS CASE, STAY HOME WITH THE "HOUSE GUEST."
THAT WAS JUST MEAN OF YOU GUYS!
WELL, THE TITANS USUALLY PATROL THE CITY ON HALLOWEEN TO MAKE SURE THE STREETS ARE SAFE FOR TRICK-OR-TREATERS...
BUT SOMEONE HAD TO STAY AT THE TOWER AND KEEP THE OLD GUY COMPANY!
WELL, I APPRECIATE YOU HELPING ME CHAPERONE THE KIDS TONIGHT.
I WOULDN'T HAVE MISSED IT FOR THE WORLD, SARAH!
KNOCK. KNOCK.
WHO'S THERE?
UM... PHILIP.
PHILIP, WHO?
"PHILIP" MY BAG WITH CANDY!
!

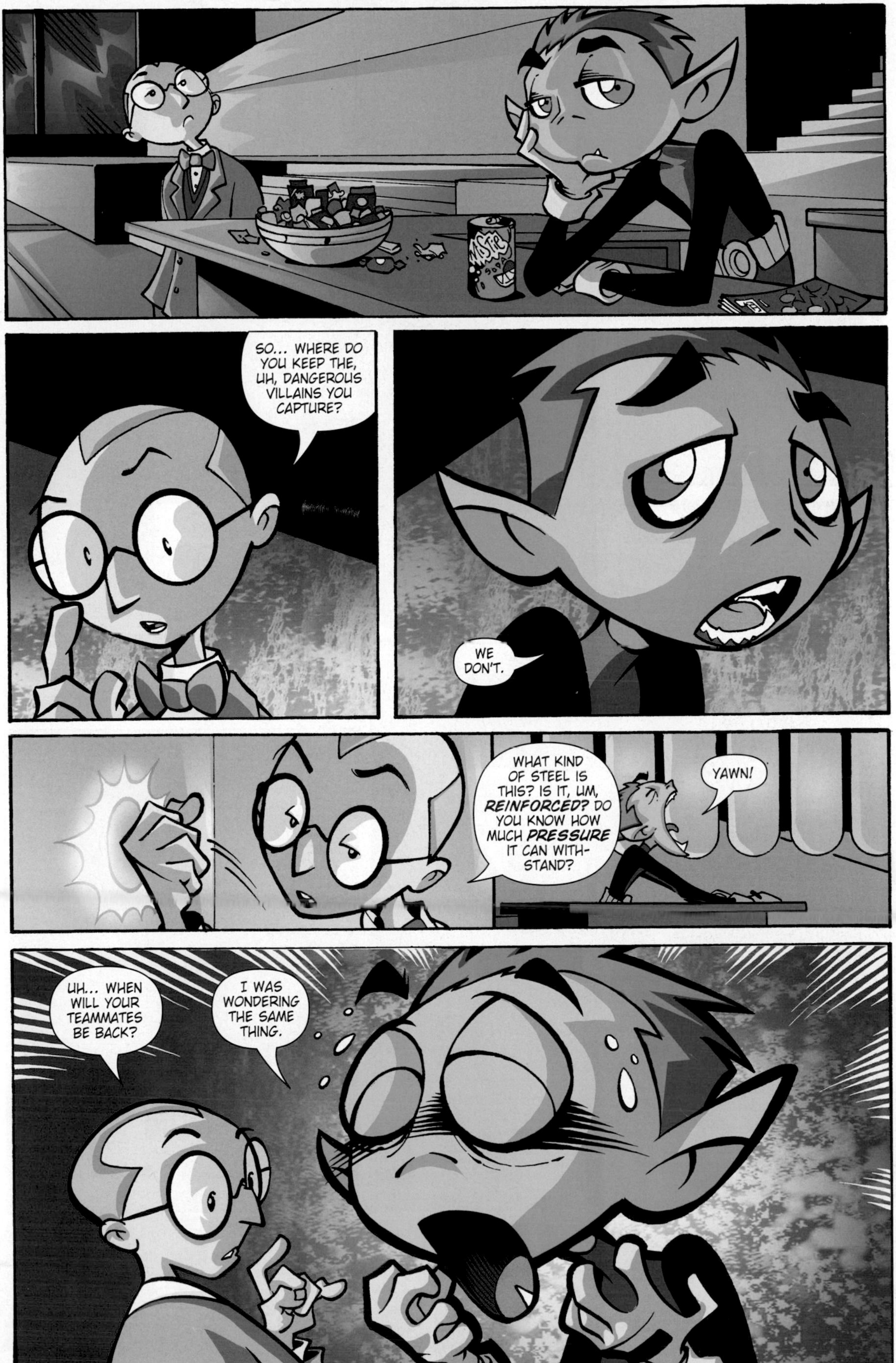
SO... WHERE DO YOU KEEP THE, UH, DANGEROUS VILLAINS YOU CAPTURE?
WE DON'T.
WHAT KIND OF STEEL IS THIS? IS IT, UM, REINFORCED? DO YOU KNOW HOW MUCH PRESSURE IT CAN WITH-STAND?
YAWN!
UH... WHEN WILL YOUR TEAMMATES BE BACK?
I WAS WONDERING THE SAME THING.

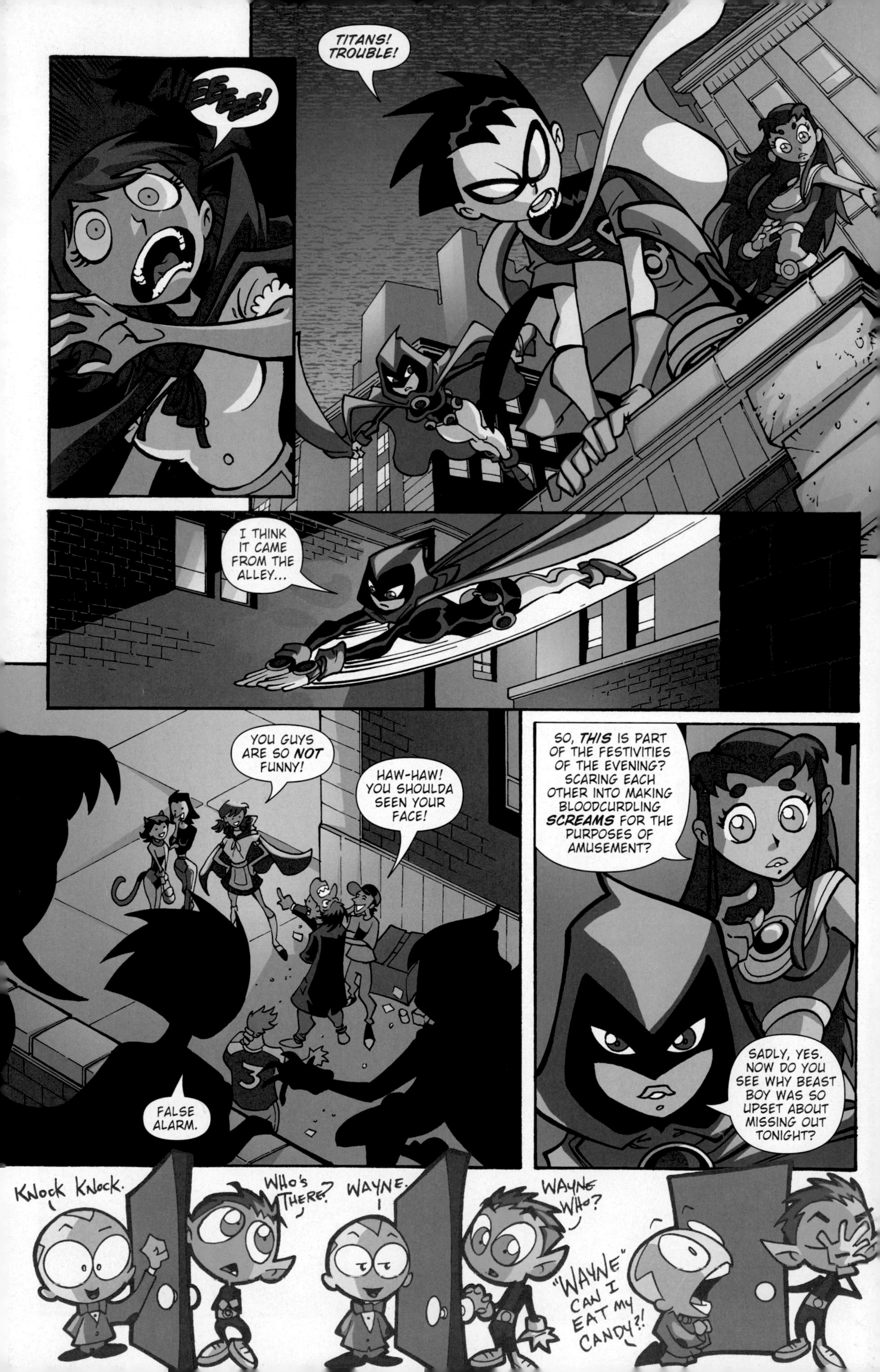
AIIEEEEEE!
TITANS! TROUBLE!
I THINK IT CAME FROM THE ALLEY...
YOU GUYS ARE SO *NOT* FUNNY!
HAW-HAW! YOU SHOULDA SEEN YOUR FACE!
FALSE ALARM.
SO, *THIS* IS PART OF THE FESTIVITIES OF THE EVENING? SCARING EACH OTHER INTO MAKING BLOODCURDLING *SCREAMS* FOR THE PURPOSES OF AMUSEMENT?
SADLY, YES. NOW DO YOU SEE WHY BEAST BOY WAS SO UPSET ABOUT MISSING OUT TONIGHT?
KNOCK KNOCK.
WHO'S THERE?
WAYNE.
WAYNE WHO?
"WAYNE" CAN I EAT MY CANDY?!

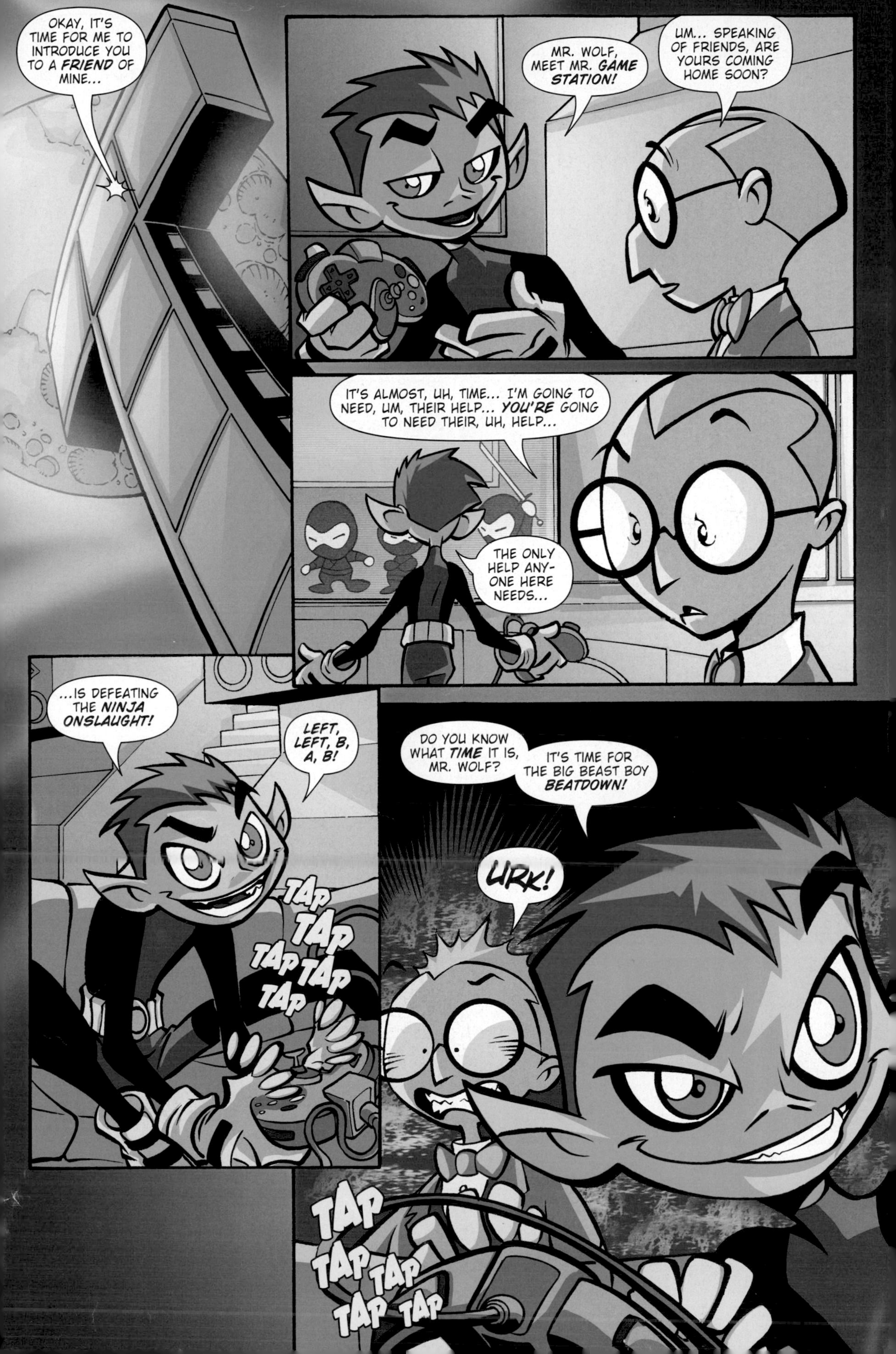
OKAY, IT'S TIME FOR ME TO INTRODUCE YOU TO A FRIEND OF MINE...
MR. WOLF, MEET MR. GAME STATION!
UM... SPEAKING OF FRIENDS, ARE YOURS COMING HOME SOON?
IT'S ALMOST, UH, TIME... I'M GOING TO NEED, UM, THEIR HELP... YOU'RE GOING TO NEED THEIR, UH, HELP...
THE ONLY HELP ANY-ONE HERE NEEDS...
...IS DEFEATING THE NINJA ONSLAUGHT!
LEFT, LEFT, B, A, B!
TAP TAP TAP TAP TAP
DO YOU KNOW WHAT TIME IT IS, MR. WOLF?
IT'S TIME FOR THE BIG BEAST BOY BEATDOWN!
URK!
TAP TAP TAP TAP TAP

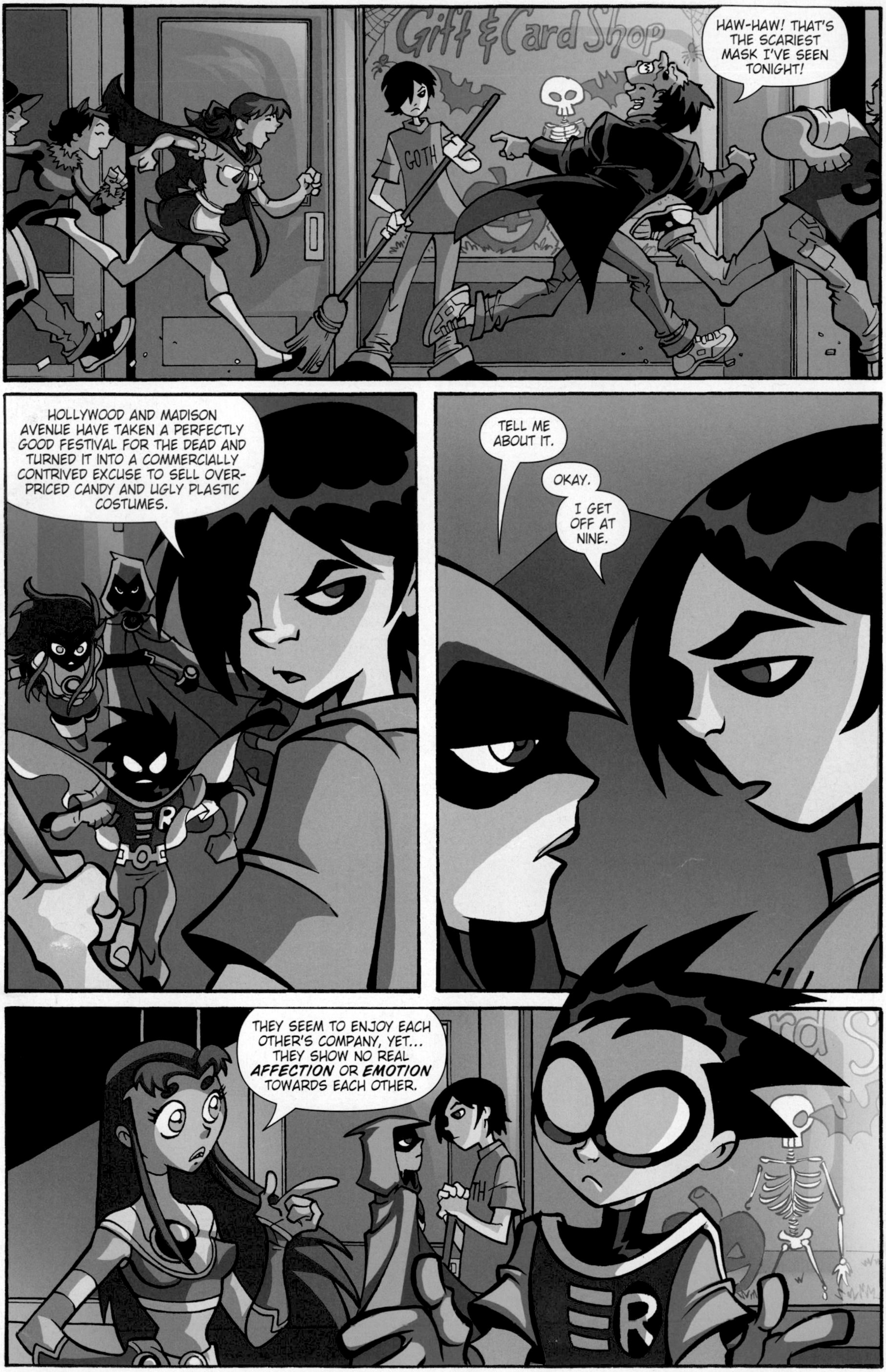
Gift & Card Shop
GOTH
HAW-HAW! THAT'S THE SCARIEST MASK I'VE SEEN TONIGHT!
HOLLYWOOD AND MADISON AVENUE HAVE TAKEN A PERFECTLY GOOD FESTIVAL FOR THE DEAD AND TURNED IT INTO A COMMERCIALLY CONTRIVED EXCUSE TO SELL OVER-PRICED CANDY AND UGLY PLASTIC COSTUMES.
TELL ME ABOUT IT.
OKAY.
I GET OFF AT NINE.
THEY SEEM TO ENJOY EACH OTHER'S COMPANY, YET... THEY SHOW NO REAL *AFFECTION* OR *EMOTION* TOWARDS EACH OTHER.

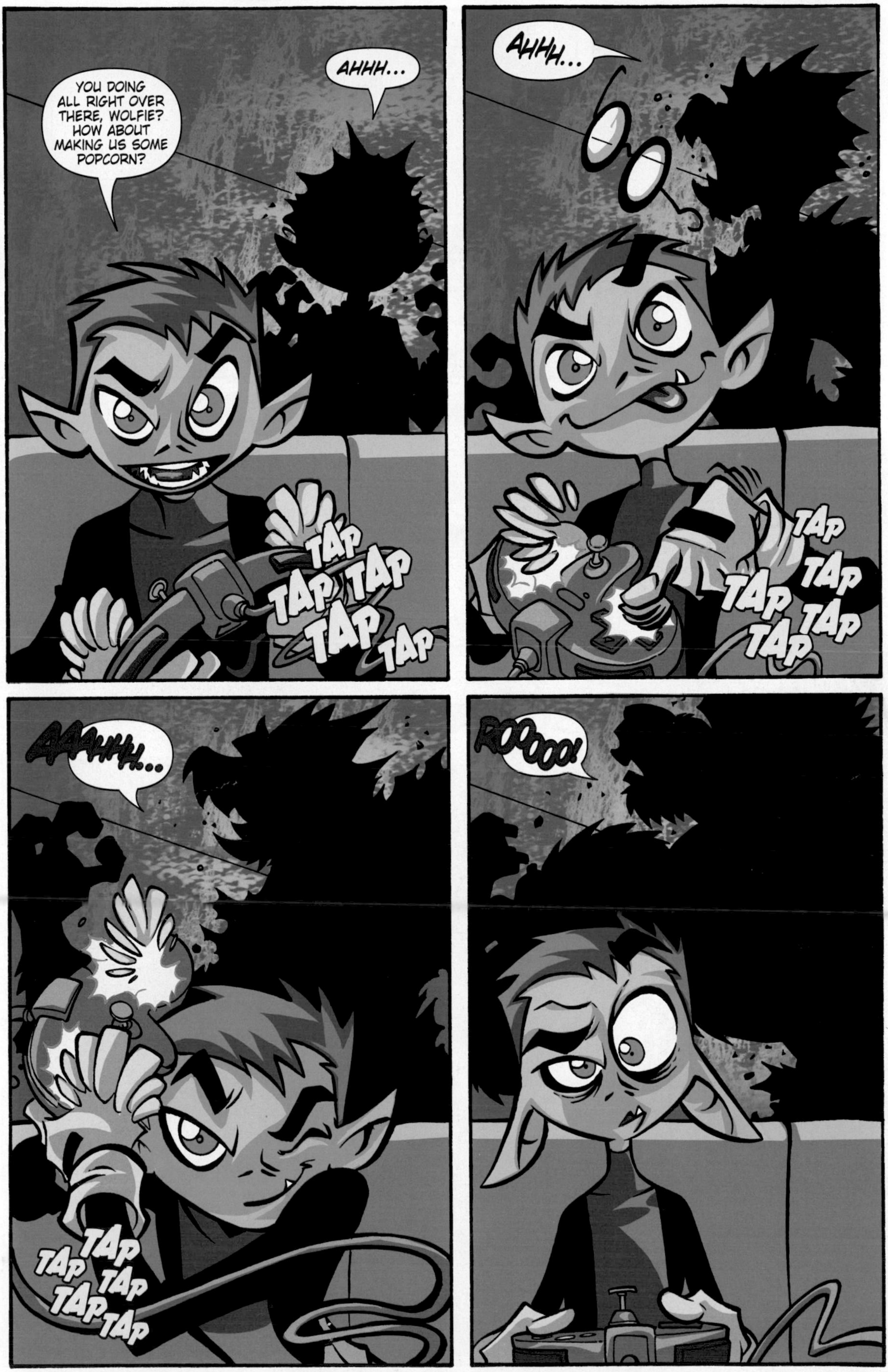
YOU DOING ALL RIGHT OVER THERE, WOLFIE? HOW ABOUT MAKING US SOME POPCORN?
AHHH...
TAP TAP TAP TAP TAP
AHHH...
TAP TAP TAP TAP TAP
AAAHHH...
TAP TAP TAP TAP TAP TAP
ROOOOO!

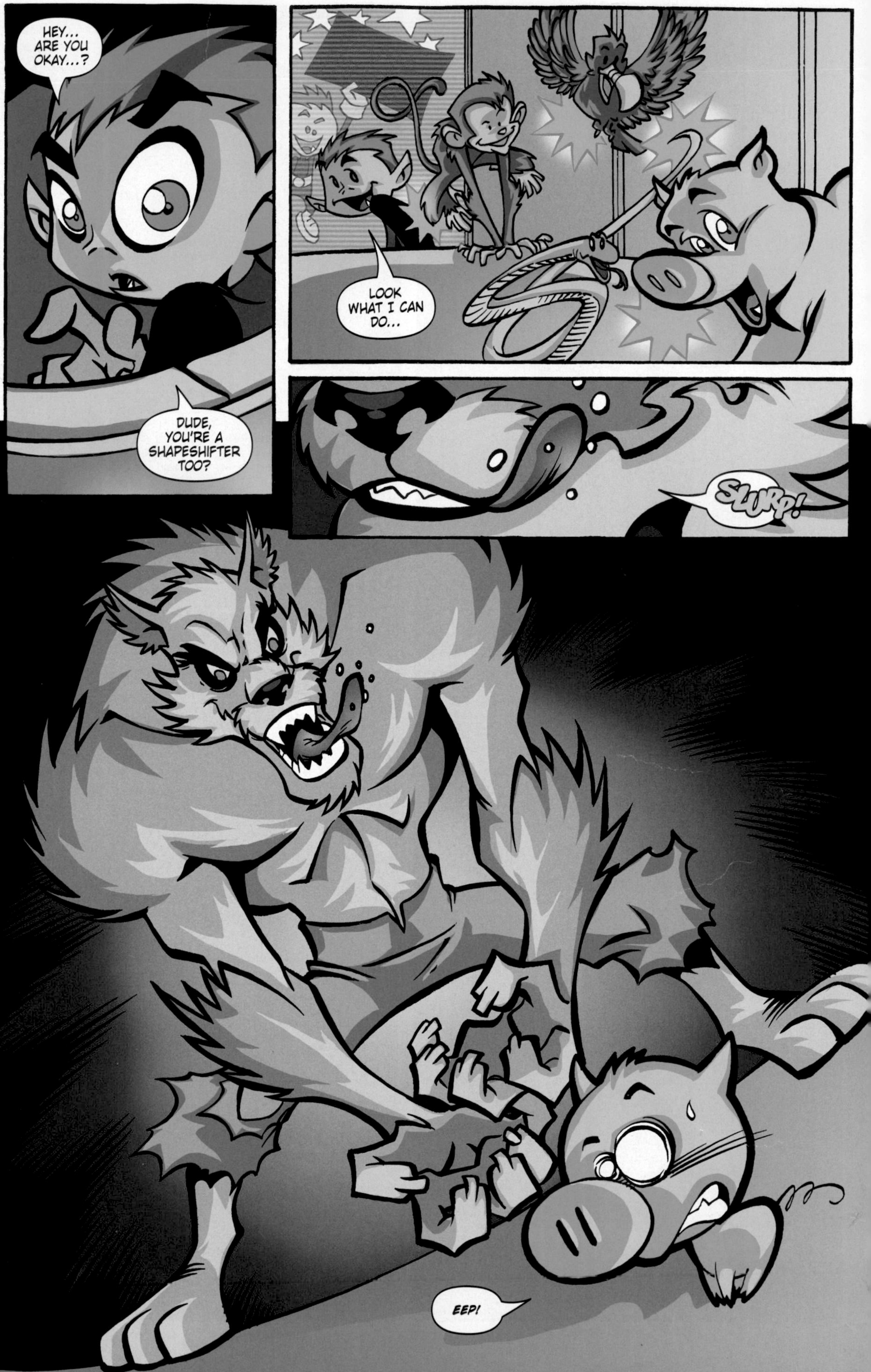

HEY... ARE YOU OKAY...?
DUDE, YOU'RE A SHAPESHIFTER TOO?
LOOK WHAT I CAN DO...
SLURP!
EEP!

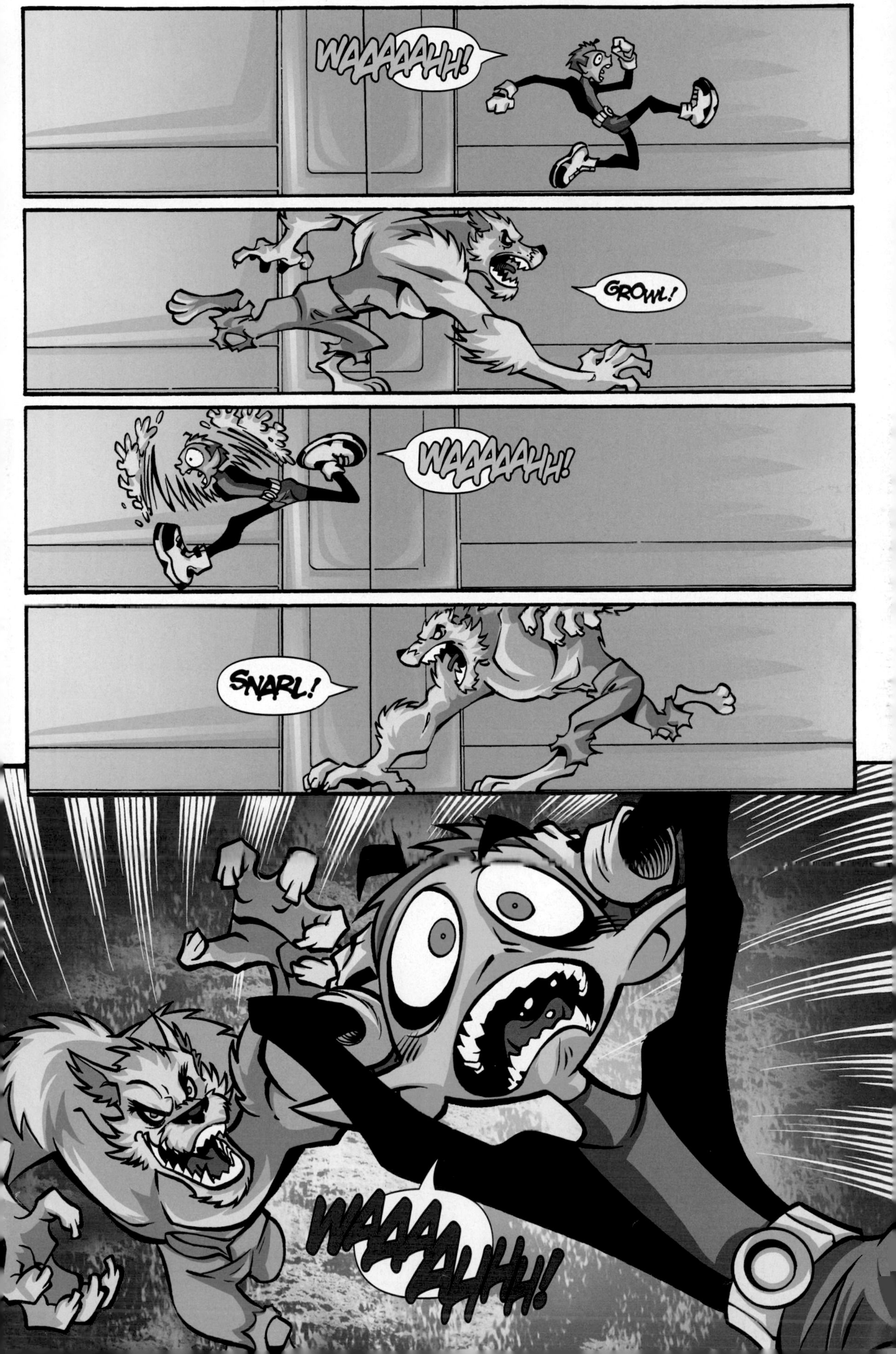
WAAAAAHH!
GROWL!
WAAAAAHH!
SNARL!
WAAAAAHHH!

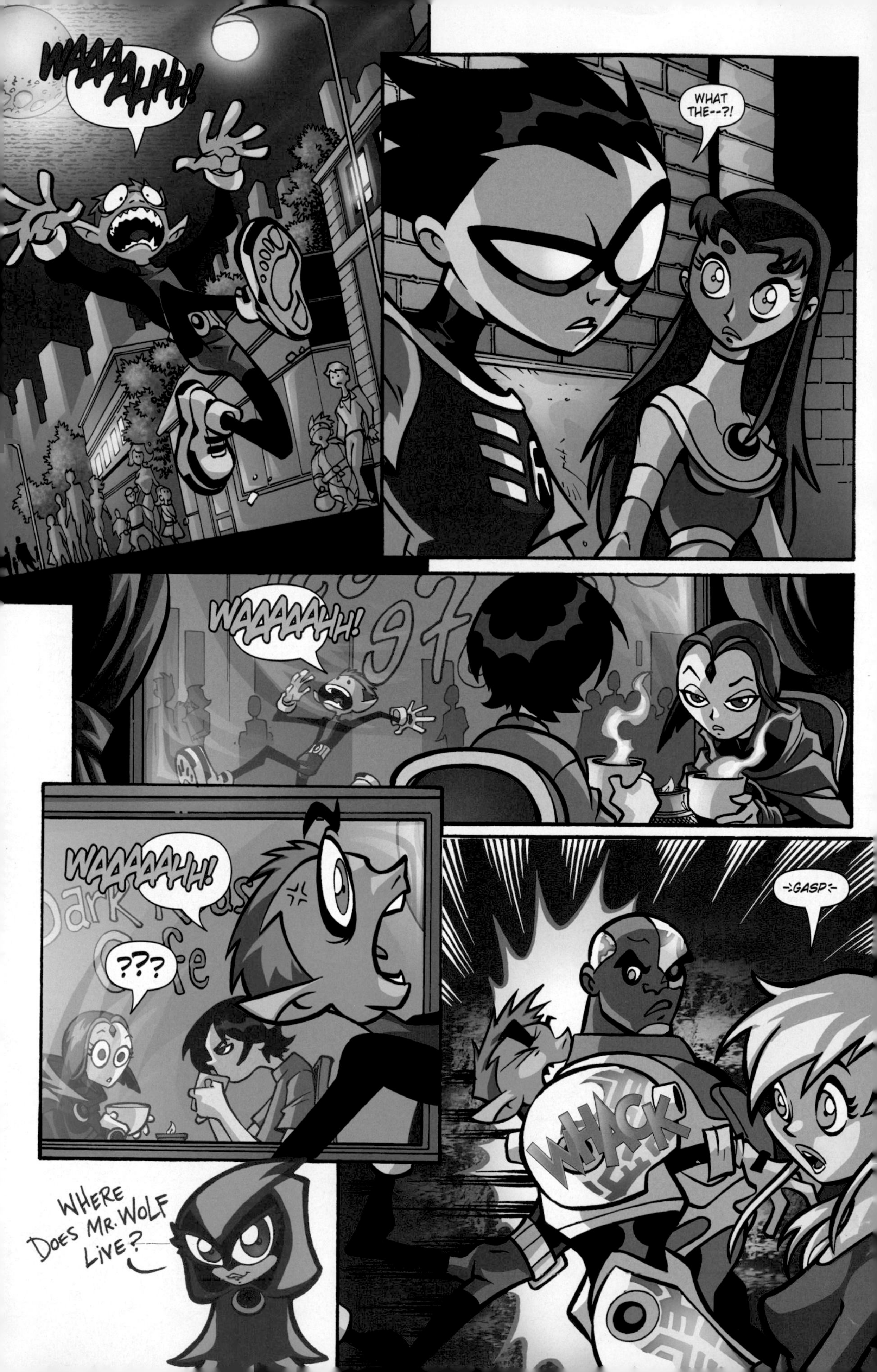
WAAAAHHH!
WHAT THE--?!
WAAAAAHH!
WAAAAAHH!
???
Dark Ros
Cafe
-GASP-
WHACK
WHERE DOES MR. WOLF LIVE?

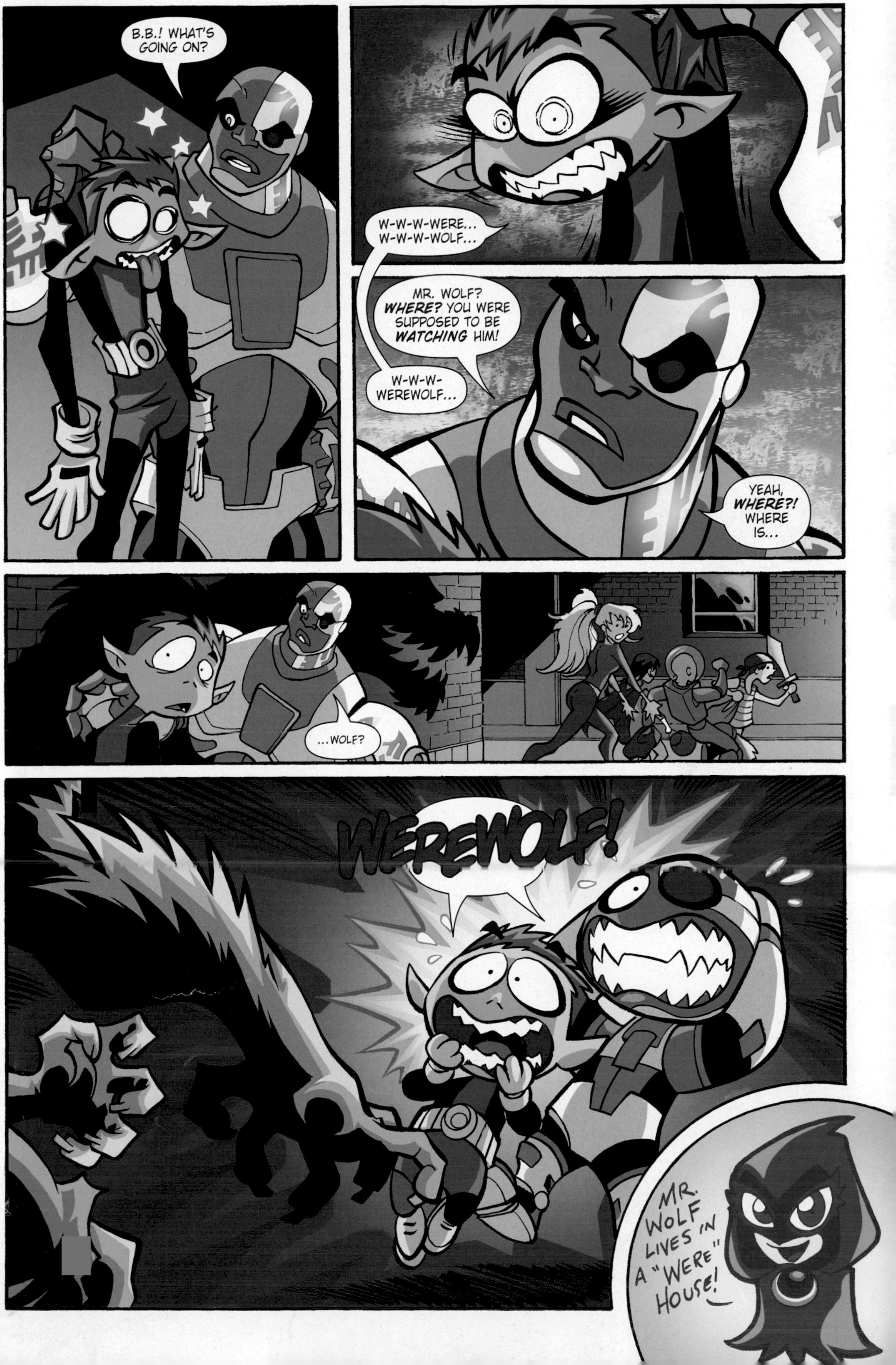
B.B.! WHAT'S GOING ON?
W-W-W-WERE... W-W-W-WOLF...
MR. WOLF? WHERE? YOU WERE SUPPOSED TO BE WATCHING HIM!
W-W-W-WEREWOLF...
YEAH, WHERE?! WHERE IS...
...WOLF?
WEREWOLF!
MR. WOLF LIVES IN A "WERE" HOUSE!

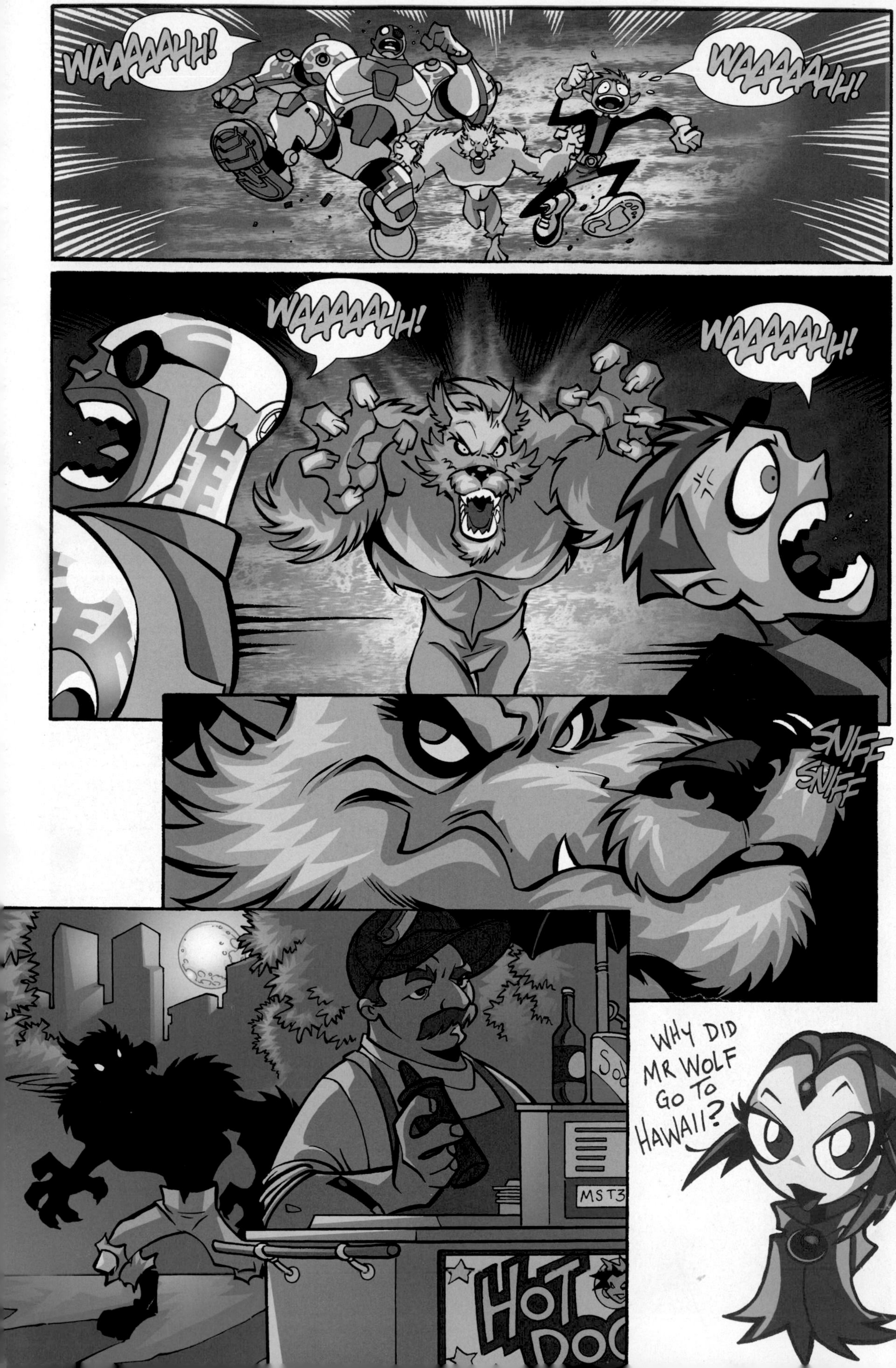
WAAAAAHH!
WAAAAAHH!
WAAAAAHH!
WAAAAAHH!
SNIFF SNIFF
MST3
HOT DOG
WHY DID MR WOLF GO TO HAWAII?

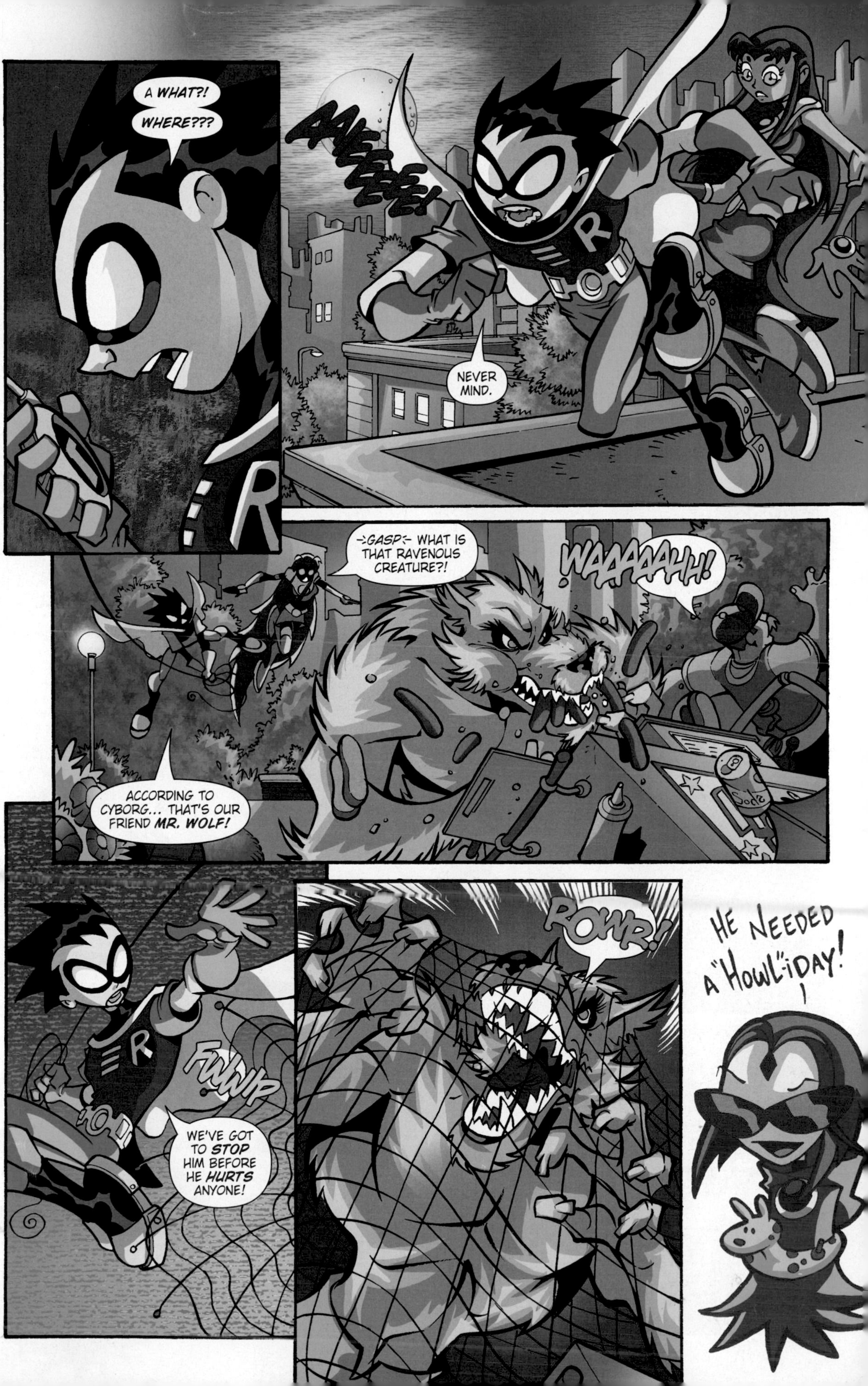
A WHAT?!
WHERE???
AAIEEEEE!
NEVER MIND.
-GASP- WHAT IS THAT RAVENOUS CREATURE?!
WAAAAAHH!
ACCORDING TO CYBORG... THAT'S OUR FRIEND MR. WOLF!
FWWIP
WE'VE GOT TO STOP HIM BEFORE HE HURTS ANYONE!
ROWR!
HE NEEDED A "HOWL"-IDAY!

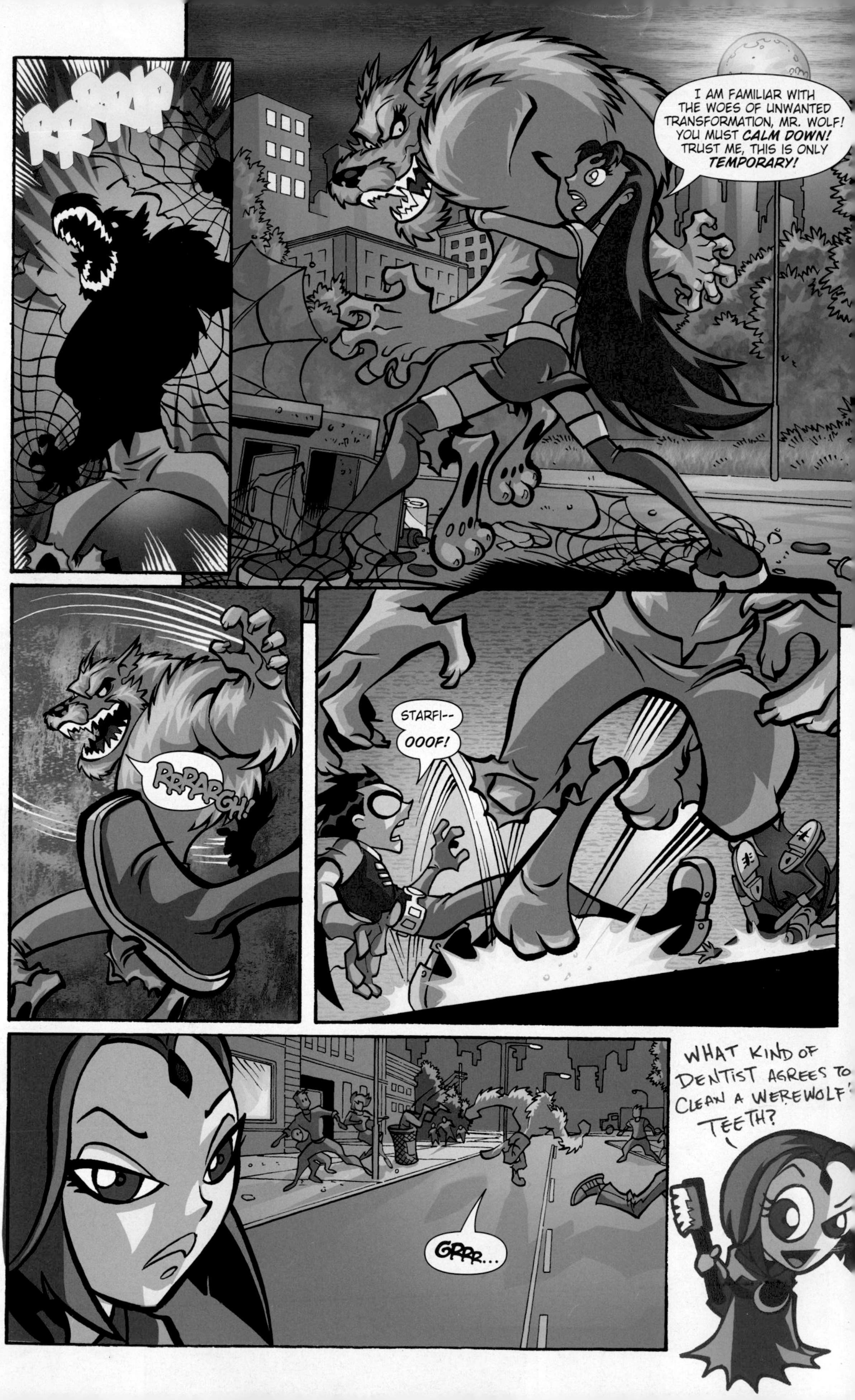
RRRRAP
I AM FAMILIAR WITH THE WOES OF UNWANTED TRANSFORMATION, MR. WOLF! YOU MUST CALM DOWN! TRUST ME, THIS IS ONLY TEMPORARY!
RRRRARGH!
STARFI--
OOOF!
GRRR...
WHAT KIND OF DENTIST AGREES TO CLEAN A WEREWOLF'S TEETH?

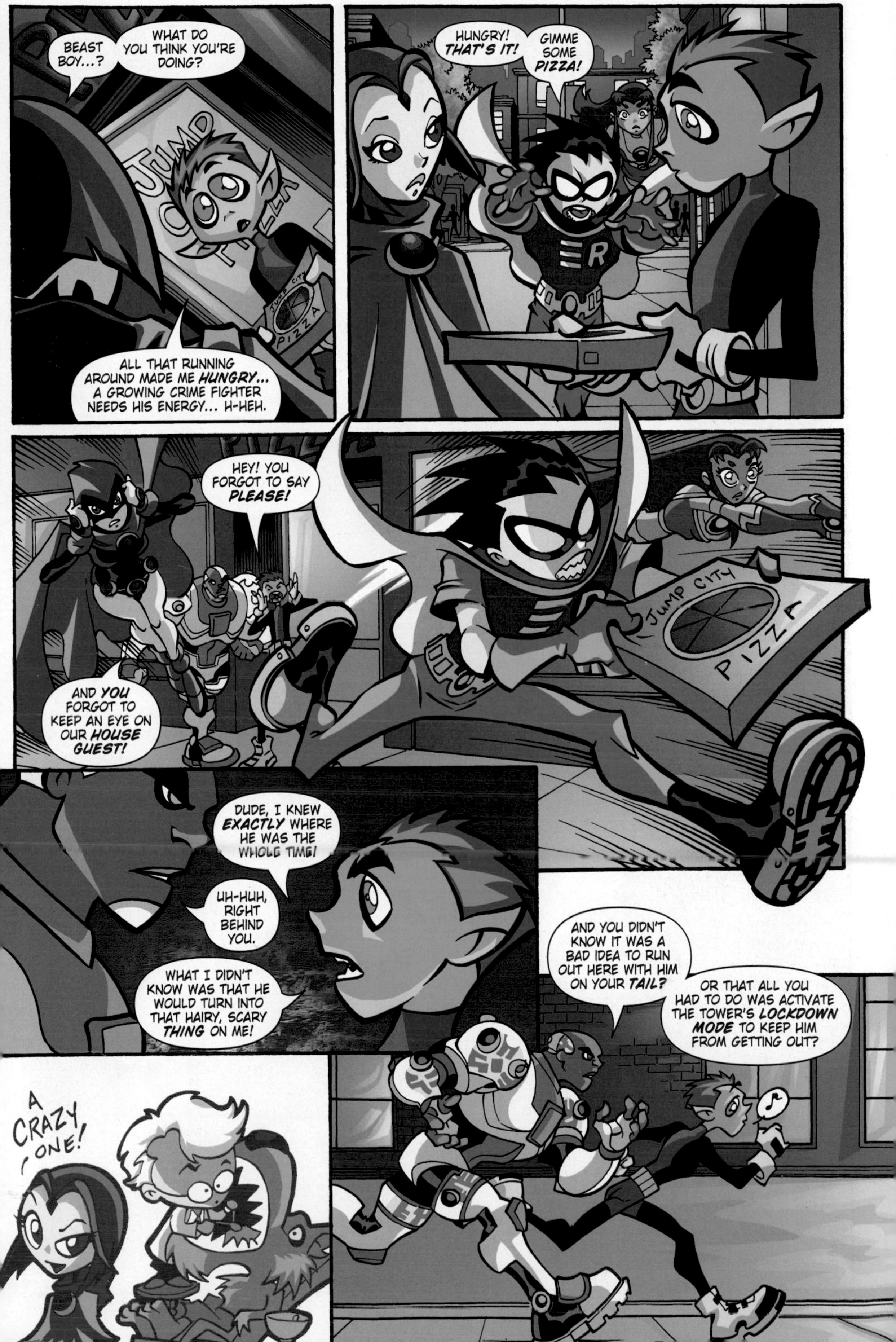
BEAST BOY...?
WHAT DO YOU THINK YOU'RE DOING?
ALL THAT RUNNING AROUND MADE ME HUNGRY... A GROWING CRIME FIGHTER NEEDS HIS ENERGY... H-HEH.
JUMP CITY PIZZA
HUNGRY! THAT'S IT!
GIMME SOME PIZZA!
HEY! YOU FORGOT TO SAY PLEASE!
AND YOU FORGOT TO KEEP AN EYE ON OUR HOUSE GUEST!
JUMP CITY PIZZA
DUDE, I KNEW EXACTLY WHERE HE WAS THE WHOLE TIME!
UH-HUH, RIGHT BEHIND YOU.
WHAT I DIDN'T KNOW WAS THAT HE WOULD TURN INTO THAT HAIRY, SCARY THING ON ME!
AND YOU DIDN'T KNOW IT WAS A BAD IDEA TO RUN OUT HERE WITH HIM ON YOUR TAIL?
OR THAT ALL YOU HAD TO DO WAS ACTIVATE THE TOWER'S LOCKDOWN MODE TO KEEP HIM FROM GETTING OUT?
A CRAZY ONE!

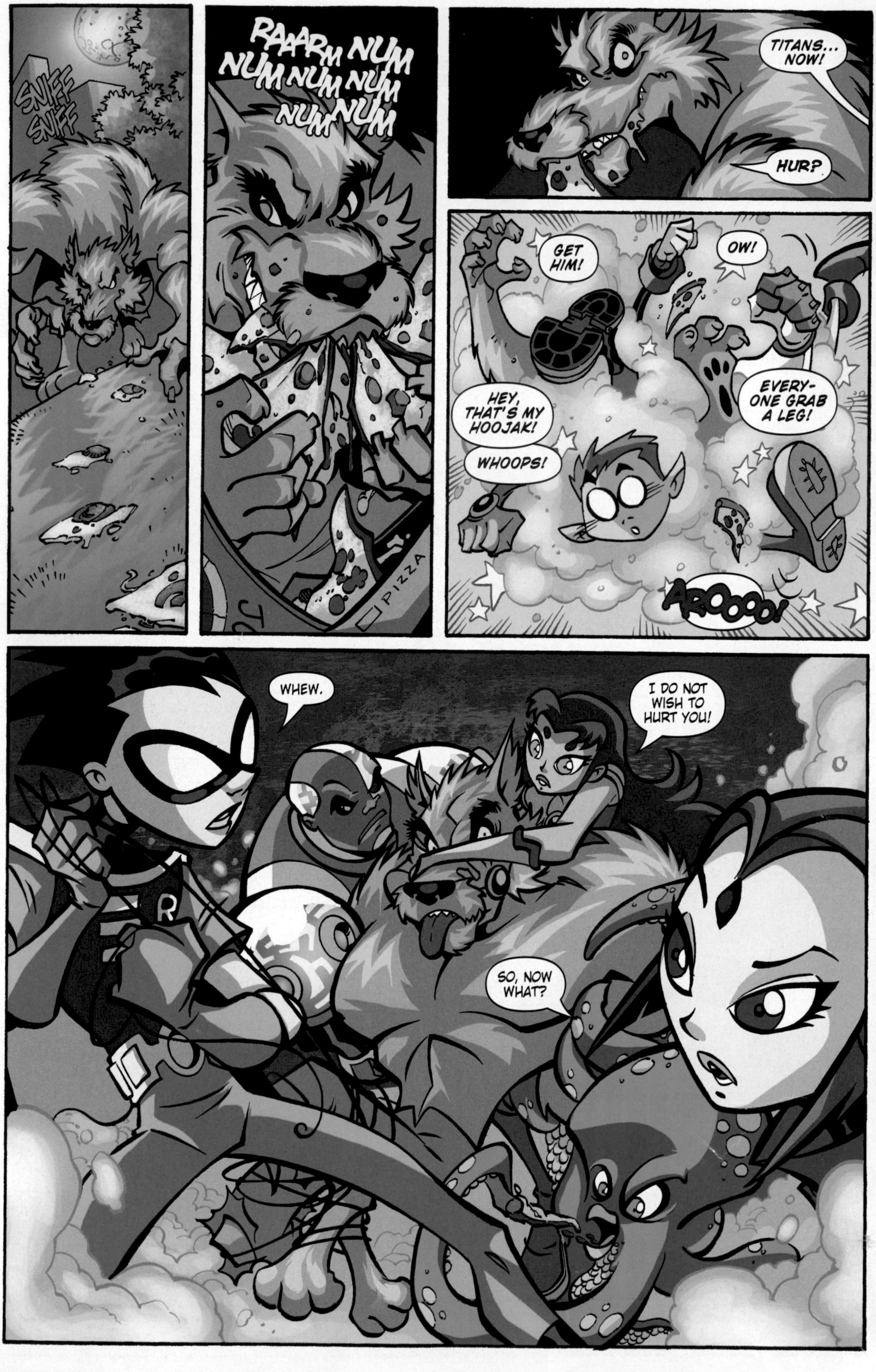
SNIFF SNIFF
RAAARM NUM NUM NUM NUM NUM NUM
TITANS... NOW!
HUR?
GET HIM!
OW!
EVERY-ONE GRAB A LEG!
HEY, THAT'S MY HOOJAK!
WHOOPS!
AROOOOO!
WHEW.
I DO NOT WISH TO HURT YOU!
SO, NOW WHAT?

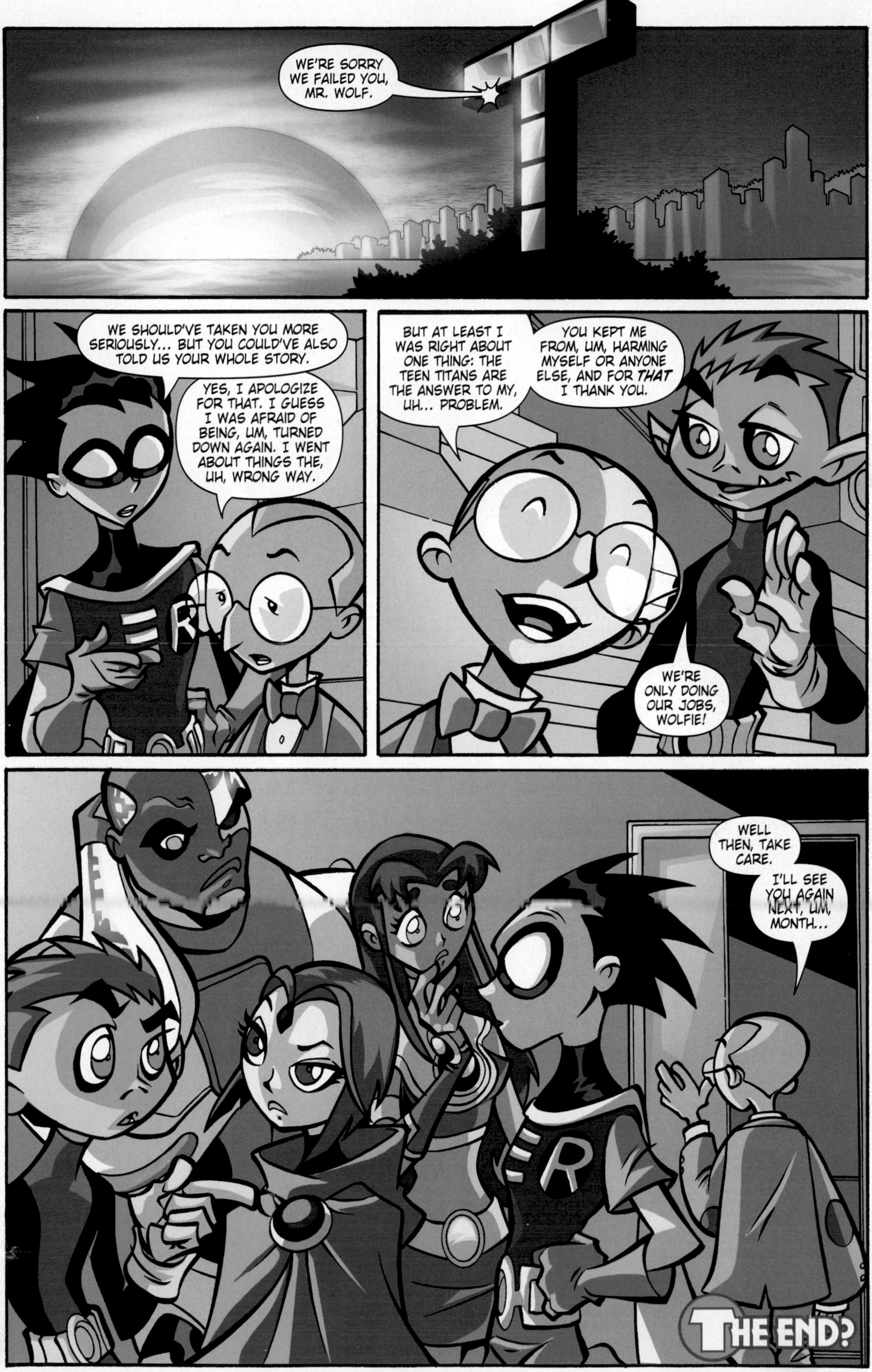
WE'RE SORRY WE FAILED YOU, MR. WOLF.
WE SHOULD'VE TAKEN YOU MORE SERIOUSLY... BUT YOU COULD'VE ALSO TOLD US YOUR WHOLE STORY.
YES, I APOLOGIZE FOR THAT. I GUESS I WAS AFRAID OF BEING, UM, TURNED DOWN AGAIN. I WENT ABOUT THINGS THE, UH, WRONG WAY.
BUT AT LEAST I WAS RIGHT ABOUT ONE THING: THE TEEN TITANS ARE THE ANSWER TO MY, UH... PROBLEM.
YOU KEPT ME FROM, UM, HARMING MYSELF OR ANYONE ELSE, AND FOR *THAT* I THANK YOU.
WE'RE ONLY DOING OUR JOBS, WOLFIE!
WELL THEN, TAKE CARE.
I'LL SEE YOU AGAIN NEXT, UM, MONTH...
THE END?

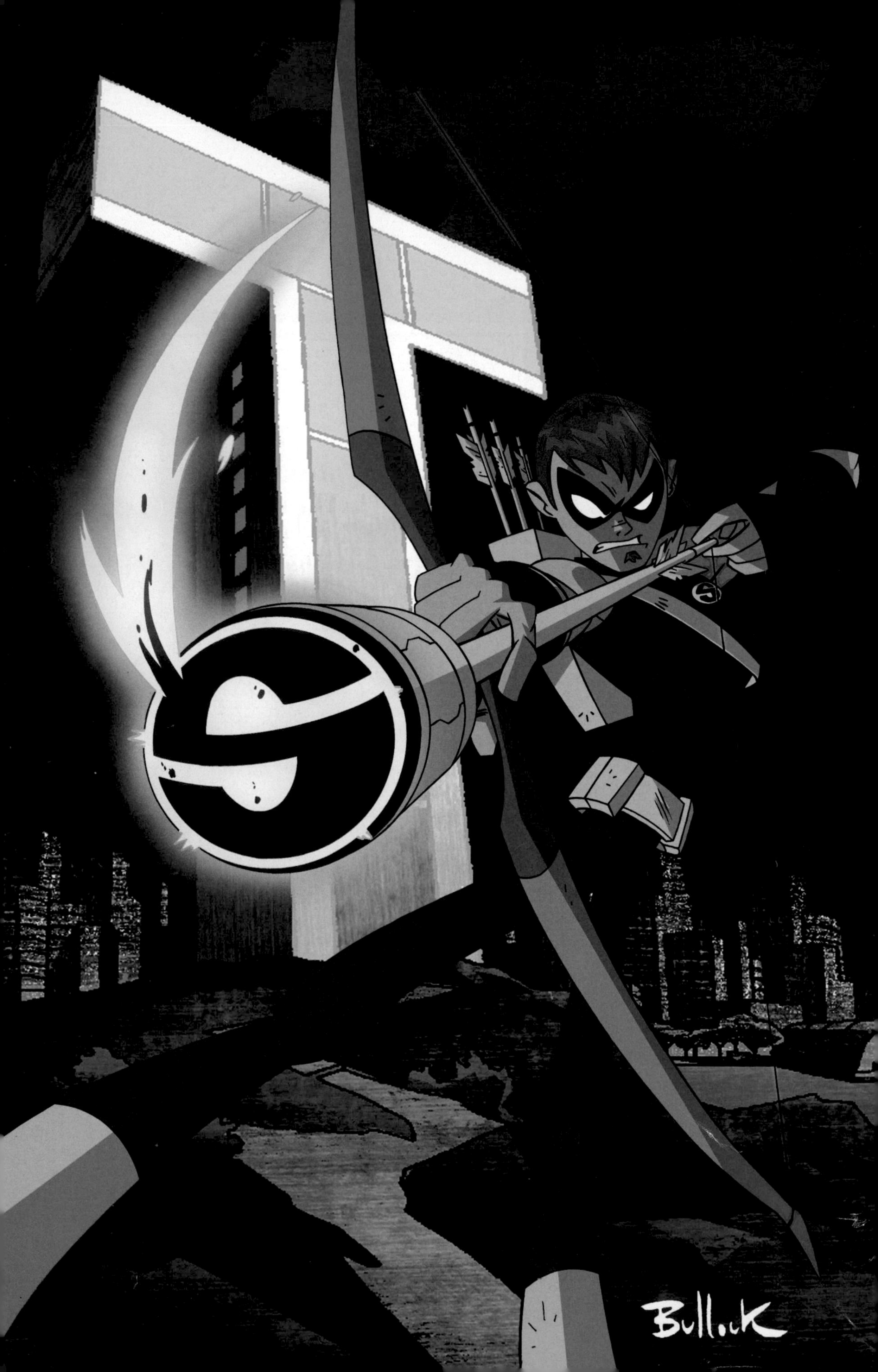
Bullock

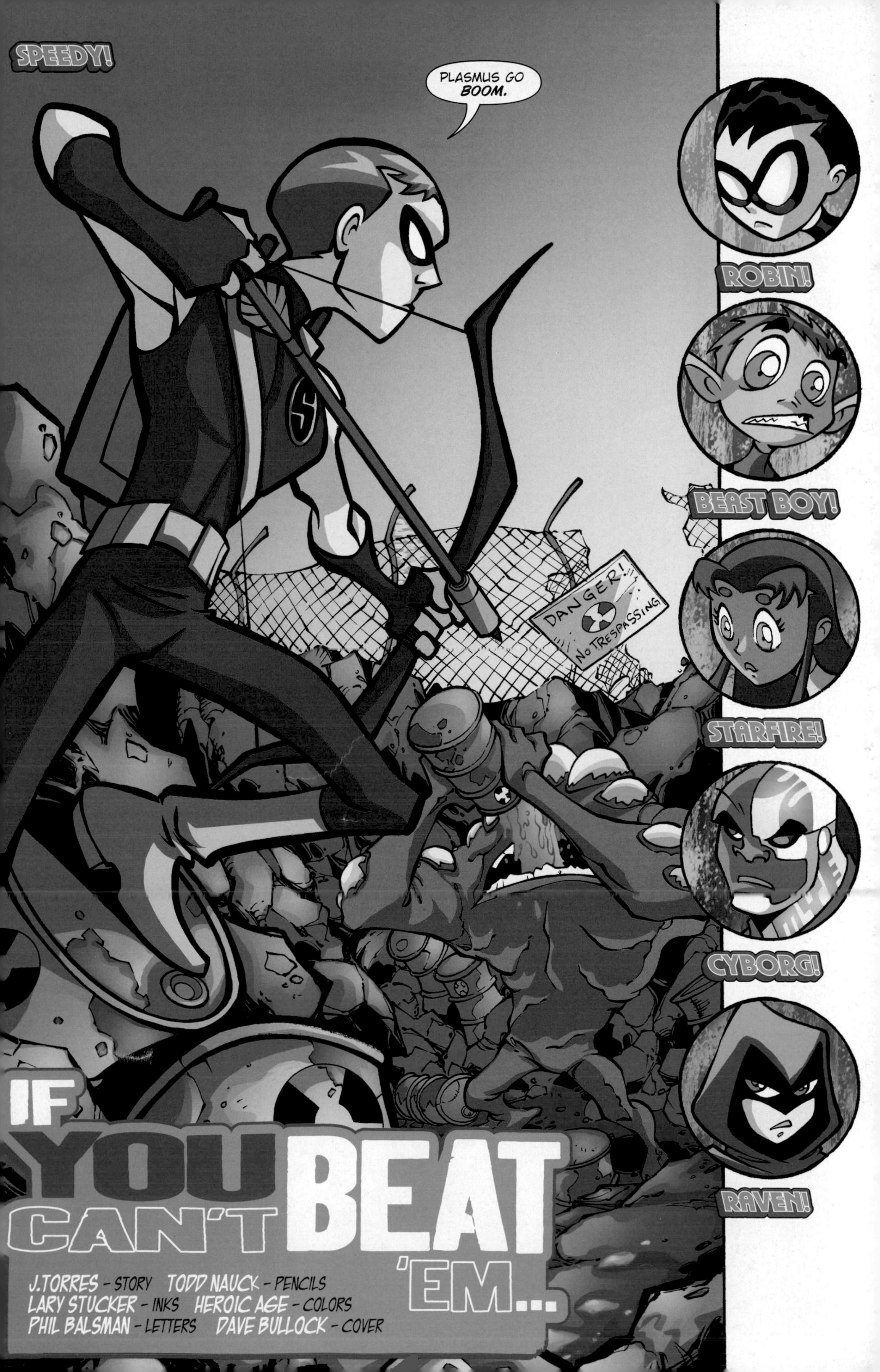

SPEEDY!
PLASMUS GO BOOM.
DANGER! NO TRESPASSING
ROBIN!
BEAST BOY!
STARFIRE!
CYBORG!
RAVEN!
IF YOU CAN'T BEAT 'EM...
J.TORRES - STORY TODD NAUCK - PENCILS
LARY STUCKER - INKS HEROIC AGE - COLORS
PHIL BALSMAN - LETTERS DAVE BULLOCK - COVER

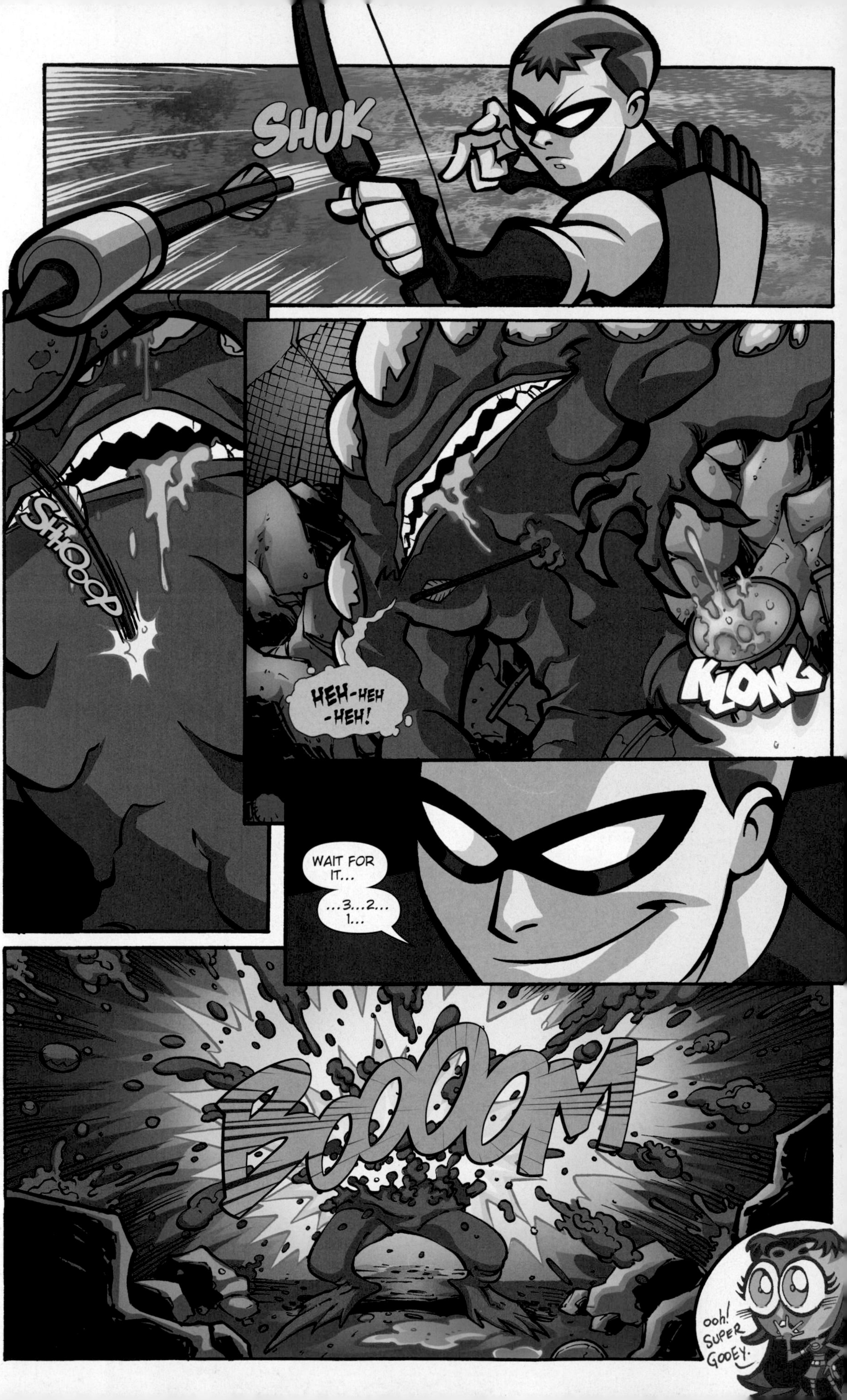
SHUK
SHOOOP
HEH-HEH
-HEH!
KLONG
WAIT FOR IT...
...3...2...
1...
BOOOOM
ooh! SUPER GOOEY.

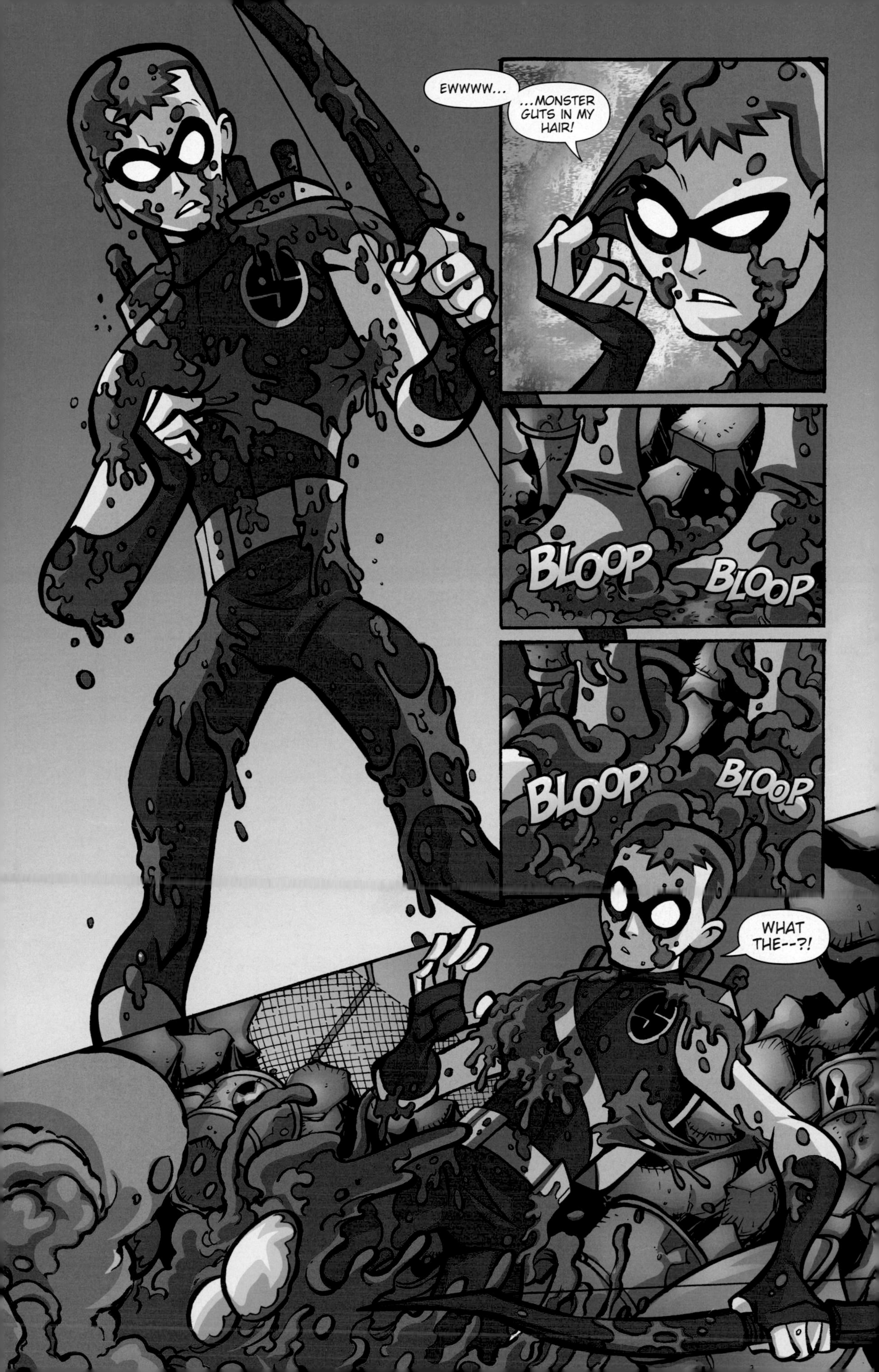
EWWWW...
...MONSTER GUTS IN MY HAIR!
BLOOP
BLOOP
BLOOP
BLOOP
WHAT THE--?!

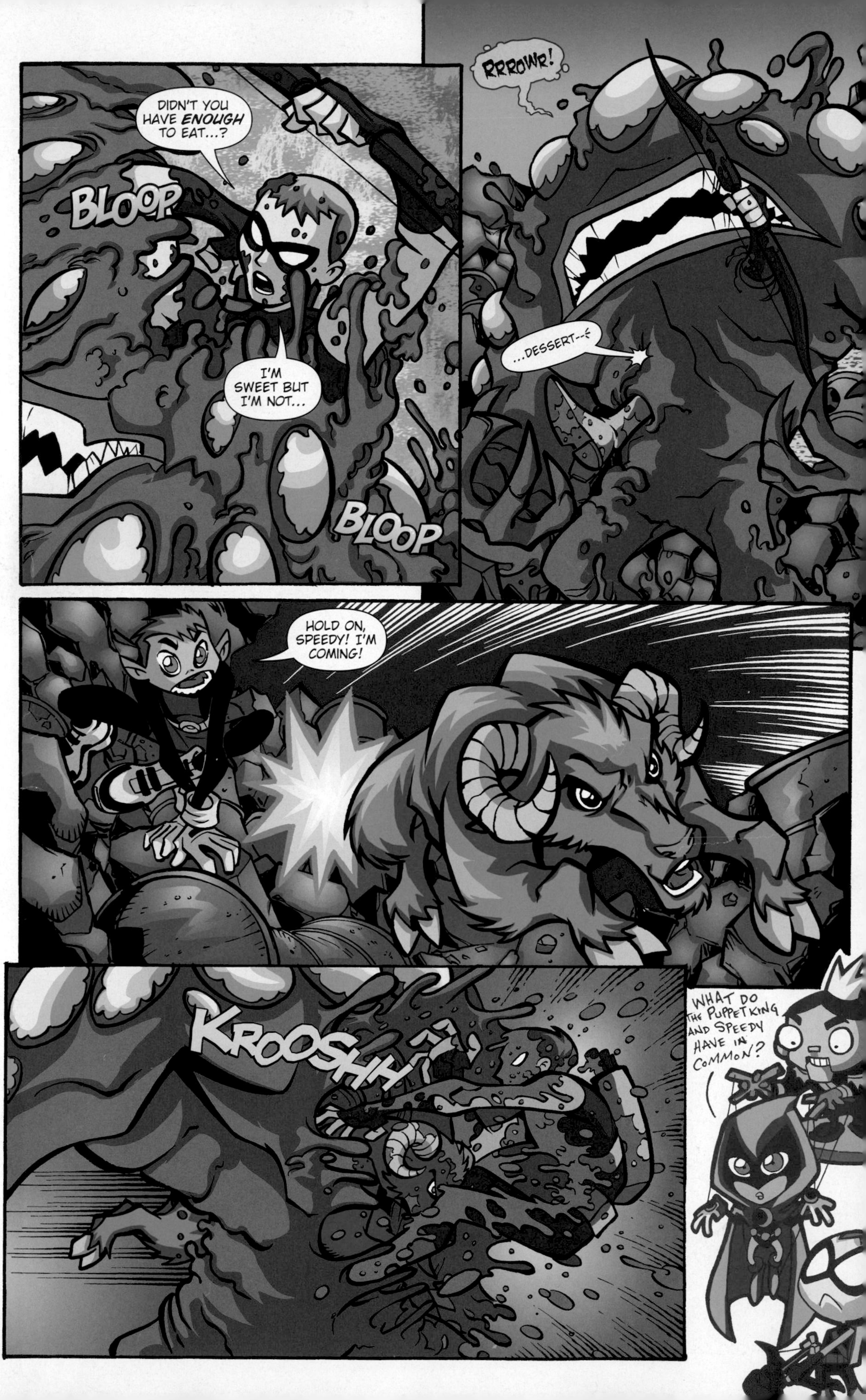

DIDN'T YOU HAVE ENOUGH TO EAT...?
BLOOP
I'M SWEET BUT I'M NOT...
BLOOP
RRROWR!
...DESSERT--!
HOLD ON, SPEEDY! I'M COMING!
KROOSHH
WHAT DO THE PUPPET KING AND SPEEDY HAVE IN COMMON?

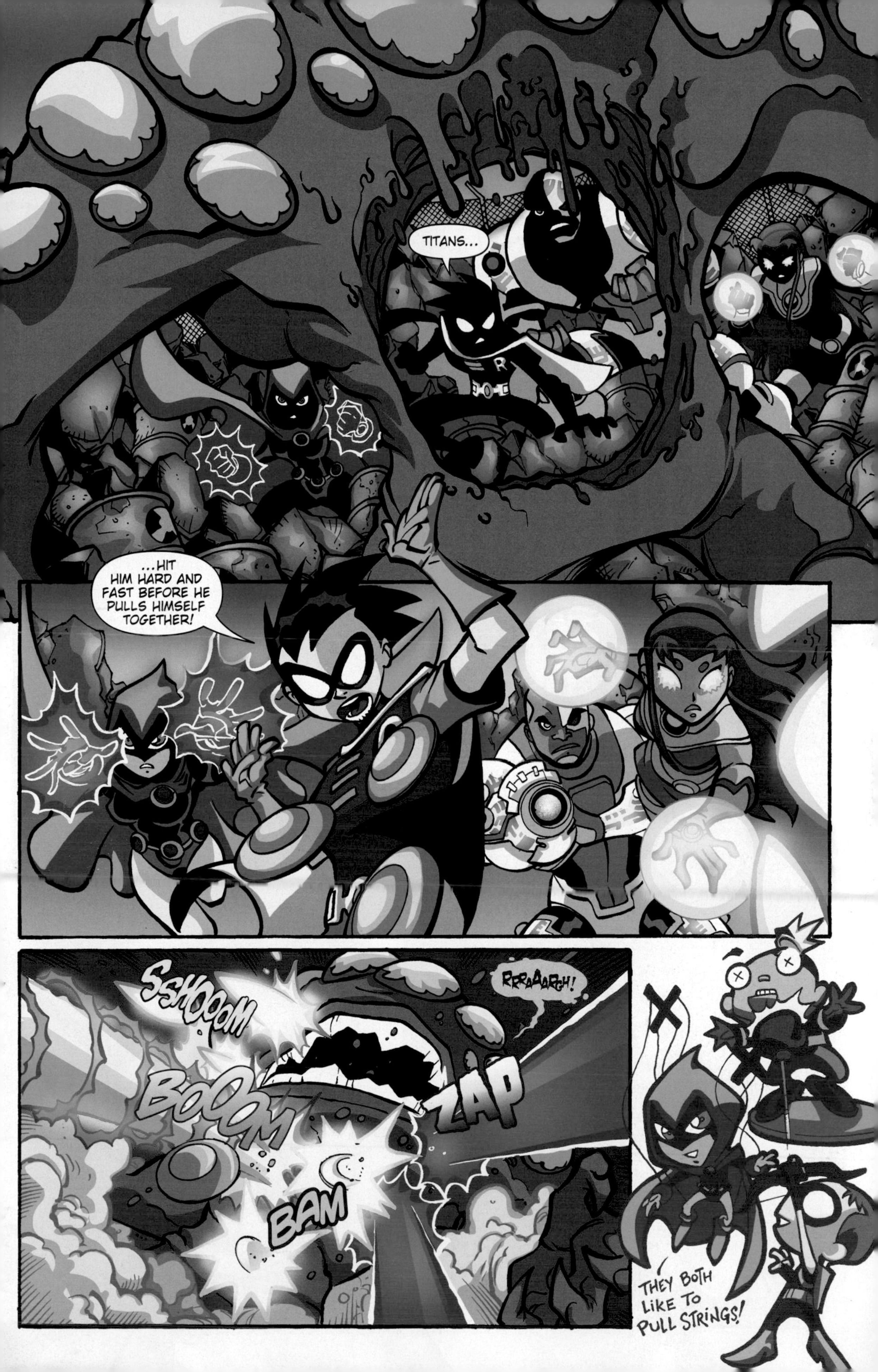
TITANS...
...HIT HIM HARD AND FAST BEFORE HE PULLS HIMSELF TOGETHER!
SSHOOOM
RRRAAARGH!
BOOOM
ZAP
BAM
THEY BOTH LIKE TO PULL STRINGS!

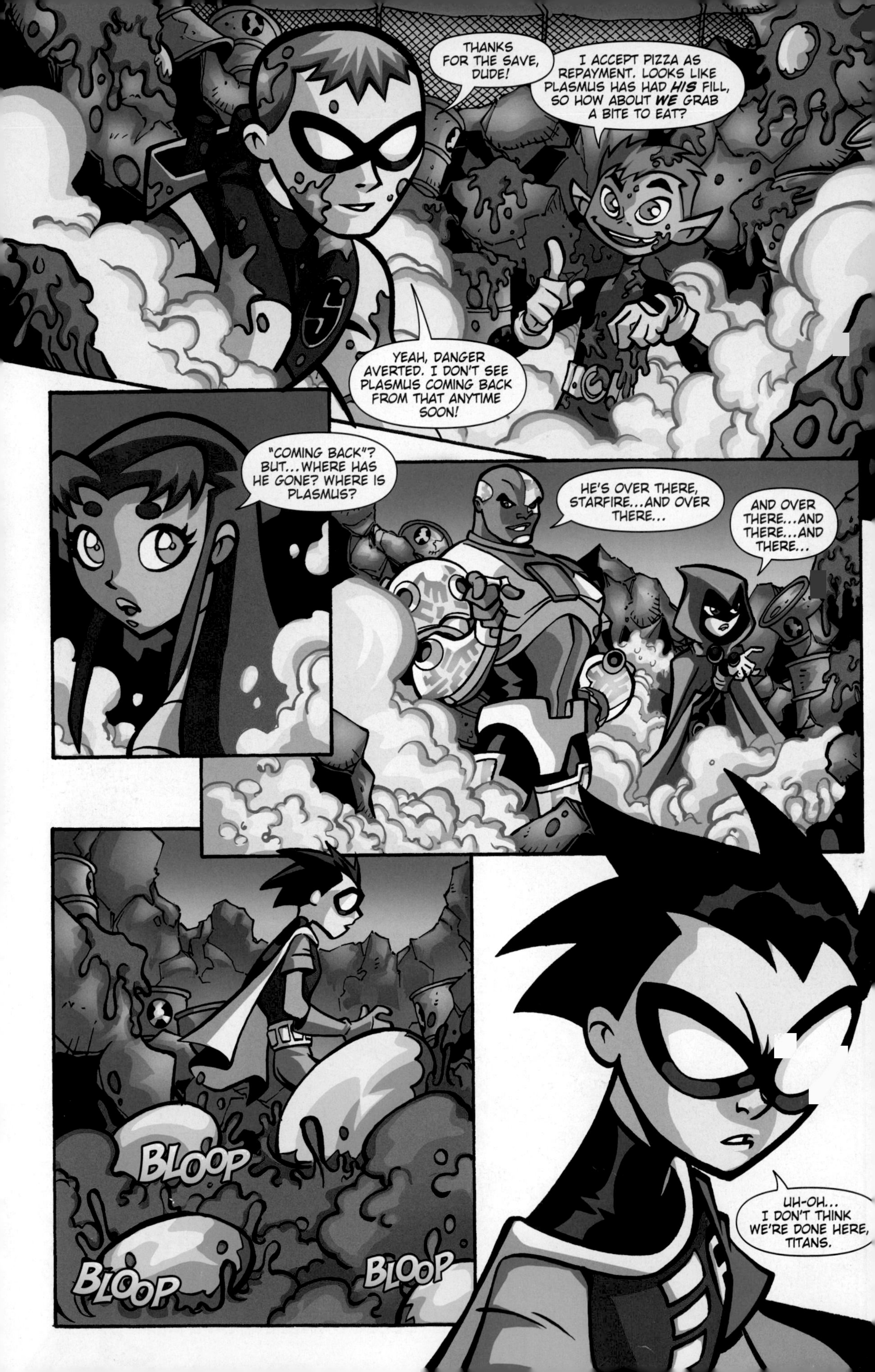
THANKS FOR THE SAVE, DUDE!
I ACCEPT PIZZA AS REPAYMENT. LOOKS LIKE PLASMUS HAS HAD *HIS* FILL, SO HOW ABOUT *WE* GRAB A BITE TO EAT?
YEAH, DANGER AVERTED. I DON'T SEE PLASMUS COMING BACK FROM THAT ANYTIME SOON!
"COMING BACK"? BUT...WHERE HAS HE GONE? WHERE IS PLASMUS?
HE'S OVER THERE, STARFIRE...AND OVER THERE...
AND OVER THERE...AND THERE...AND THERE...
BLOOP
BLOOP
BLOOP
UH-OH... I DON'T THINK WE'RE DONE HERE, TITANS.

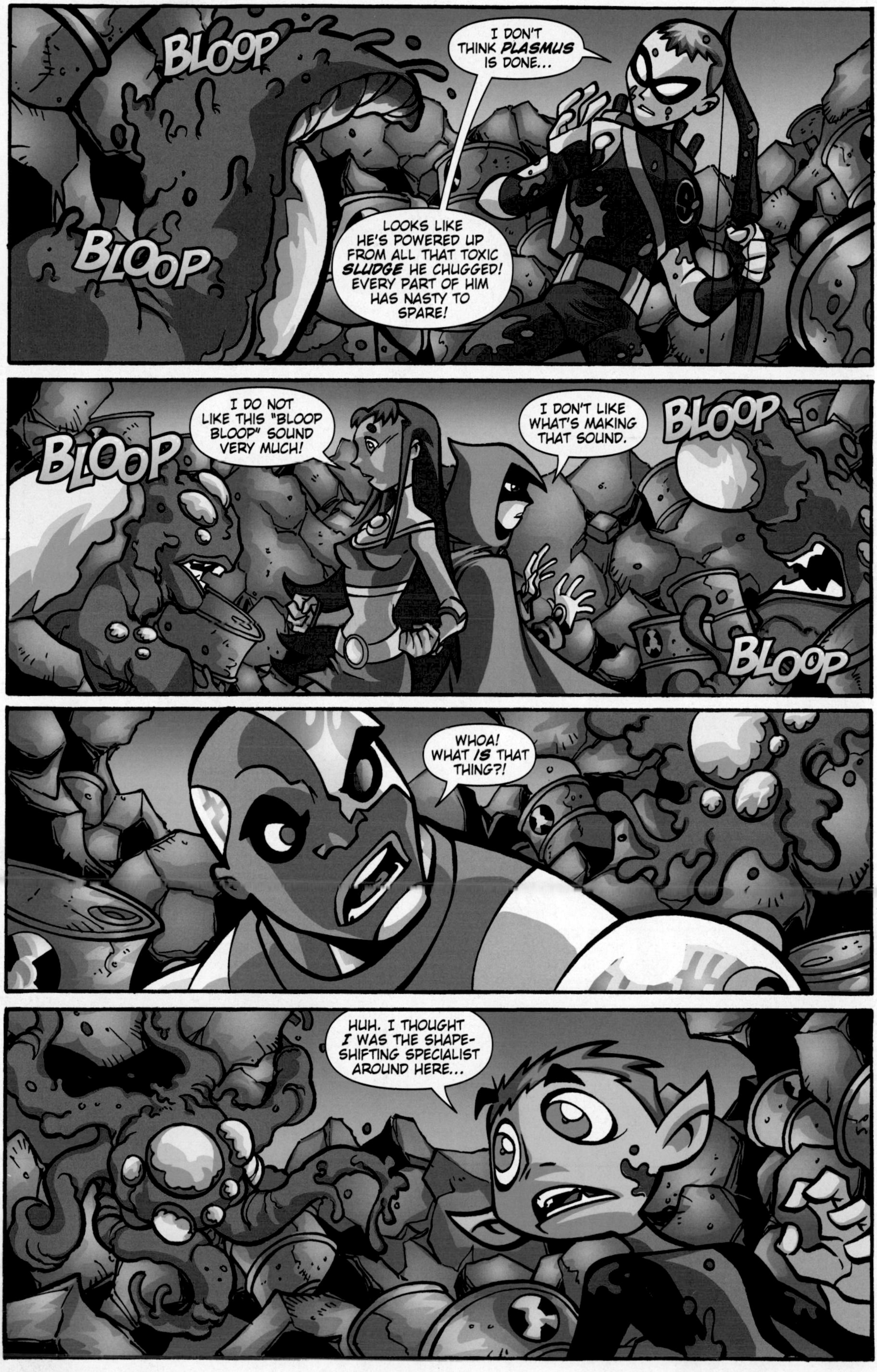
BLOOP
BLOOP
I DON'T THINK PLASMUS IS DONE...
LOOKS LIKE HE'S POWERED UP FROM ALL THAT TOXIC SLUDGE HE CHUGGED! EVERY PART OF HIM HAS NASTY TO SPARE!
BLOOP
I DO NOT LIKE THIS "BLOOP BLOOP" SOUND VERY MUCH!
I DON'T LIKE WHAT'S MAKING THAT SOUND.
BLOOP
BLOOP
WHOA! WHAT IS THAT THING?!
HUH. I THOUGHT I WAS THE SHAPE-SHIFTING SPECIALIST AROUND HERE...

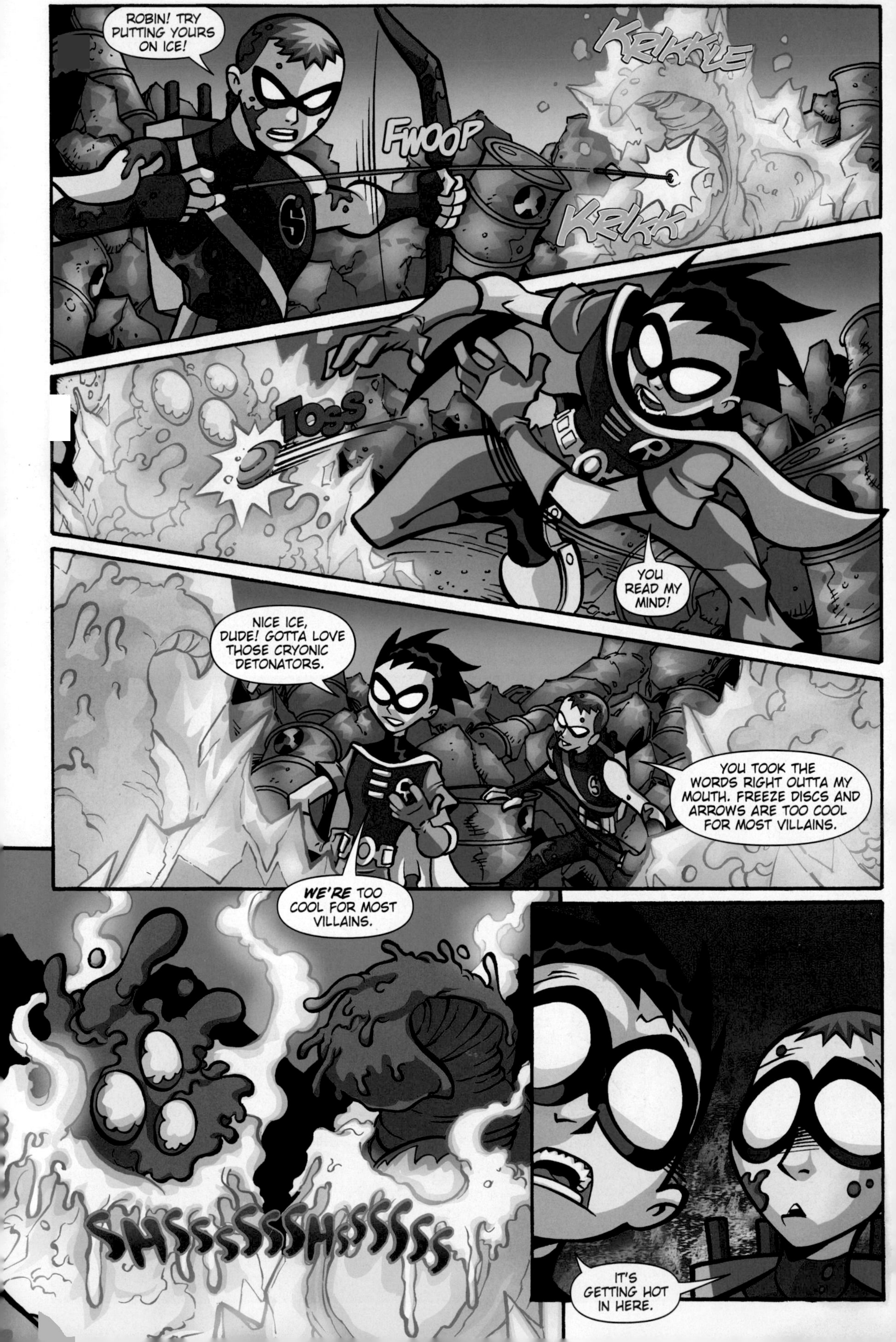
ROBIN! TRY PUTTING YOURS ON ICE!
FWOOP
KRIKKLE
KRIKK
TOSS
YOU READ MY MIND!
NICE ICE, DUDE! GOTTA LOVE THOSE CRYONIC DETONATORS.
YOU TOOK THE WORDS RIGHT OUTTA MY MOUTH. FREEZE DISCS AND ARROWS ARE TOO COOL FOR MOST VILLAINS.
WE'RE TOO COOL FOR MOST VILLAINS.
SHSSSSSSHSSSSSS
IT'S GETTING HOT IN HERE.

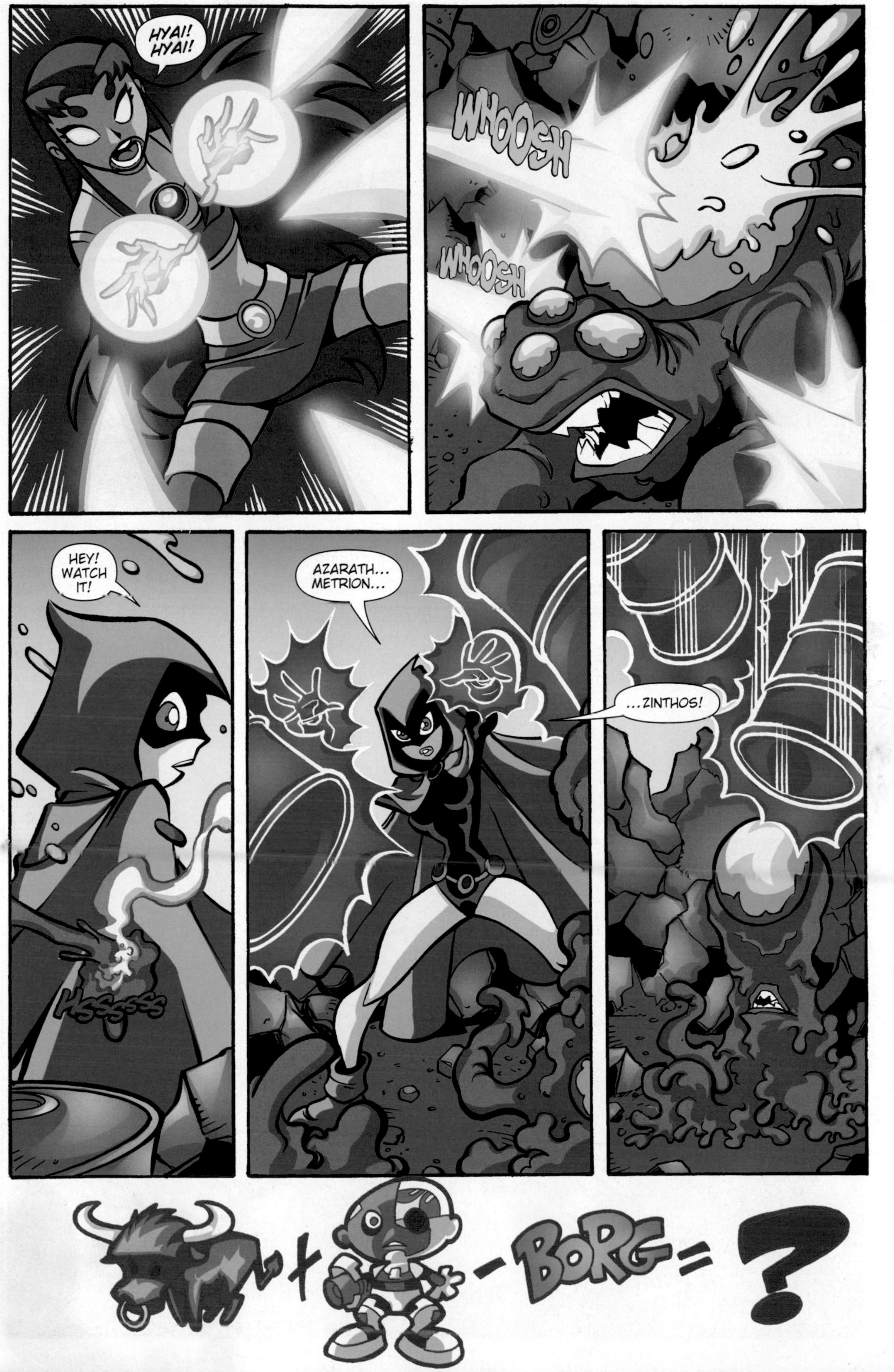
HYAI! HYAI!
WHOOSH
WHOOSH
HEY! WATCH IT!
HSSSSS
AZARATH... METRION...
...ZINTHOS!
BORG

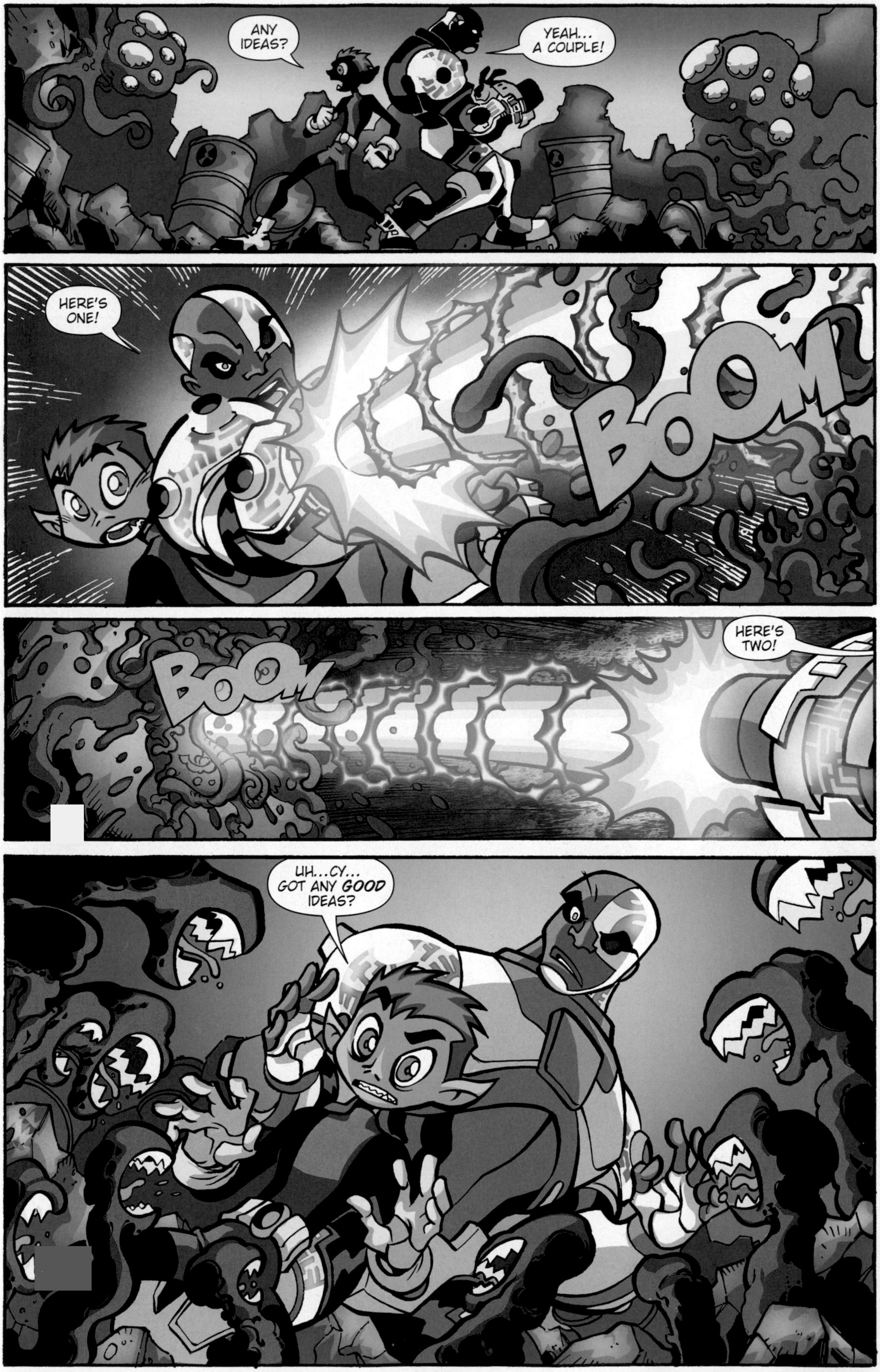
ANY IDEAS?
YEAH... A COUPLE!
HERE'S ONE!
BOOM
BOOM
HERE'S TWO!
UH...CY... GOT ANY GOOD IDEAS?

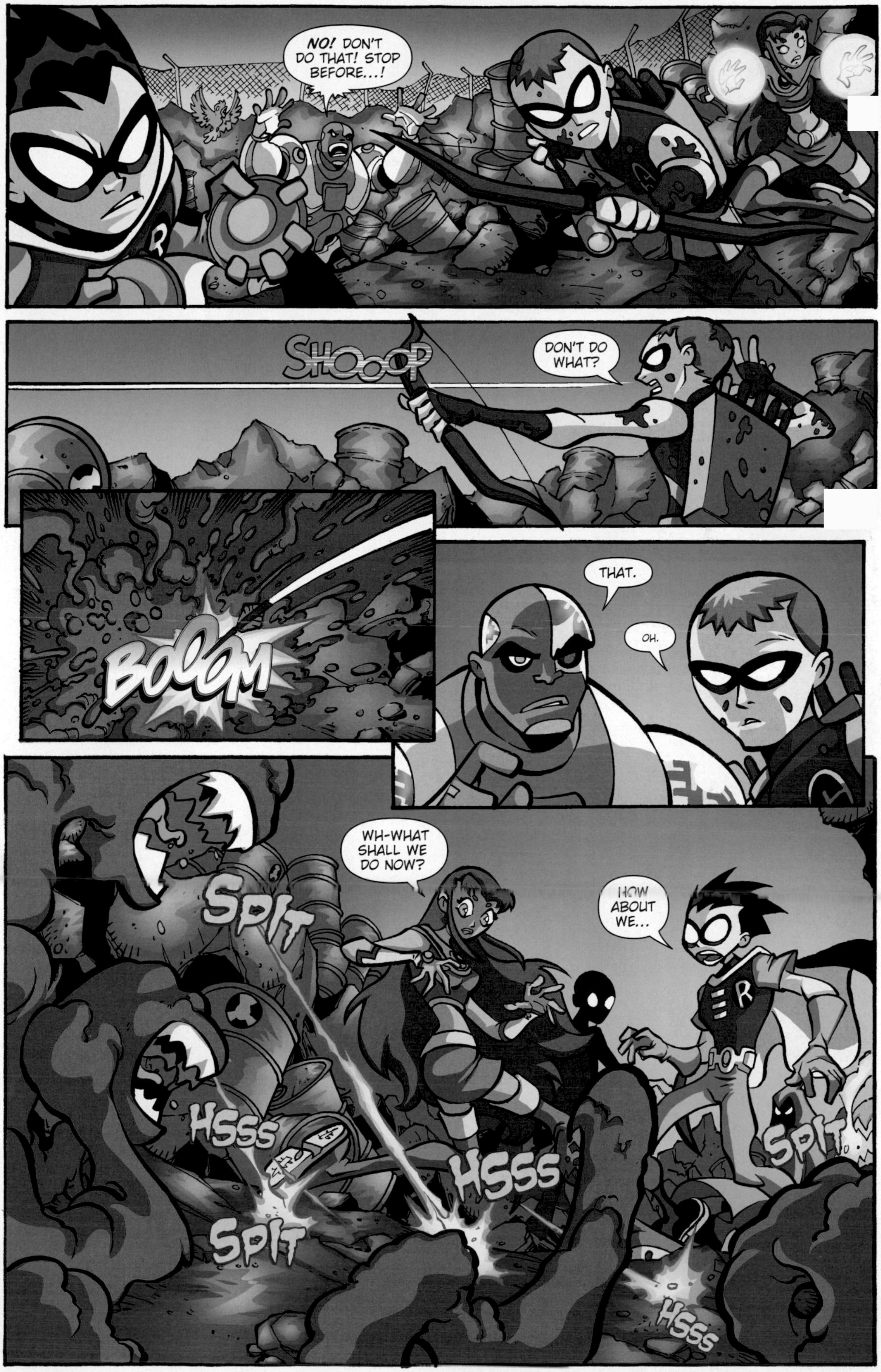
NO! DON'T DO THAT! STOP BEFORE...!
SHOOOP
DON'T DO WHAT?
BOOOM
THAT.
OH.
WH-WHAT SHALL WE DO NOW?
HOW ABOUT WE...
SPIT
HSSS
HSSS
SPIT
SPIT
HSSS

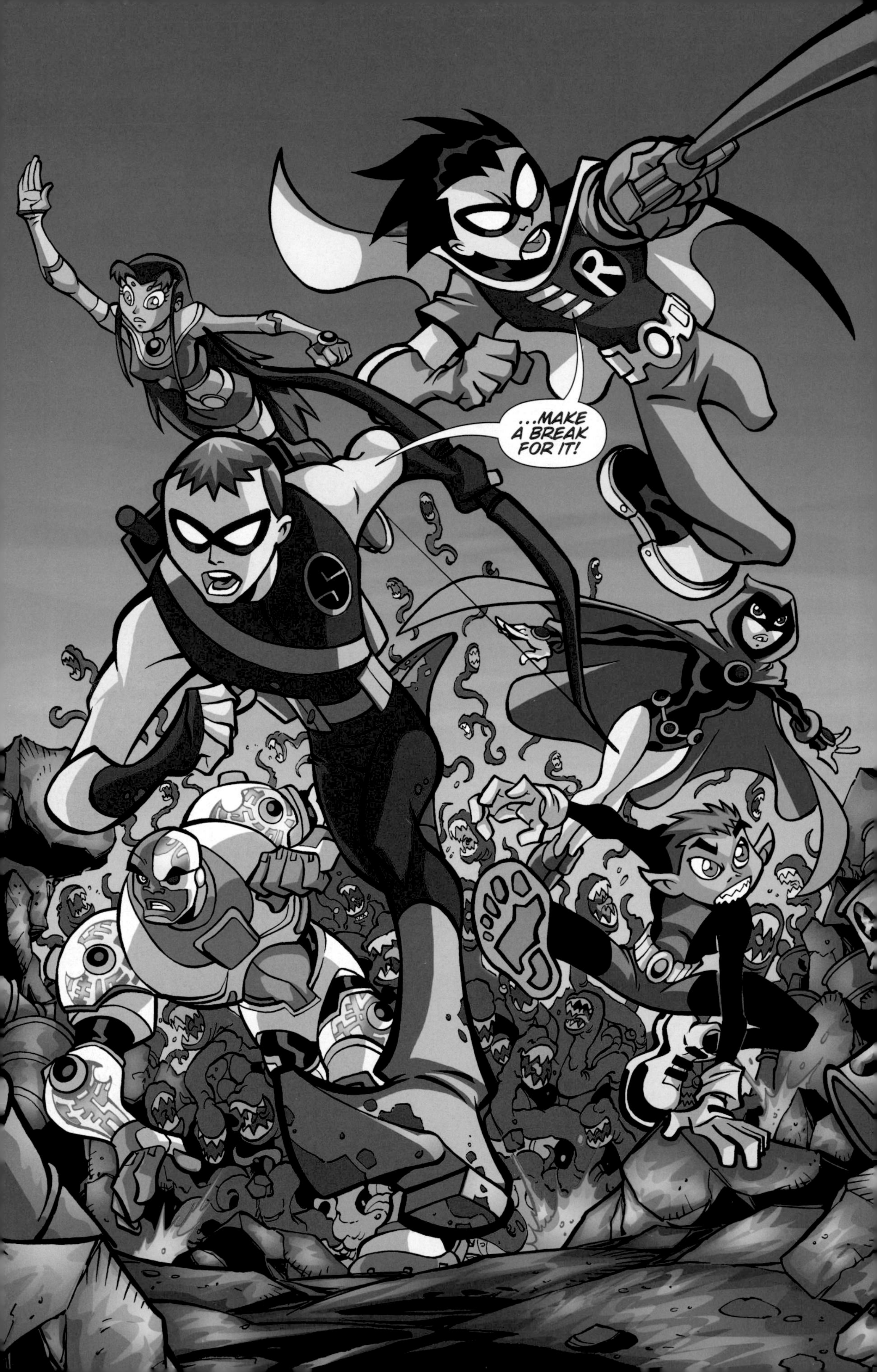
...MAKE A BREAK FOR IT!

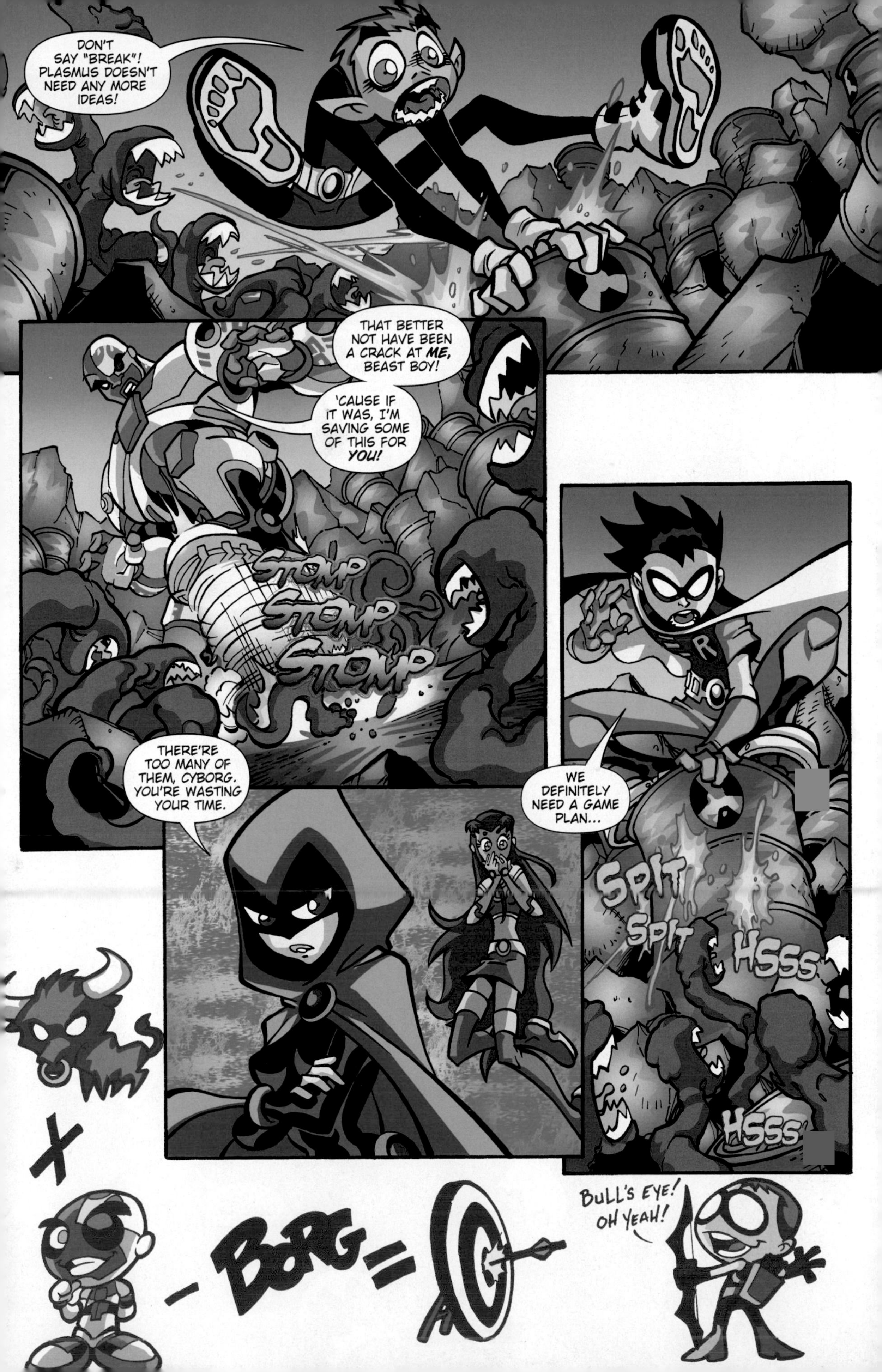
DON'T SAY "BREAK"! PLASMUS DOESN'T NEED ANY MORE IDEAS!
THAT BETTER NOT HAVE BEEN A CRACK AT ME, BEAST BOY!
'CAUSE IF IT WAS, I'M SAVING SOME OF THIS FOR YOU!
STOMP STOMP STOMP
THERE'RE TOO MANY OF THEM, CYBORG. YOU'RE WASTING YOUR TIME.
WE DEFINITELY NEED A GAME PLAN...
SPIT SPIT HSSS
HSSS
BULL'S EYE! OH YEAH!
- BORG =

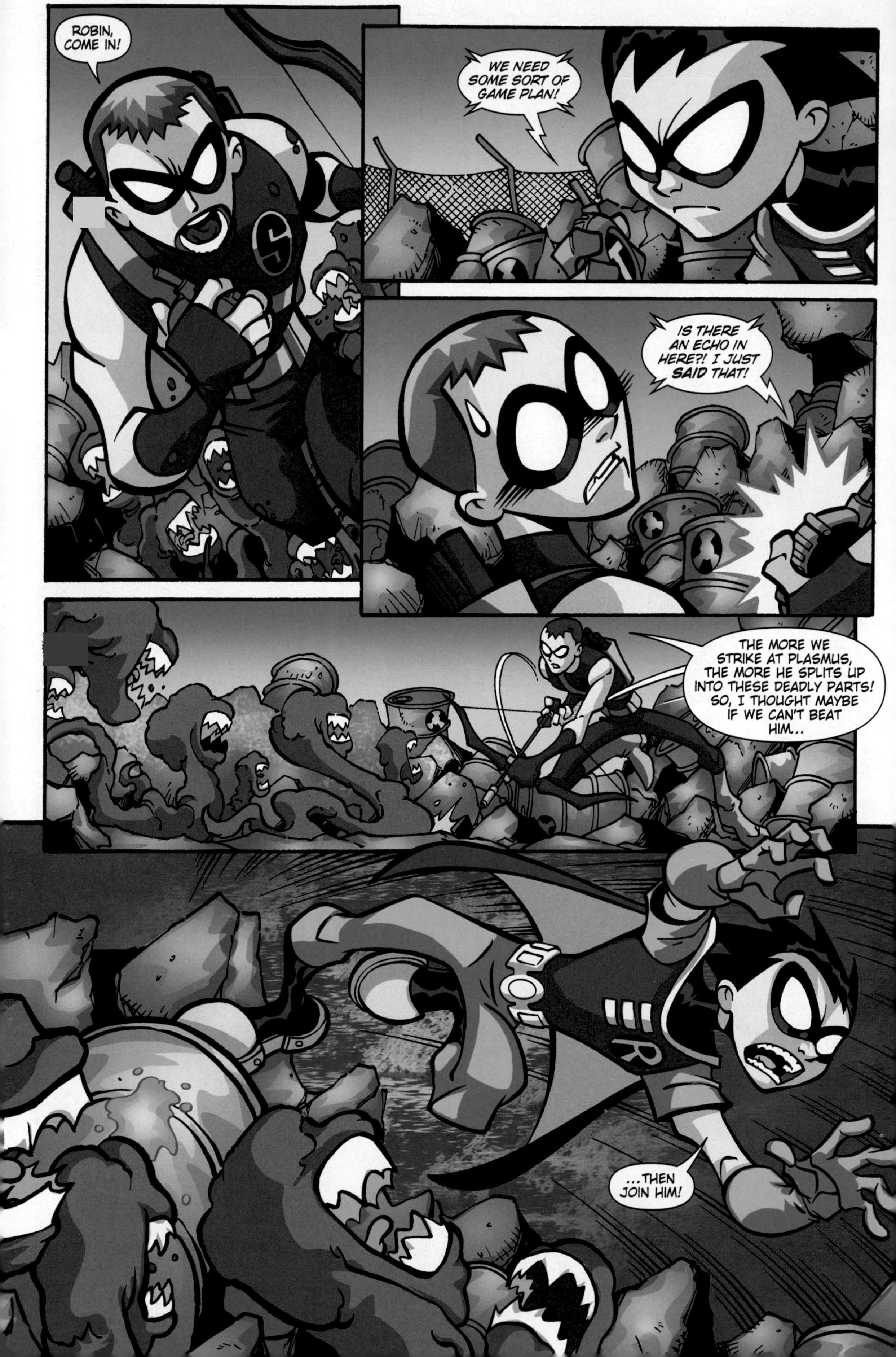
ROBIN, COME IN!
WE NEED SOME SORT OF GAME PLAN!
IS THERE AN ECHO IN HERE?! I JUST SAID THAT!
THE MORE WE STRIKE AT PLASMUS, THE MORE HE SPLITS UP INTO THESE DEADLY PARTS! SO, I THOUGHT MAYBE IF WE CAN'T BEAT HIM...
...THEN JOIN HIM!

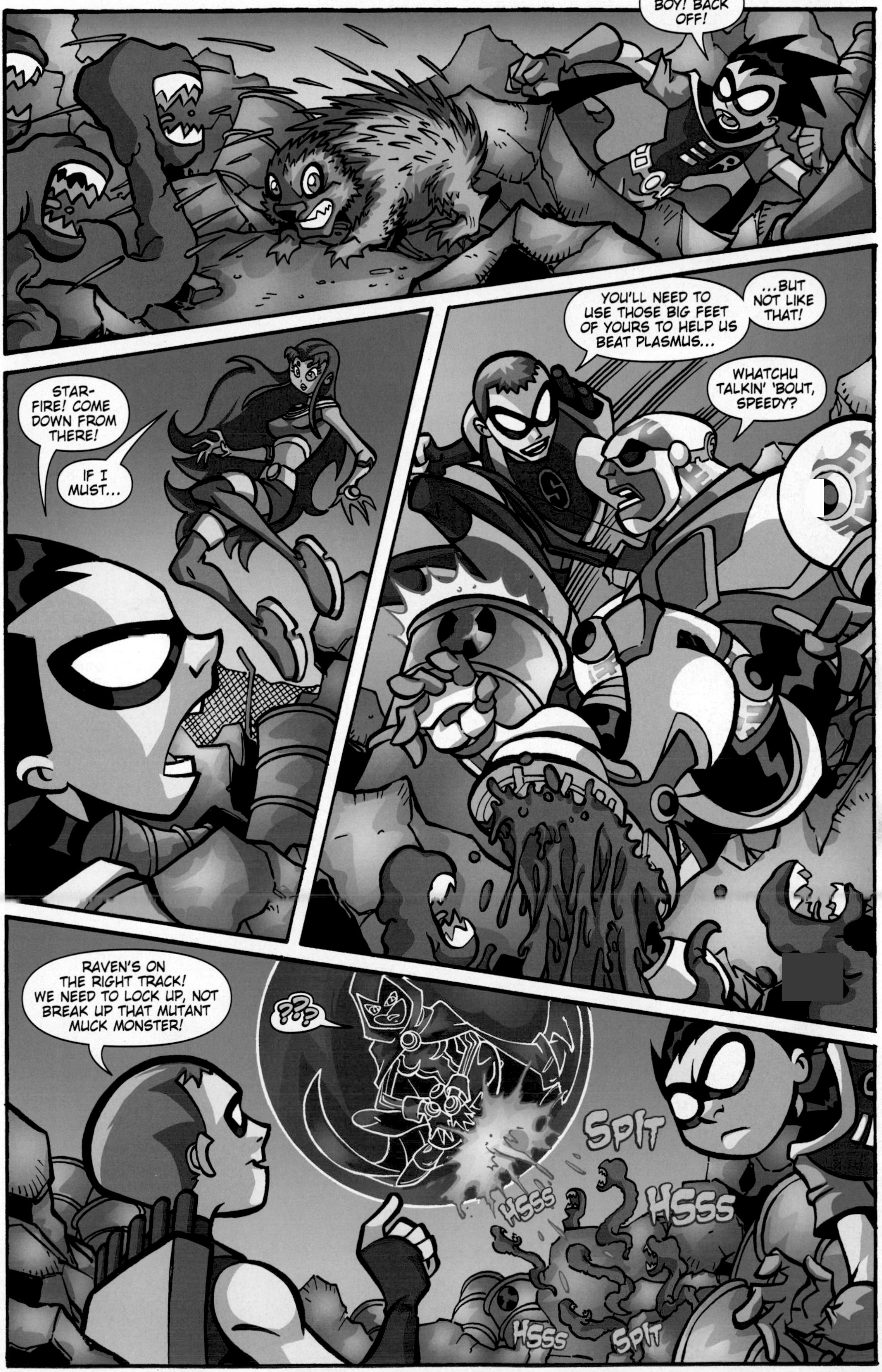
NO, BEAST BOY! BACK OFF!
YOU'LL NEED TO USE THOSE BIG FEET OF YOURS TO HELP US BEAT PLASMUS...
...BUT NOT LIKE THAT!
WHATCHU TALKIN' 'BOUT, SPEEDY?
STAR-FIRE! COME DOWN FROM THERE!
IF I MUST...
RAVEN'S ON THE RIGHT TRACK! WE NEED TO LOCK UP, NOT BREAK UP THAT MUTANT MUCK MONSTER!
???
SPIT
HSSS
HSSS
HSSS
SPIT

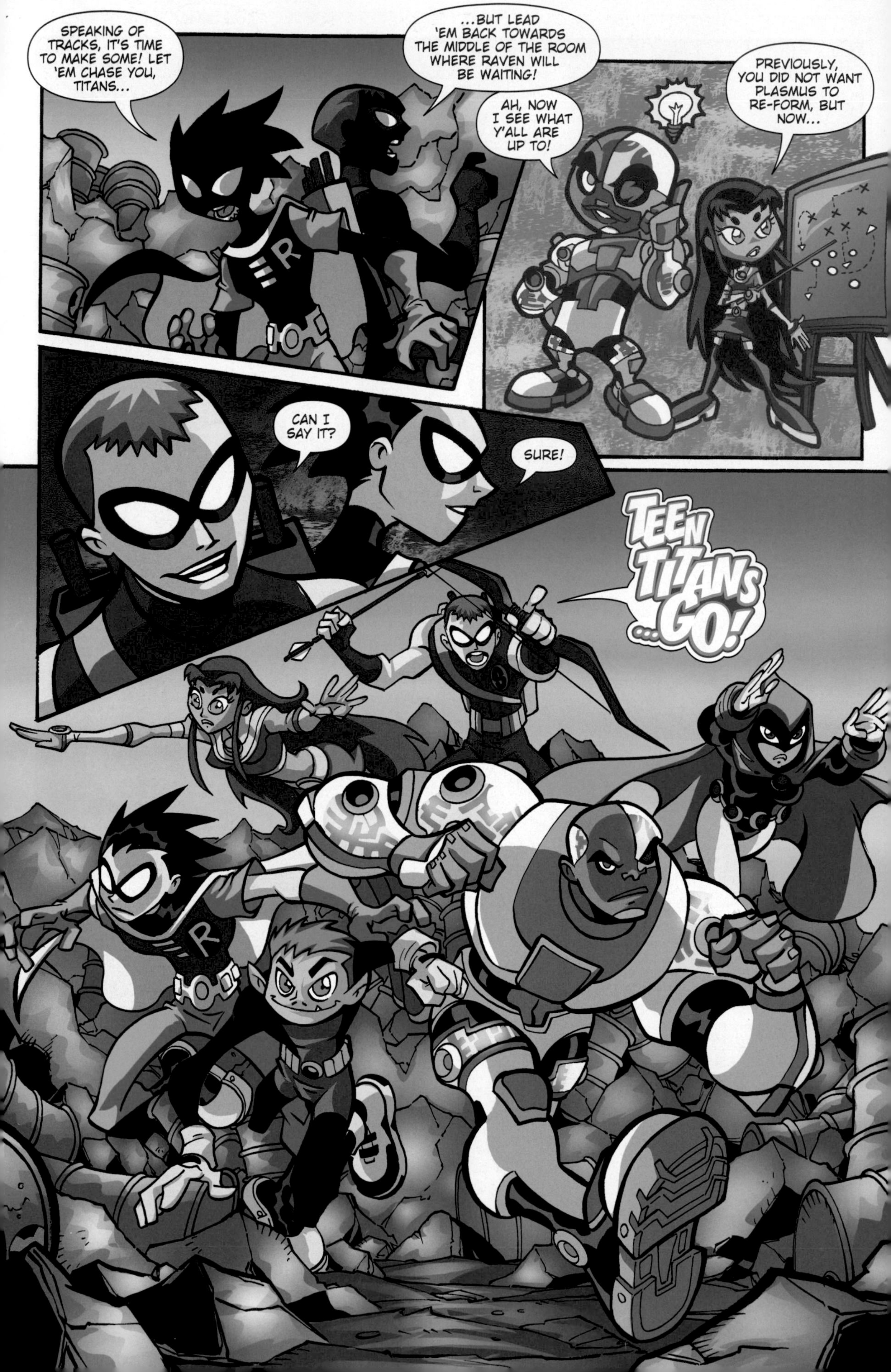
SPEAKING OF TRACKS, IT'S TIME TO MAKE SOME! LET 'EM CHASE YOU, TITANS...
...BUT LEAD 'EM BACK TOWARDS THE MIDDLE OF THE ROOM WHERE RAVEN WILL BE WAITING!
AH, NOW I SEE WHAT Y'ALL ARE UP TO!
PREVIOUSLY, YOU DID NOT WANT PLASMUS TO RE-FORM, BUT NOW...
CAN I SAY IT?
SURE!
TEEN TITANS ...GO!

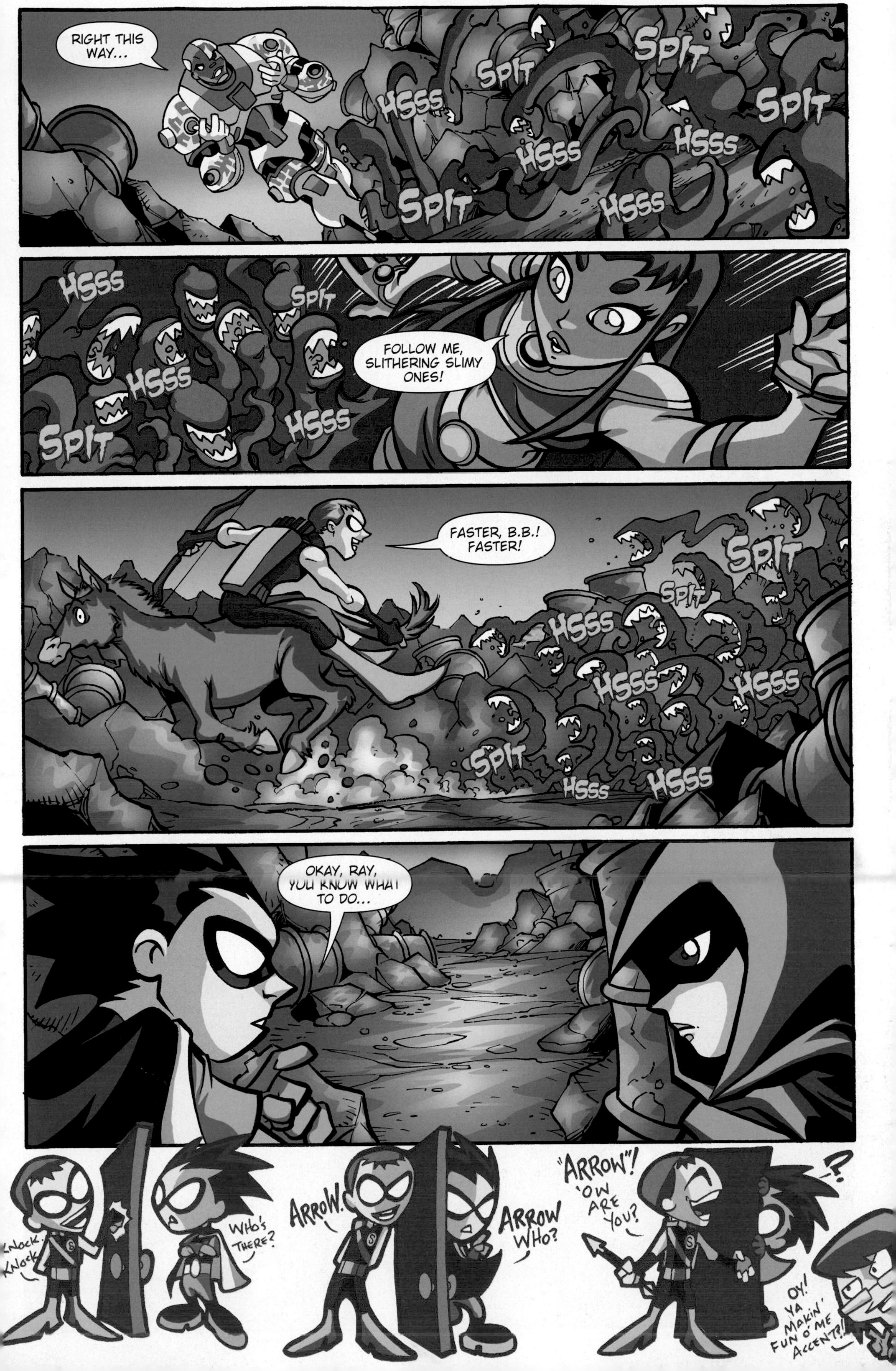
RIGHT THIS WAY...
HSSS
SPIT
SPIT
SPIT
SPIT
HSSS
HSSS
SPIT
HSSS
HSSS
SPIT
HSSS
FOLLOW ME, SLITHERING SLIMY ONES!
HSSS
SPIT
FASTER, B.B.! FASTER!
SPIT
SPIT
HSSS
HSSS
HSSS
SPIT
HSSS
HSSS
OKAY, RAY, YOU KNOW WHAT TO DO...
KNOCK KNOCK
WHO'S THERE?
ARROW.
ARROW WHO?
"ARROW"! 'OW ARE YOU?
?
OY! YA MAKIN' FUN O' ME ACCENT?!

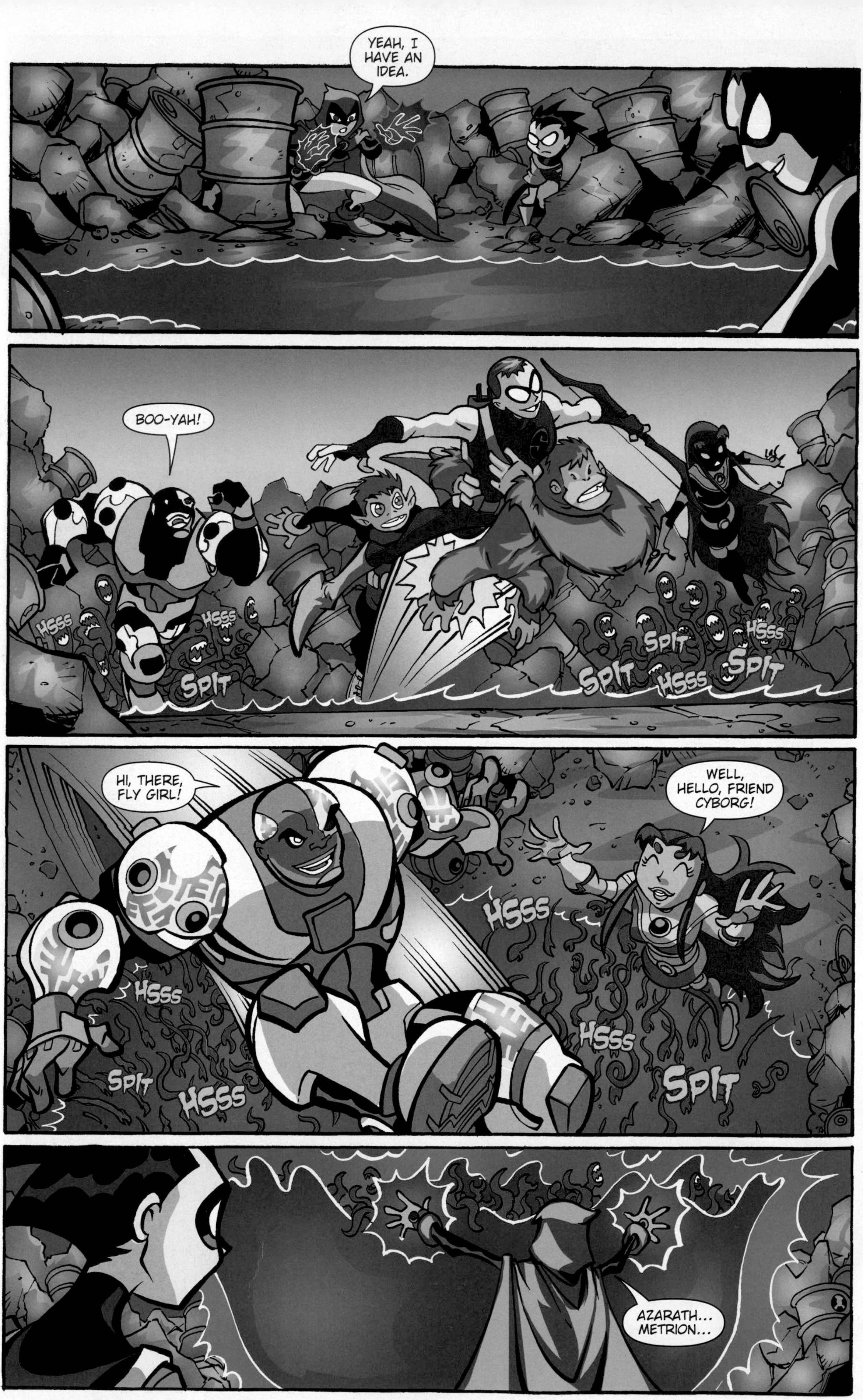
YEAH, I HAVE AN IDEA.
BOO-YAH!
HSSS
HSSS
SPIT
SPIT
HSSS
SPIT
HSSS
SPIT
HI, THERE, FLY GIRL!
WELL, HELLO, FRIEND CYBORG!
HSSS
HSSS
HSSS
SPIT
HSSS
SPIT
AZARATH... METRION...

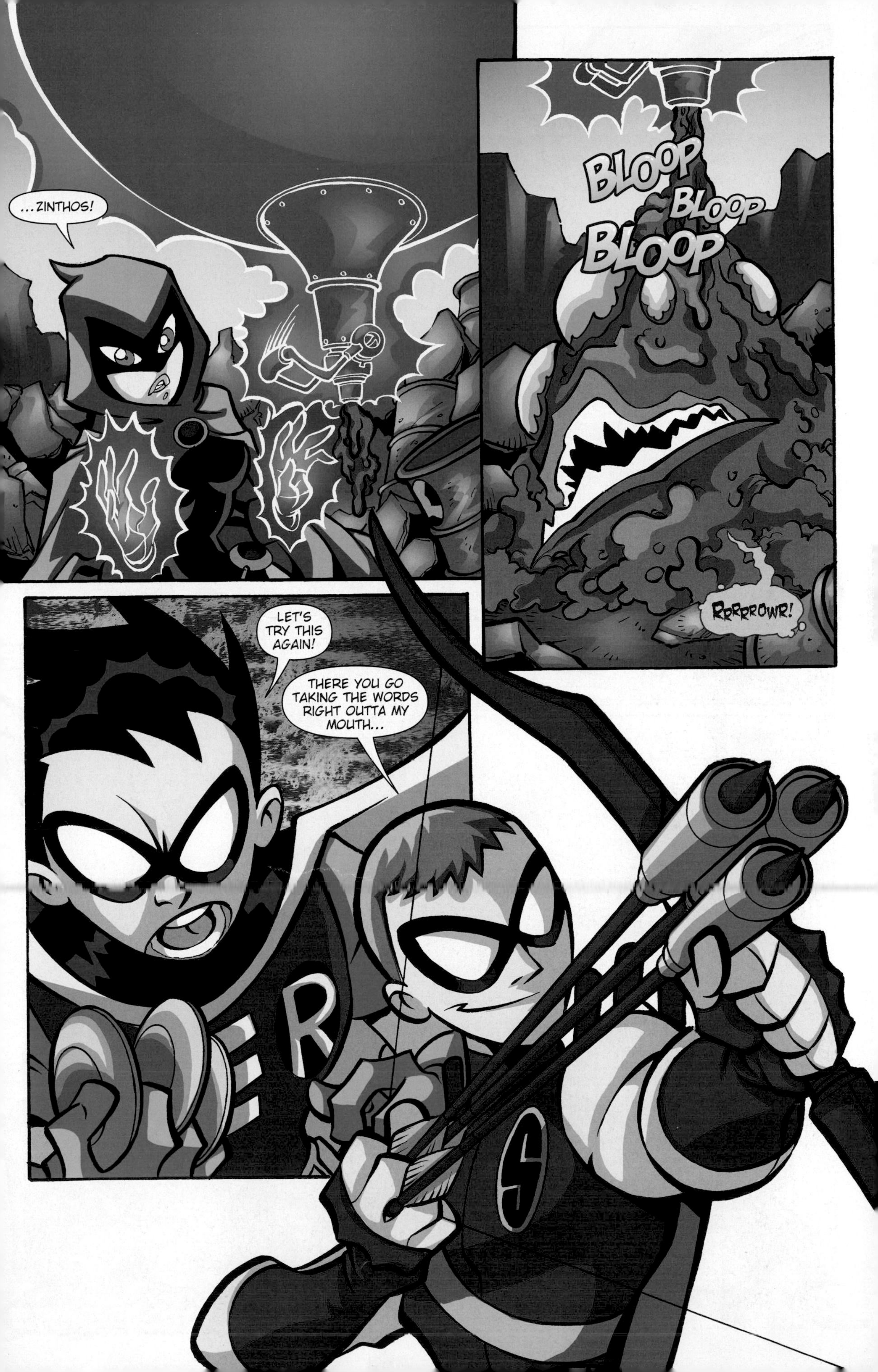

...ZINTHOS!
BLOOP
BLOOP
BLOOP
RRRRROWR!
LET'S TRY THIS AGAIN!
THERE YOU GO TAKING THE WORDS RIGHT OUTTA MY MOUTH...

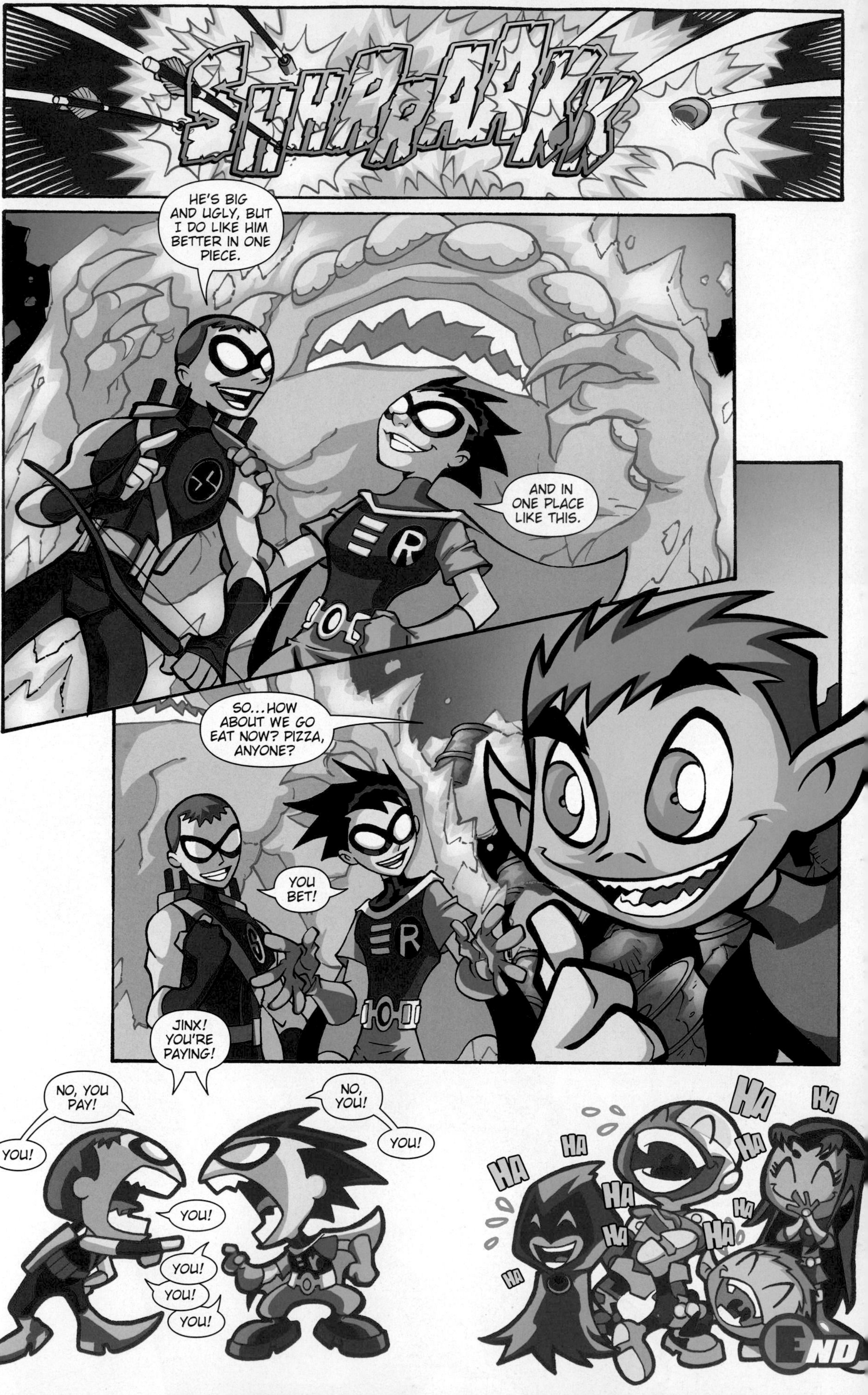
SHHRAAAKK
HE'S BIG AND UGLY, BUT I DO LIKE HIM BETTER IN ONE PIECE.
AND IN ONE PLACE LIKE THIS.
SO...HOW ABOUT WE GO EAT NOW? PIZZA, ANYONE?
YOU BET!
JINX! YOU'RE PAYING!
NO, YOU PAY!
YOU!
NO, YOU!
YOU!
YOU!
YOU!
YOU!
YOU!
HA
HA
HA
HA
HA
HA
HA
HA
HA
HA
END

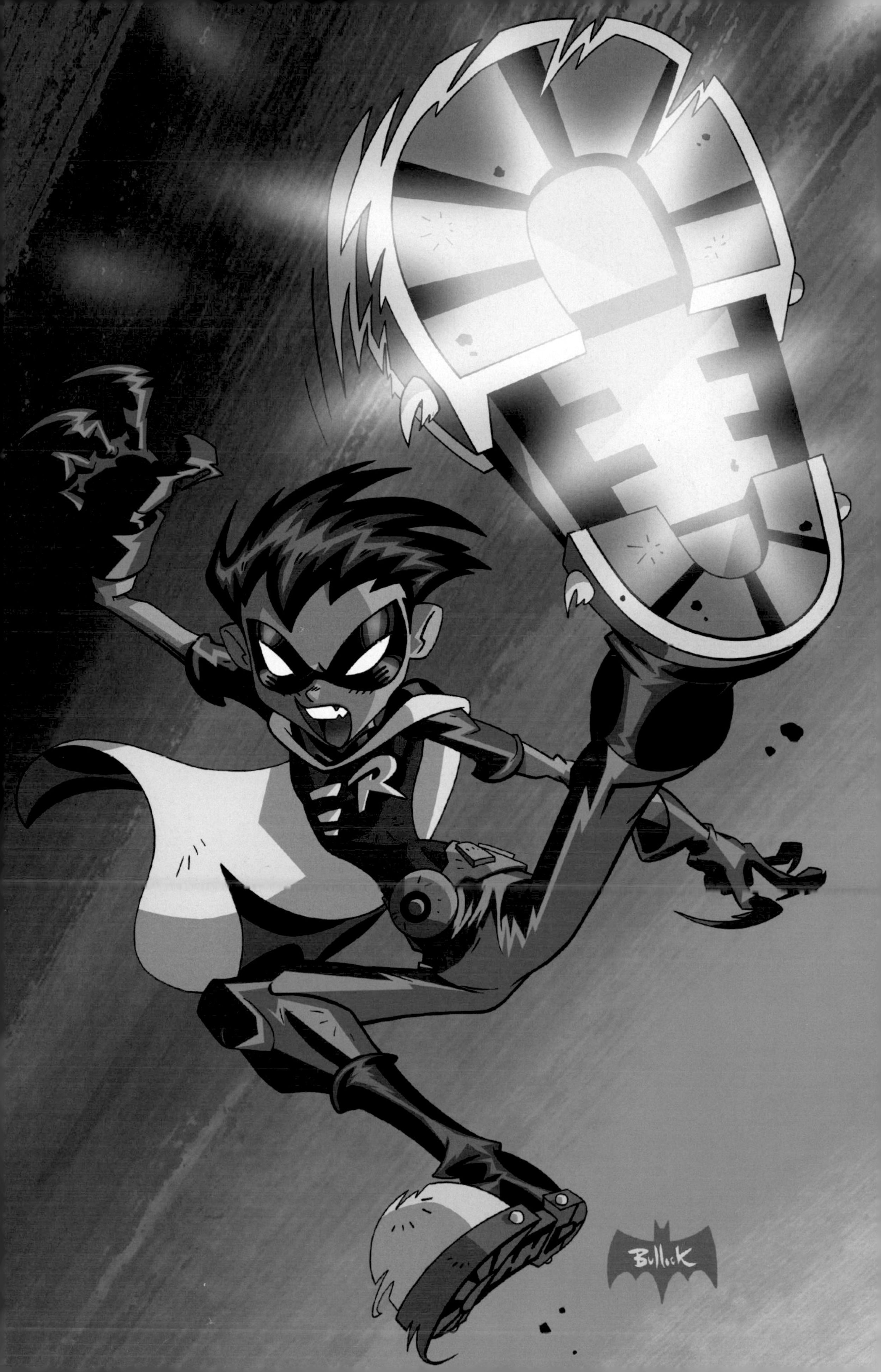
Bullock

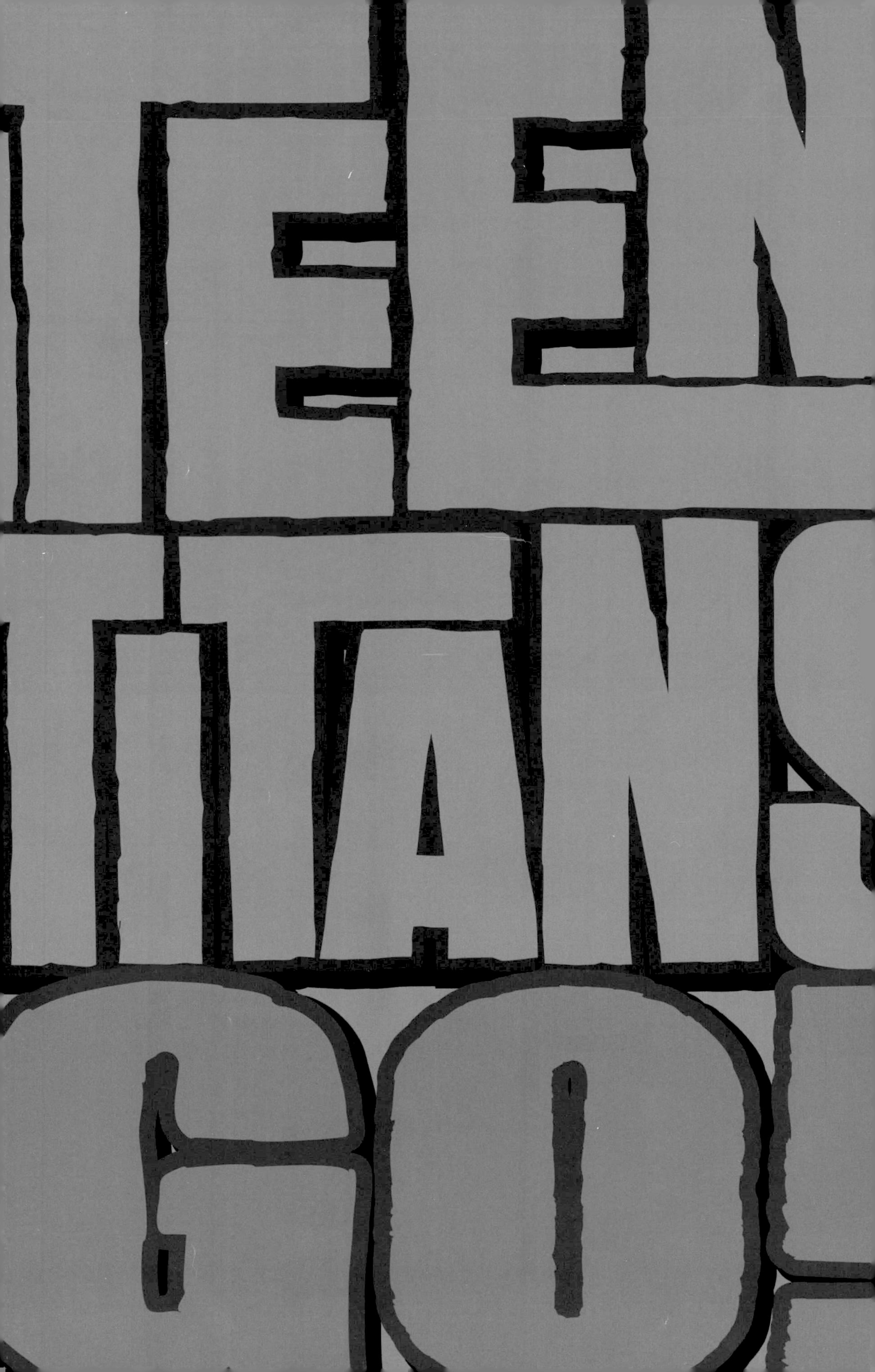

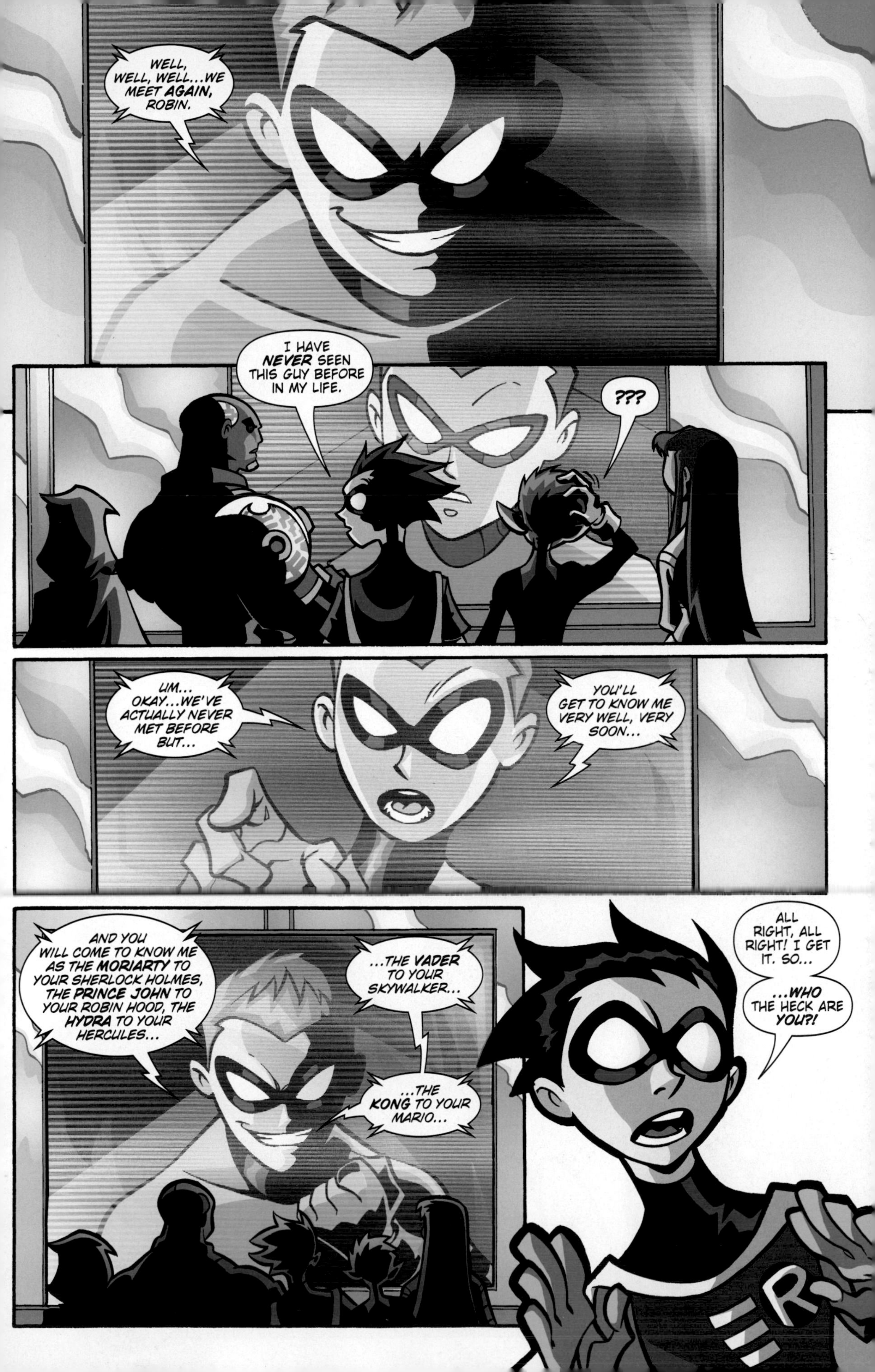
WELL, WELL, WELL...WE MEET AGAIN, ROBIN.
I HAVE NEVER SEEN THIS GUY BEFORE IN MY LIFE.
???
UM... OKAY...WE'VE ACTUALLY NEVER MET BEFORE BUT...
YOU'LL GET TO KNOW ME VERY WELL, VERY SOON...
AND YOU WILL COME TO KNOW ME AS THE MORIARTY TO YOUR SHERLOCK HOLMES, THE PRINCE JOHN TO YOUR ROBIN HOOD, THE HYDRA TO YOUR HERCULES...
...THE VADER TO YOUR SKYWALKER...
...THE KONG TO YOUR MARIO...
ALL RIGHT, ALL RIGHT! I GET IT. SO...
...WHO THE HECK ARE YOU?!

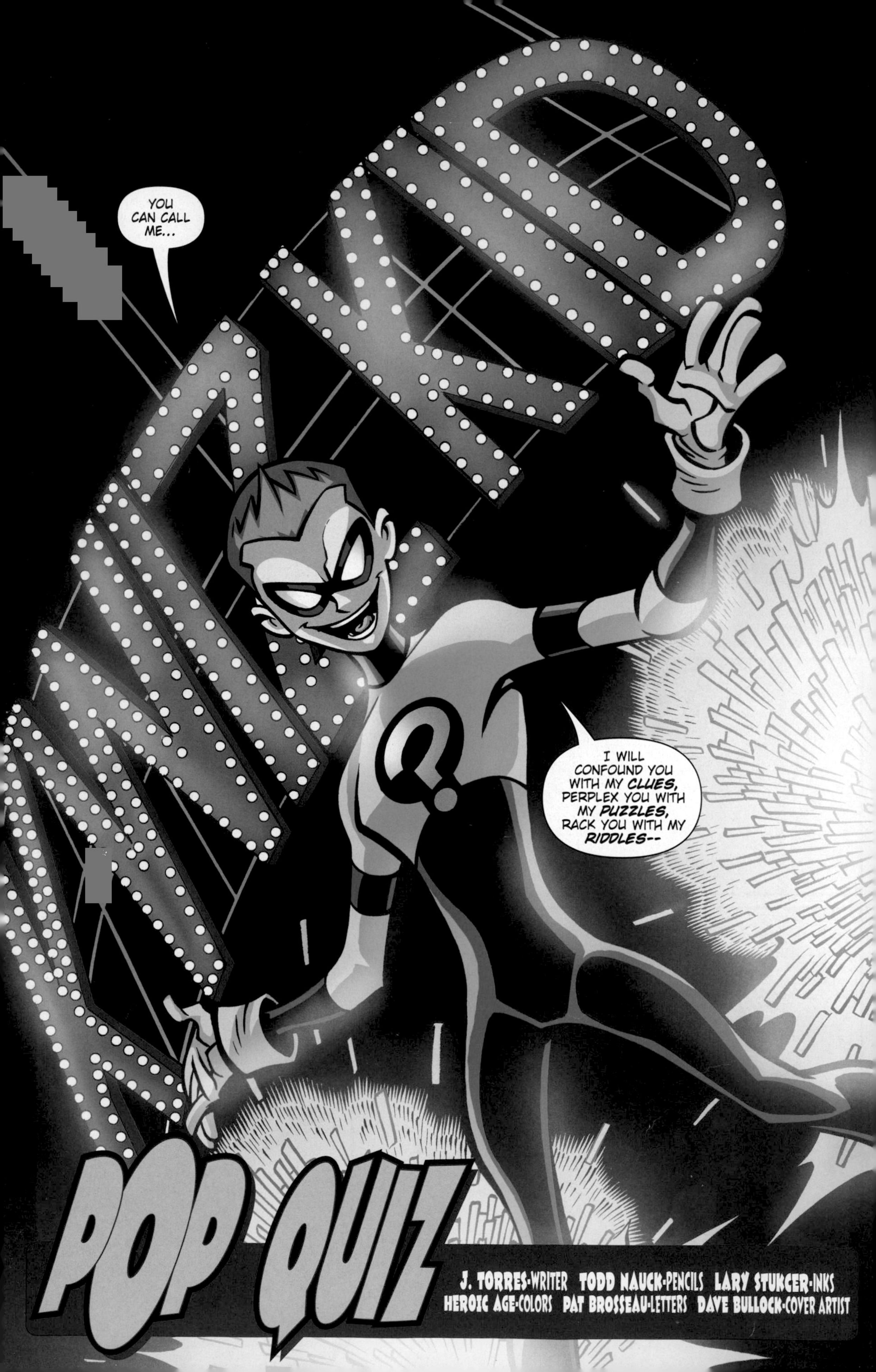
YOU CAN CALL ME...
KID
I WILL CONFOUND YOU WITH MY CLUES, PERPLEX YOU WITH MY PUZZLES, RACK YOU WITH MY RIDDLES--
POP QUIZ
J. TORRES-WRITER TODD NAUCK-PENCILS LARY STUCKER-INKS
HEROIC AGE-COLORS PAT BROSSEAU-LETTERS DAVE BULLOCK-COVER ARTIST

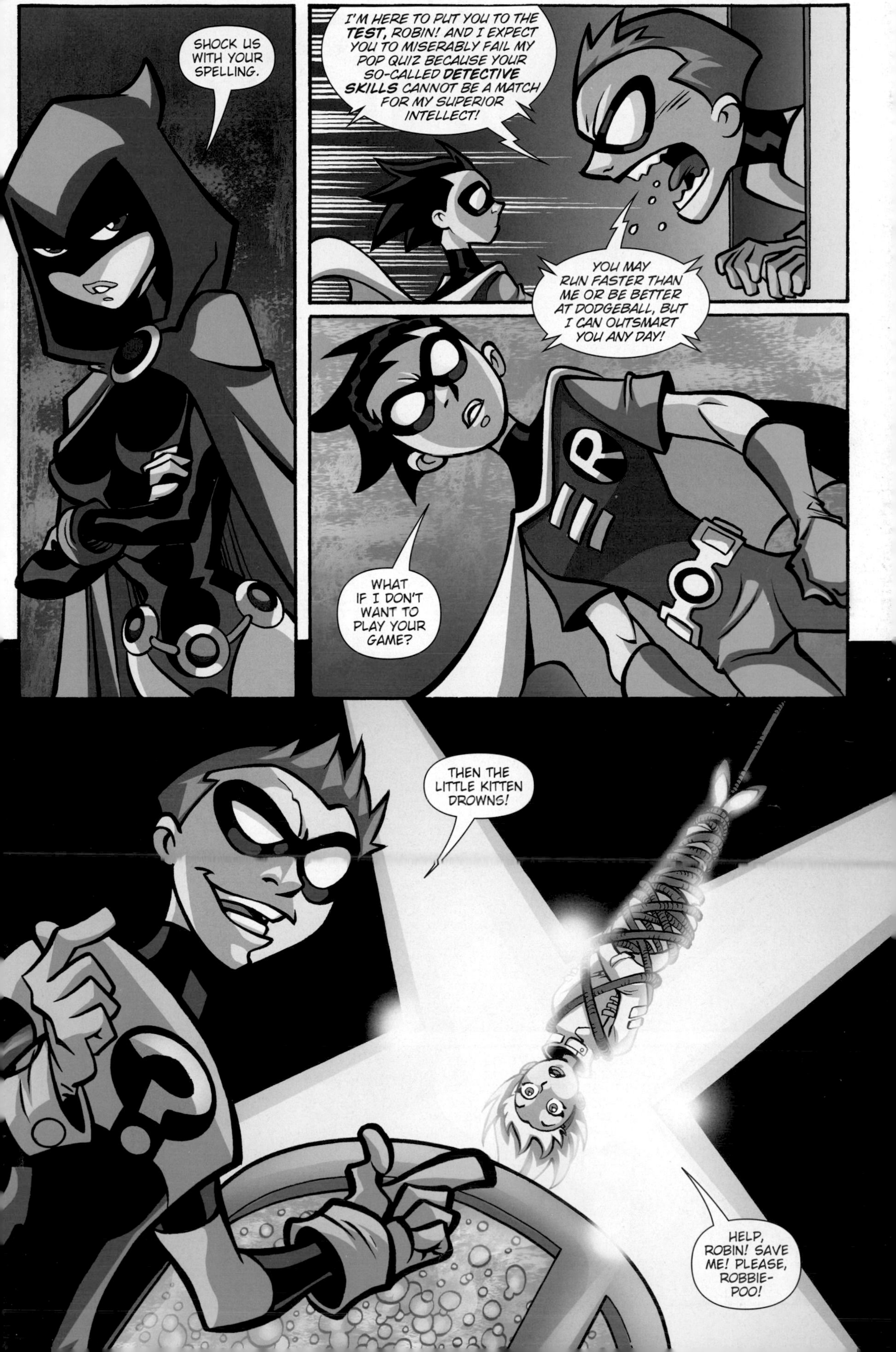
SHOCK US WITH YOUR SPELLING.
I'M HERE TO PUT YOU TO THE TEST, ROBIN! AND I EXPECT YOU TO MISERABLY FAIL MY POP QUIZ BECAUSE YOUR SO-CALLED DETECTIVE SKILLS CANNOT BE A MATCH FOR MY SUPERIOR INTELLECT!
YOU MAY RUN FASTER THAN ME OR BE BETTER AT DODGEBALL, BUT I CAN OUTSMART YOU ANY DAY!
WHAT IF I DON'T WANT TO PLAY YOUR GAME?
THEN THE LITTLE KITTEN DROWNS!
HELP, ROBIN! SAVE ME! PLEASE, ROBBIE-POO!

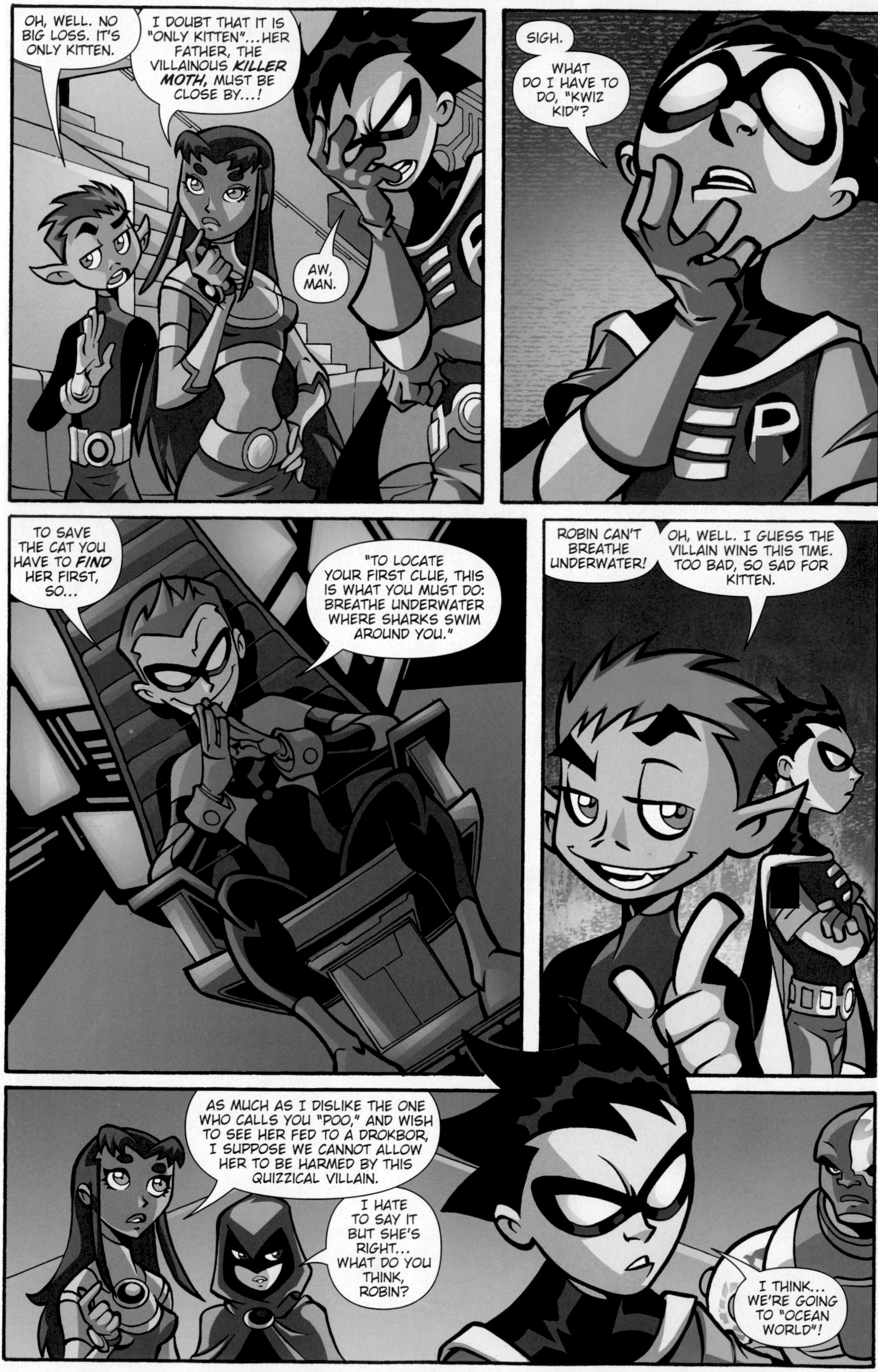
OH, WELL. NO BIG LOSS. IT'S ONLY KITTEN.
I DOUBT THAT IT IS "ONLY KITTEN"...HER FATHER, THE VILLAINOUS KILLER MOTH, MUST BE CLOSE BY...!
AW, MAN.
SIGH.
WHAT DO I HAVE TO DO, "KWIZ KID"?
TO SAVE THE CAT YOU HAVE TO FIND HER FIRST, SO...
"TO LOCATE YOUR FIRST CLUE, THIS IS WHAT YOU MUST DO: BREATHE UNDERWATER WHERE SHARKS SWIM AROUND YOU."
ROBIN CAN'T BREATHE UNDERWATER!
OH, WELL. I GUESS THE VILLAIN WINS THIS TIME. TOO BAD, SO SAD FOR KITTEN.
AS MUCH AS I DISLIKE THE ONE WHO CALLS YOU "POO," AND WISH TO SEE HER FED TO A DROKBOR, I SUPPOSE WE CANNOT ALLOW HER TO BE HARMED BY THIS QUIZZICAL VILLAIN.
I HATE TO SAY IT BUT SHE'S RIGHT... WHAT DO YOU THINK, ROBIN?
I THINK... WE'RE GOING TO "OCEAN WORLD"!

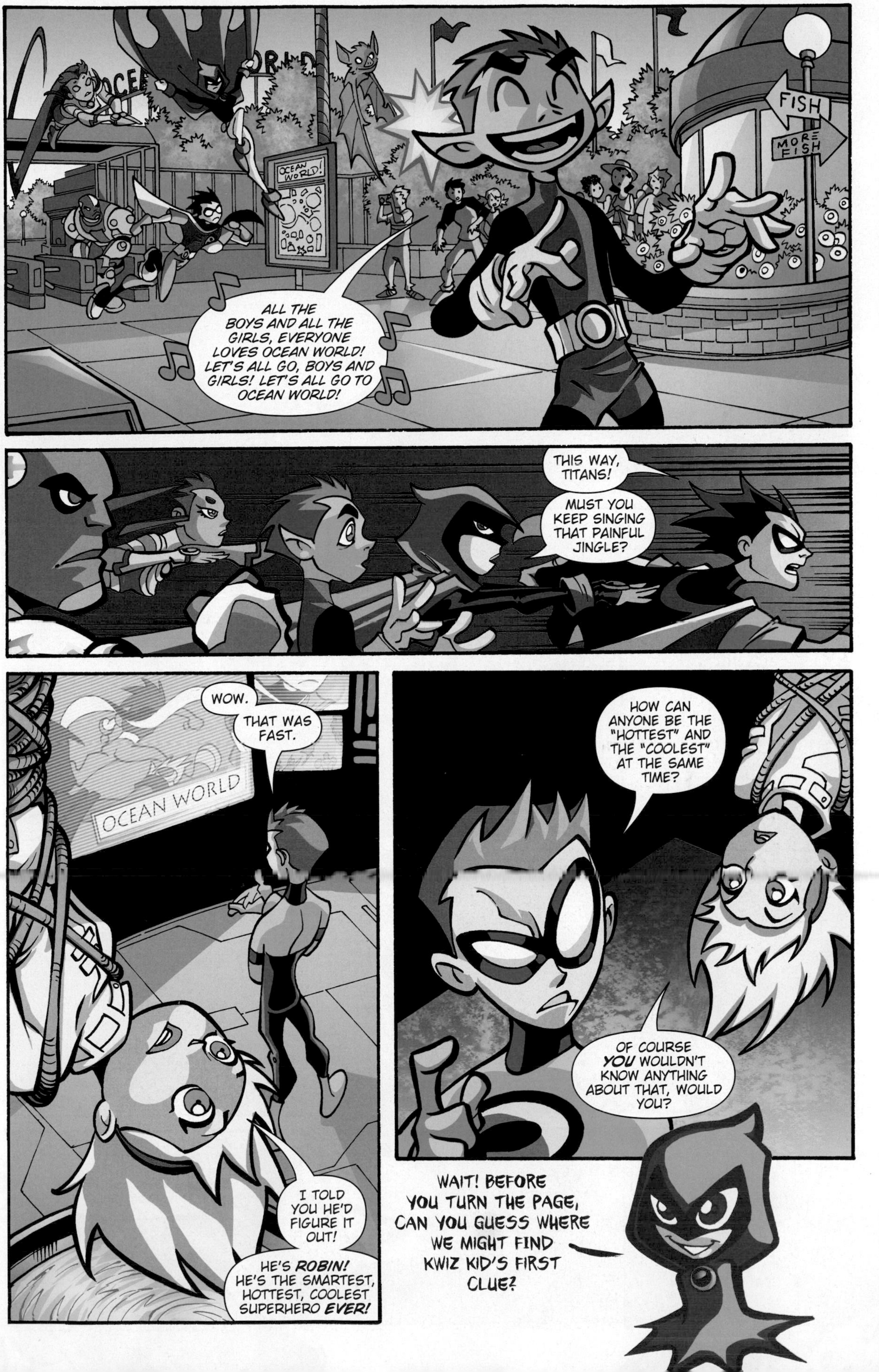
OCEAN WORLD
OCEAN WORLD!
FISH
MORE FISH
ALL THE BOYS AND ALL THE GIRLS, EVERYONE LOVES OCEAN WORLD! LET'S ALL GO, BOYS AND GIRLS! LET'S ALL GO TO OCEAN WORLD!
THIS WAY, TITANS!
MUST YOU KEEP SINGING THAT PAINFUL JINGLE?
WOW.
THAT WAS FAST.
OCEAN WORLD
I TOLD YOU HE'D FIGURE IT OUT!
HE'S ROBIN! HE'S THE SMARTEST, HOTTEST, COOLEST SUPERHERO EVER!
HOW CAN ANYONE BE THE "HOTTEST" AND THE "COOLEST" AT THE SAME TIME?
OF COURSE YOU WOULDN'T KNOW ANYTHING ABOUT THAT, WOULD YOU?
WAIT! BEFORE YOU TURN THE PAGE, CAN YOU GUESS WHERE WE MIGHT FIND KWIZ KID'S FIRST CLUE?

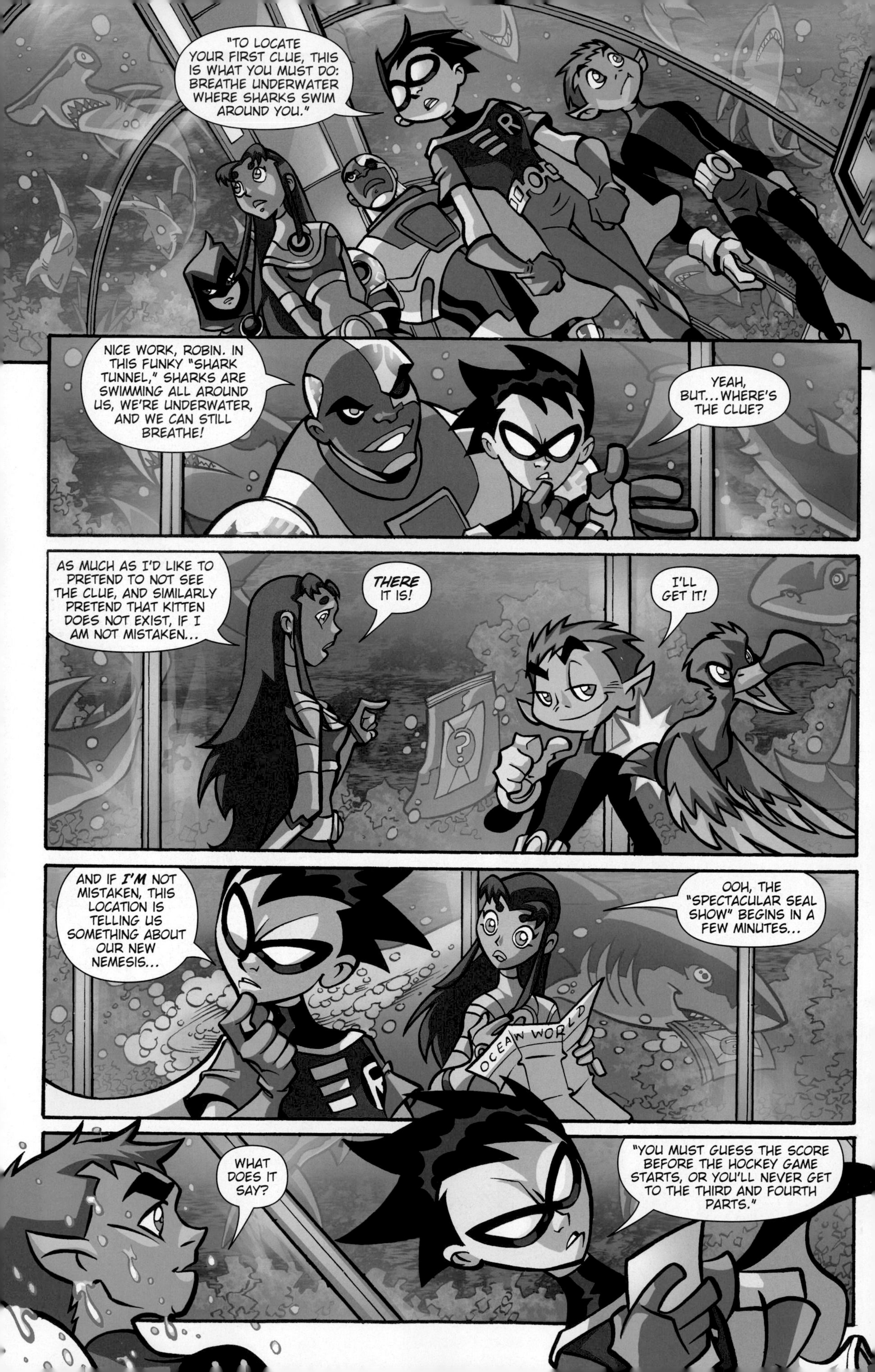
"TO LOCATE YOUR FIRST CLUE, THIS IS WHAT YOU MUST DO: BREATHE UNDERWATER WHERE SHARKS SWIM AROUND YOU."
NICE WORK, ROBIN. IN THIS FUNKY "SHARK TUNNEL," SHARKS ARE SWIMMING ALL AROUND US, WE'RE UNDERWATER, AND WE CAN STILL BREATHE!
YEAH, BUT...WHERE'S THE CLUE?
AS MUCH AS I'D LIKE TO PRETEND TO NOT SEE THE CLUE, AND SIMILARLY PRETEND THAT KITTEN DOES NOT EXIST, IF I AM NOT MISTAKEN...
THERE IT IS!
I'LL GET IT!
AND IF *I'M* NOT MISTAKEN, THIS LOCATION IS TELLING US SOMETHING ABOUT OUR NEW NEMESIS...
OOH, THE "SPECTACULAR SEAL SHOW" BEGINS IN A FEW MINUTES...
OCEAN WORLD
WHAT DOES IT SAY?
"YOU MUST GUESS THE SCORE BEFORE THE HOCKEY GAME STARTS, OR YOU'LL NEVER GET TO THE THIRD AND FOURTH PARTS."

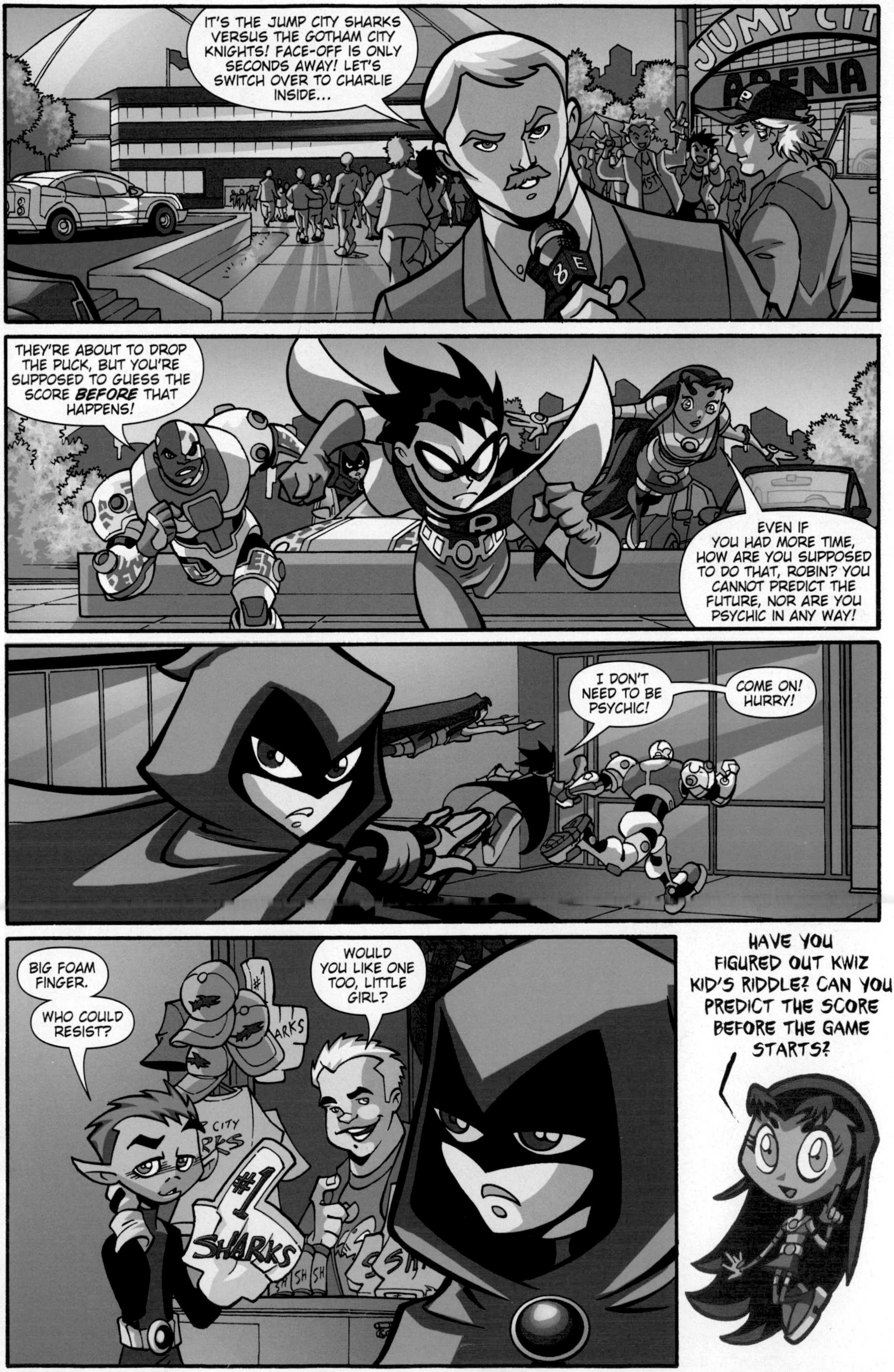
IT'S THE JUMP CITY SHARKS VERSUS THE GOTHAM CITY KNIGHTS! FACE-OFF IS ONLY SECONDS AWAY! LET'S SWITCH OVER TO CHARLIE INSIDE...
ARENA
THEY'RE ABOUT TO DROP THE PUCK, BUT YOU'RE SUPPOSED TO GUESS THE SCORE *BEFORE* THAT HAPPENS!
EVEN IF YOU HAD MORE TIME, HOW ARE YOU SUPPOSED TO DO THAT, ROBIN? YOU CANNOT PREDICT THE FUTURE, NOR ARE YOU PSYCHIC IN ANY WAY!
I DON'T NEED TO BE PSYCHIC!
COME ON! HURRY!
BIG FOAM FINGER.
WHO COULD RESIST?
WOULD YOU LIKE ONE TOO, LITTLE GIRL?
#1
SHARKS
HAVE YOU FIGURED OUT KWIZ KID'S RIDDLE? CAN YOU PREDICT THE SCORE BEFORE THE GAME STARTS?

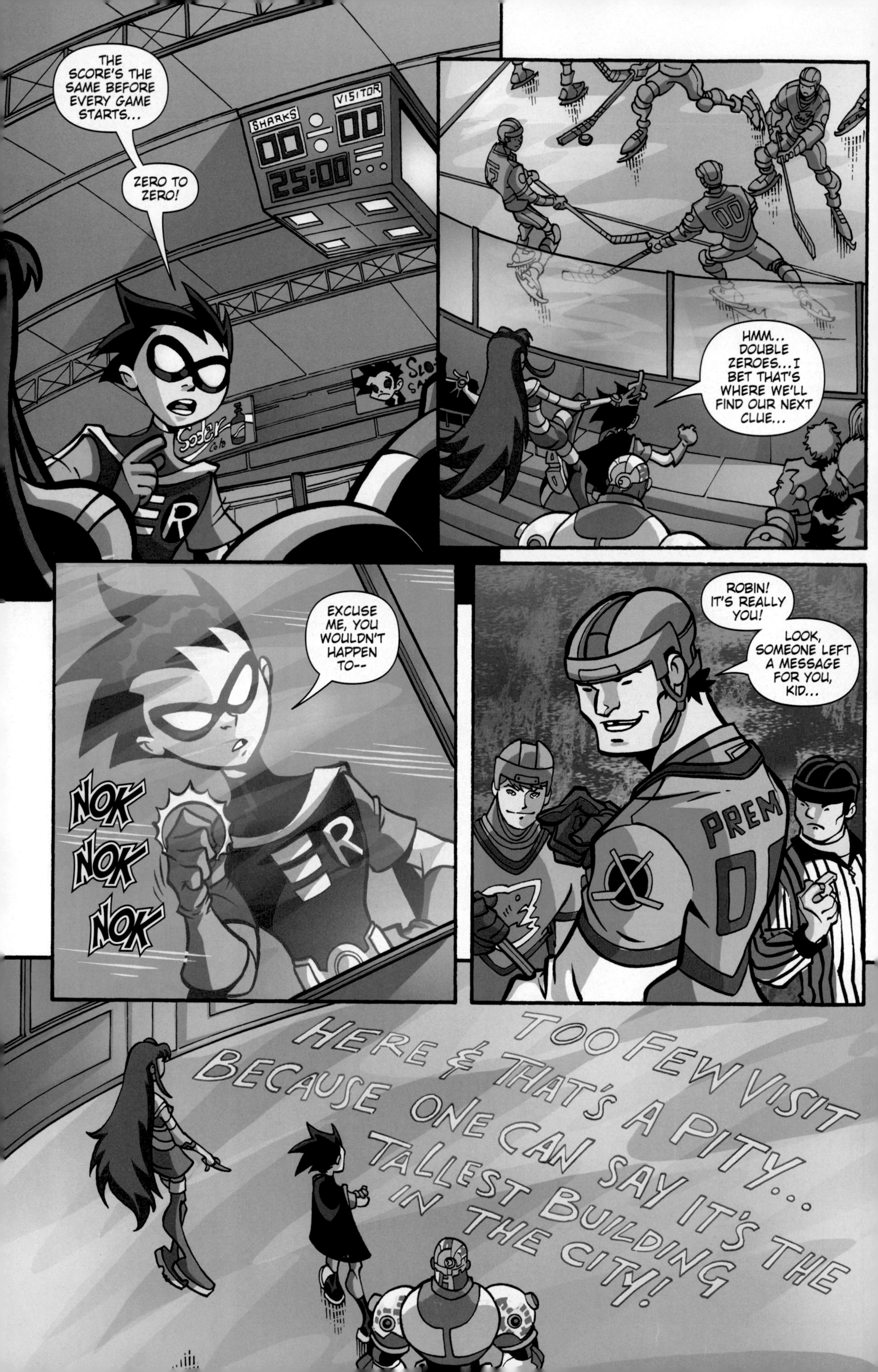
THE SCORE'S THE SAME BEFORE EVERY GAME STARTS...
ZERO TO ZERO!
SHARKS
VISITOR
00
00
25:00
HMM... DOUBLE ZEROES...I BET THAT'S WHERE WE'LL FIND OUR NEXT CLUE...
EXCUSE ME, YOU WOULDN'T HAPPEN TO--
NOK
NOK
NOK
ROBIN! IT'S REALLY YOU!
LOOK, SOMEONE LEFT A MESSAGE FOR YOU, KID...
PREM
TOO FEW VISIT HERE & THAT'S A PITY... BECAUSE ONE CAN SAY IT'S THE TALLEST BUILDING IN THE CITY!

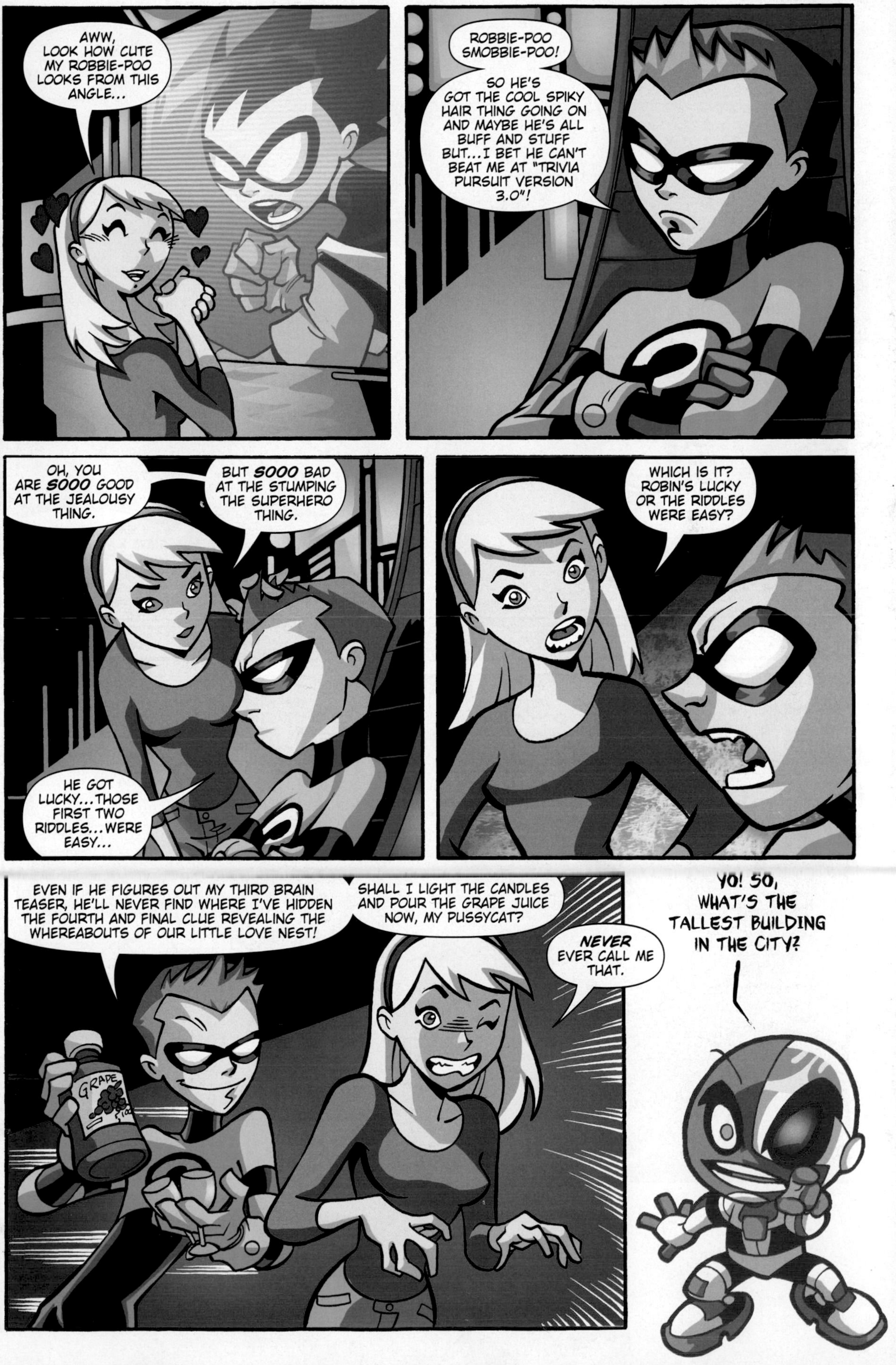
AWW, LOOK HOW CUTE MY ROBBIE-POO LOOKS FROM THIS ANGLE...
ROBBIE-POO SMOBBIE-POO!
SO HE'S GOT THE COOL SPIKY HAIR THING GOING ON AND MAYBE HE'S ALL BUFF AND STUFF BUT...I BET HE CAN'T BEAT ME AT "TRIVIA PURSUIT VERSION 3.0"!
OH, YOU ARE SOOO GOOD AT THE JEALOUSY THING.
BUT SOOO BAD AT THE STUMPING THE SUPERHERO THING.
HE GOT LUCKY...THOSE FIRST TWO RIDDLES...WERE EASY...
WHICH IS IT? ROBIN'S LUCKY OR THE RIDDLES WERE EASY?
EVEN IF HE FIGURES OUT MY THIRD BRAIN TEASER, HE'LL NEVER FIND WHERE I'VE HIDDEN THE FOURTH AND FINAL CLUE REVEALING THE WHEREABOUTS OF OUR LITTLE LOVE NEST!
SHALL I LIGHT THE CANDLES AND POUR THE GRAPE JUICE NOW, MY PUSSYCAT?
NEVER EVER CALL ME THAT.
GRAPE
YO! SO, WHAT'S THE TALLEST BUILDING IN THE CITY?

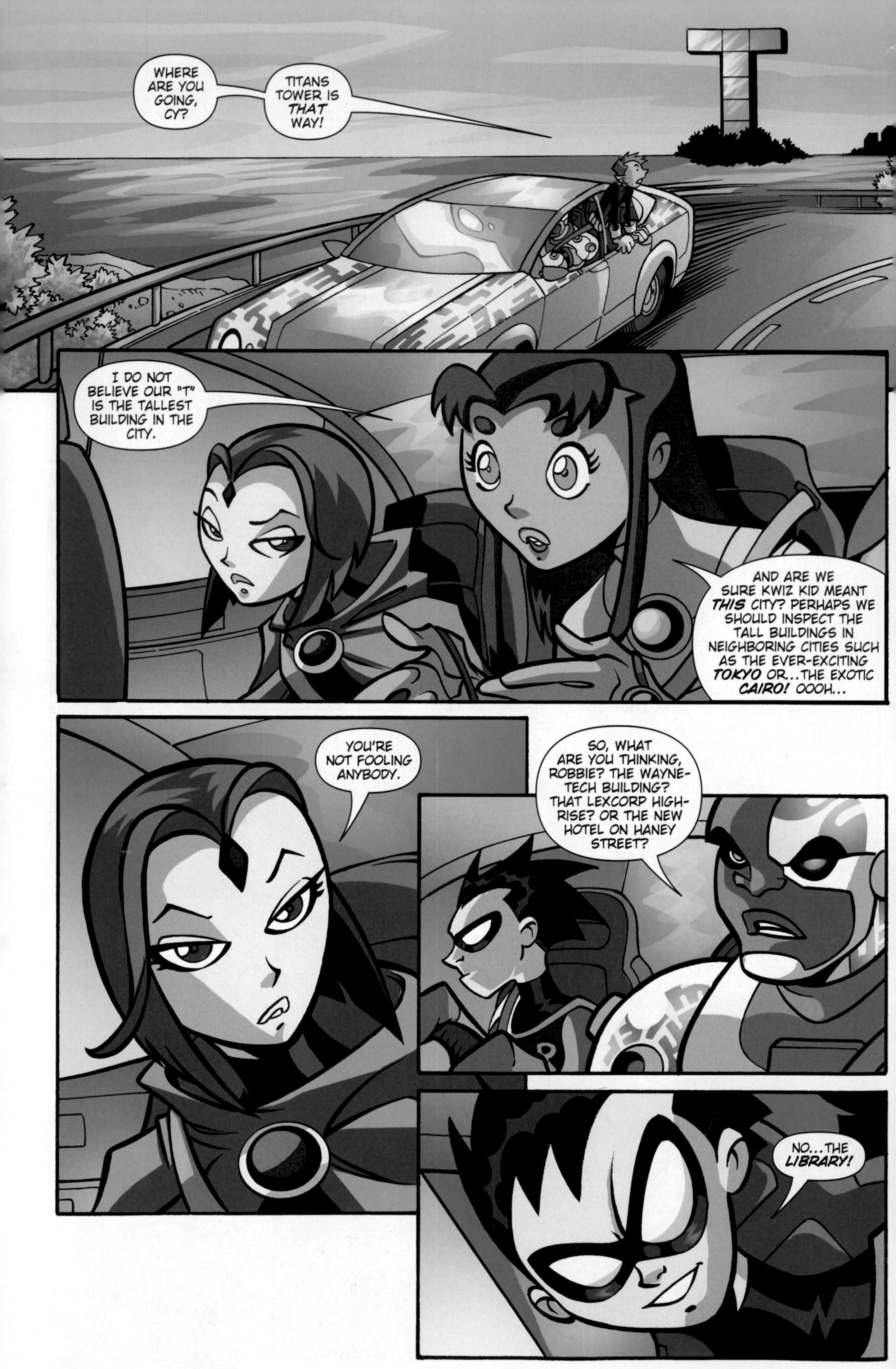
WHERE ARE YOU GOING, CY?
TITANS TOWER IS *THAT* WAY!
I DO NOT BELIEVE OUR "T" IS THE TALLEST BUILDING IN THE CITY.
AND ARE WE SURE KWIZ KID MEANT *THIS* CITY? PERHAPS WE SHOULD INSPECT THE TALL BUILDINGS IN NEIGHBORING CITIES SUCH AS THE EVER-EXCITING *TOKYO* OR...THE EXOTIC *CAIRO!* OOOH...
YOU'RE NOT FOOLING ANYBODY.
SO, WHAT ARE YOU THINKING, ROBBIE? THE WAYNE-TECH BUILDING? THAT LEXCORP HIGH-RISE? OR THE NEW HOTEL ON HANEY STREET?
NO...THE *LIBRARY!*

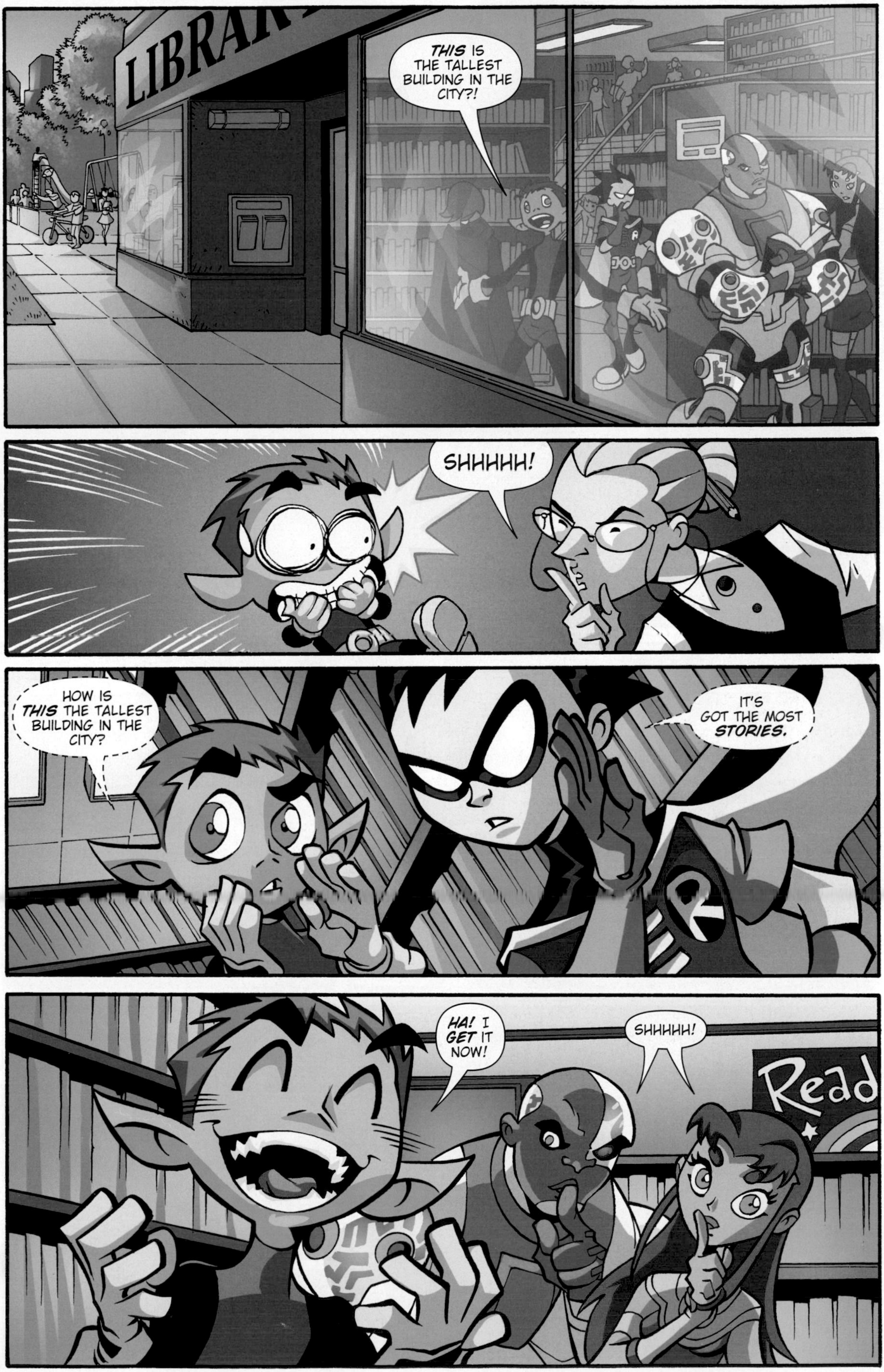
LIBRAR
THIS IS THE TALLEST BUILDING IN THE CITY?!
SHHHHH!
HOW IS THIS THE TALLEST BUILDING IN THE CITY?
IT'S GOT THE MOST STORIES.
HA! I GET IT NOW!
SHHHHH!
Read

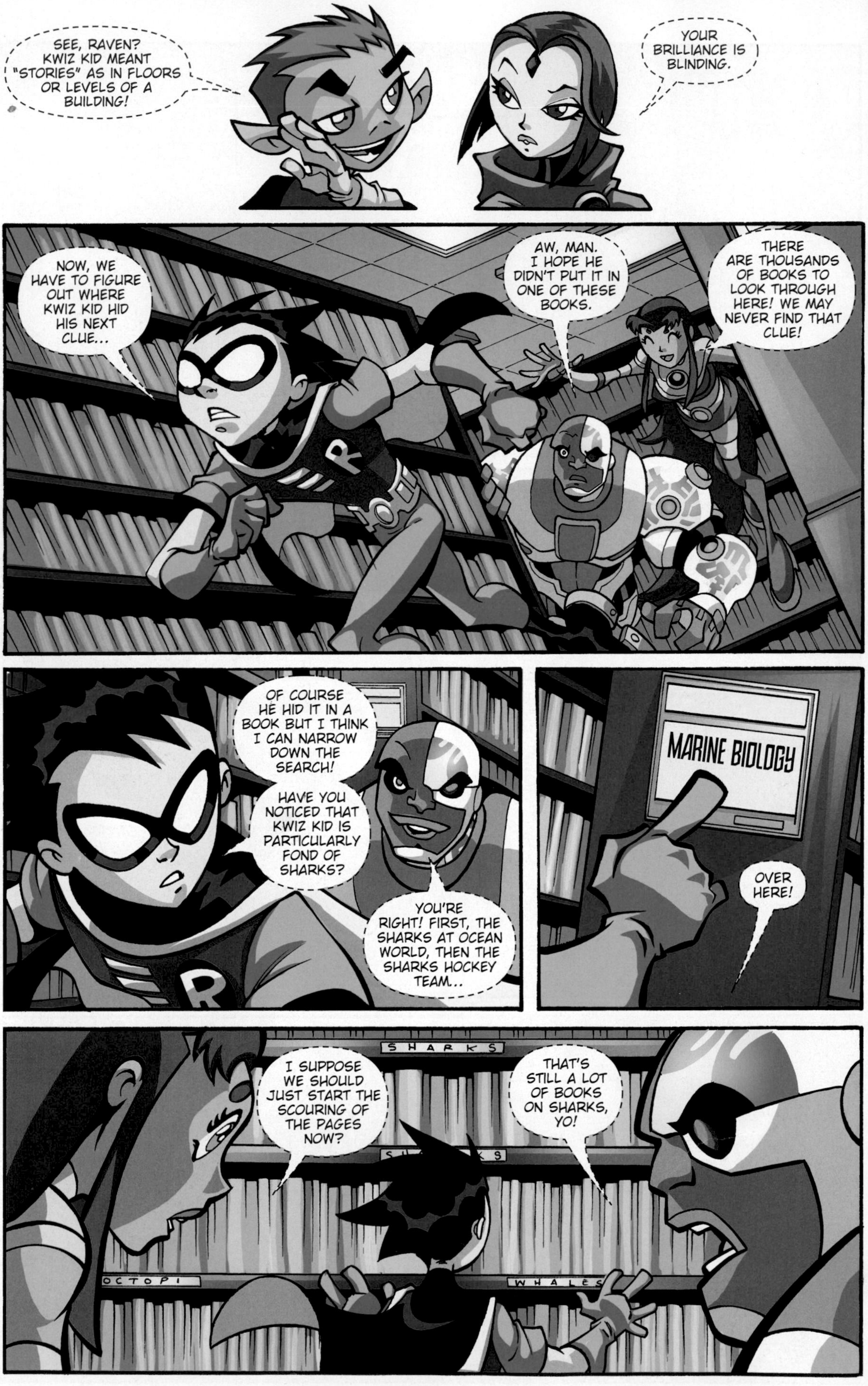
SEE, RAVEN? KWIZ KID MEANT "STORIES" AS IN FLOORS OR LEVELS OF A BUILDING!
YOUR BRILLIANCE IS BLINDING.
NOW, WE HAVE TO FIGURE OUT WHERE KWIZ KID HID HIS NEXT CLUE...
AW, MAN. I HOPE HE DIDN'T PUT IT IN ONE OF THESE BOOKS.
THERE ARE THOUSANDS OF BOOKS TO LOOK THROUGH HERE! WE MAY NEVER FIND THAT CLUE!
OF COURSE HE HID IT IN A BOOK BUT I THINK I CAN NARROW DOWN THE SEARCH!
HAVE YOU NOTICED THAT KWIZ KID IS PARTICULARLY FOND OF SHARKS?
YOU'RE RIGHT! FIRST, THE SHARKS AT OCEAN WORLD, THEN THE SHARKS HOCKEY TEAM...
MARINE BIOLOGY
OVER HERE!
SHARKS
I SUPPOSE WE SHOULD JUST START THE SCOURING OF THE PAGES NOW?
THAT'S STILL A LOT OF BOOKS ON SHARKS, YO!
OCTOPI
WHALES

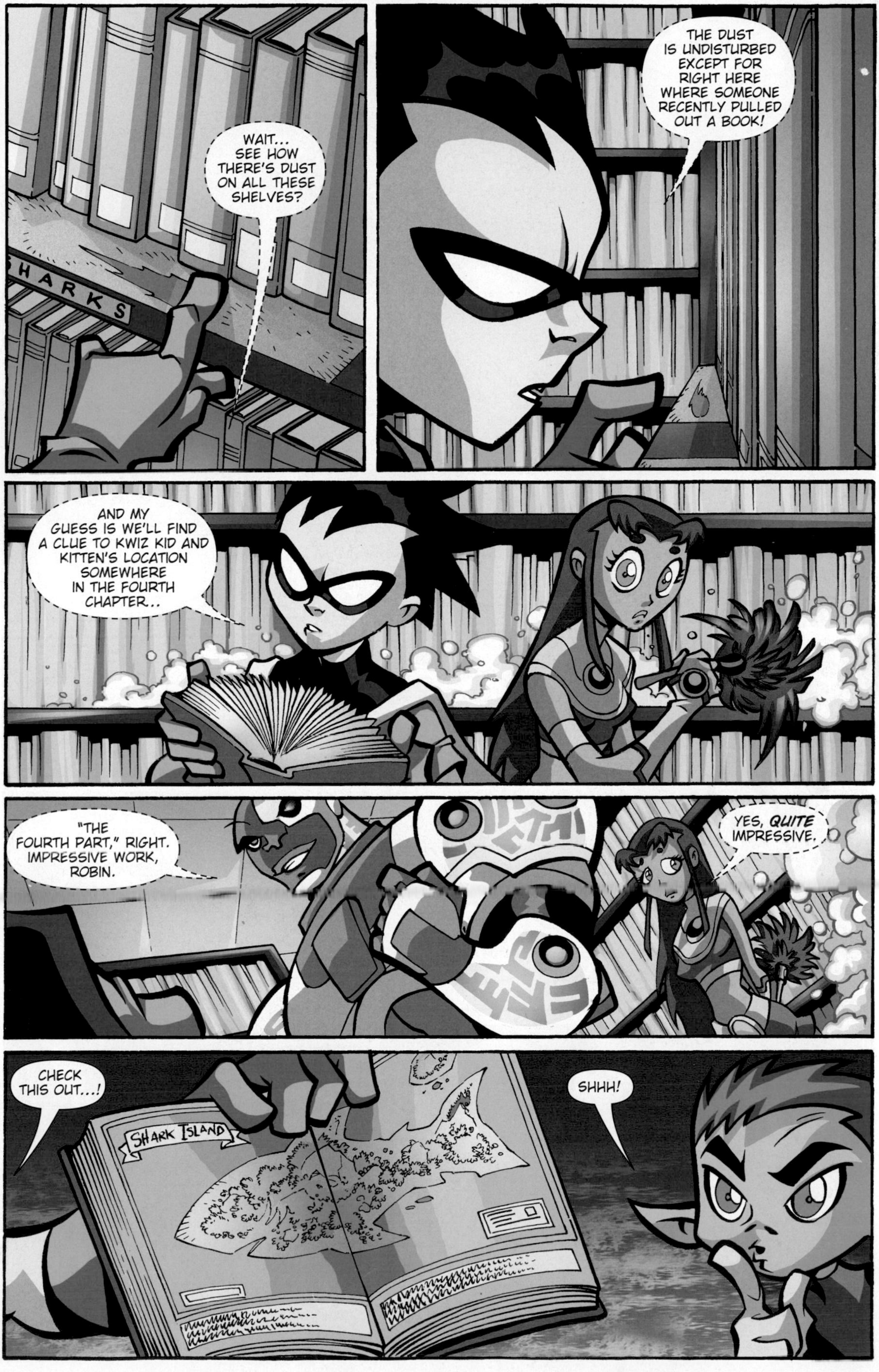

SHARKS
WAIT... SEE HOW THERE'S DUST ON ALL THESE SHELVES?
THE DUST IS UNDISTURBED EXCEPT FOR RIGHT HERE WHERE SOMEONE RECENTLY PULLED OUT A BOOK!
AND MY GUESS IS WE'LL FIND A CLUE TO KWIZ KID AND KITTEN'S LOCATION SOMEWHERE IN THE FOURTH CHAPTER...
"THE FOURTH PART," RIGHT. IMPRESSIVE WORK, ROBIN.
YES, *QUITE* IMPRESSIVE.
CHECK THIS OUT...!
SHARK ISLAND
SHHH!

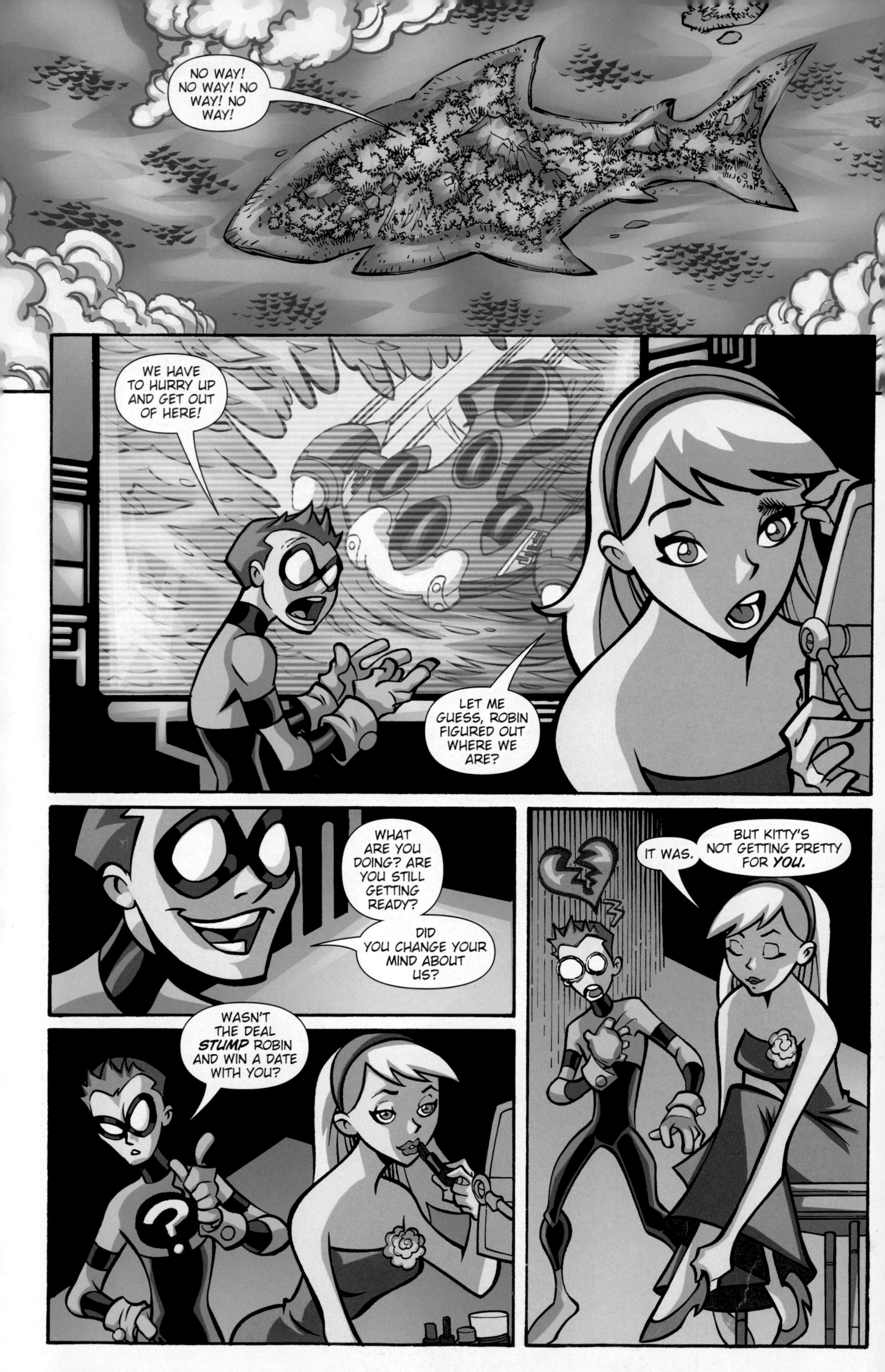
NO WAY! NO WAY! NO WAY! NO WAY!
WE HAVE TO HURRY UP AND GET OUT OF HERE!
LET ME GUESS, ROBIN FIGURED OUT WHERE WE ARE?
WHAT ARE YOU DOING? ARE YOU STILL GETTING READY?
DID YOU CHANGE YOUR MIND ABOUT US?
WASN'T THE DEAL STUMP ROBIN AND WIN A DATE WITH YOU?
IT WAS.
BUT KITTY'S NOT GETTING PRETTY FOR YOU.

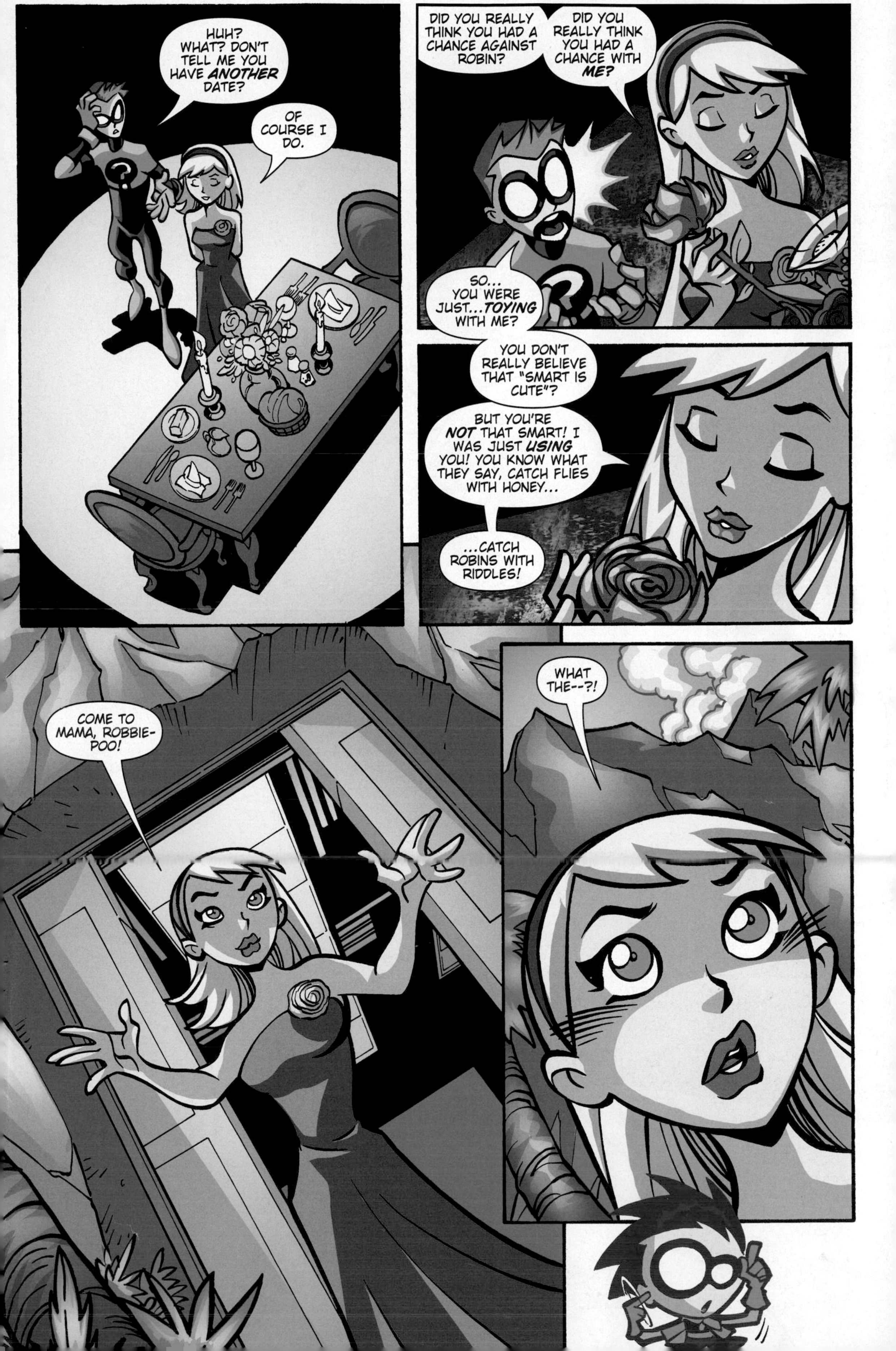
HUH? WHAT? DON'T TELL ME YOU HAVE ANOTHER DATE?
OF COURSE I DO.
DID YOU REALLY THINK YOU HAD A CHANCE AGAINST ROBIN?
DID YOU REALLY THINK YOU HAD A CHANCE WITH ME?
SO... YOU WERE JUST...TOYING WITH ME?
YOU DON'T REALLY BELIEVE THAT "SMART IS CUTE"?
BUT YOU'RE NOT THAT SMART! I WAS JUST USING YOU! YOU KNOW WHAT THEY SAY, CATCH FLIES WITH HONEY...
...CATCH ROBINS WITH RIDDLES!
COME TO MAMA, ROBBIE-POO!
WHAT THE--?!

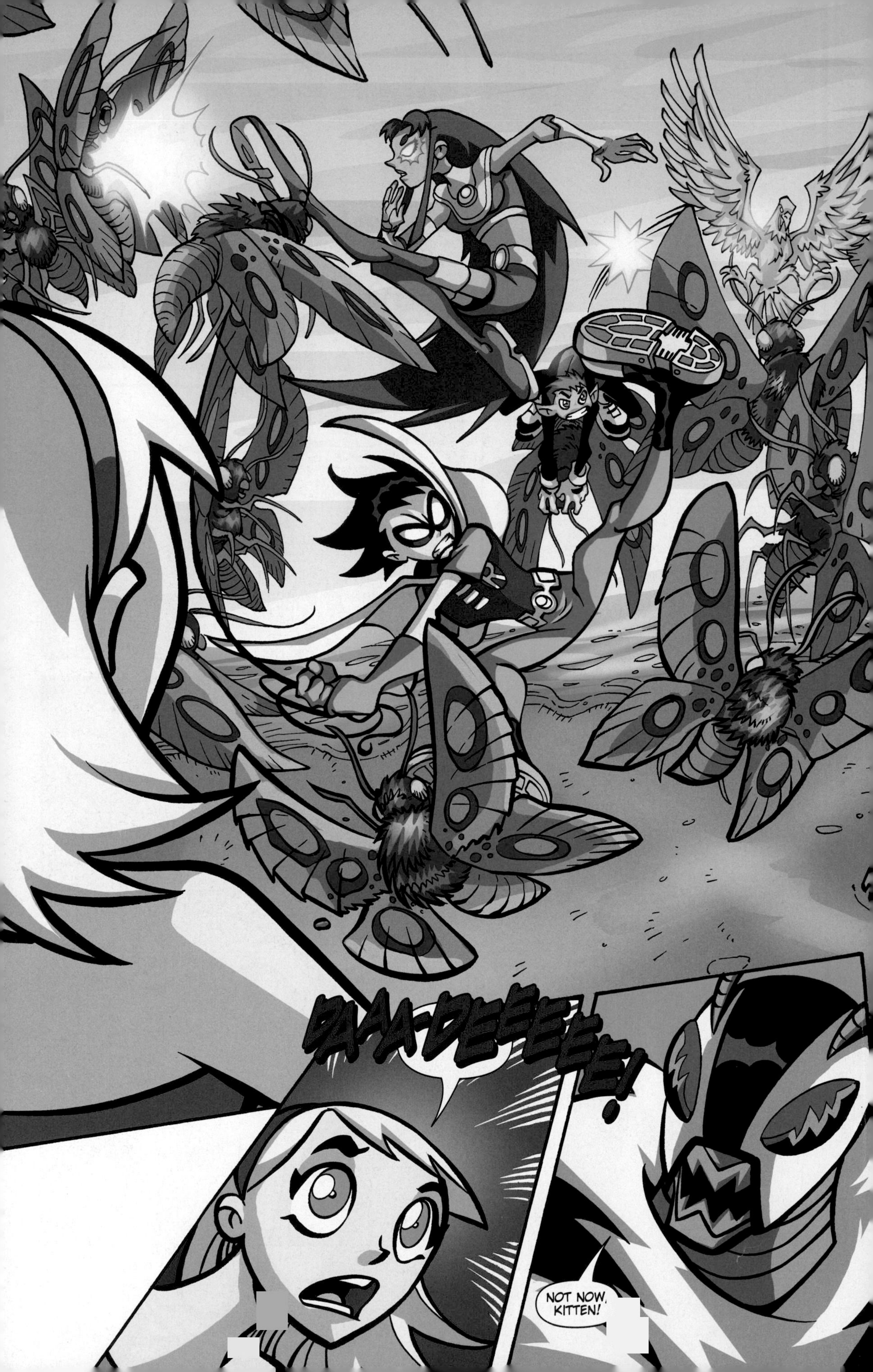
DAAA-DEEEEEE!
NOT NOW, KITTEN!

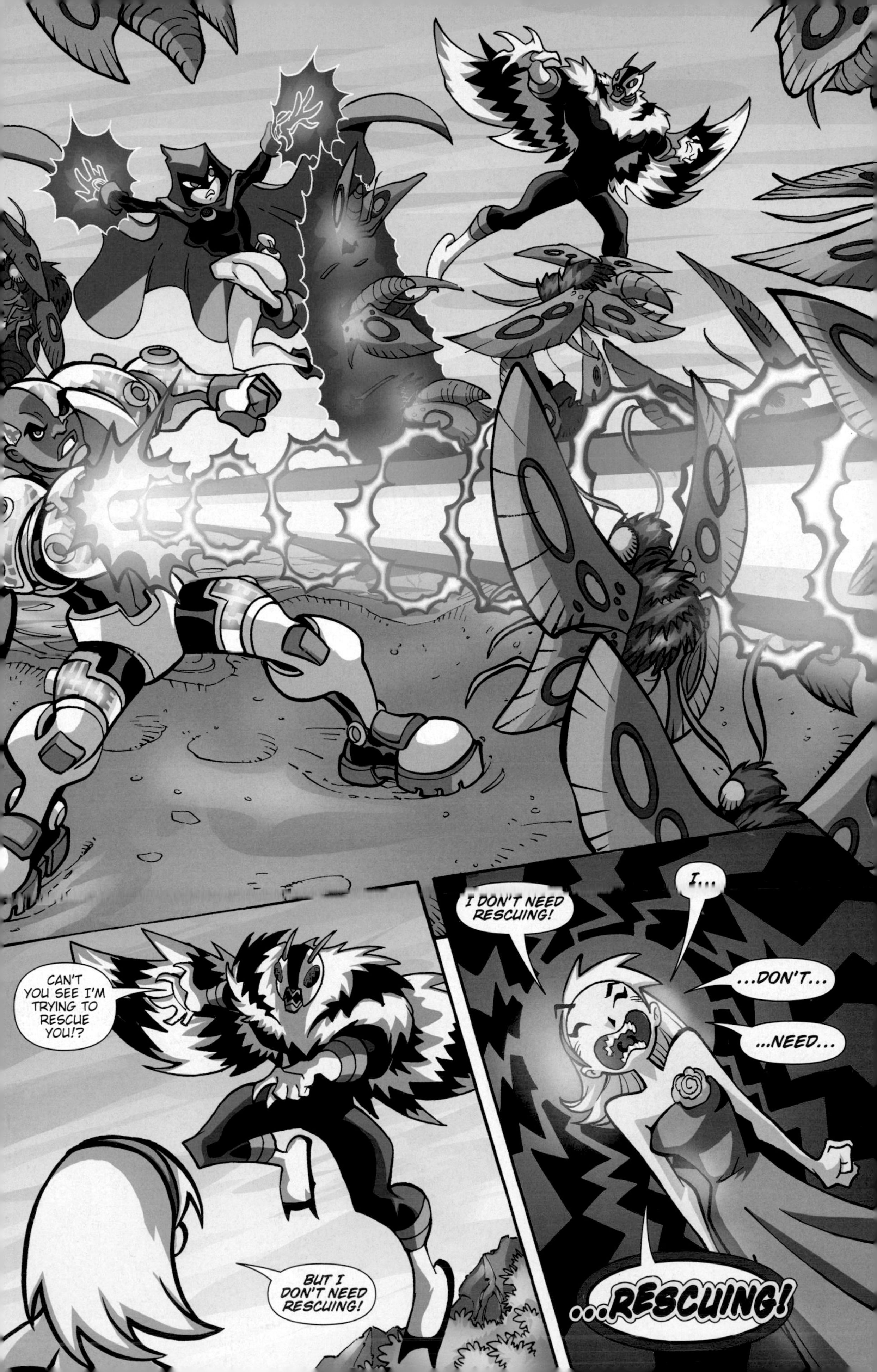

CAN'T YOU SEE I'M TRYING TO RESCUE YOU!?
BUT I DON'T NEED RESCUING!
I DON'T NEED RESCUING!
I...
...DON'T...
...NEED...
...RESCUING!

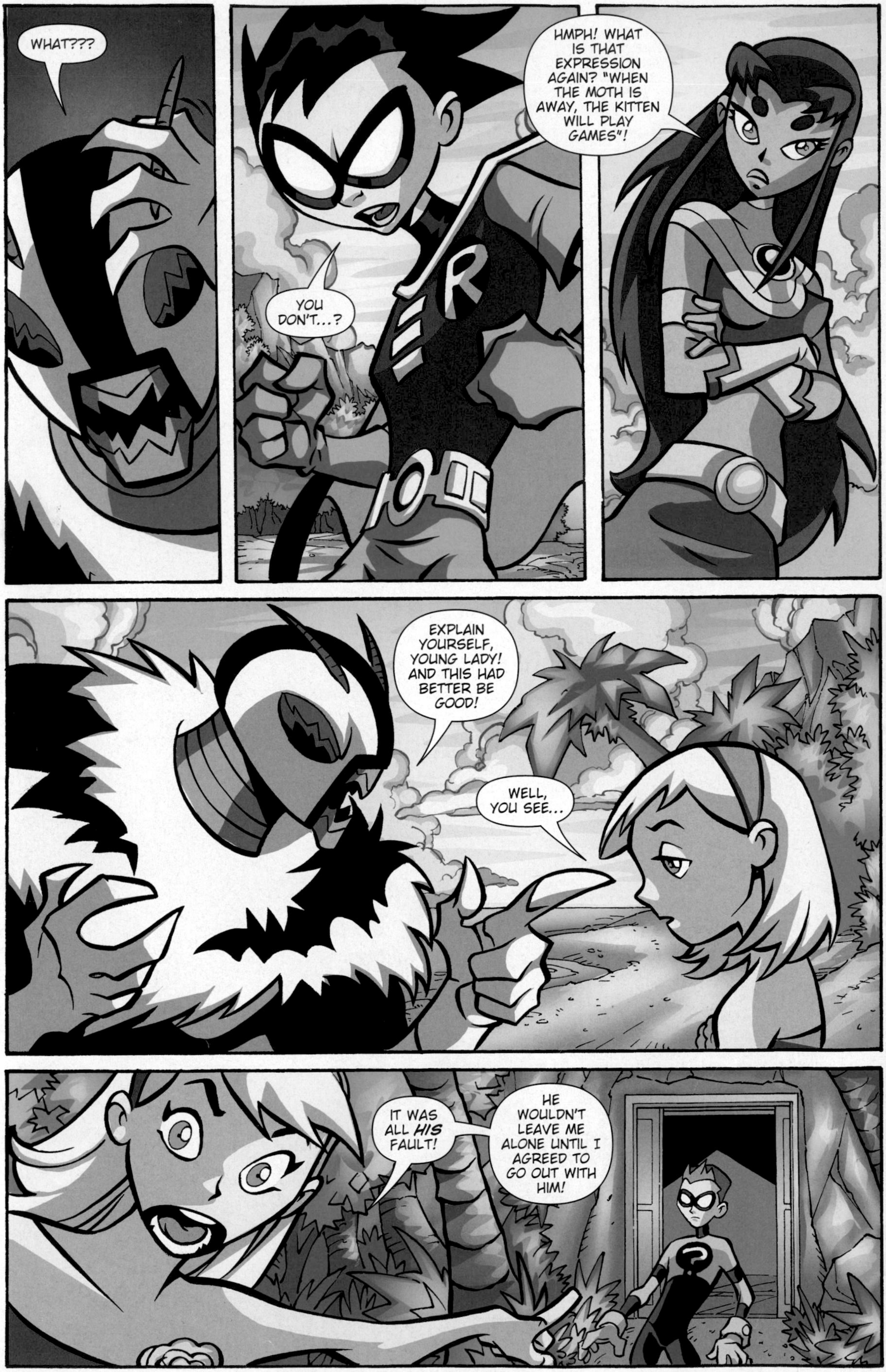
WHAT???
YOU DON'T...?
HMPH! WHAT IS THAT EXPRESSION AGAIN? "WHEN THE MOTH IS AWAY, THE KITTEN WILL PLAY GAMES"!
EXPLAIN YOURSELF, YOUNG LADY! AND THIS HAD BETTER BE GOOD!
WELL, YOU SEE...
IT WAS ALL *HIS* FAULT!
HE WOULDN'T LEAVE ME ALONE UNTIL I AGREED TO GO OUT WITH HIM!

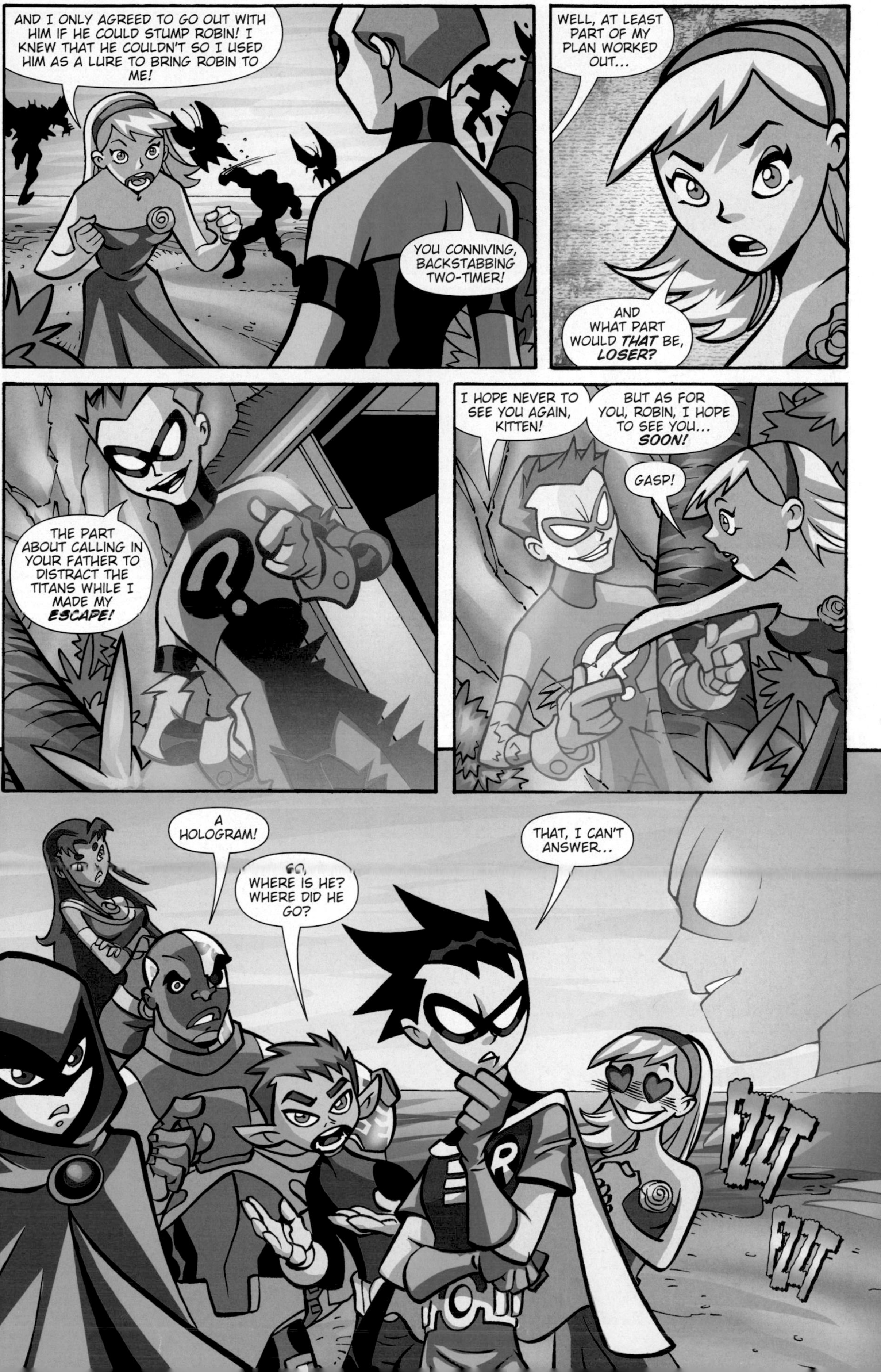
AND I ONLY AGREED TO GO OUT WITH HIM IF HE COULD STUMP ROBIN! I KNEW THAT HE COULDN'T SO I USED HIM AS A LURE TO BRING ROBIN TO ME!
YOU CONNIVING, BACKSTABBING TWO-TIMER!
WELL, AT LEAST PART OF MY PLAN WORKED OUT...
AND WHAT PART WOULD THAT BE, LOSER?
THE PART ABOUT CALLING IN YOUR FATHER TO DISTRACT THE TITANS WHILE I MADE MY ESCAPE!
I HOPE NEVER TO SEE YOU AGAIN, KITTEN!
BUT AS FOR YOU, ROBIN, I HOPE TO SEE YOU... SOON!
GASP!
A HOLOGRAM!
SO, WHERE IS HE? WHERE DID HE GO?
THAT, I CAN'T ANSWER...
FZZT
FZZT

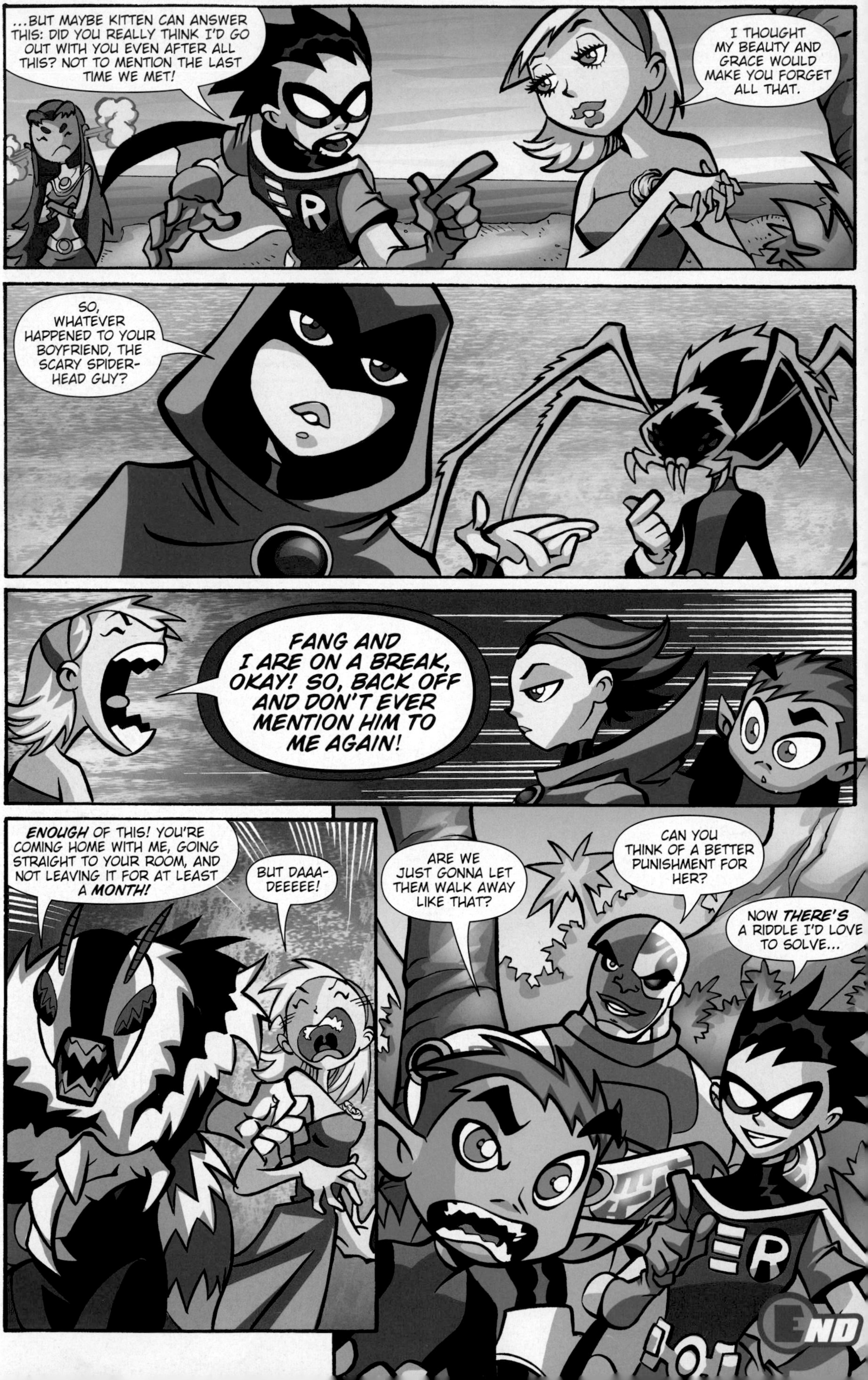

...BUT MAYBE KITTEN CAN ANSWER THIS: DID YOU REALLY THINK I'D GO OUT WITH YOU EVEN AFTER ALL THIS? NOT TO MENTION THE LAST TIME WE MET!
I THOUGHT MY BEAUTY AND GRACE WOULD MAKE YOU FORGET ALL THAT.
SO, WHATEVER HAPPENED TO YOUR BOYFRIEND, THE SCARY SPIDER-HEAD GUY?
FANG AND I ARE ON A BREAK, OKAY! SO, BACK OFF AND DON'T EVER MENTION HIM TO ME AGAIN!
ENOUGH OF THIS! YOU'RE COMING HOME WITH ME, GOING STRAIGHT TO YOUR ROOM, AND NOT LEAVING IT FOR AT LEAST A MONTH!
BUT DAAA-DEEEEE!
ARE WE JUST GONNA LET THEM WALK AWAY LIKE THAT?
CAN YOU THINK OF A BETTER PUNISHMENT FOR HER?
NOW THERE'S A RIDDLE I'D LOVE TO SOLVE...
END

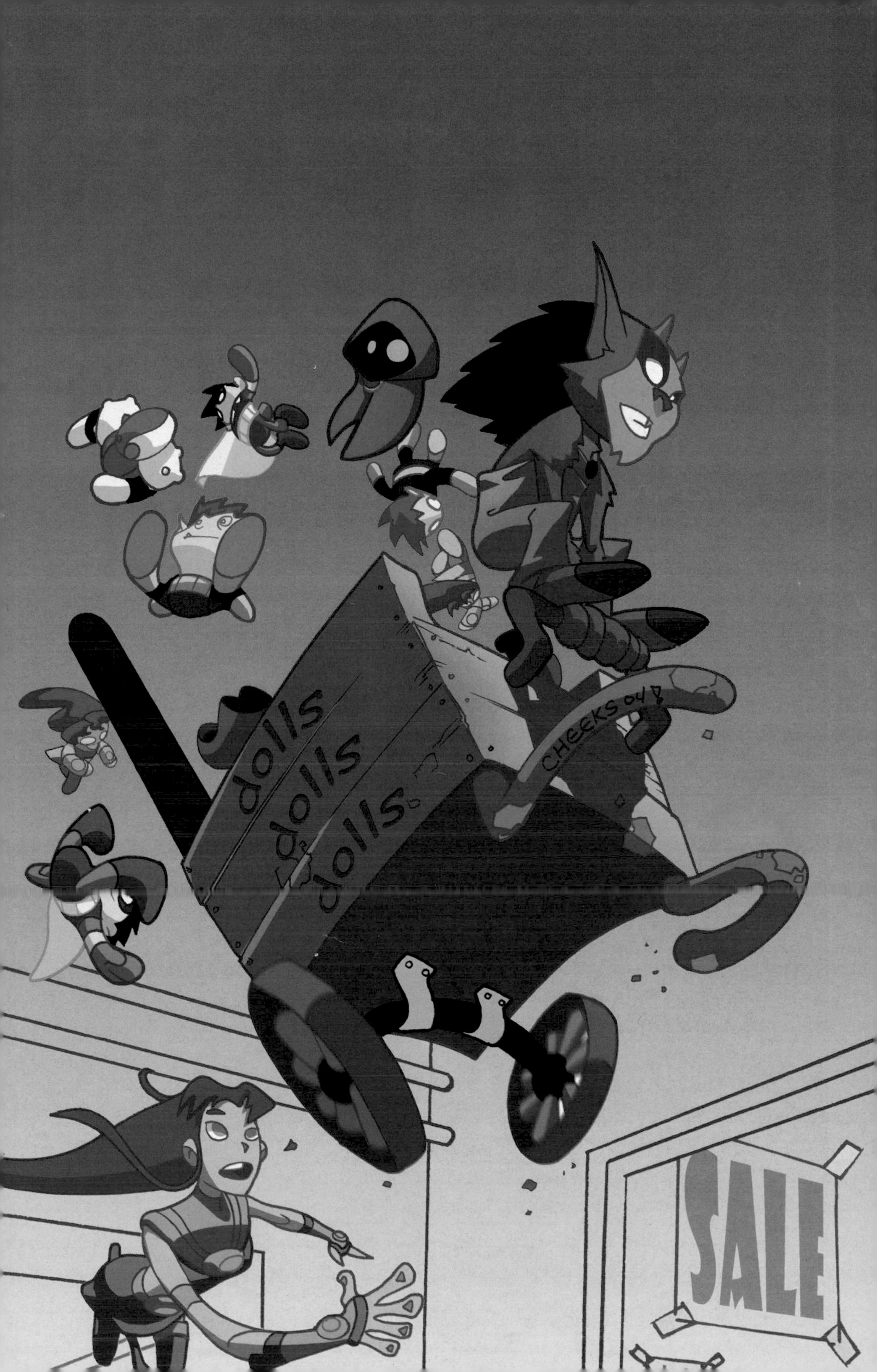
dolls
dolls
dolls
CHEEKS 04
SALE

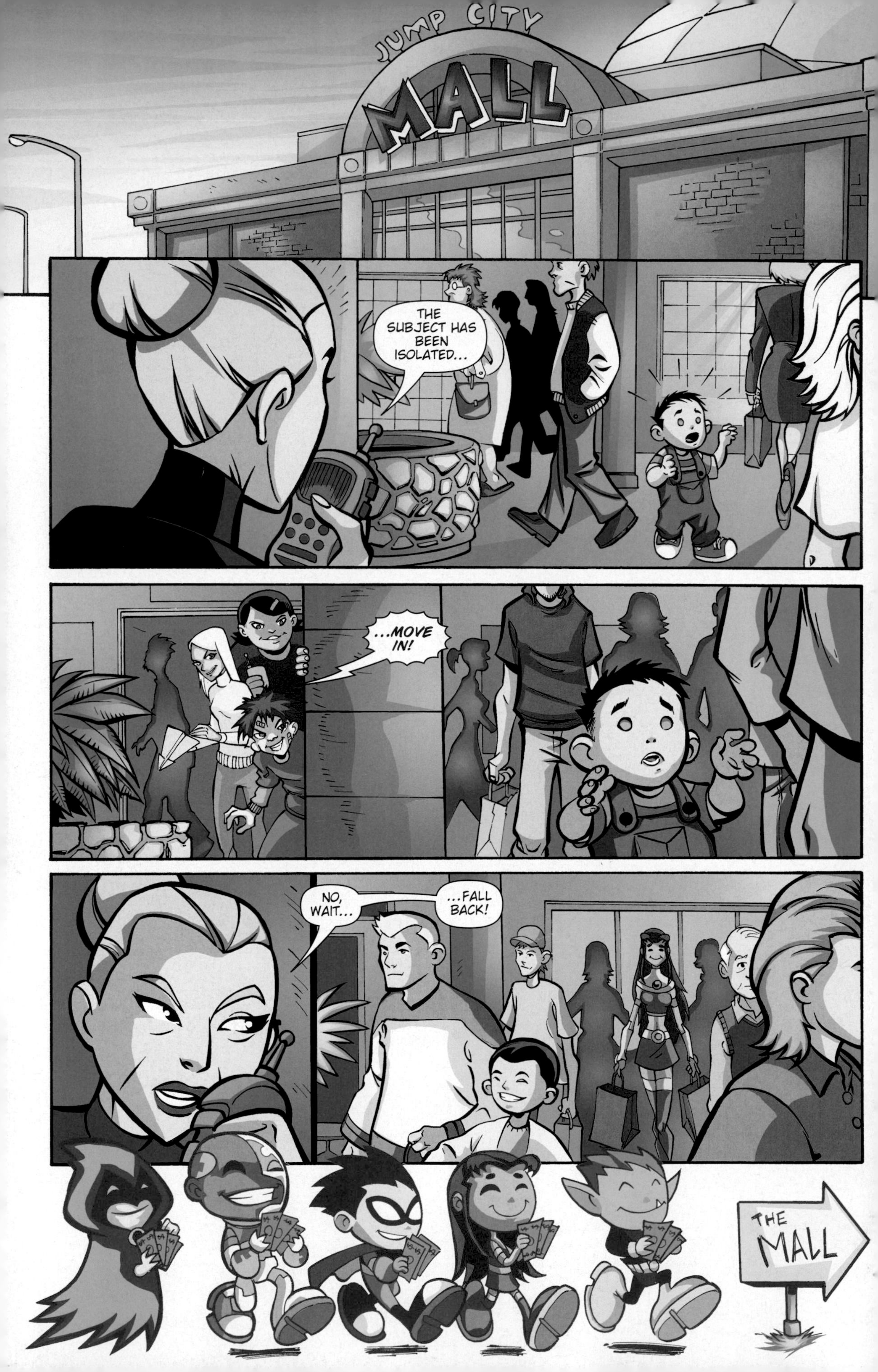
JUMP CITY
MALL
THE SUBJECT HAS BEEN ISOLATED...
...MOVE IN!
NO, WAIT...
...FALL BACK!
THE MALL

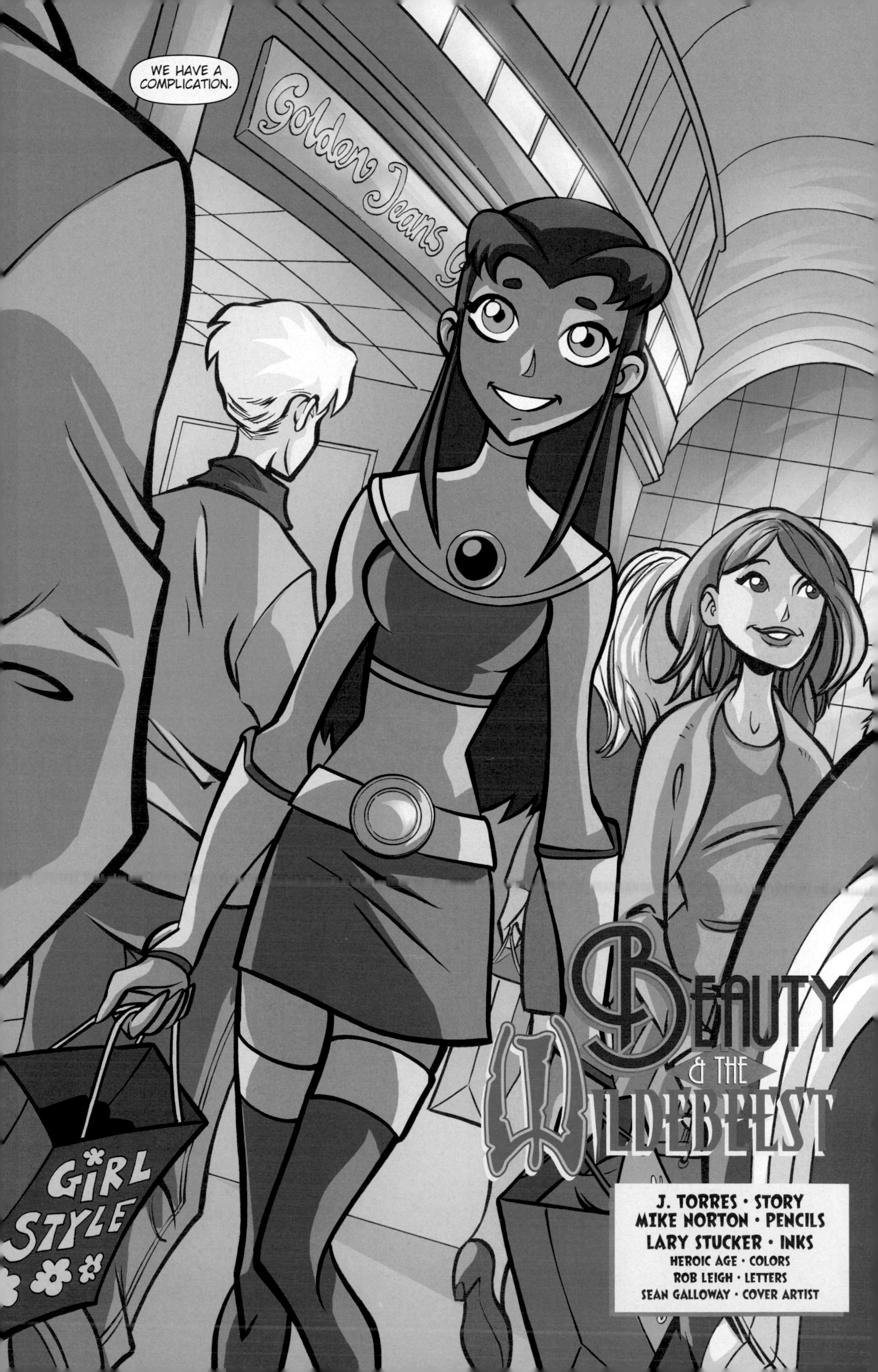
WE HAVE A COMPLICATION.
Golden Jeans
BEAUTY & THE WILDEBEEST
J. TORRES • STORY
MIKE NORTON • PENCILS
LARY STUCKER • INKS
HEROIC AGE • COLORS
ROB LEIGH • LETTERS
SEAN GALLOWAY • COVER ARTIST
GIRL STYLE

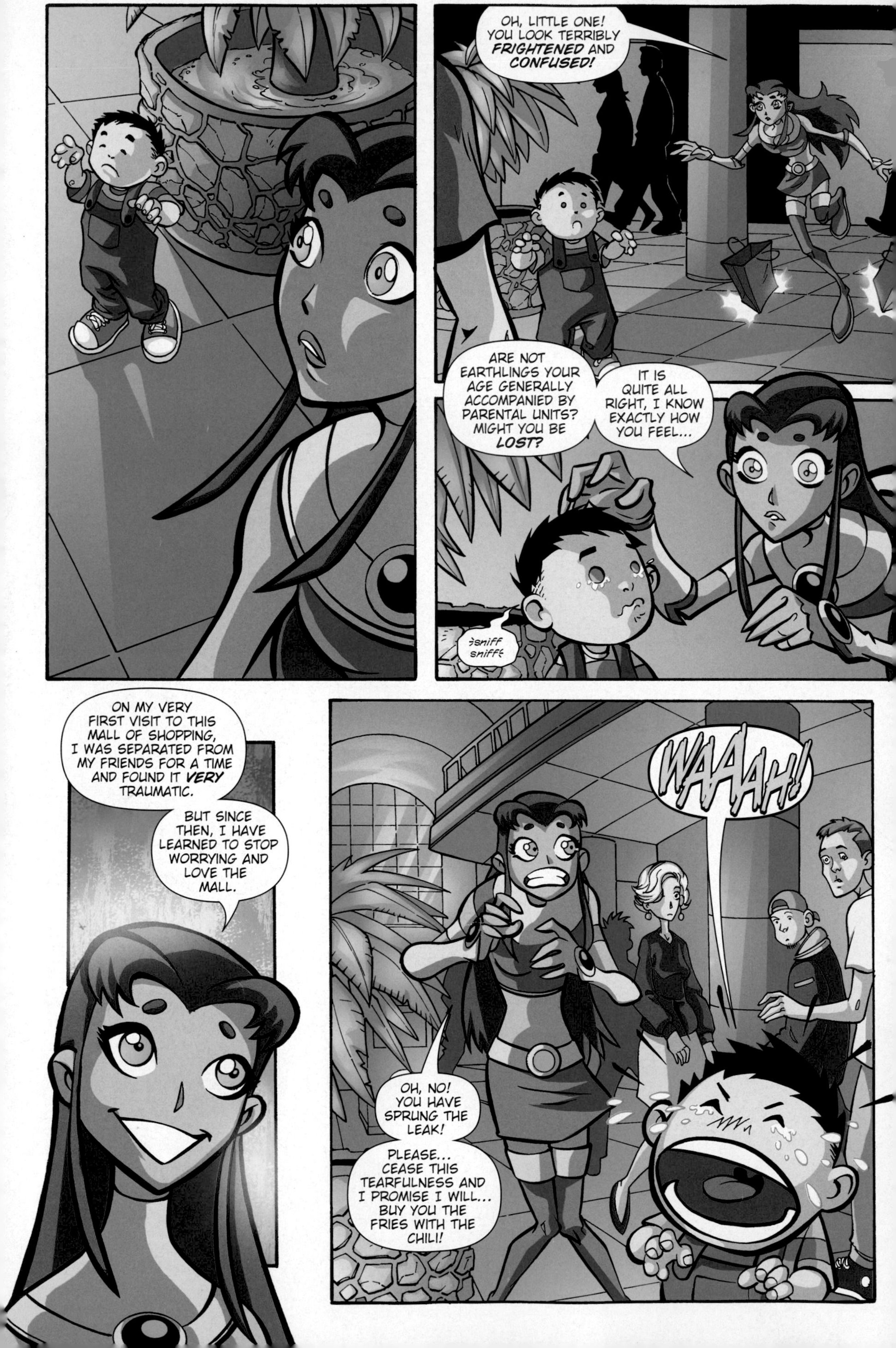
OH, LITTLE ONE! YOU LOOK TERRIBLY FRIGHTENED AND CONFUSED!
ARE NOT EARTHLINGS YOUR AGE GENERALLY ACCOMPANIED BY PARENTAL UNITS? MIGHT YOU BE LOST?
IT IS QUITE ALL RIGHT, I KNOW EXACTLY HOW YOU FEEL...
sniff sniff
ON MY VERY FIRST VISIT TO THIS MALL OF SHOPPING, I WAS SEPARATED FROM MY FRIENDS FOR A TIME AND FOUND IT VERY TRAUMATIC.
BUT SINCE THEN, I HAVE LEARNED TO STOP WORRYING AND LOVE THE MALL.
WAAAH!
OH, NO! YOU HAVE SPRUNG THE LEAK!
PLEASE... CEASE THIS TEARFULNESS AND I PROMISE I WILL... BUY YOU THE FRIES WITH THE CHILI!

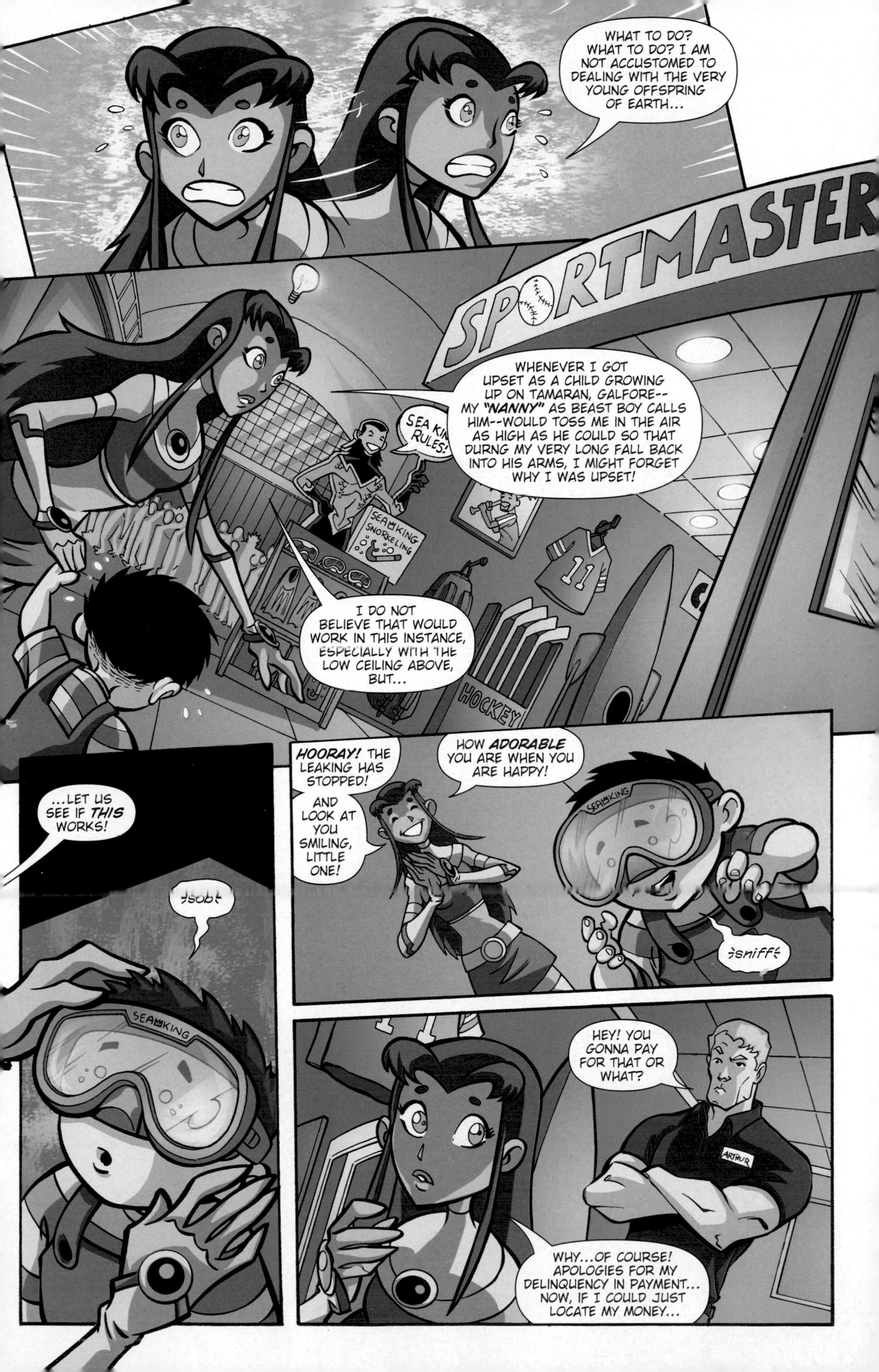
WHAT TO DO? WHAT TO DO? I AM NOT ACCUSTOMED TO DEALING WITH THE VERY YOUNG OFFSPRING OF EARTH...
SPORTMASTER
WHENEVER I GOT UPSET AS A CHILD GROWING UP ON TAMARAN, GALFORE-- MY "NANNY" AS BEAST BOY CALLS HIM--WOULD TOSS ME IN THE AIR AS HIGH AS HE COULD SO THAT DURNG MY VERY LONG FALL BACK INTO HIS ARMS, I MIGHT FORGET WHY I WAS UPSET!
SEA KING RULES!
SEA KING SNORKELING
11
I DO NOT BELIEVE THAT WOULD WORK IN THIS INSTANCE, ESPECIALLY WITH THE LOW CEILING ABOVE, BUT...
HOCKEY
...LET US SEE IF THIS WORKS!
sob
SEA KING
HOORAY! THE LEAKING HAS STOPPED!
AND LOOK AT YOU SMILING, LITTLE ONE!
HOW ADORABLE YOU ARE WHEN YOU ARE HAPPY!
SEA KING
sniff
HEY! YOU GONNA PAY FOR THAT OR WHAT?
ARTHUR
WHY...OF COURSE! APOLOGIES FOR MY DELINQUENCY IN PAYMENT... NOW, IF I COULD JUST LOCATE MY MONEY...

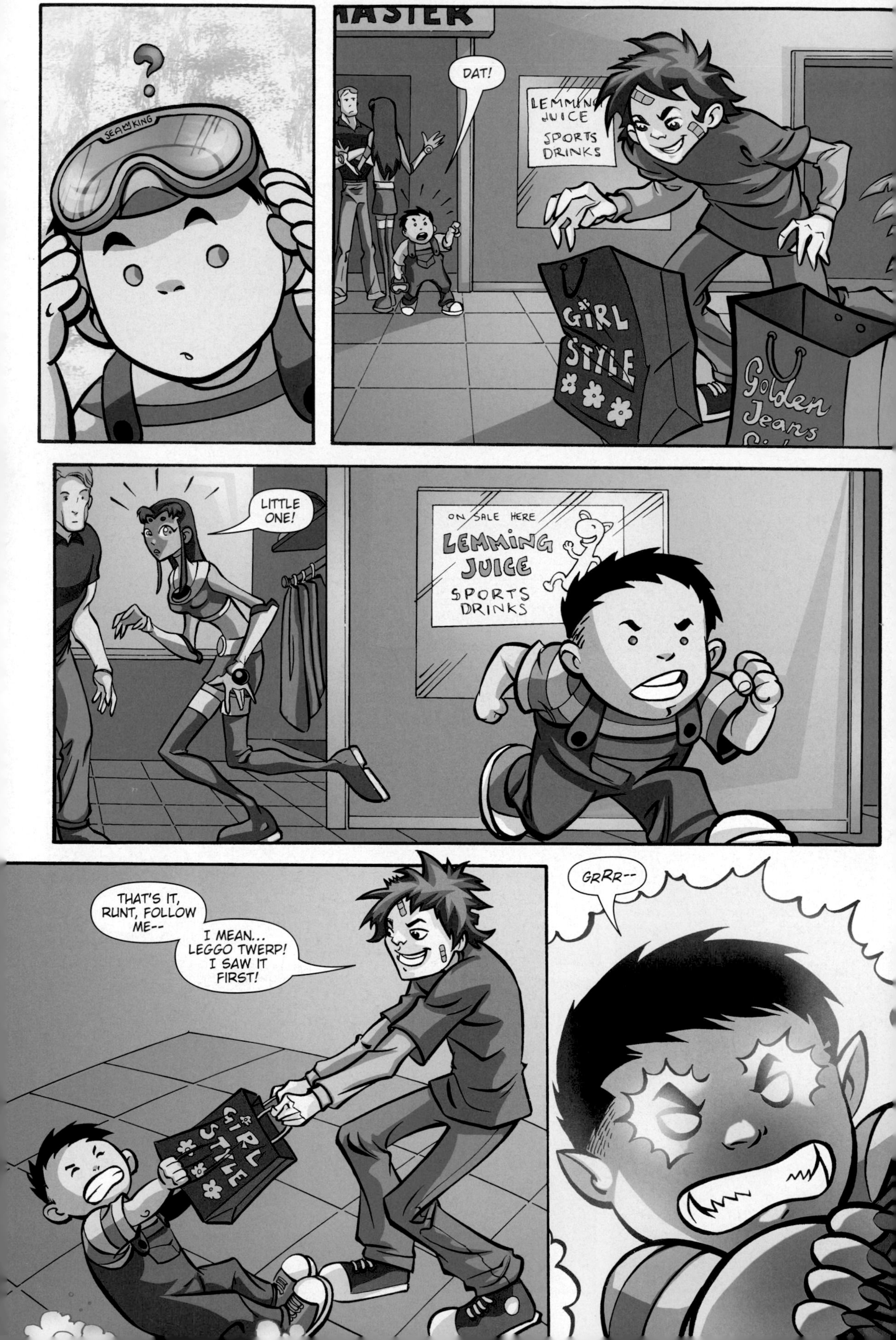

SEA KING
?
MASTER
DAT!
LEMMING JUICE SPORTS DRINKS
GIRL STYLE
Golden Jeans
LITTLE ONE!
ON SALE HERE
LEMMING JUICE
SPORTS DRINKS
THAT'S IT, RUNT, FOLLOW ME--
I MEAN... LEGGO TWERP! I SAW IT FIRST!
GIRL STYLE
GRRR--

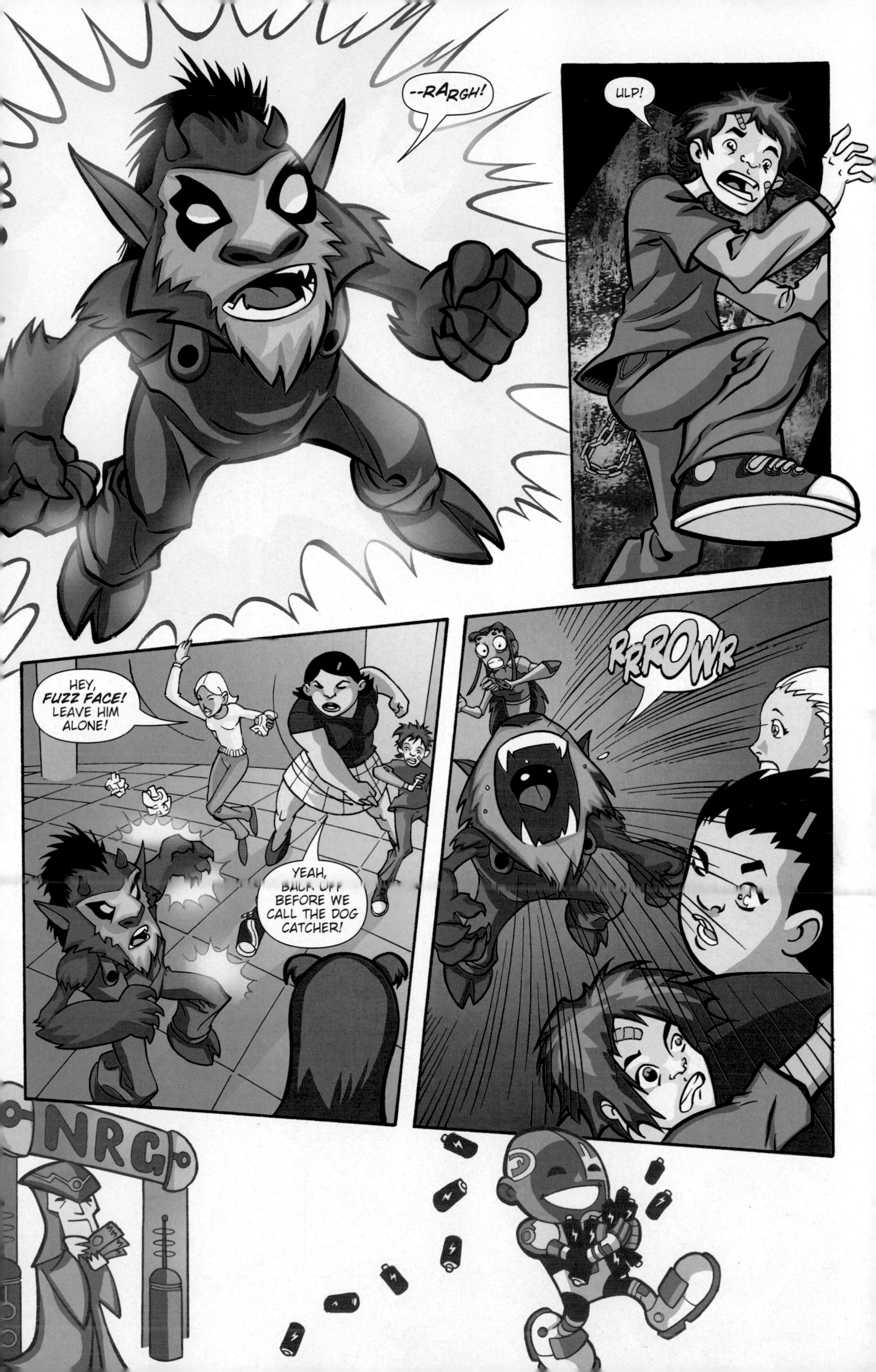
--RARGH!
ULP!
HEY, FUZZ FACE! LEAVE HIM ALONE!
YEAH, BACK OFF BEFORE WE CALL THE DOG CATCHER!
RRROWR
NRG

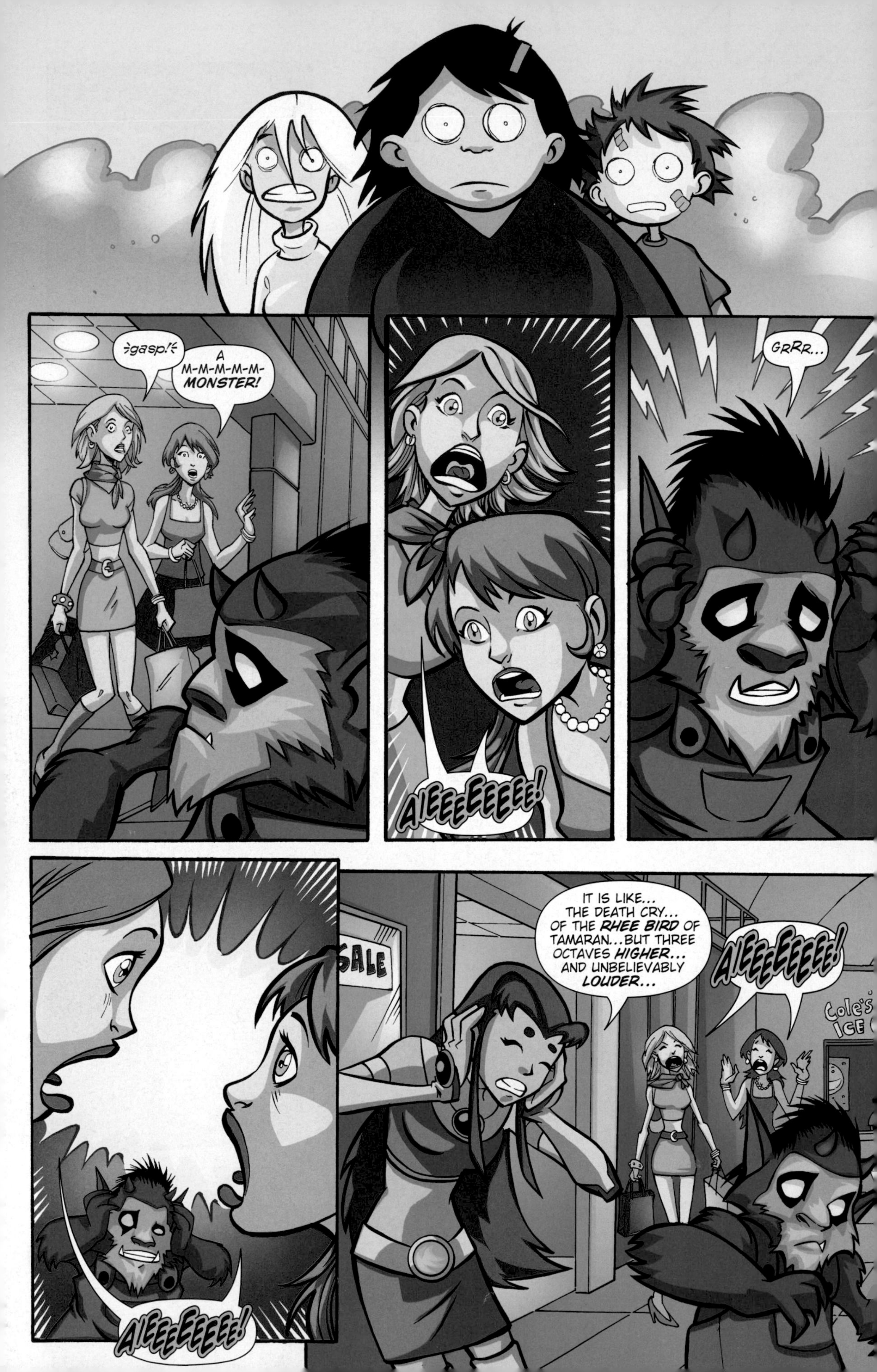

gasp!
A M-M-M-M-M-MONSTER!
AIEEEEEEEE!
GRRR...
AIEEEEEEEE!
IT IS LIKE... THE DEATH CRY... OF THE RHEE BIRD OF TAMARAN... BUT THREE OCTAVES HIGHER... AND UNBELIEVABLY LOUDER...
AIEEEEEEEE!
SALE
Cole's ICE

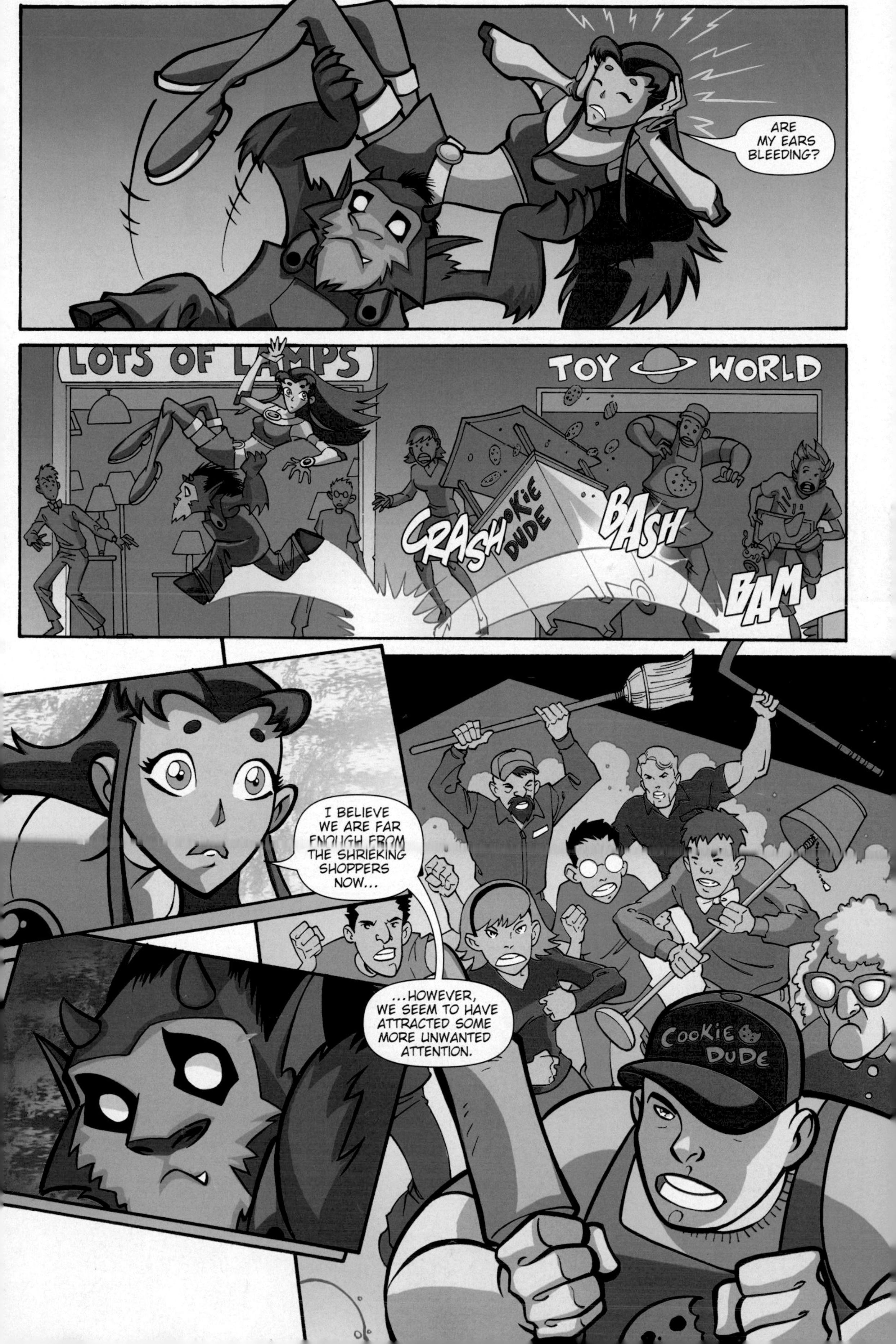
ARE MY EARS BLEEDING?
LOTS OF LAMPS
TOY WORLD
CRASH
COOKIE DUDE
BASH
BAM
I BELIEVE WE ARE FAR ENOUGH FROM THE SHRIEKING SHOPPERS NOW...
...HOWEVER, WE SEEM TO HAVE ATTRACTED SOME MORE UNWANTED ATTENTION.
COOKIE DUDE

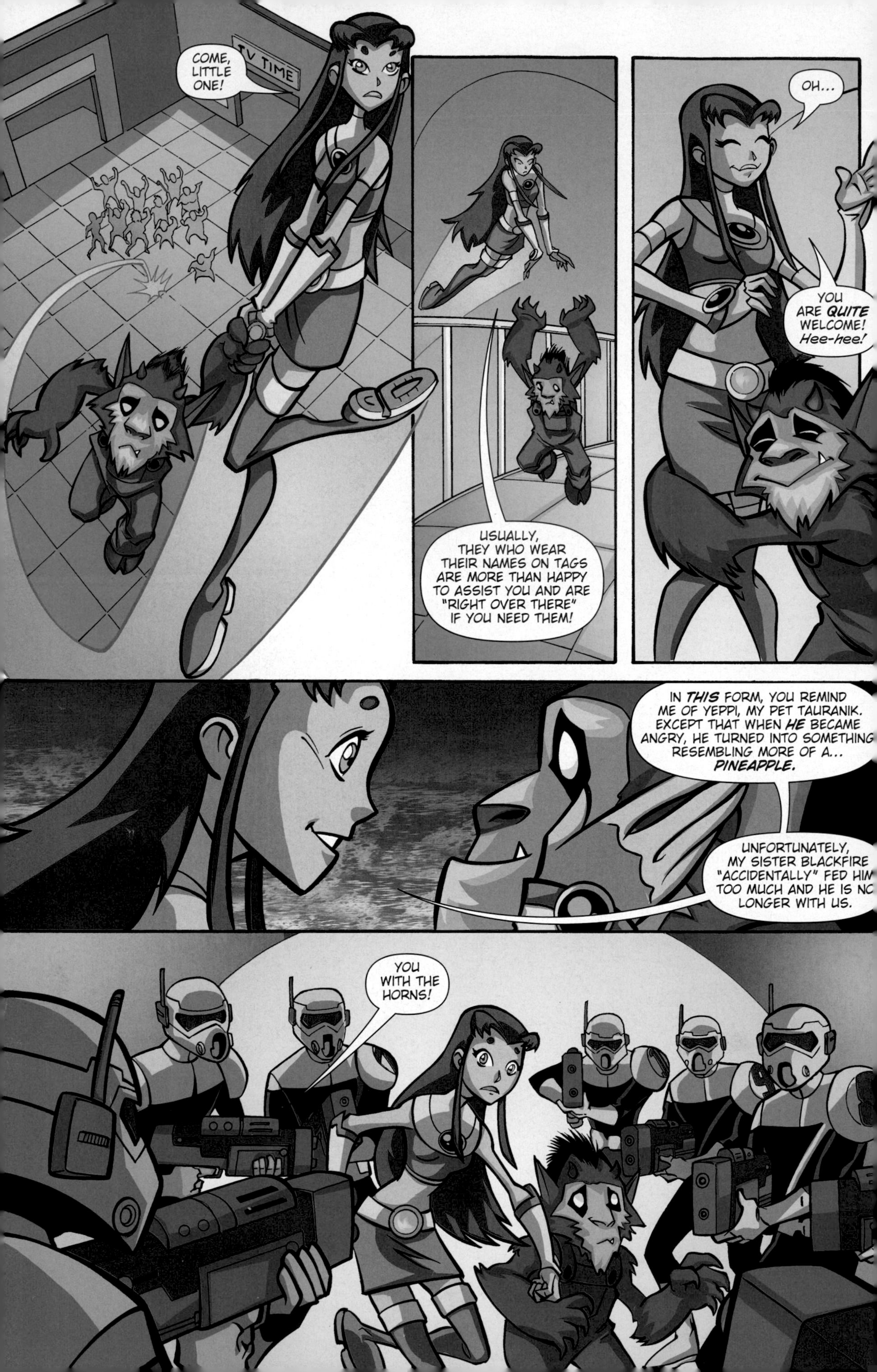

COME, LITTLE ONE!
TV TIME
USUALLY, THEY WHO WEAR THEIR NAMES ON TAGS ARE MORE THAN HAPPY TO ASSIST YOU AND ARE "RIGHT OVER THERE" IF YOU NEED THEM!
OH...
YOU ARE **QUITE** WELCOME! *Hee-hee!*
IN **THIS** FORM, YOU REMIND ME OF YEPPI, MY PET TAURANIK. EXCEPT THAT WHEN **HE** BECAME ANGRY, HE TURNED INTO SOMETHING RESEMBLING MORE OF A... **PINEAPPLE.**
UNFORTUNATELY, MY SISTER BLACKFIRE "ACCIDENTALLY" FED HIM TOO MUCH AND HE IS NO LONGER WITH US.
YOU WITH THE HORNS!

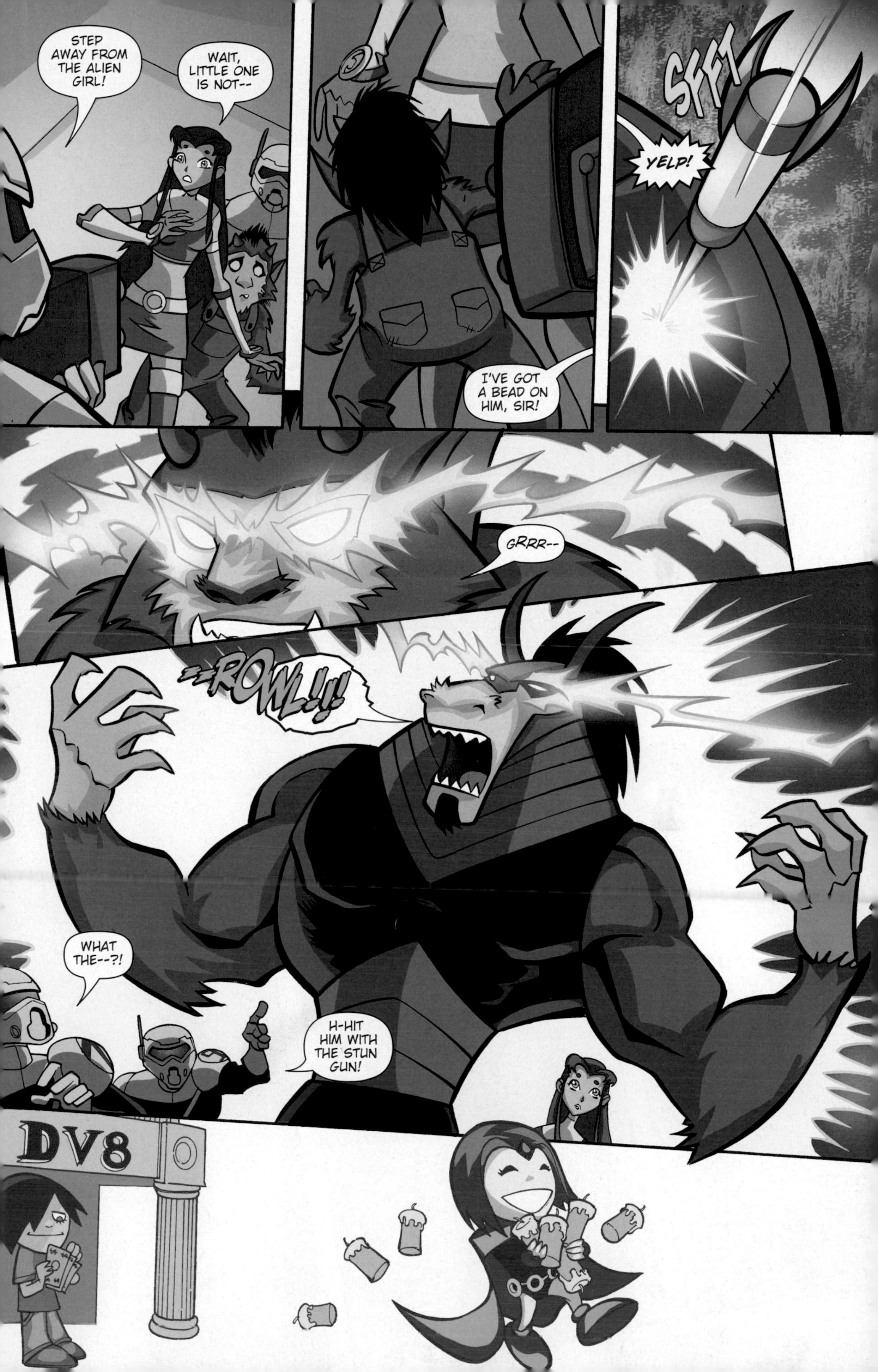
STEP AWAY FROM THE ALIEN GIRL!
WAIT, LITTLE ONE IS NOT--
SFFT
YELP!
I'VE GOT A BEAD ON HIM, SIR!
GRRR--
--ROWL!!!
WHAT THE--?!
H-HIT HIM WITH THE STUN GUN!
DV8

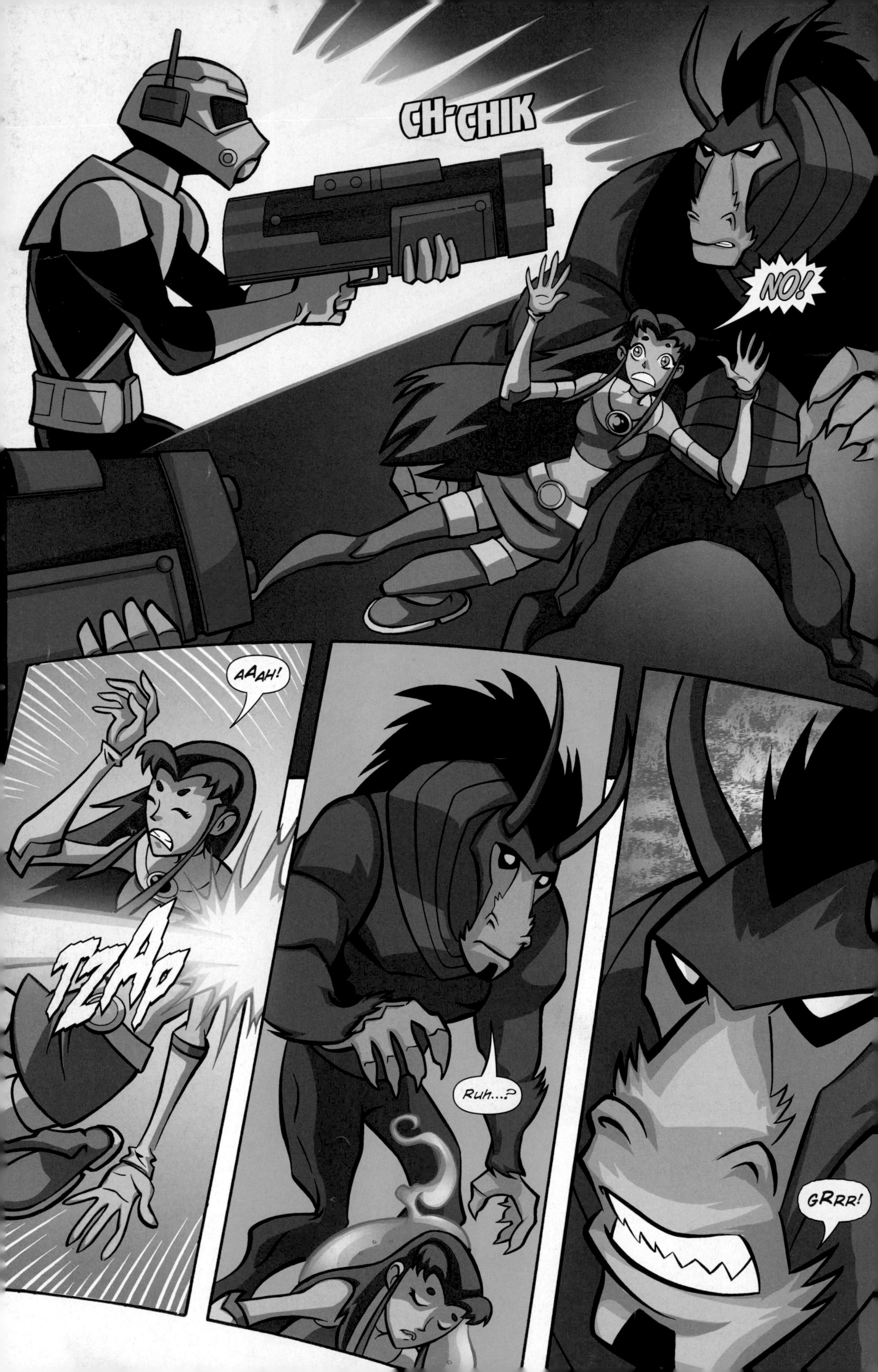
CH-CHIK
NO!
AAAH!
TZAP
Ruh...?
GRRR!

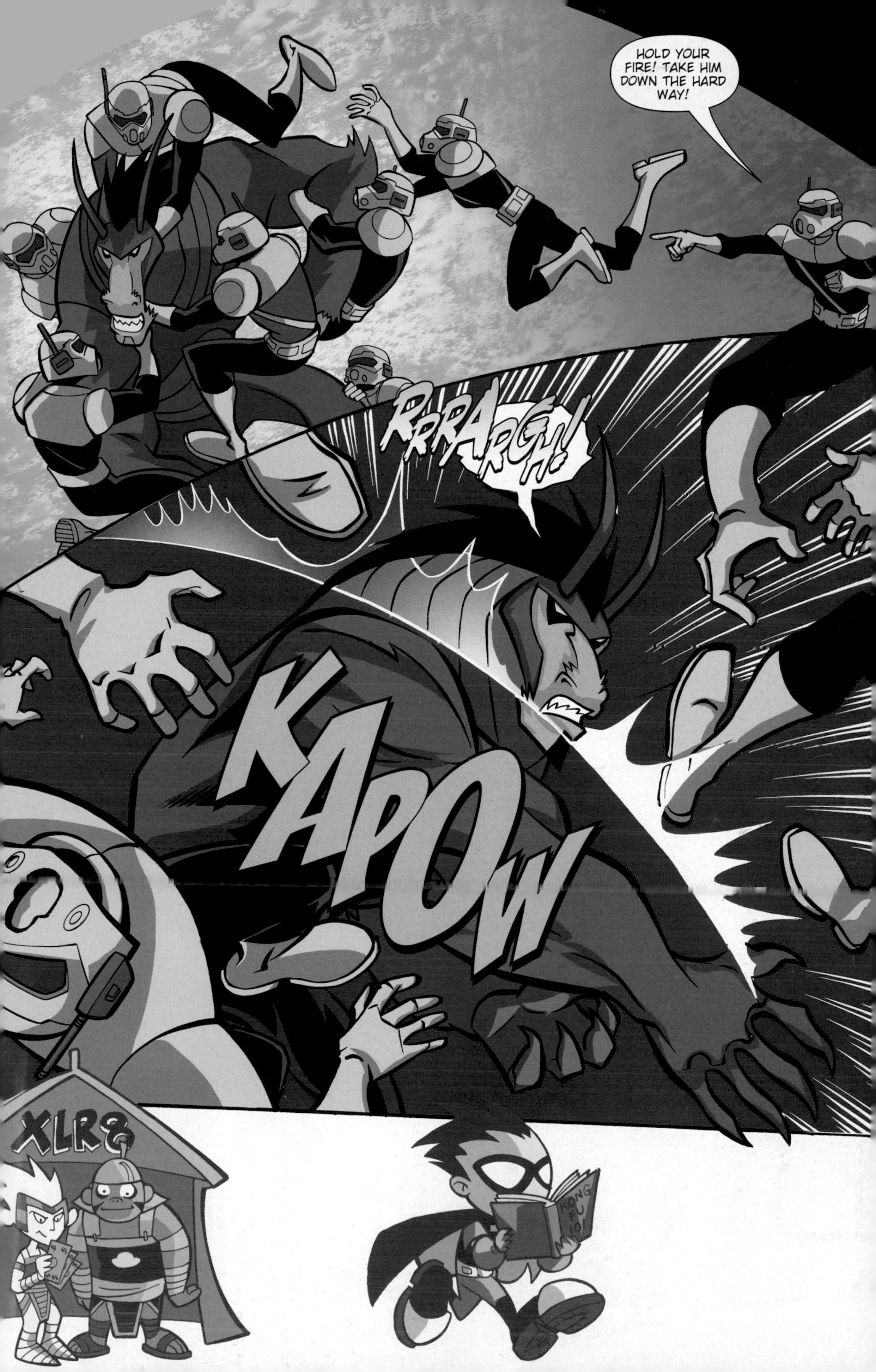
HOLD YOUR FIRE! TAKE HIM DOWN THE HARD WAY!
RRRRARGH!
KAPOW
XLR8
KONG FU 101

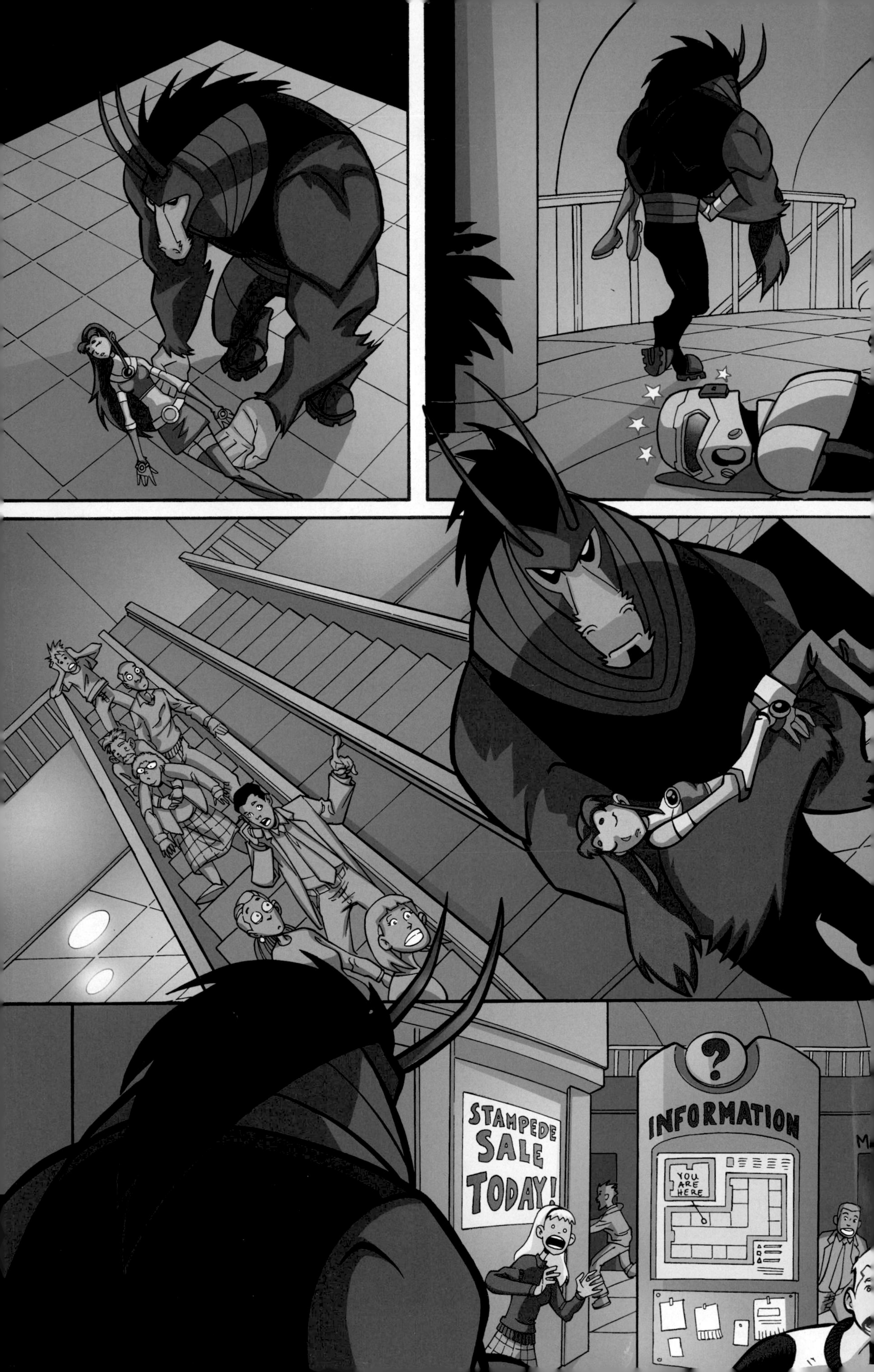
STAMPEDE SALE TODAY!
INFORMATION
YOU ARE HERE

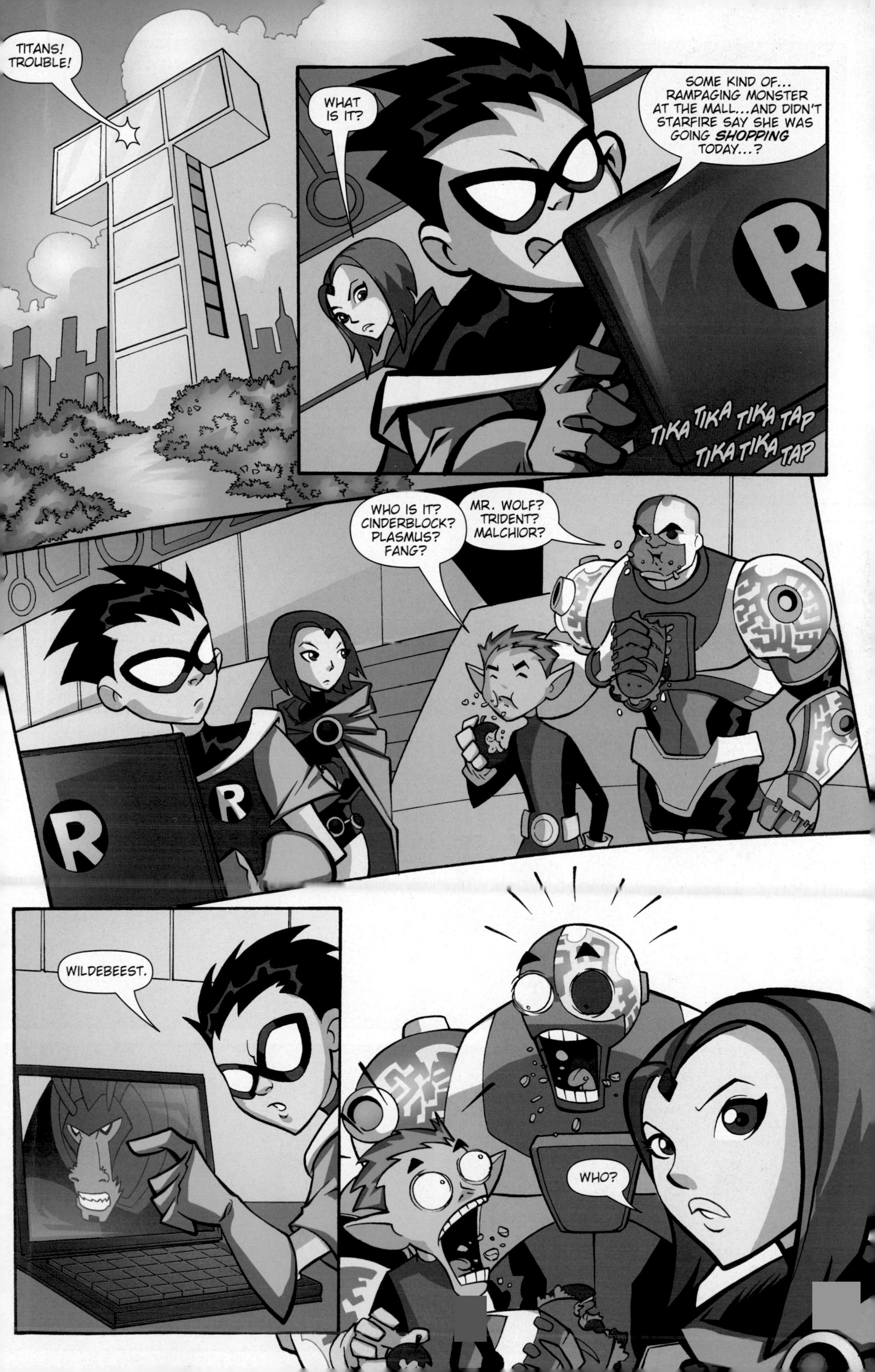
TITANS! TROUBLE!
WHAT IS IT?
SOME KIND OF... RAMPAGING MONSTER AT THE MALL...AND DIDN'T STARFIRE SAY SHE WAS GOING SHOPPING TODAY...?
TIKA TIKA TIKA TAP
TIKA TIKA TAP
WHO IS IT? CINDERBLOCK? PLASMUS? FANG?
MR. WOLF? TRIDENT? MALCHIOR?
WILDEBEEST.
WHO?

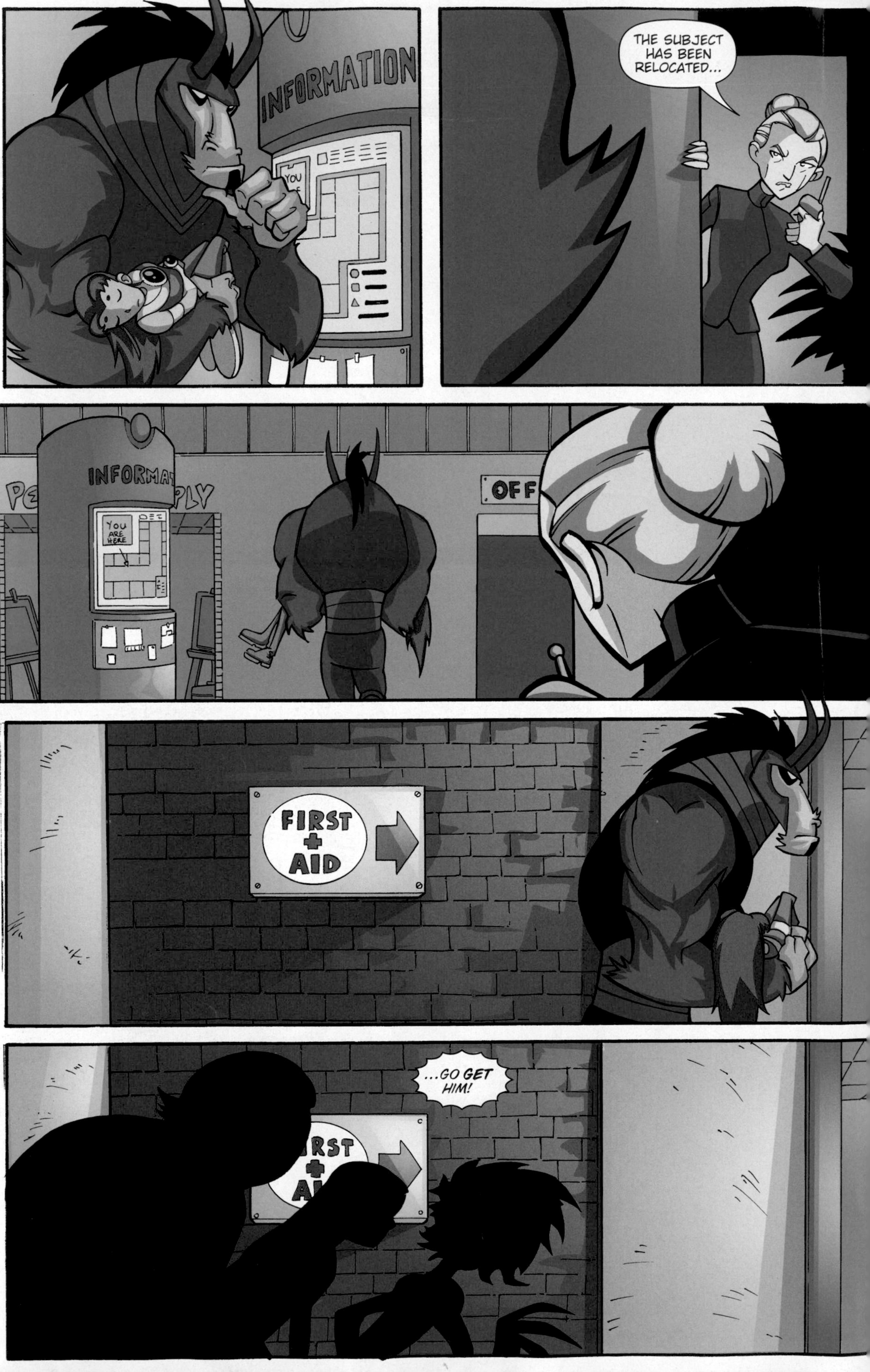
INFORMATION
YOU
THE SUBJECT HAS BEEN RELOCATED...
INFORMA
YOU ARE HERE
OFF
FIRST + AID
...GO GET HIM!

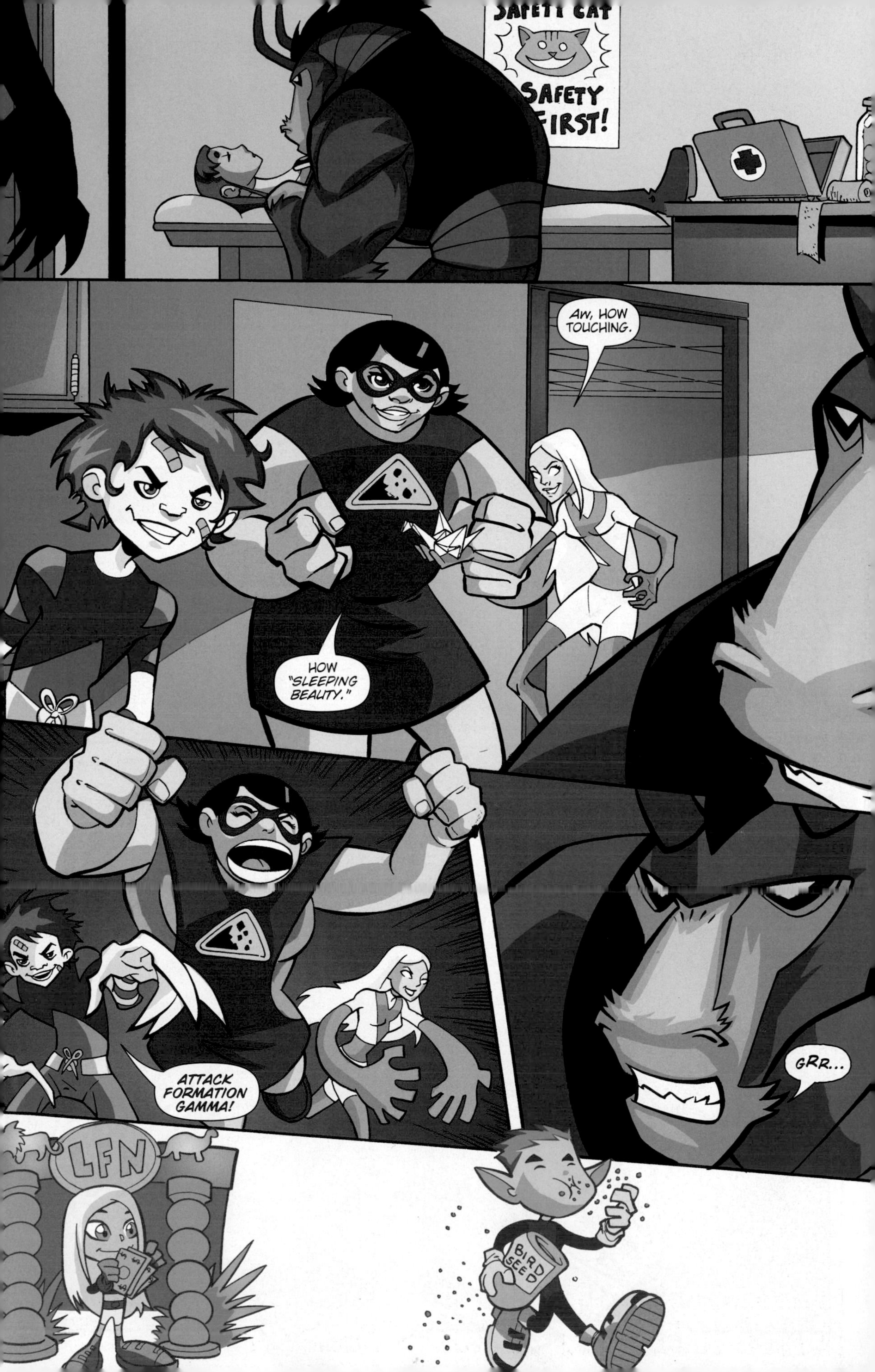
SAFETY CAT
SAFETY FIRST!
AW, HOW TOUCHING.
HOW "SLEEPING BEAUTY."
ATTACK FORMATION GAMMA!
GRR...
LFN
BIRD SEED

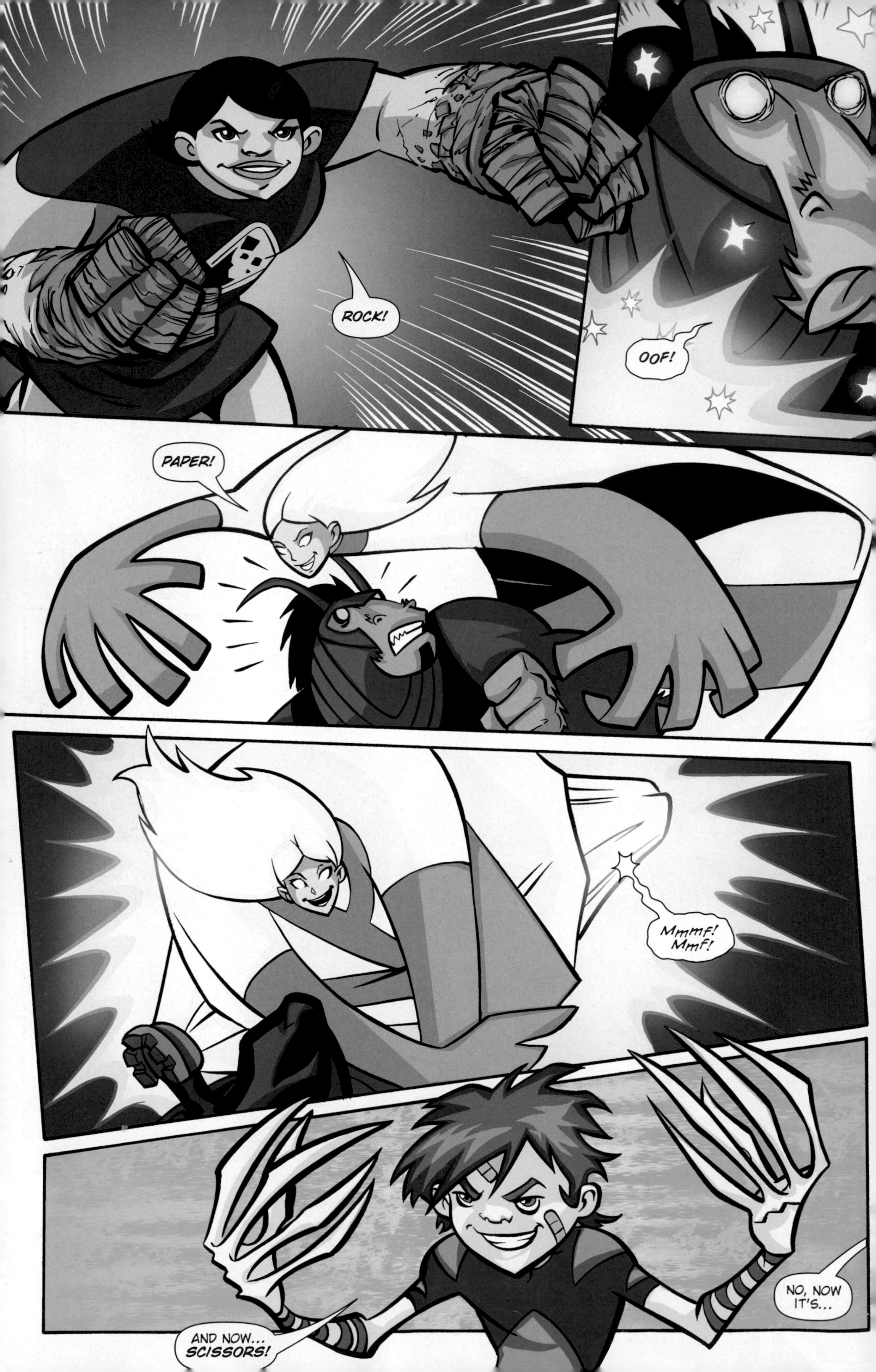
ROCK!
OOF!
PAPER!
Mmmf! Mmf!
AND NOW... SCISSORS!
NO, NOW IT'S...

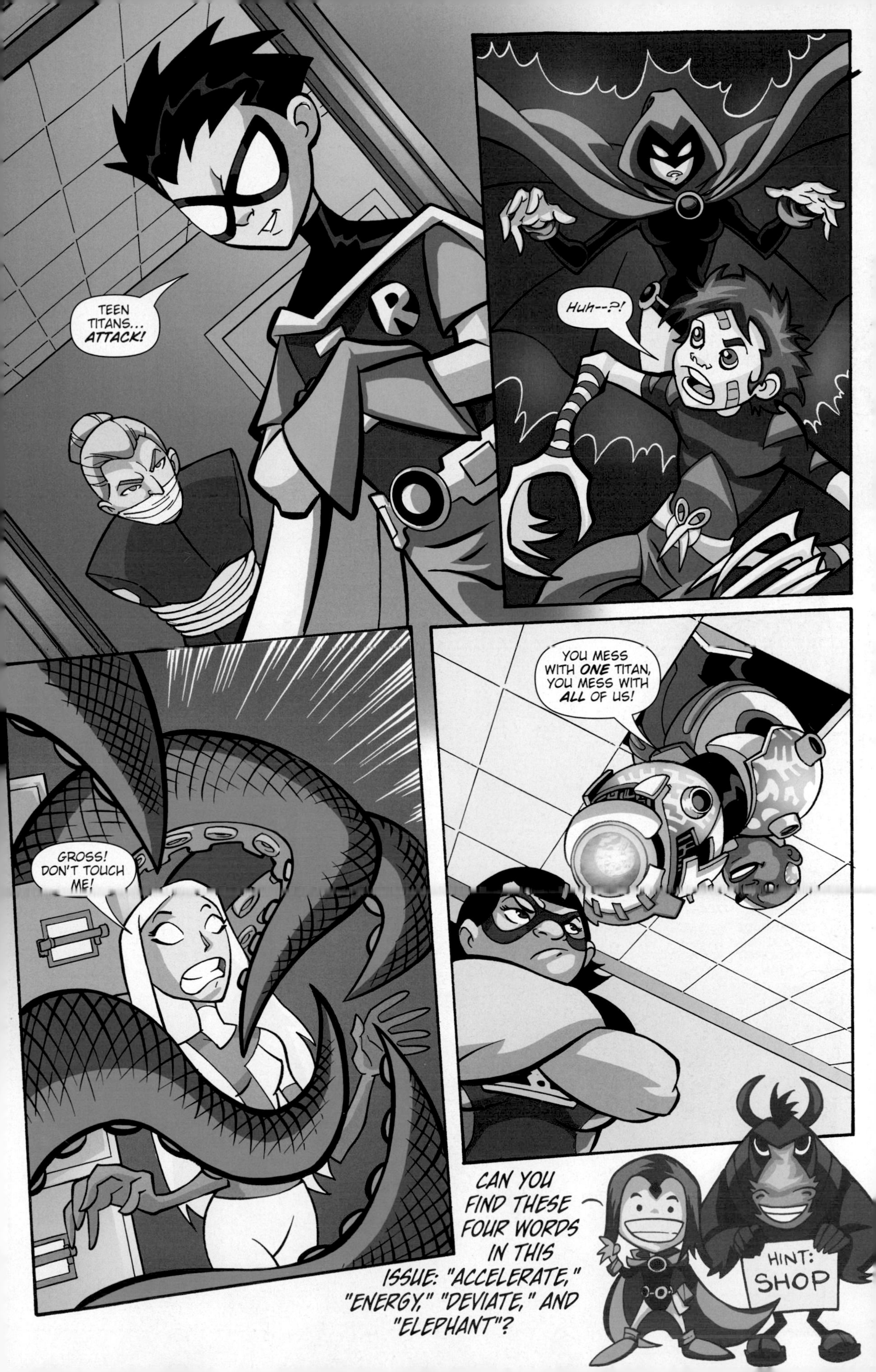

TEEN TITANS... ATTACK!
Huh--?!
GROSS! DON'T TOUCH ME!
YOU MESS WITH ONE TITAN, YOU MESS WITH ALL OF US!
CAN YOU FIND THESE FOUR WORDS IN THIS ISSUE: "ACCELERATE," "ENERGY," "DEVIATE," AND "ELEPHANT"?
HINT: SHOP

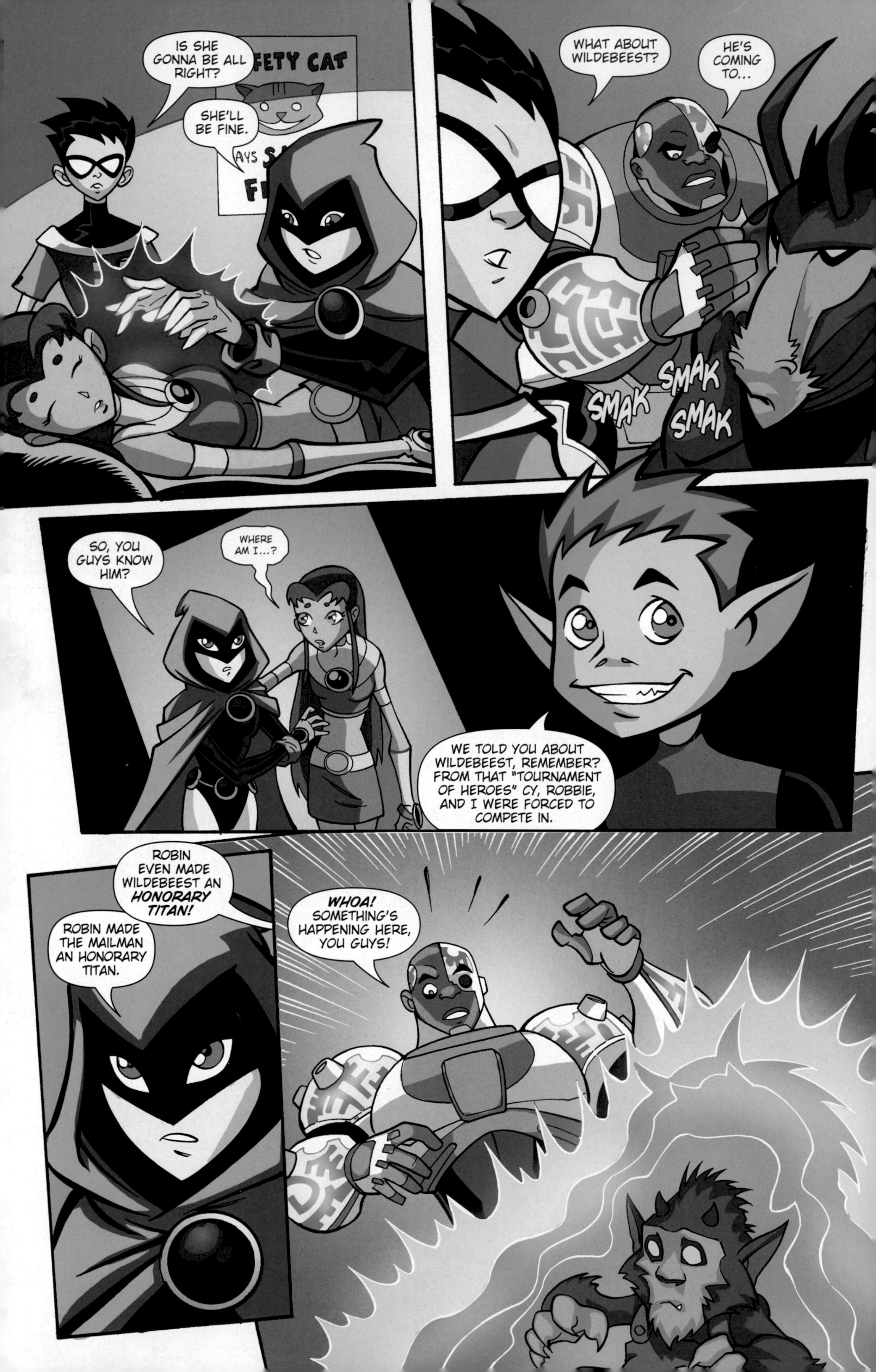
IS SHE GONNA BE ALL RIGHT?
SHE'LL BE FINE.
FETY CAT
WHAT ABOUT WILDEBEEST?
HE'S COMING TO...
SMAK
SMAK
SMAK
SO, YOU GUYS KNOW HIM?
WHERE AM I...?
WE TOLD YOU ABOUT WILDEBEEST, REMEMBER? FROM THAT "TOURNAMENT OF HEROES" CY, ROBBIE, AND I WERE FORCED TO COMPETE IN.
ROBIN EVEN MADE WILDEBEEST AN HONORARY TITAN!
ROBIN MADE THE MAILMAN AN HONORARY TITAN.
WHOA! SOMETHING'S HAPPENING HERE, YOU GUYS!

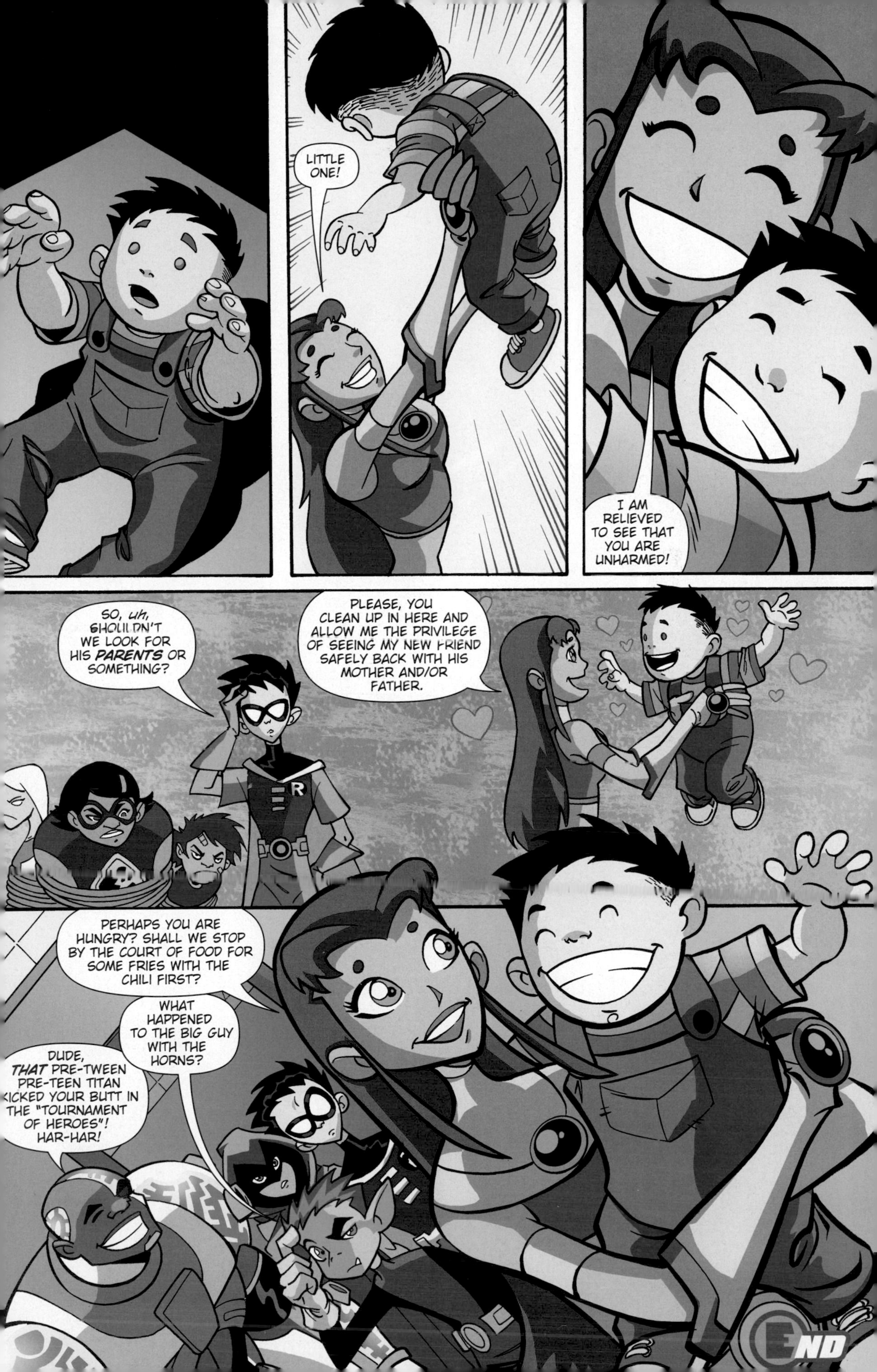
LITTLE ONE!
I AM RELIEVED TO SEE THAT YOU ARE UNHARMED!
SO, uh, SHOULDN'T WE LOOK FOR HIS PARENTS OR SOMETHING?
PLEASE, YOU CLEAN UP IN HERE AND ALLOW ME THE PRIVILEGE OF SEEING MY NEW FRIEND SAFELY BACK WITH HIS MOTHER AND/OR FATHER.
PERHAPS YOU ARE HUNGRY? SHALL WE STOP BY THE COURT OF FOOD FOR SOME FRIES WITH THE CHILI FIRST?
WHAT HAPPENED TO THE BIG GUY WITH THE HORNS?
DUDE, THAT PRE-TWEEN PRE-TEEN TITAN KICKED YOUR BUTT IN THE "TOURNAMENT OF HEROES"! HAR-HAR!
END

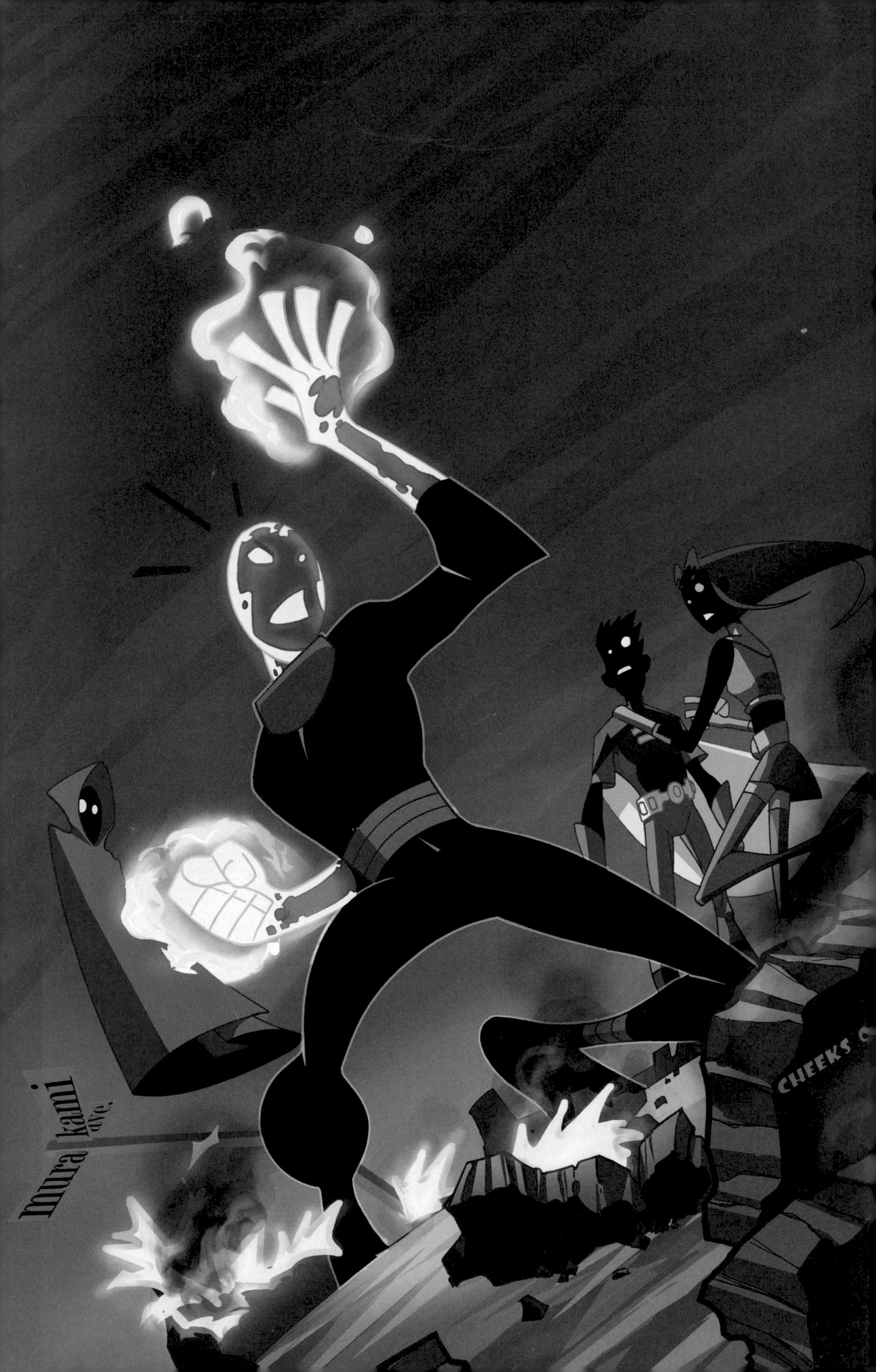

murakami ave.
CHEEKS

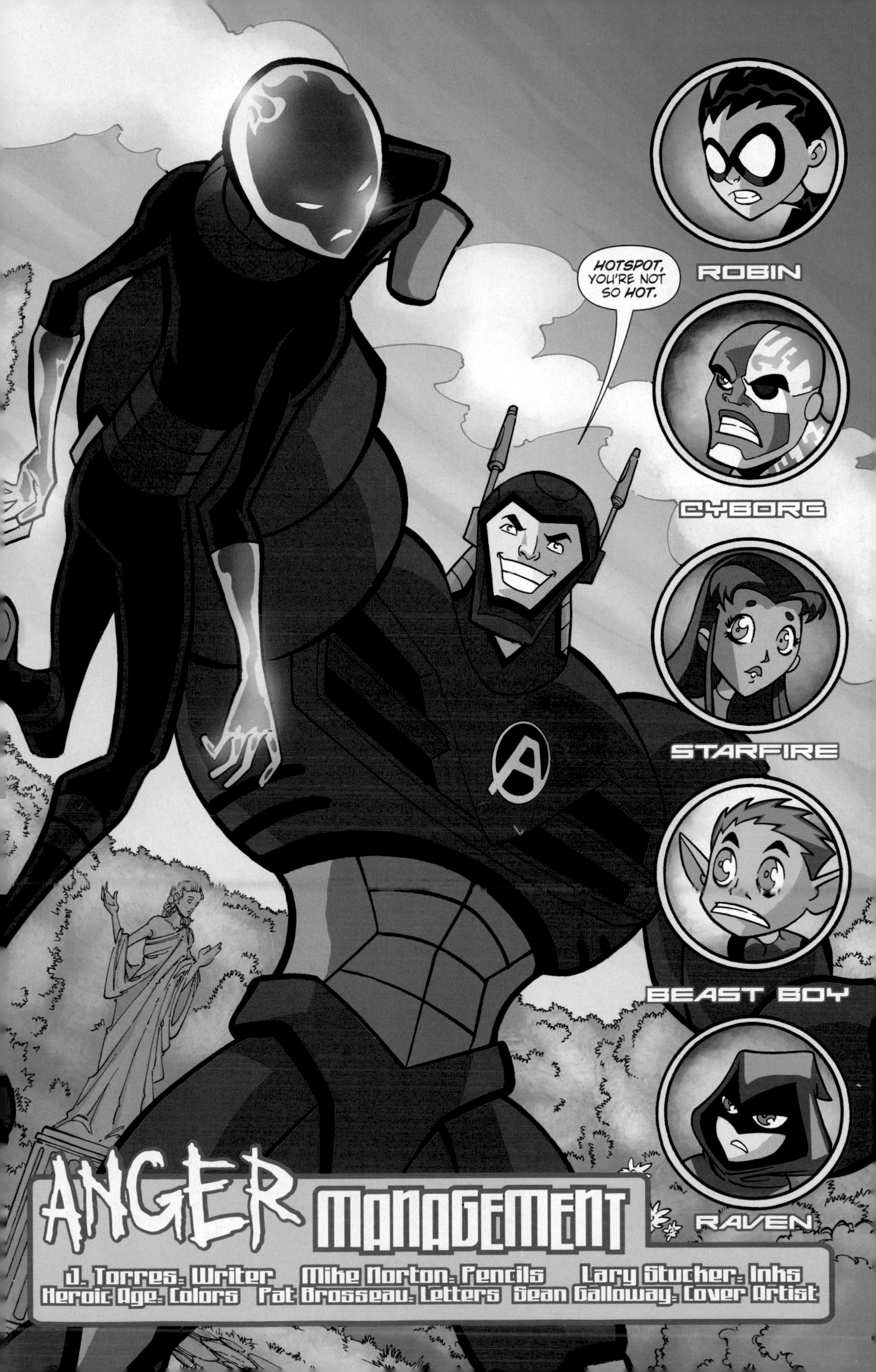

HOTSPOT, YOU'RE NOT SO HOT.
ROBIN
CYBORG
STARFIRE
BEAST BOY
RAVEN
ANGER MANAGEMENT
J. Torres: Writer Mike Norton: Pencils Lary Stucker: Inks
Heroic Age: Colors Pat Brosseau: Letters Sean Galloway: Cover Artist

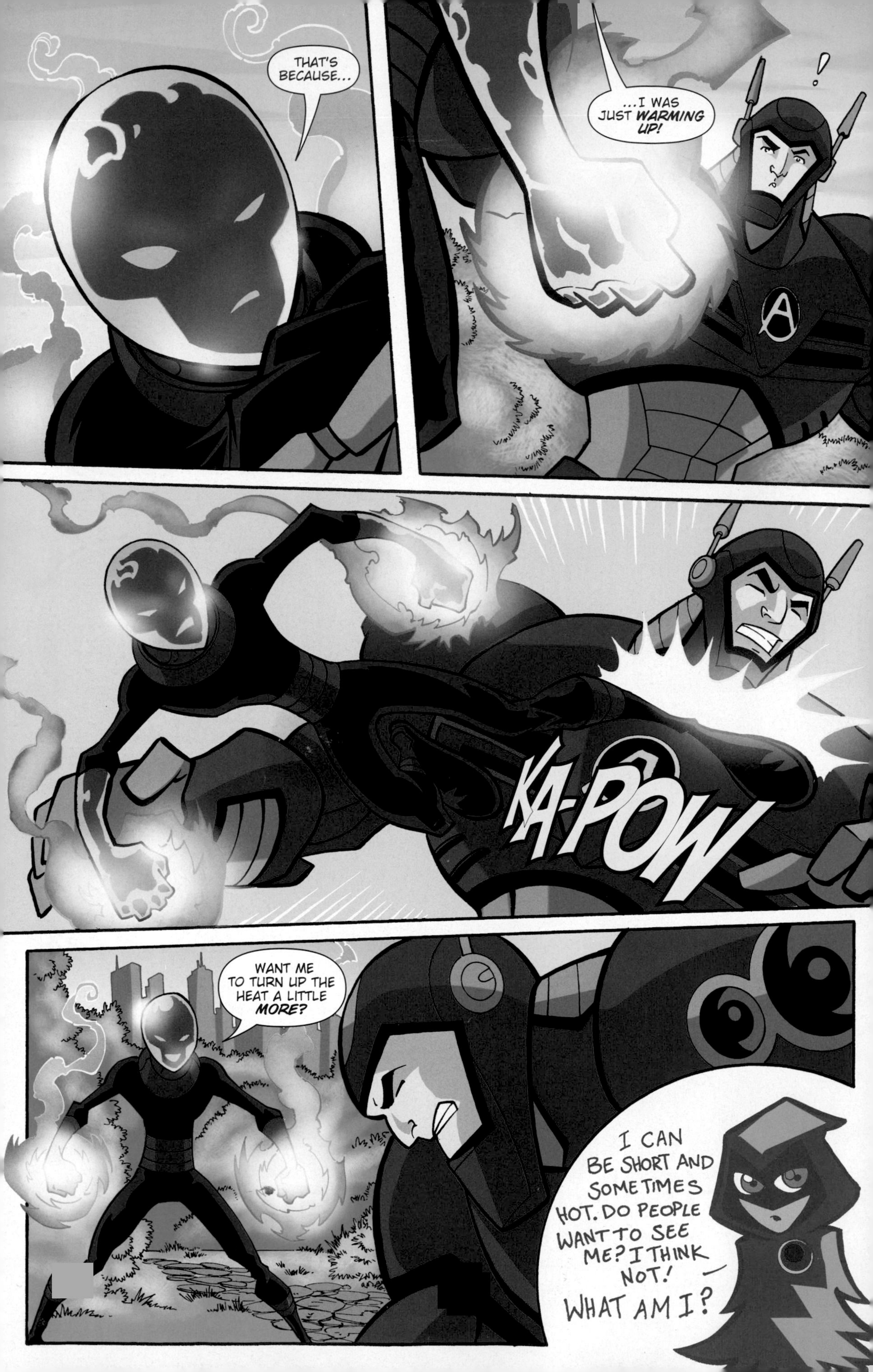
THAT'S BECAUSE...
...I WAS JUST **WARMING UP!**
!
KA-POW
WANT ME TO TURN UP THE HEAT A LITTLE **MORE?**
I CAN BE SHORT AND SOMETIMES HOT. DO PEOPLE WANT TO SEE ME? I THINK NOT!
WHAT AM I?

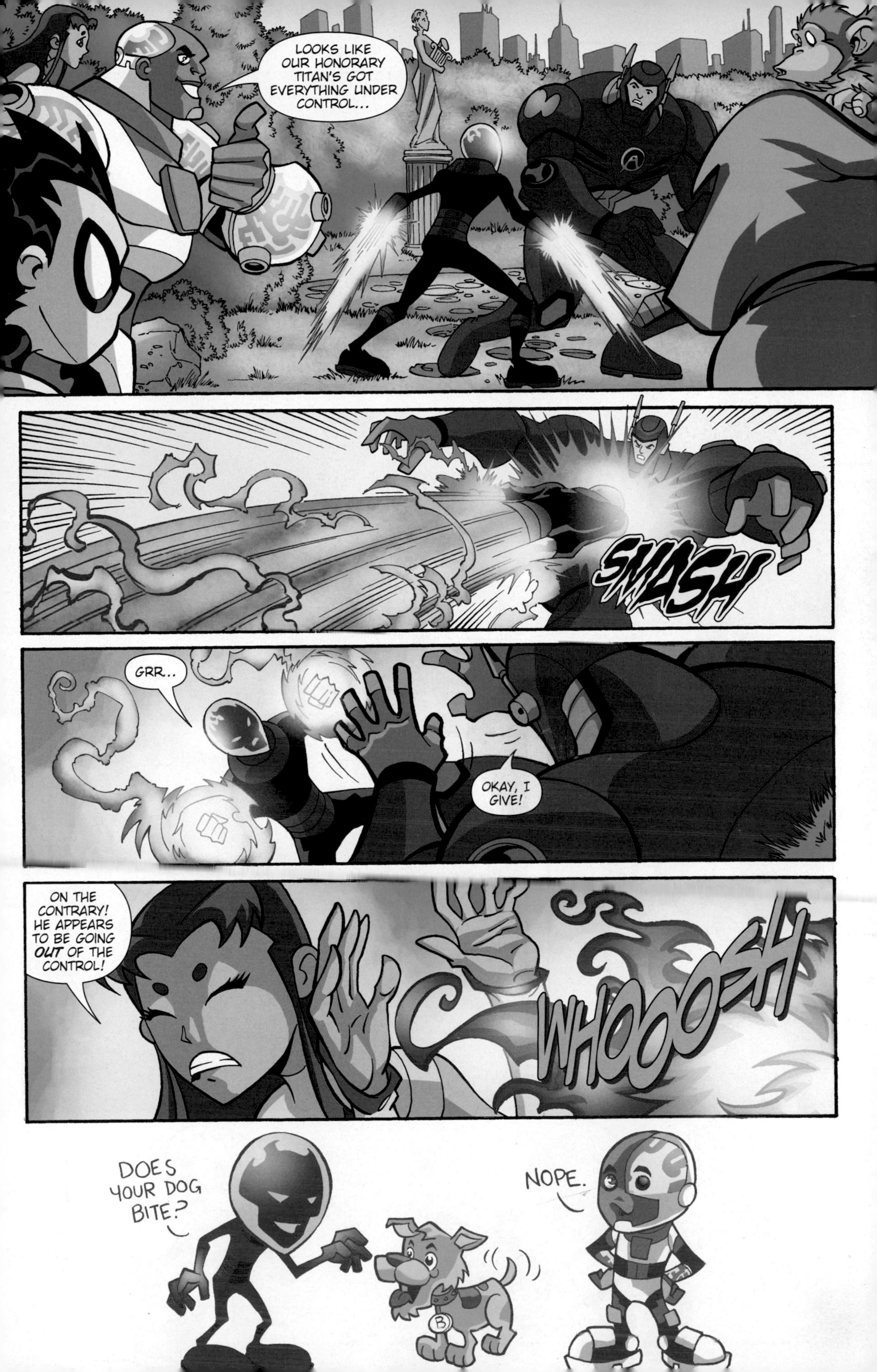
LOOKS LIKE OUR HONORARY TITAN'S GOT EVERYTHING UNDER CONTROL...
SMASH
GRR...
OKAY, I GIVE!
ON THE CONTRARY! HE APPEARS TO BE GOING OUT OF THE CONTROL!
WHOOOOSH
DOES YOUR DOG BITE?
NOPE.

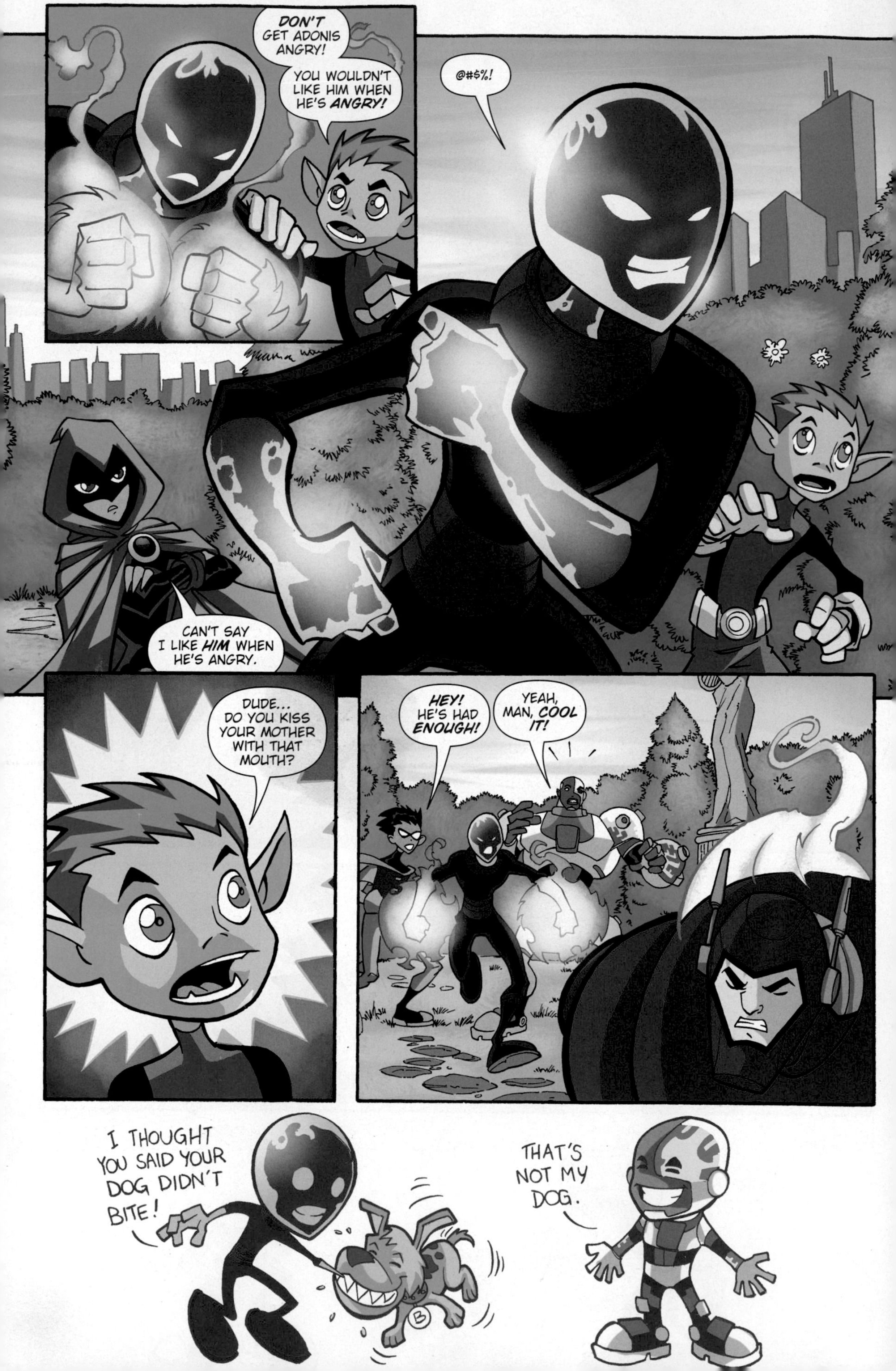

DON'T GET ADONIS ANGRY!
YOU WOULDN'T LIKE HIM WHEN HE'S ANGRY!
@#$%!
CAN'T SAY I LIKE HIM WHEN HE'S ANGRY.
DUDE... DO YOU KISS YOUR MOTHER WITH THAT MOUTH?
HEY! HE'S HAD ENOUGH!
YEAH, MAN, COOL IT!
I THOUGHT YOU SAID YOUR DOG DIDN'T BITE!
THAT'S NOT MY DOG.

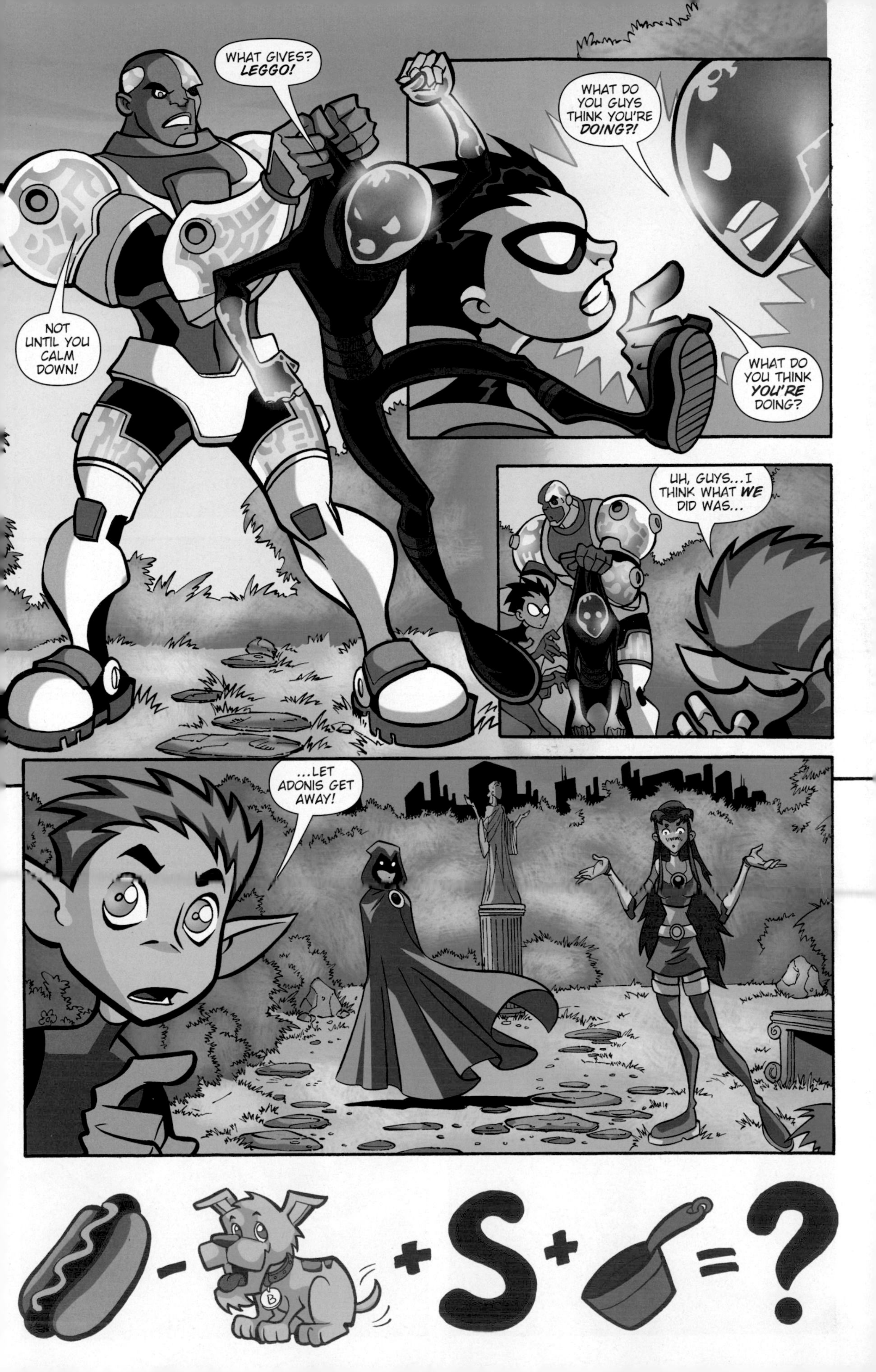

WHAT GIVES? LEGGO!
NOT UNTIL YOU CALM DOWN!
WHAT DO YOU GUYS THINK YOU'RE DOING?!
WHAT DO YOU THINK YOU'RE DOING?
UH, GUYS...I THINK WHAT WE DID WAS...
...LET ADONIS GET AWAY!
S
B

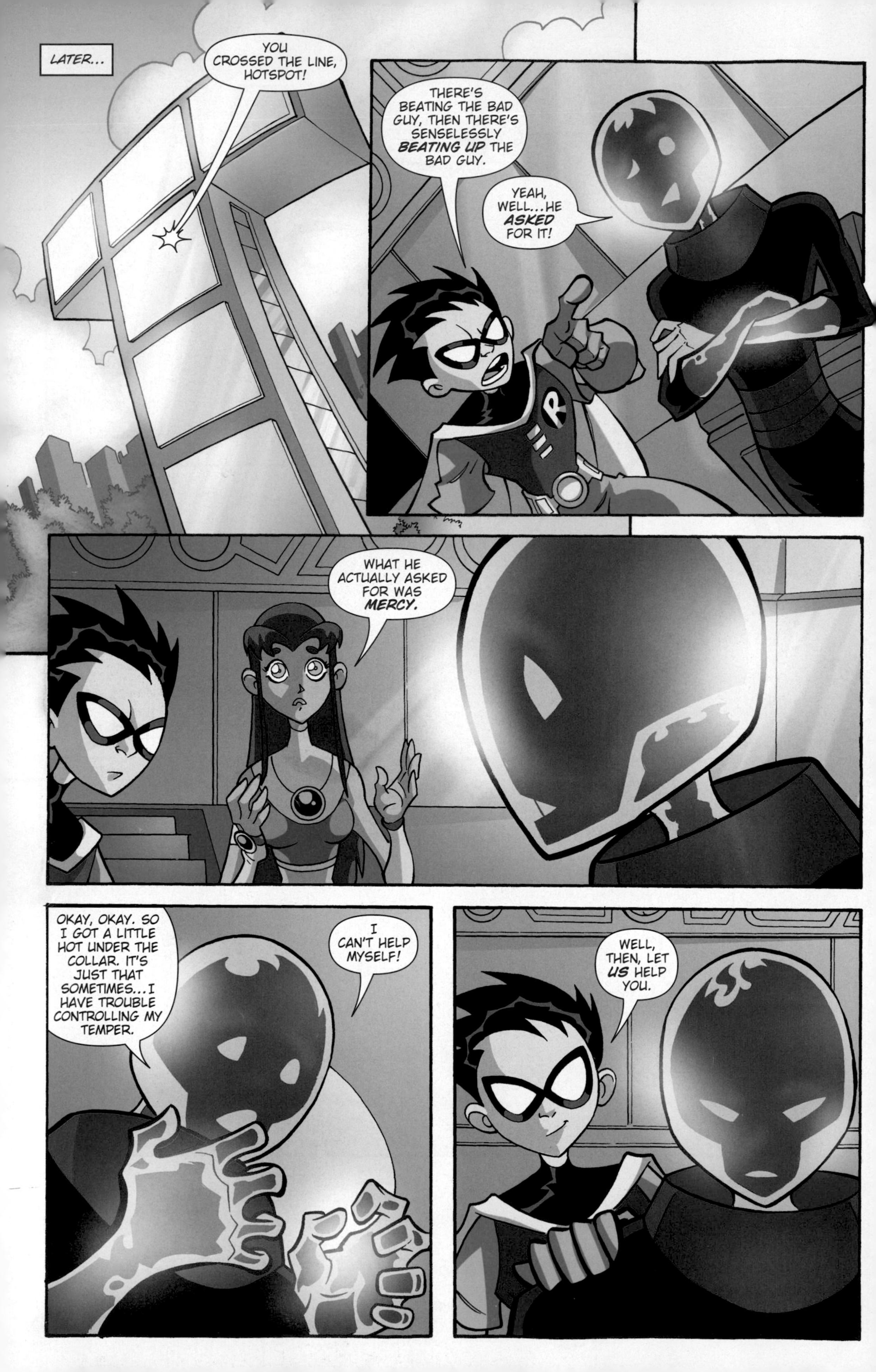
LATER...
YOU CROSSED THE LINE, HOTSPOT!
THERE'S BEATING THE BAD GUY, THEN THERE'S SENSELESSLY BEATING UP THE BAD GUY.
YEAH, WELL...HE ASKED FOR IT!
WHAT HE ACTUALLY ASKED FOR WAS MERCY.
OKAY, OKAY. SO I GOT A LITTLE HOT UNDER THE COLLAR. IT'S JUST THAT SOMETIMES...I HAVE TROUBLE CONTROLLING MY TEMPER.
I CAN'T HELP MYSELF!
WELL, THEN, LET US HELP YOU.

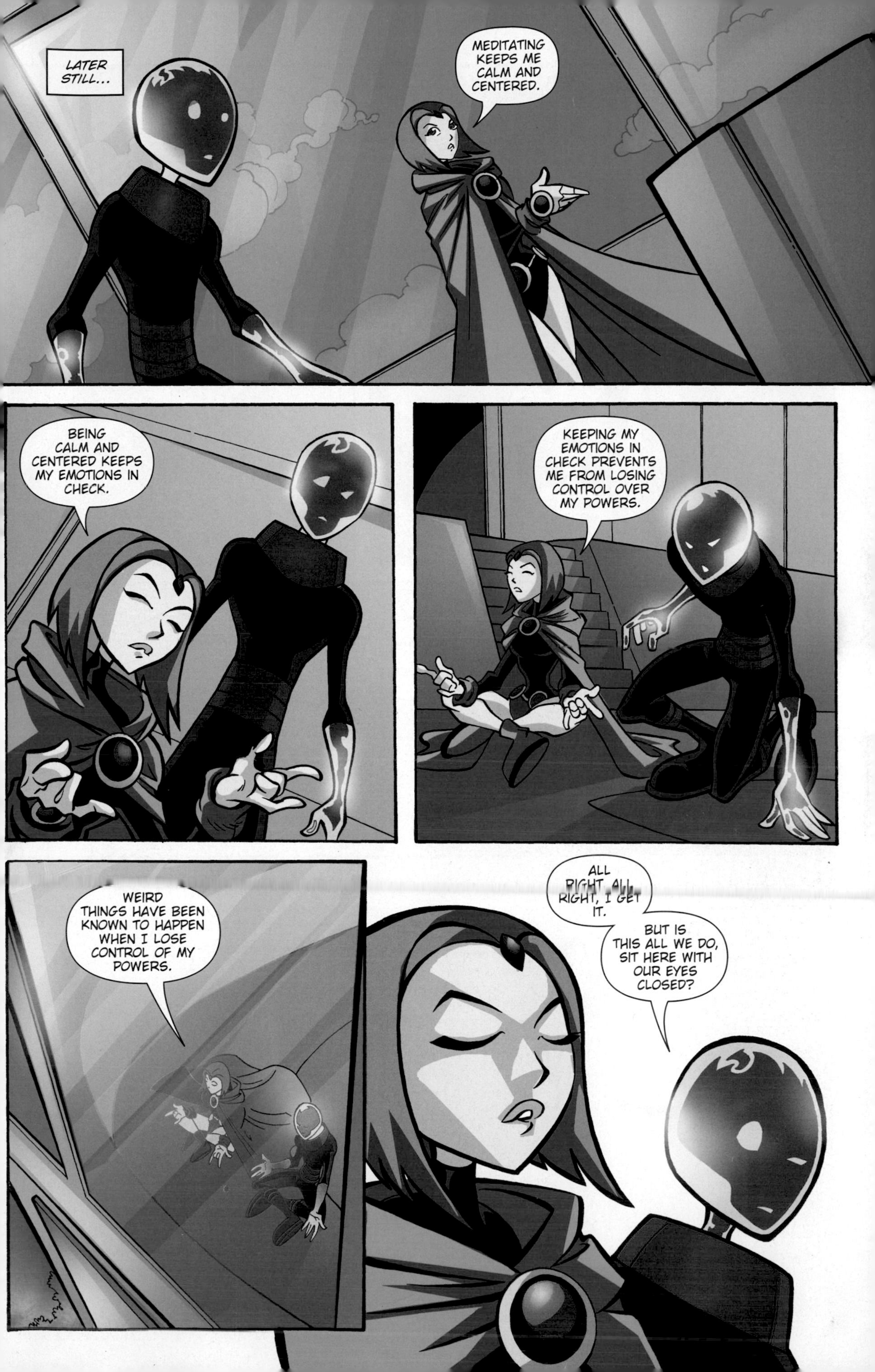
LATER STILL...
MEDITATING KEEPS ME CALM AND CENTERED.
BEING CALM AND CENTERED KEEPS MY EMOTIONS IN CHECK.
KEEPING MY EMOTIONS IN CHECK PREVENTS ME FROM LOSING CONTROL OVER MY POWERS.
WEIRD THINGS HAVE BEEN KNOWN TO HAPPEN WHEN I LOSE CONTROL OF MY POWERS.
ALL RIGHT ALL RIGHT, I GET IT.
BUT IS THIS ALL WE DO, SIT HERE WITH OUR EYES CLOSED?

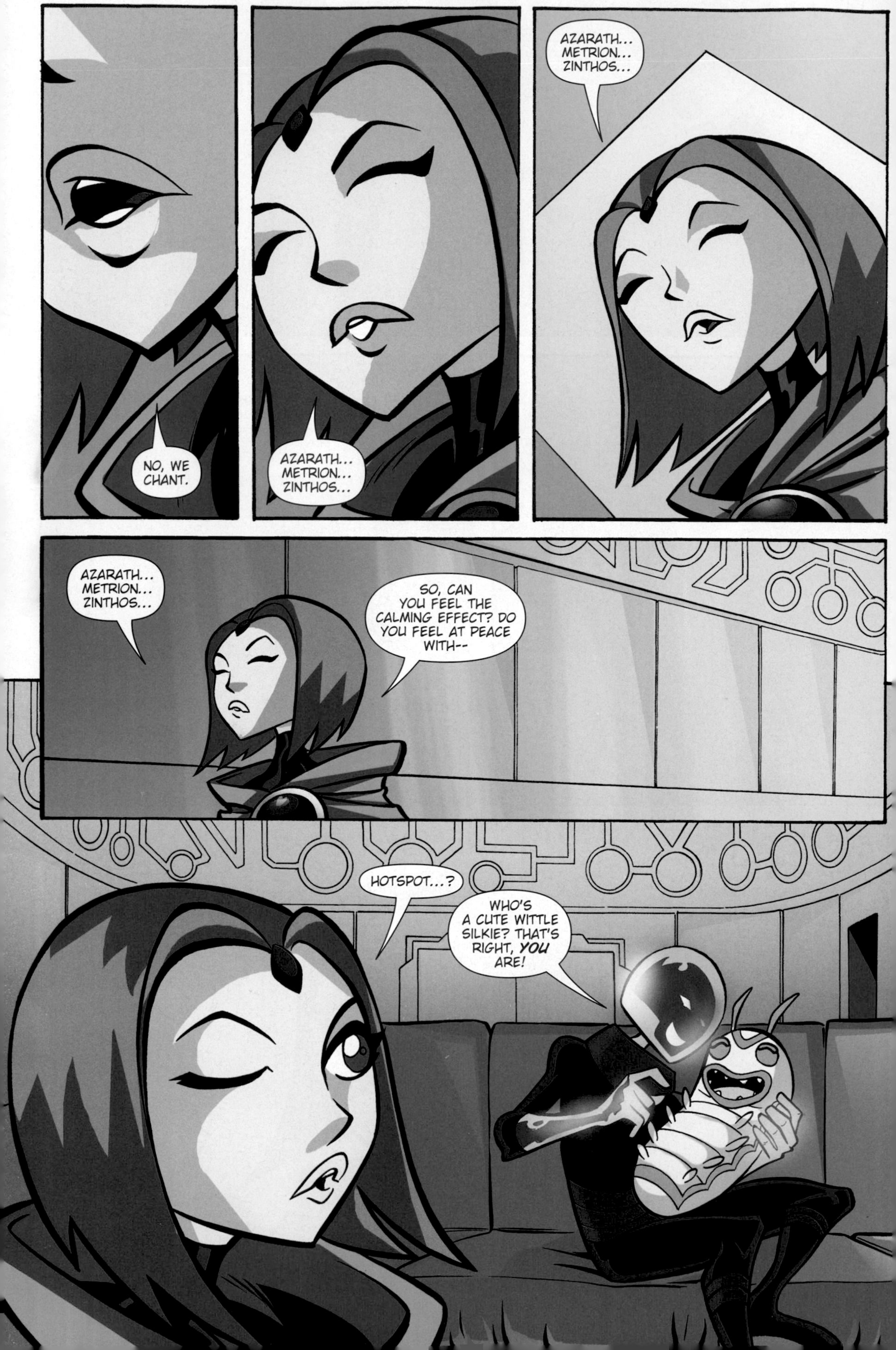
NO, WE CHANT.
AZARATH... METRION... ZINTHOS...
AZARATH... METRION... ZINTHOS...
AZARATH... METRION... ZINTHOS...
SO, CAN YOU FEEL THE CALMING EFFECT? DO YOU FEEL AT PEACE WITH--
HOTSPOT...?
WHO'S A CUTE WITTLE SILKIE? THAT'S RIGHT, ***YOU*** ARE!

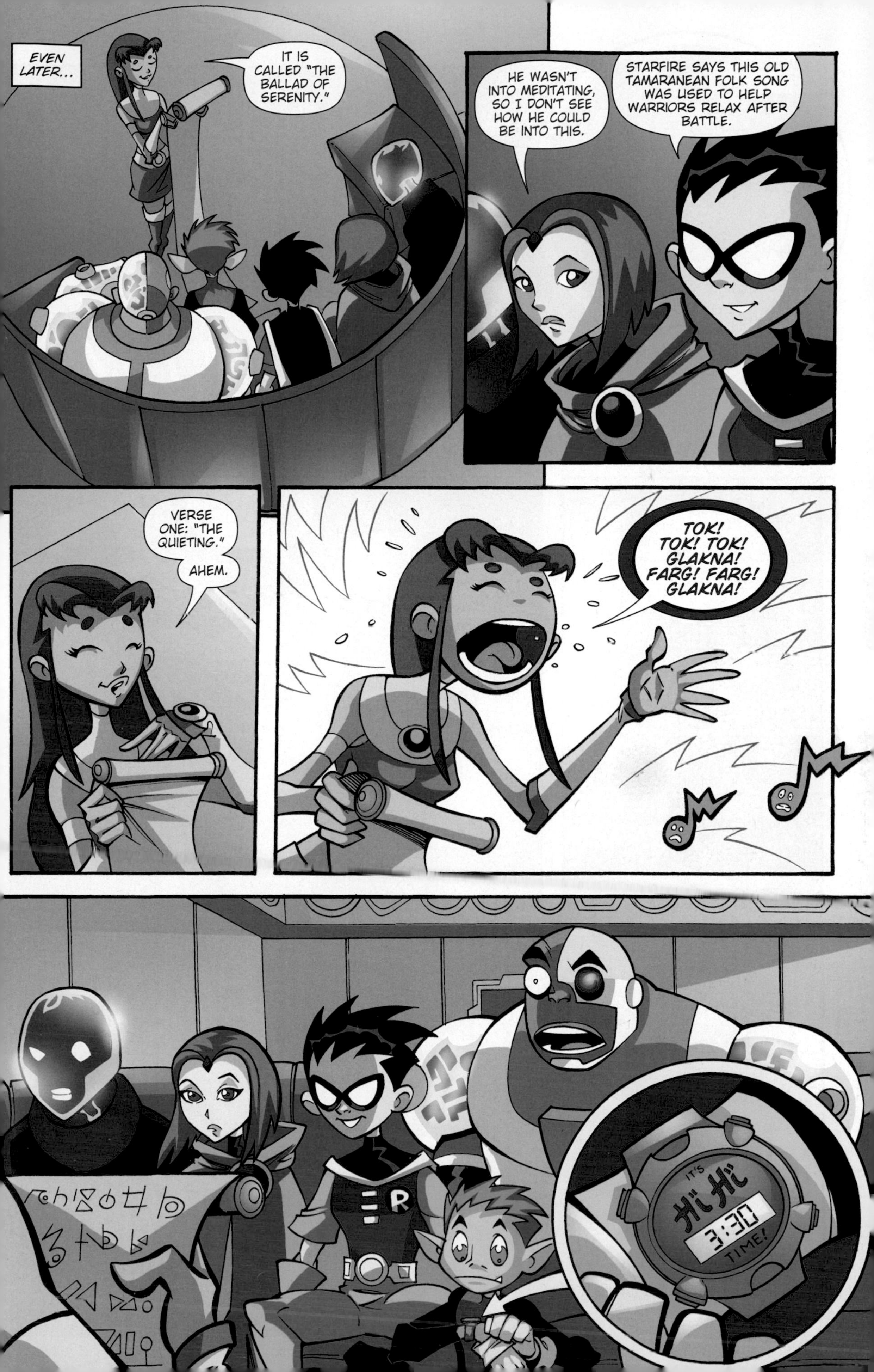
EVEN LATER...
IT IS CALLED "THE BALLAD OF SERENITY."
STARFIRE SAYS THIS OLD TAMARANEAN FOLK SONG WAS USED TO HELP WARRIORS RELAX AFTER BATTLE.
HE WASN'T INTO MEDITATING, SO I DON'T SEE HOW HE COULD BE INTO THIS.
VERSE ONE: "THE QUIETING."
AHEM.
TOK! TOK! TOK! GLAKNA! FARG! FARG! GLAKNA!
IT'S
3:30
TIME!

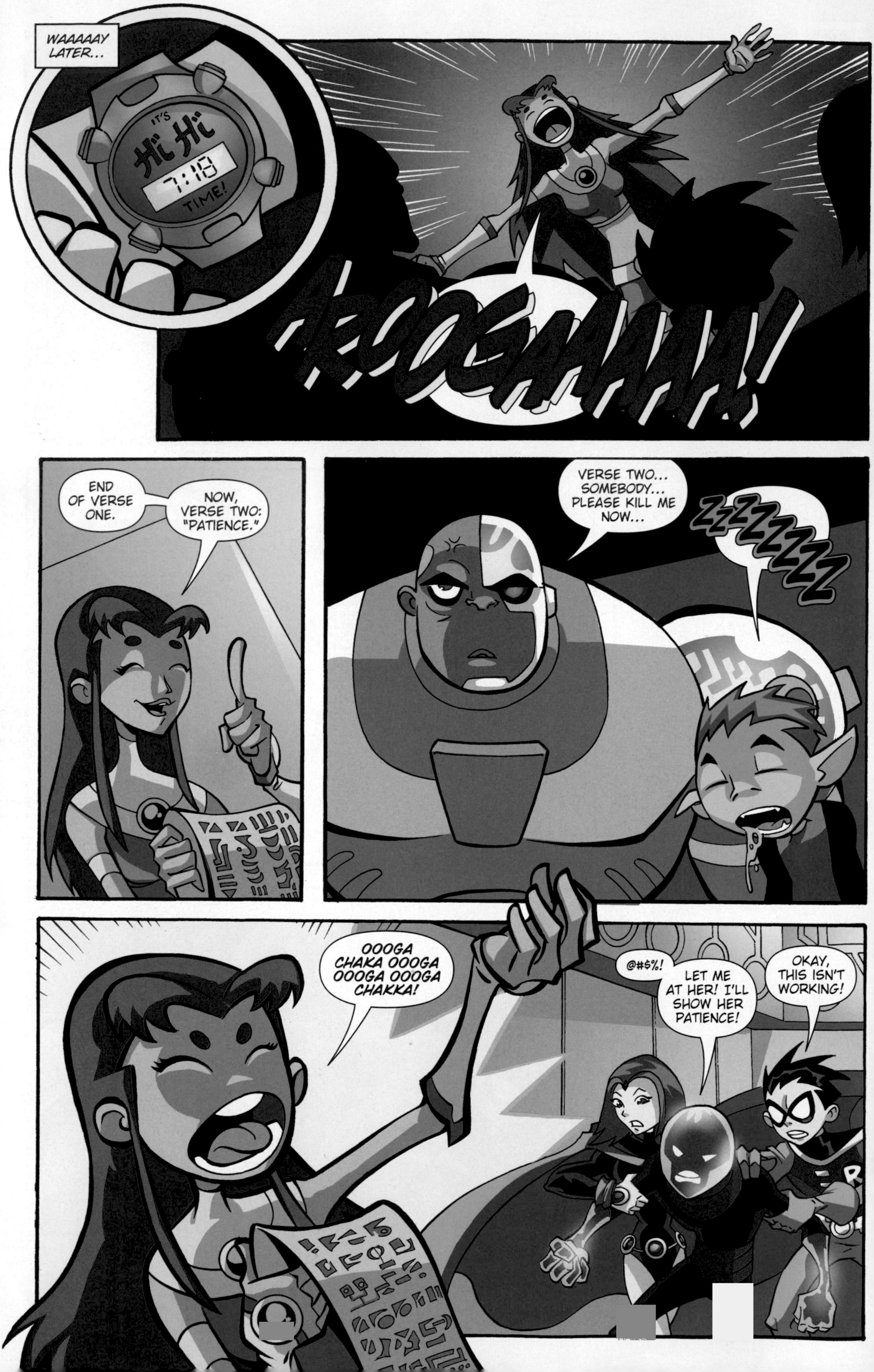
WAAAAAY LATER...
IT'S Hi Hi 7:18 TIME!
AROOGAAAAAA!
END OF VERSE ONE.
NOW, VERSE TWO: "PATIENCE."
VERSE TWO... SOMEBODY... PLEASE KILL ME NOW...
ZZZZZZZZ
OOOGA CHAKA OOOGA OOOGA OOOGA CHAKKA!
@#$%!
LET ME AT HER! I'LL SHOW HER PATIENCE!
OKAY, THIS ISN'T WORKING!

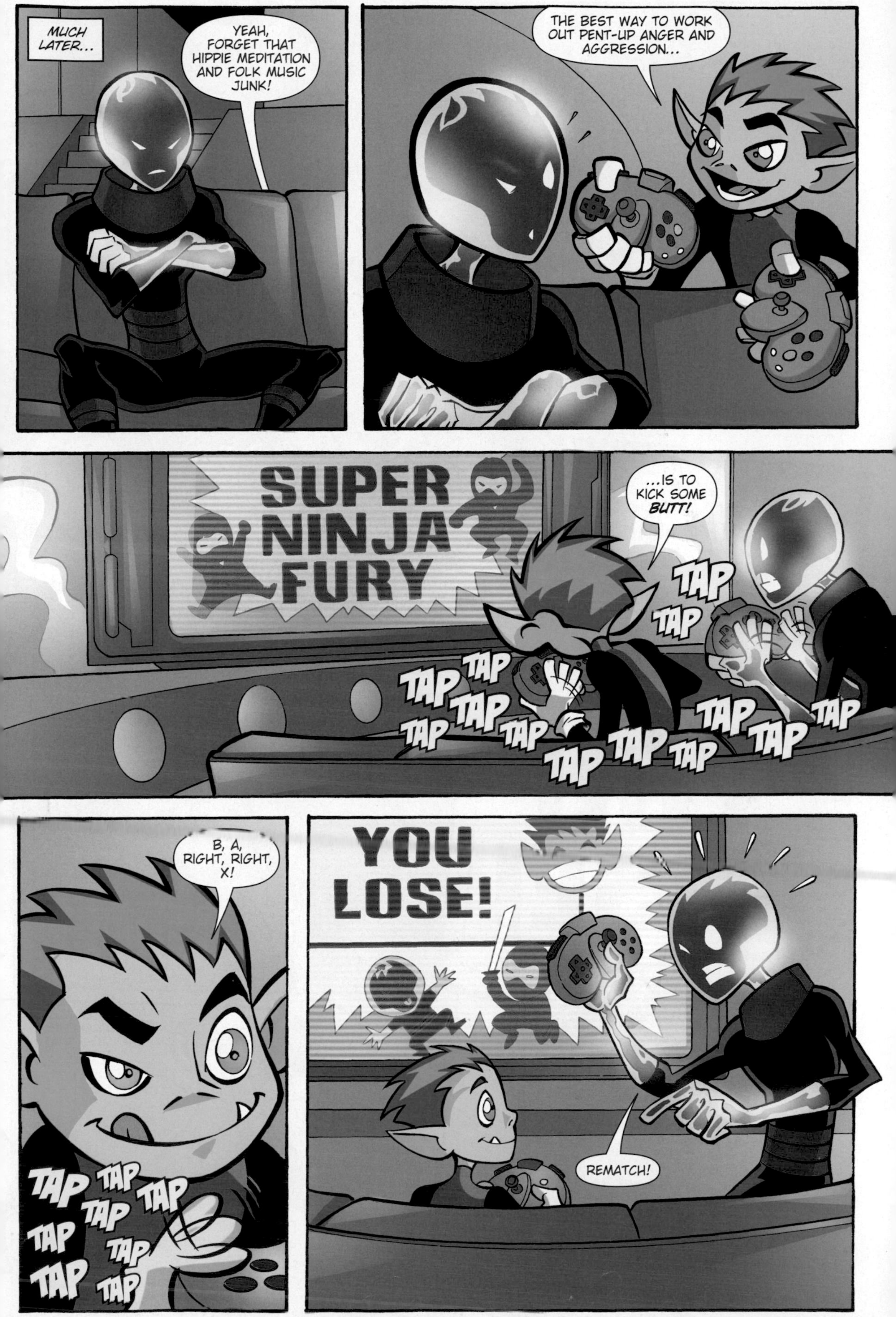

MUCH LATER...
YEAH, FORGET THAT HIPPIE MEDITATION AND FOLK MUSIC JUNK!
THE BEST WAY TO WORK OUT PENT-UP ANGER AND AGGRESSION...
SUPER NINJA FURY
...IS TO KICK SOME BUTT!
TAP TAP
TAP TAP TAP TAP TAP TAP TAP TAP TAP TAP TAP TAP
B, A, RIGHT, RIGHT, X!
TAP TAP TAP TAP TAP TAP TAP TAP
YOU LOSE!
REMATCH!

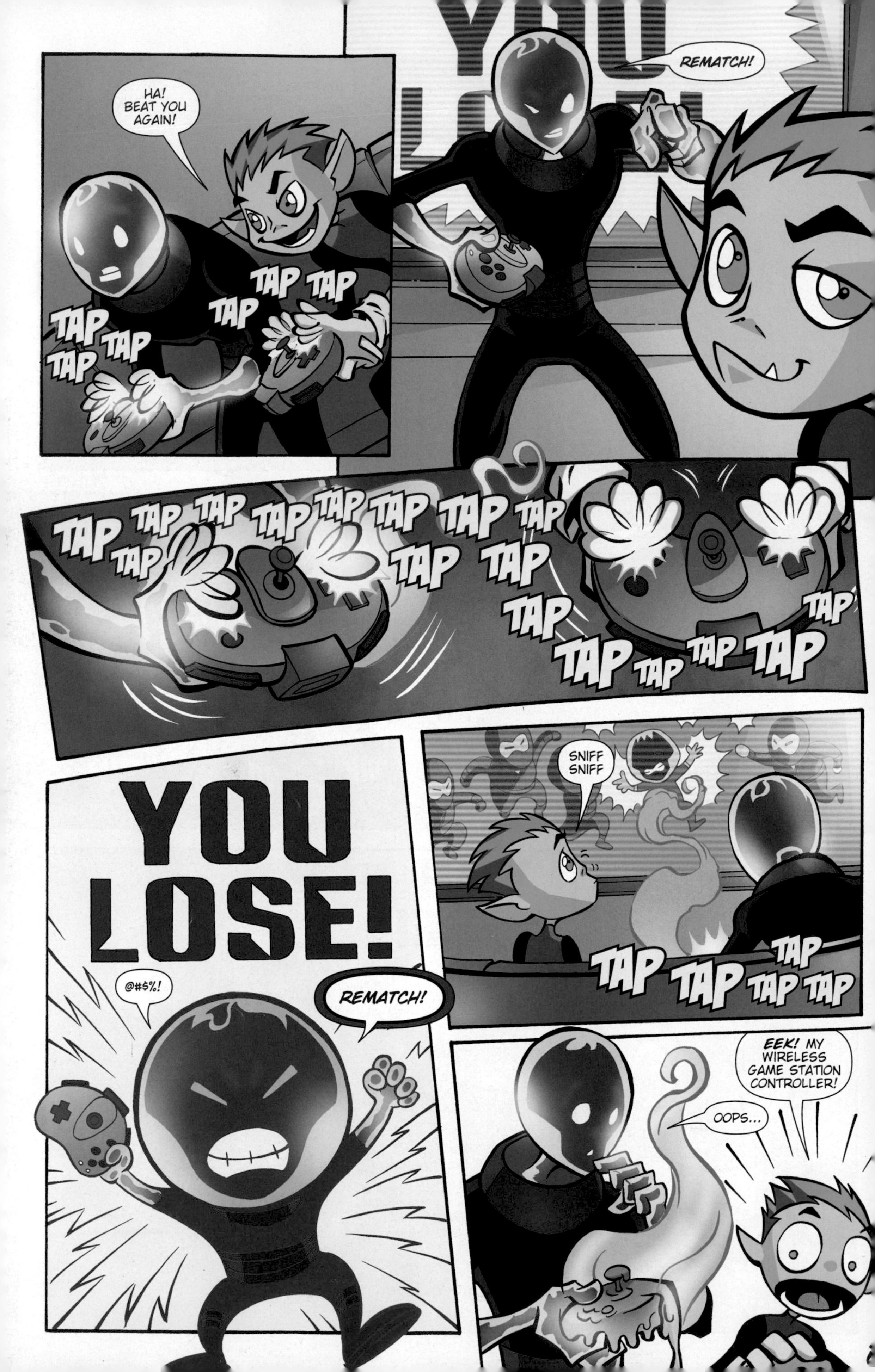

HA! BEAT YOU AGAIN!
TAP TAP TAP TAP TAP TAP
REMATCH!
TAP TAP TAP TAP TAP TAP TAP TAP TAP TAP TAP TAP TAP TAP TAP TAP
YOU LOSE!
@#$%!
REMATCH!
SNIFF SNIFF
TAP TAP TAP TAP TAP
EEK! MY WIRELESS GAME STATION CONTROLLER!
OOPS...

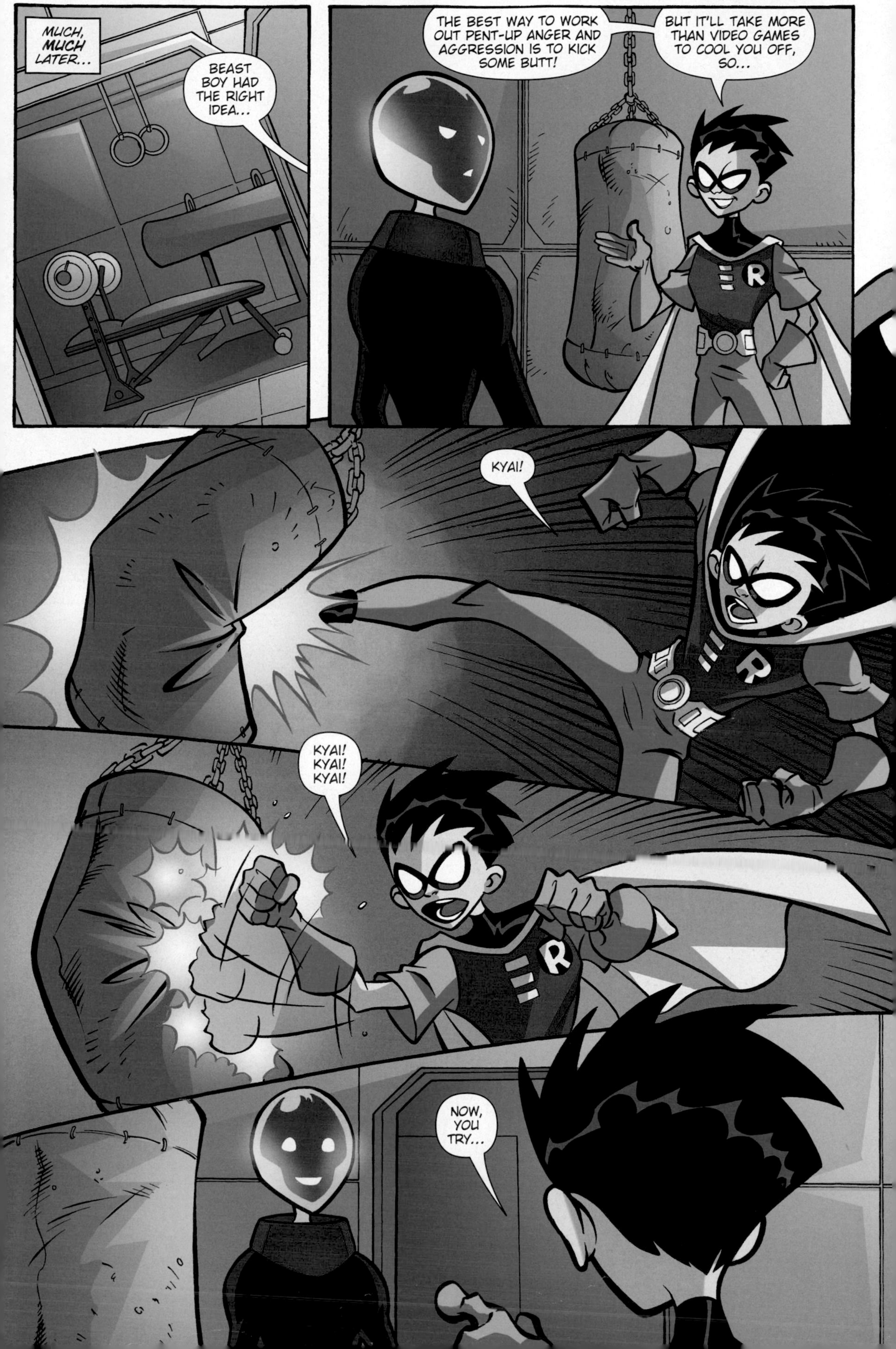
MUCH, MUCH LATER...
BEAST BOY HAD THE RIGHT IDEA...
THE BEST WAY TO WORK OUT PENT-UP ANGER AND AGGRESSION IS TO KICK SOME BUTT!
BUT IT'LL TAKE MORE THAN VIDEO GAMES TO COOL YOU OFF, SO...
KYAI!
KYAI! KYAI! KYAI!
NOW, YOU TRY...

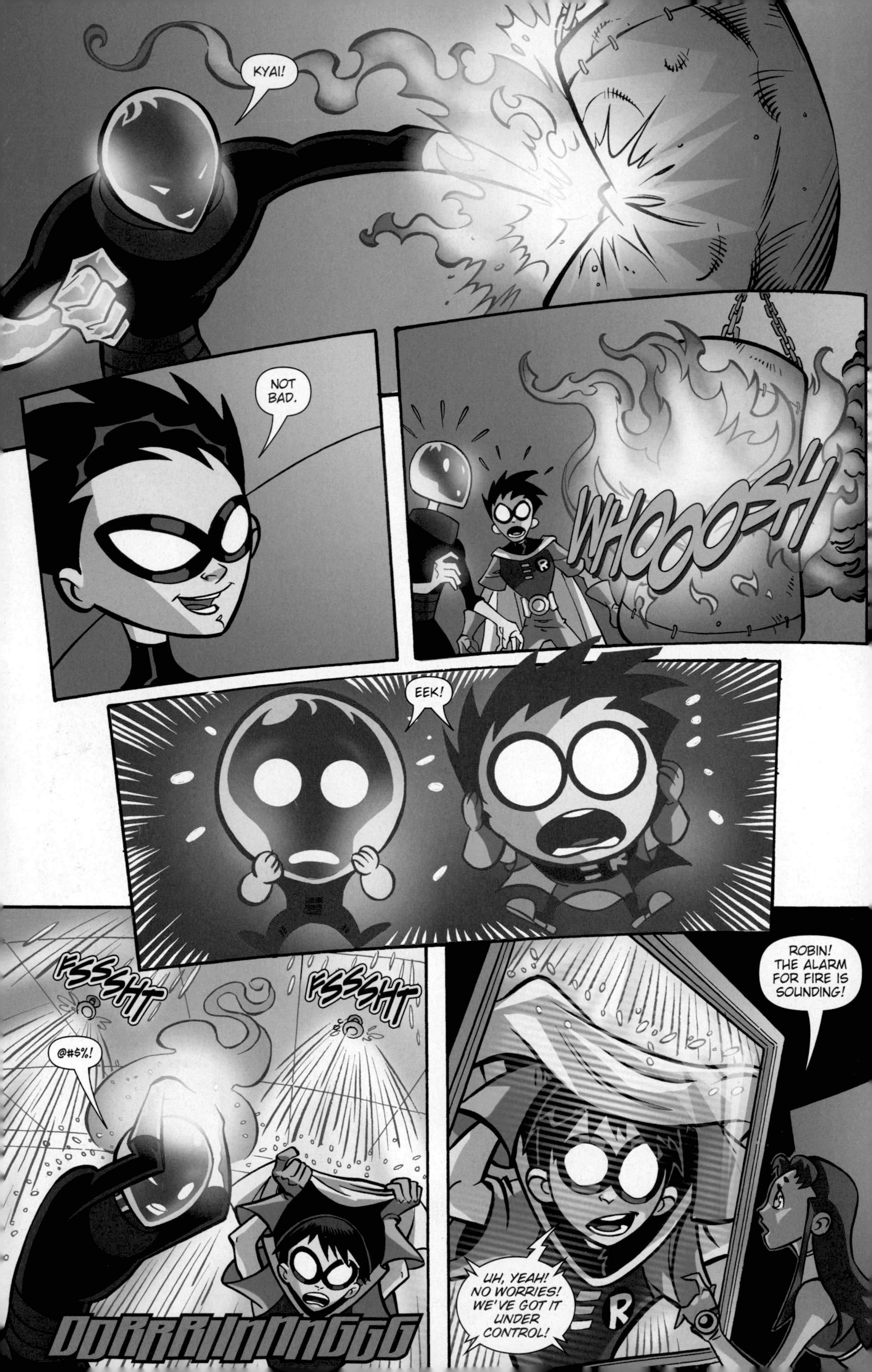
KYAI!
NOT BAD.
WHOOOOSH
EEK!
FSSSHT
FSSSHT
@#$%!
DDRRRIINNNGGG
ROBIN! THE ALARM FOR FIRE IS SOUNDING!
UH, YEAH! NO WORRIES! WE'VE GOT IT UNDER CONTROL!

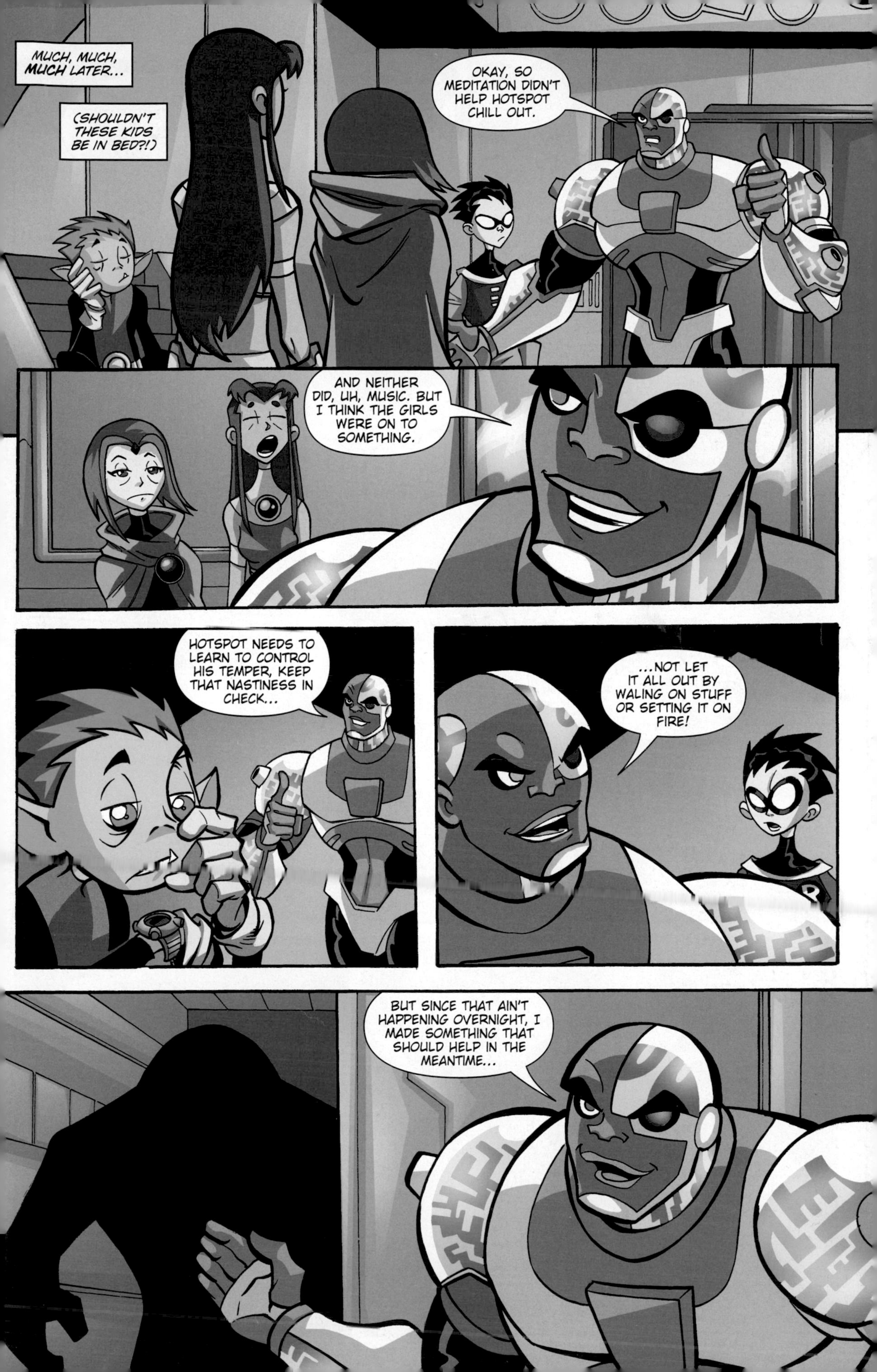
MUCH, MUCH, MUCH LATER...
(SHOULDN'T THESE KIDS BE IN BED?!)
OKAY, SO MEDITATION DIDN'T HELP HOTSPOT CHILL OUT.
AND NEITHER DID, UH, MUSIC. BUT I THINK THE GIRLS WERE ON TO SOMETHING.
HOTSPOT NEEDS TO LEARN TO CONTROL HIS TEMPER, KEEP THAT NASTINESS IN CHECK...
...NOT LET IT ALL OUT BY WALING ON STUFF OR SETTING IT ON FIRE!
BUT SINCE THAT AIN'T HAPPENING OVERNIGHT, I MADE SOMETHING THAT SHOULD HELP IN THE MEANTIME...

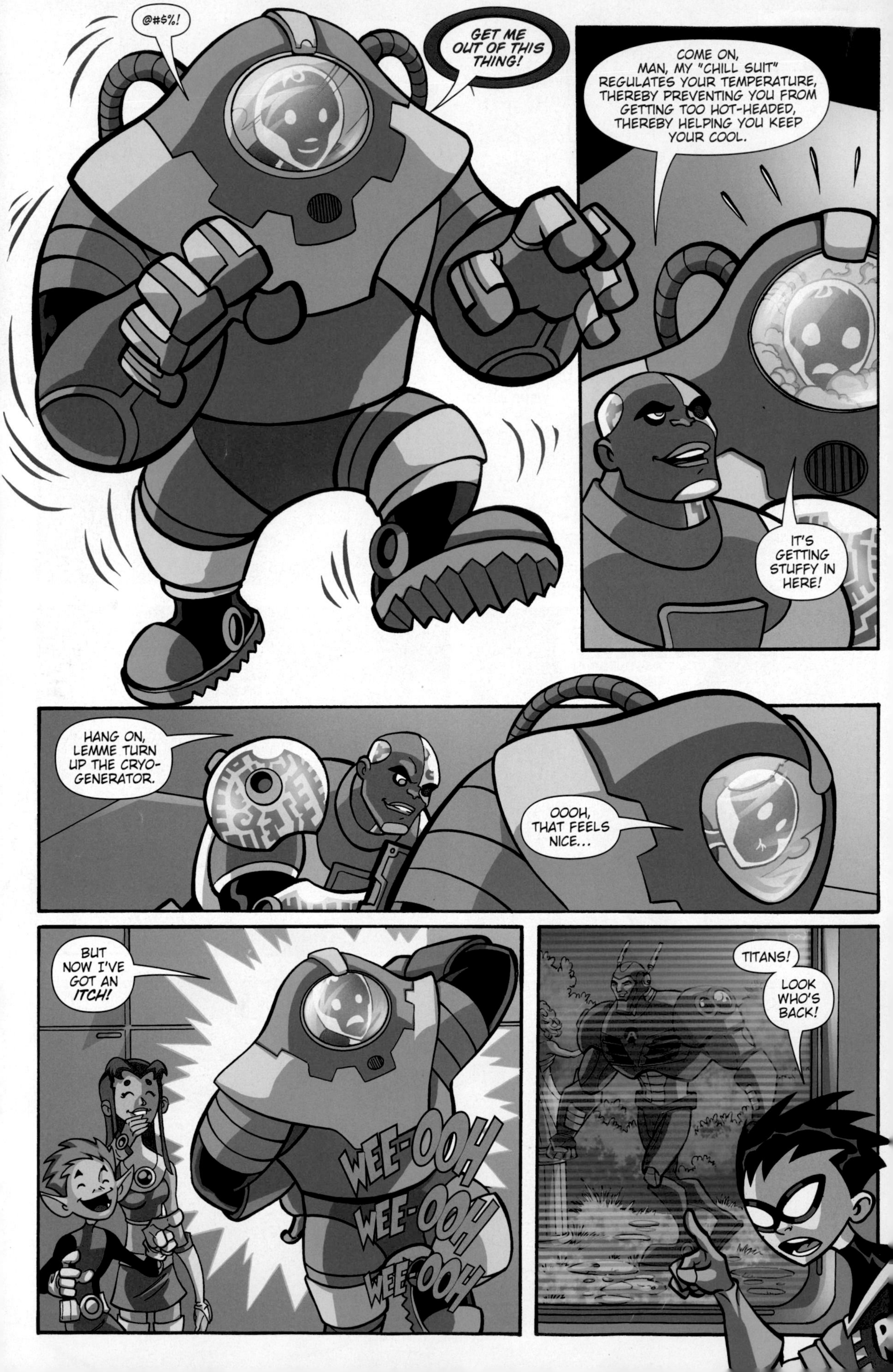
@#$%!
GET ME OUT OF THIS THING!
COME ON, MAN, MY "CHILL SUIT" REGULATES YOUR TEMPERATURE, THEREBY PREVENTING YOU FROM GETTING TOO HOT-HEADED, THEREBY HELPING YOU KEEP YOUR COOL.
IT'S GETTING STUFFY IN HERE!
HANG ON, LEMME TURN UP THE CRYO-GENERATOR.
OOOH, THAT FEELS NICE...
BUT NOW I'VE GOT AN *ITCH!*
WEE-OOH
WEE-OOH
WEE-OOH
TITANS!
LOOK WHO'S BACK!

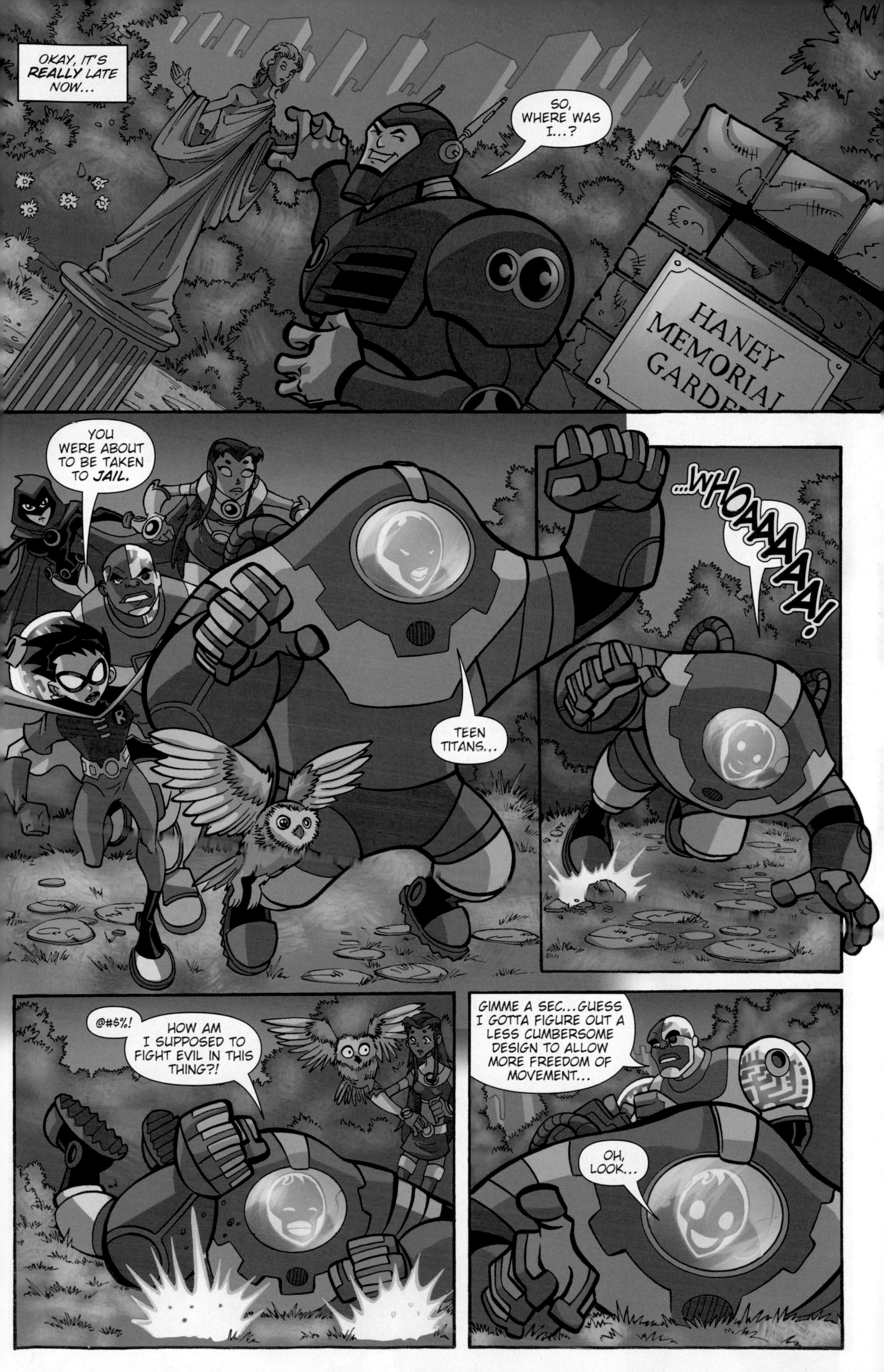

OKAY, IT'S **REALLY** LATE NOW...
SO, WHERE WAS I...?
HANEY MEMORIAL GARDE
YOU WERE ABOUT TO BE TAKEN TO **JAIL.**
TEEN TITANS...
...WHOAAAAAA!
@#$%!
HOW AM I SUPPOSED TO FIGHT EVIL IN THIS THING?!
GIMME A SEC...GUESS I GOTTA FIGURE OUT A LESS CUMBERSOME DESIGN TO ALLOW MORE FREEDOM OF MOVEMENT...
OH, LOOK...

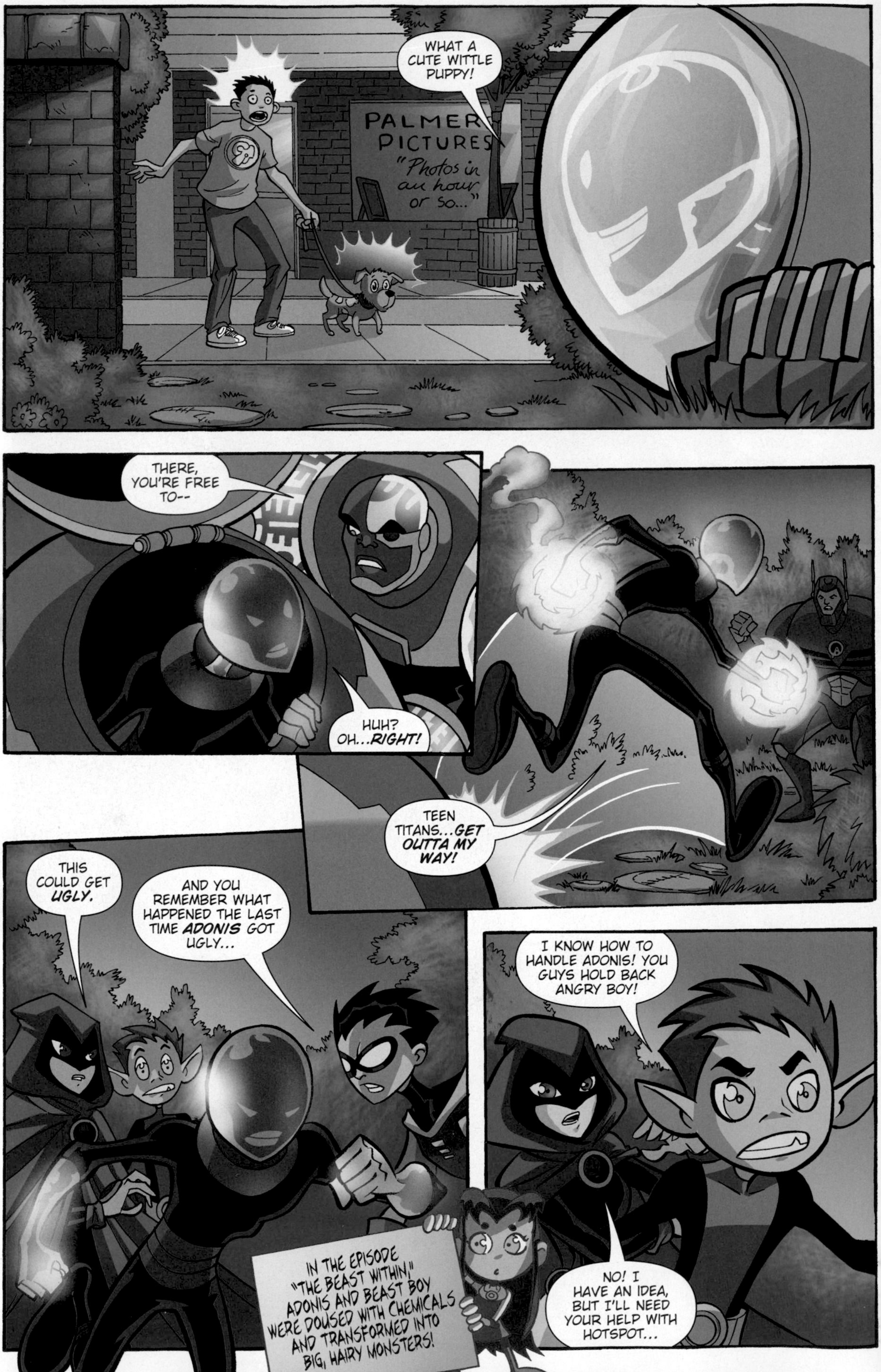
WHAT A CUTE WITTLE PUPPY!
PALMER PICTURES "Photos in an hour or so..."
THERE, YOU'RE FREE TO--
HUH? OH...RIGHT!
TEEN TITANS...GET OUTTA MY WAY!
THIS COULD GET UGLY.
AND YOU REMEMBER WHAT HAPPENED THE LAST TIME ADONIS GOT UGLY...
IN THE EPISODE "THE BEAST WITHIN," ADONIS AND BEAST BOY WERE DOUSED WITH CHEMICALS AND TRANSFORMED INTO BIG, HAIRY MONSTERS!
I KNOW HOW TO HANDLE ADONIS! YOU GUYS HOLD BACK ANGRY BOY!
NO! I HAVE AN IDEA, BUT I'LL NEED YOUR HELP WITH HOTSPOT...

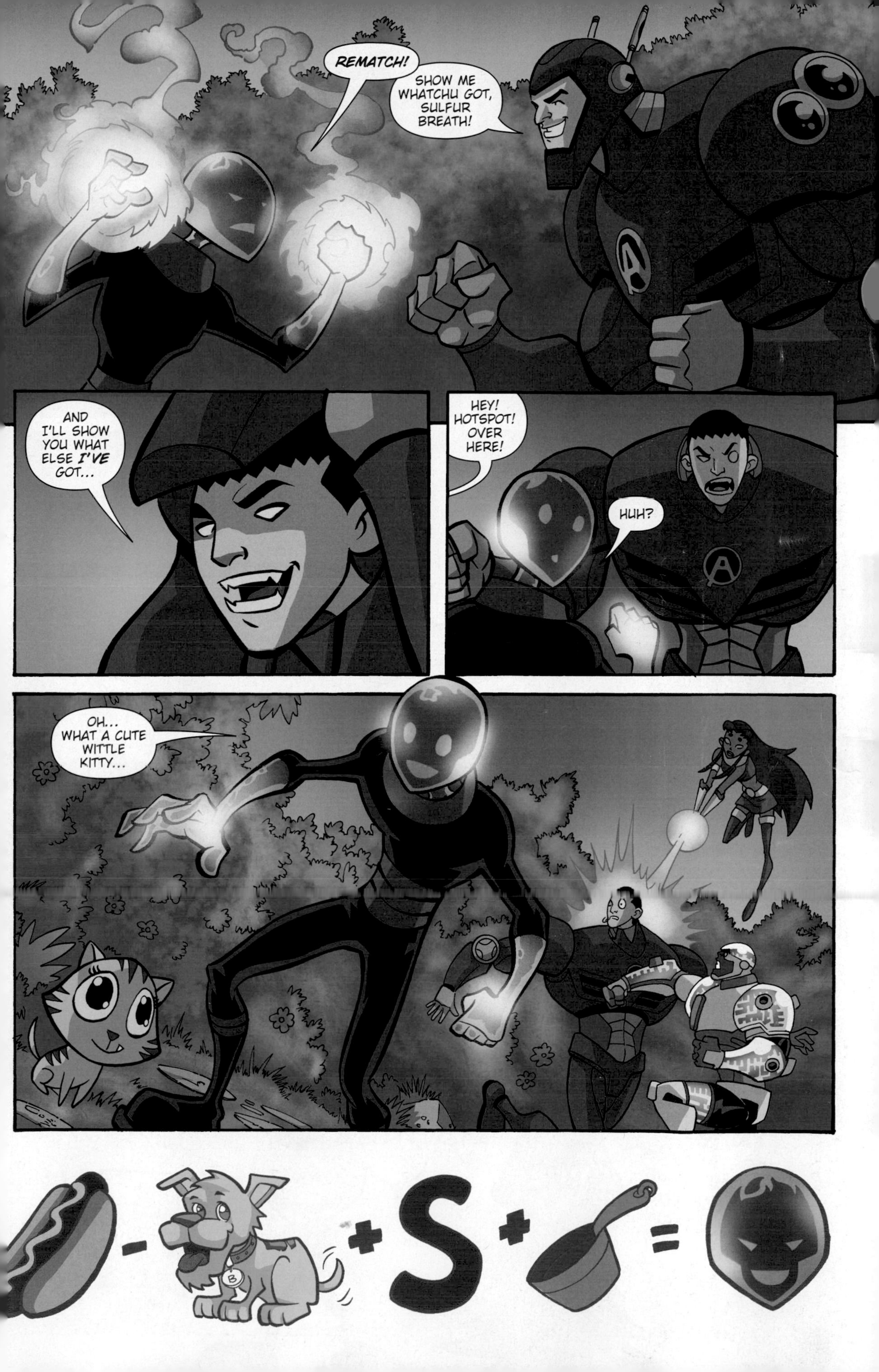
REMATCH!
SHOW ME WHATCHU GOT, SULFUR BREATH!
AND I'LL SHOW YOU WHAT ELSE I'VE GOT...
HEY! HOTSPOT! OVER HERE!
HUH?
OH... WHAT A CUTE WITTLE KITTY...
- + S + =

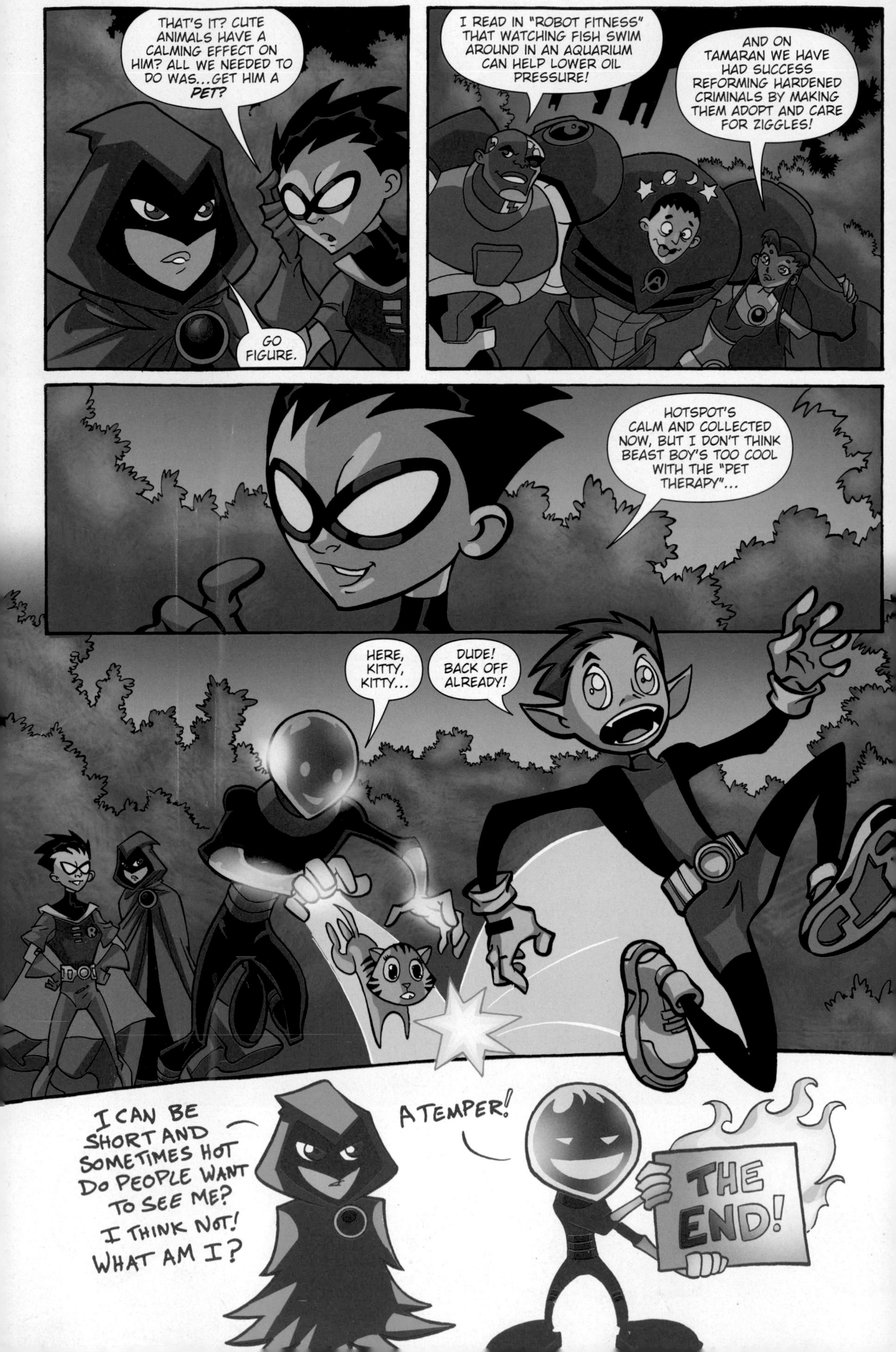
THAT'S IT? CUTE ANIMALS HAVE A CALMING EFFECT ON HIM? ALL WE NEEDED TO DO WAS...GET HIM A PET?
GO FIGURE.
I READ IN "ROBOT FITNESS" THAT WATCHING FISH SWIM AROUND IN AN AQUARIUM CAN HELP LOWER OIL PRESSURE!
AND ON TAMARAN WE HAVE HAD SUCCESS REFORMING HARDENED CRIMINALS BY MAKING THEM ADOPT AND CARE FOR ZIGGLES!
HOTSPOT'S CALM AND COLLECTED NOW, BUT I DON'T THINK BEAST BOY'S TOO COOL WITH THE "PET THERAPY"...
HERE, KITTY, KITTY...
DUDE! BACK OFF ALREADY!
I CAN BE SHORT AND SOMETIMES HOT DO PEOPLE WANT TO SEE ME? I THINK NOT! WHAT AM I?
A TEMPER!
THE END!

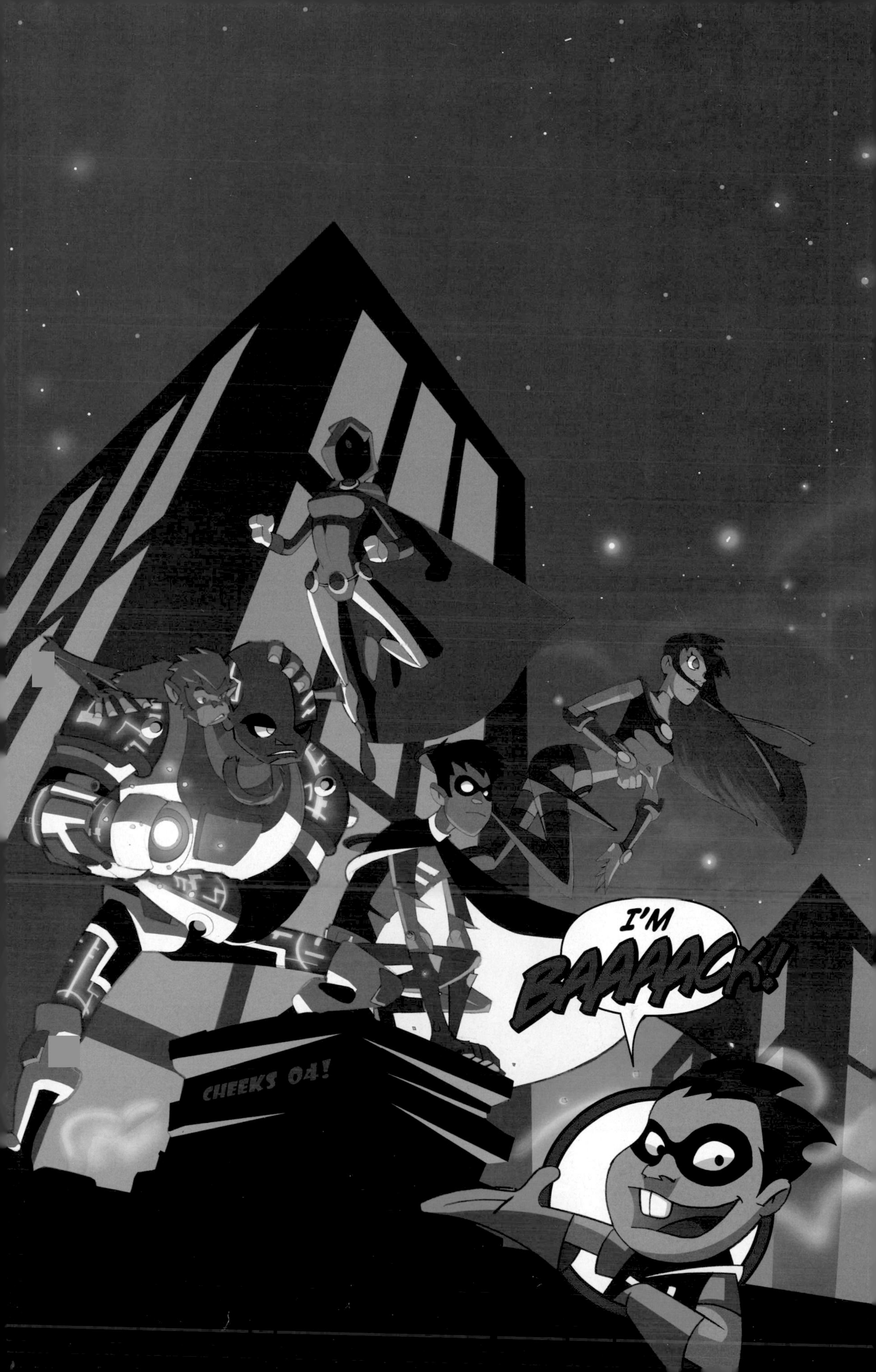
I'M BAAAACK!
CHEEKS 04!

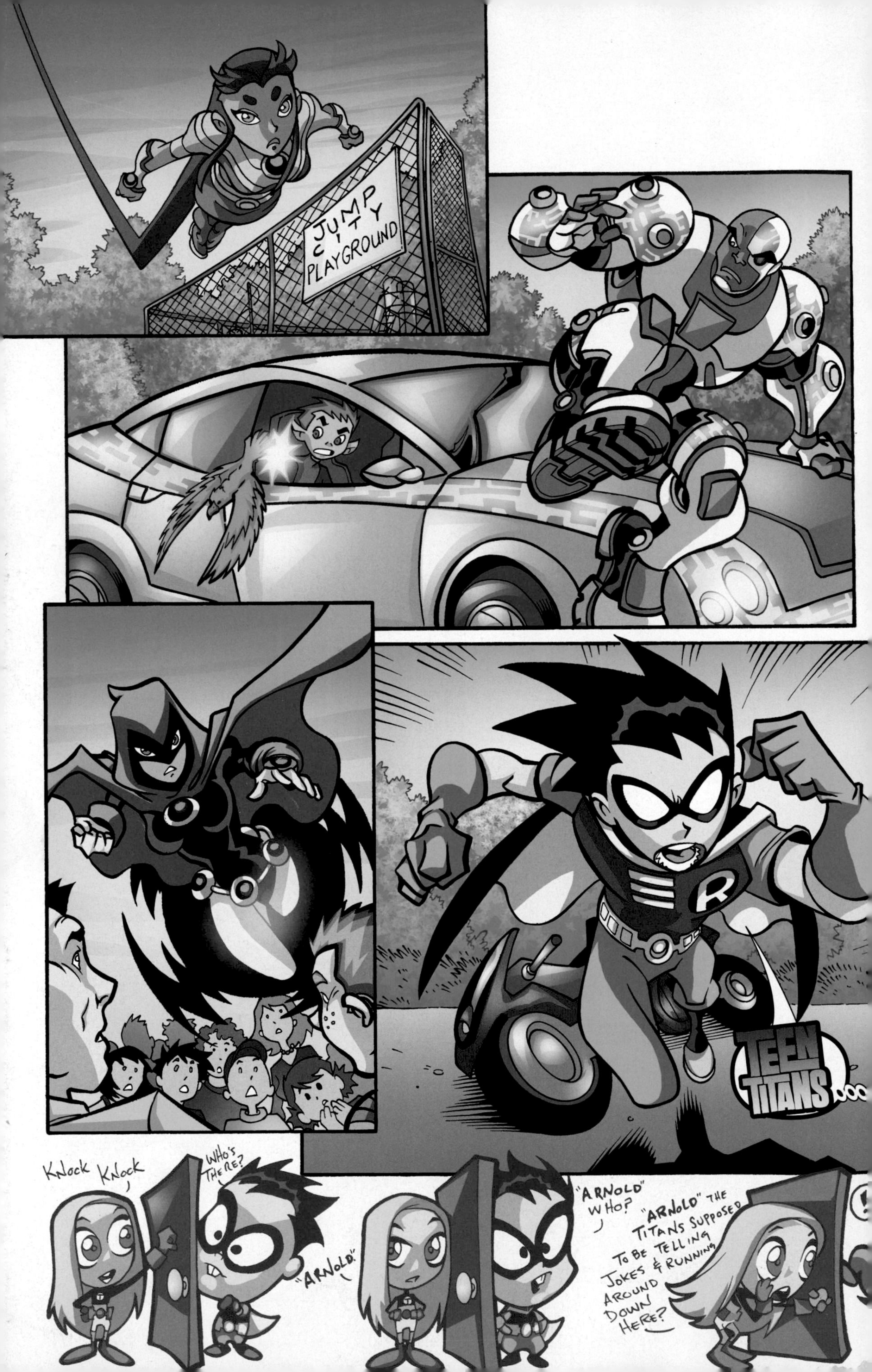
JUMP CITY PLAYGROUND
TEEN TITANS...
KNOCK KNOCK
WHO'S THERE?
"ARNOLD"
"ARNOLD" WHO?
"ARNOLD" THE TITANS SUPPOSED TO BE TELLING JOKES & RUNNING AROUND DOWN HERE?
!

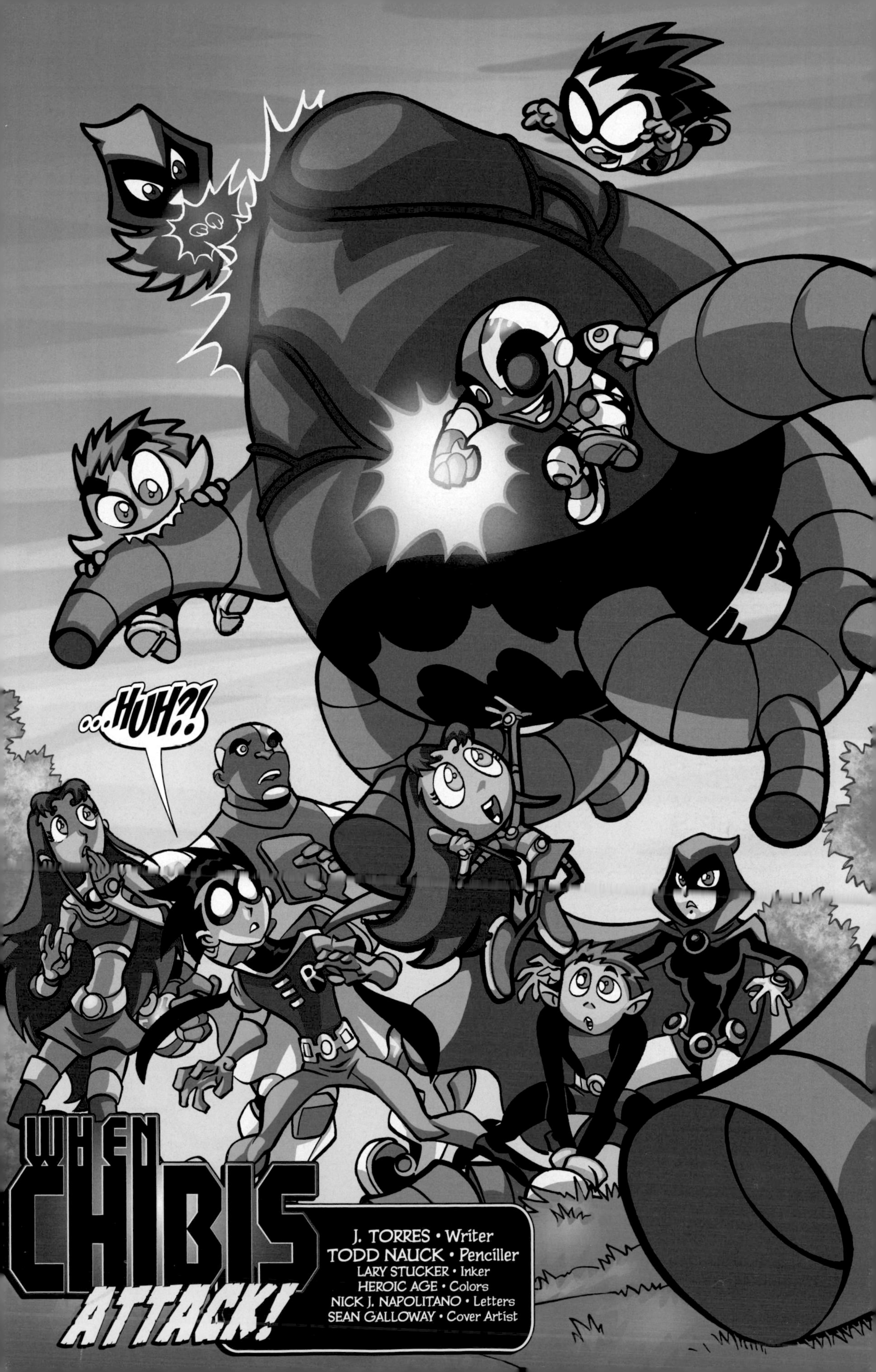
...HUH?!
WHEN CHIBIS ATTACK!
J. TORRES • Writer
TODD NAUCK • Penciller
LARY STUCKER • Inker
HEROIC AGE • Colors
NICK J. NAPOLITANO • Letters
SEAN GALLOWAY • Cover Artist

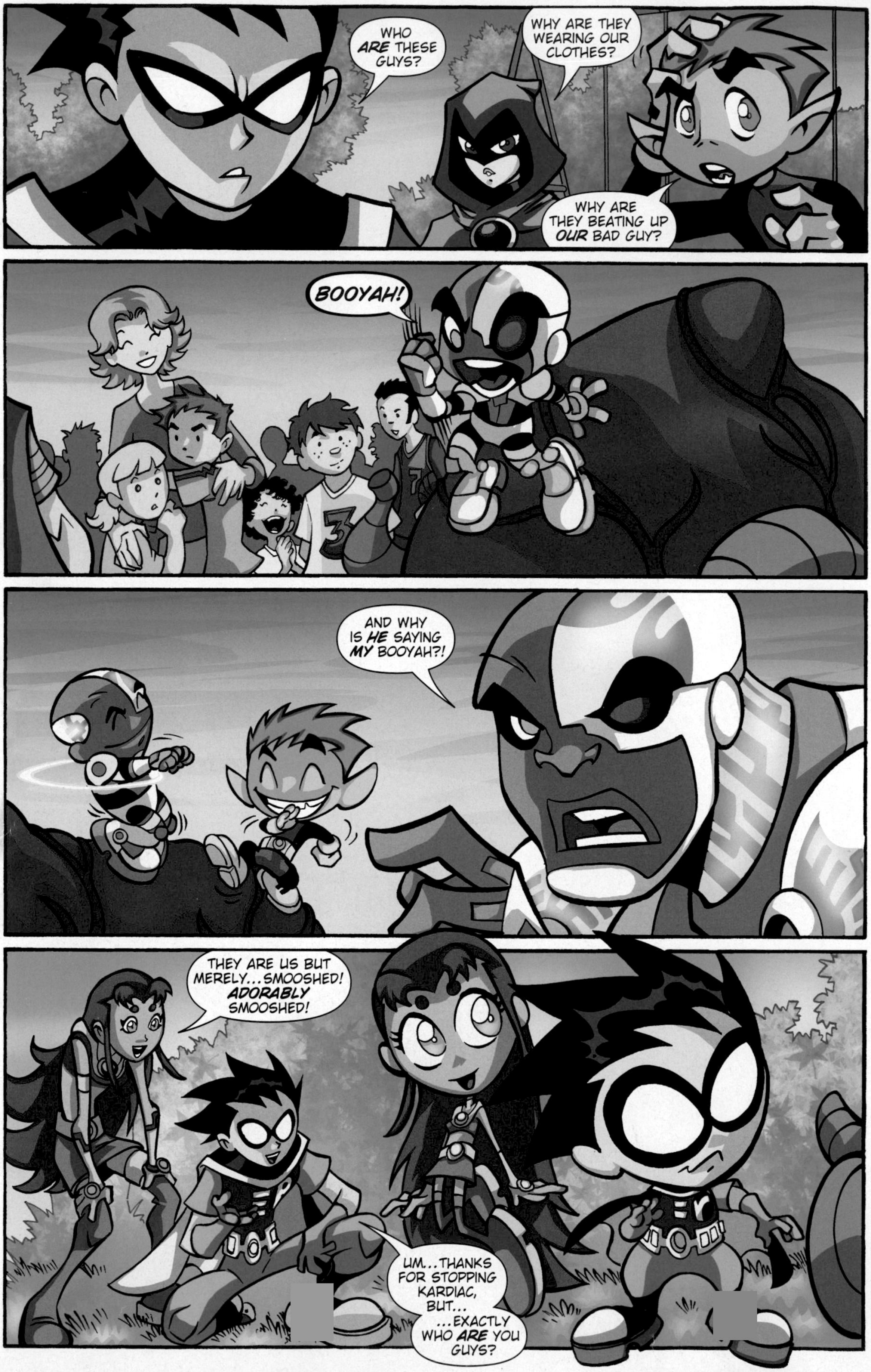
WHO ARE THESE GUYS?
WHY ARE THEY WEARING OUR CLOTHES?
WHY ARE THEY BEATING UP OUR BAD GUY?
BOOYAH!
AND WHY IS HE SAYING MY BOOYAH?!
THEY ARE US BUT MERELY...SMOOSHED! ADORABLY SMOOSHED!
UM...THANKS FOR STOPPING KARDIAC, BUT...
...EXACTLY WHO ARE YOU GUYS?

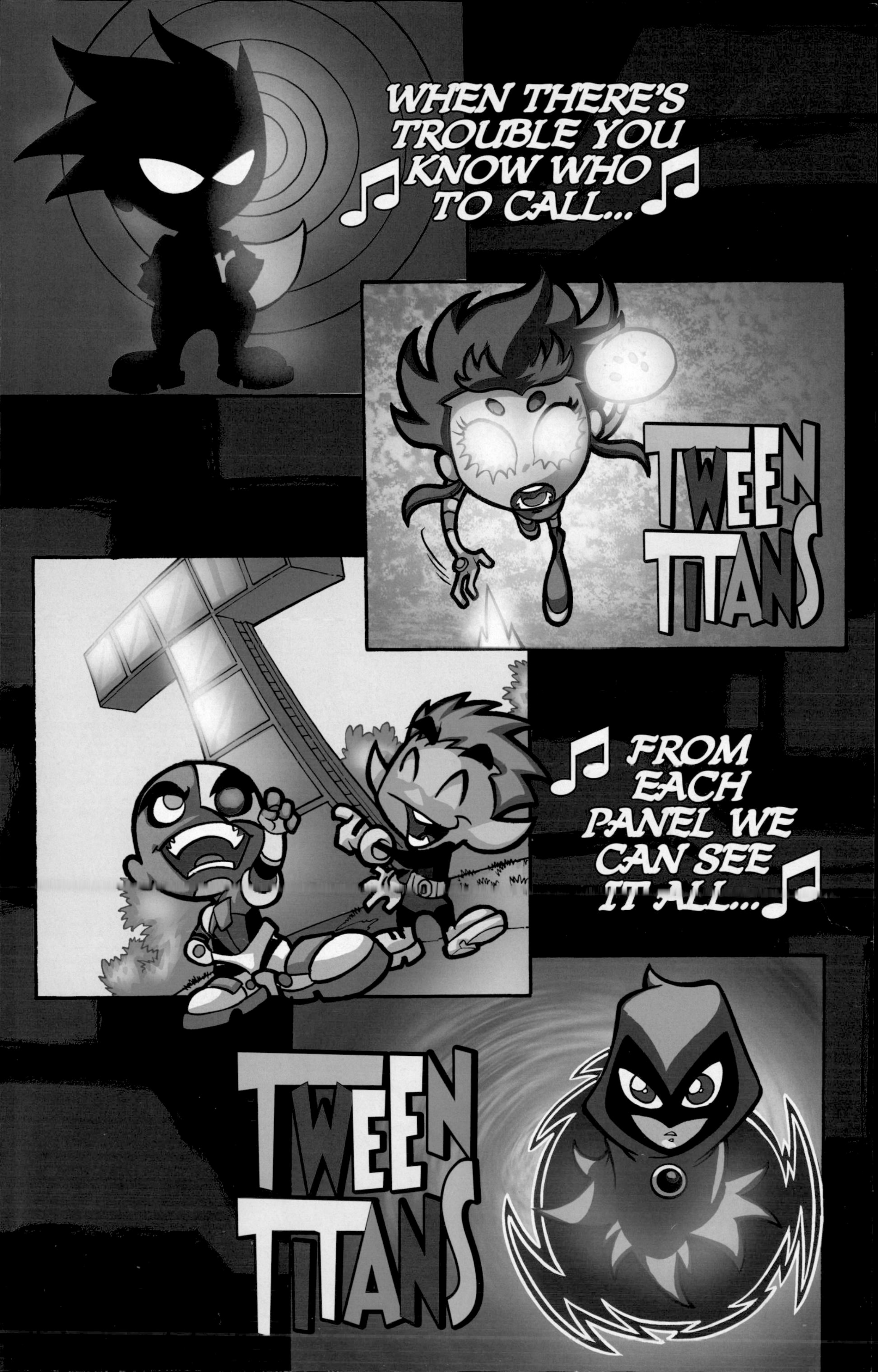
WHEN THERE'S TROUBLE YOU KNOW WHO TO CALL...
TWEEN TITANS
FROM EACH PANEL WE CAN SEE IT ALL...
TWEEN TITANS

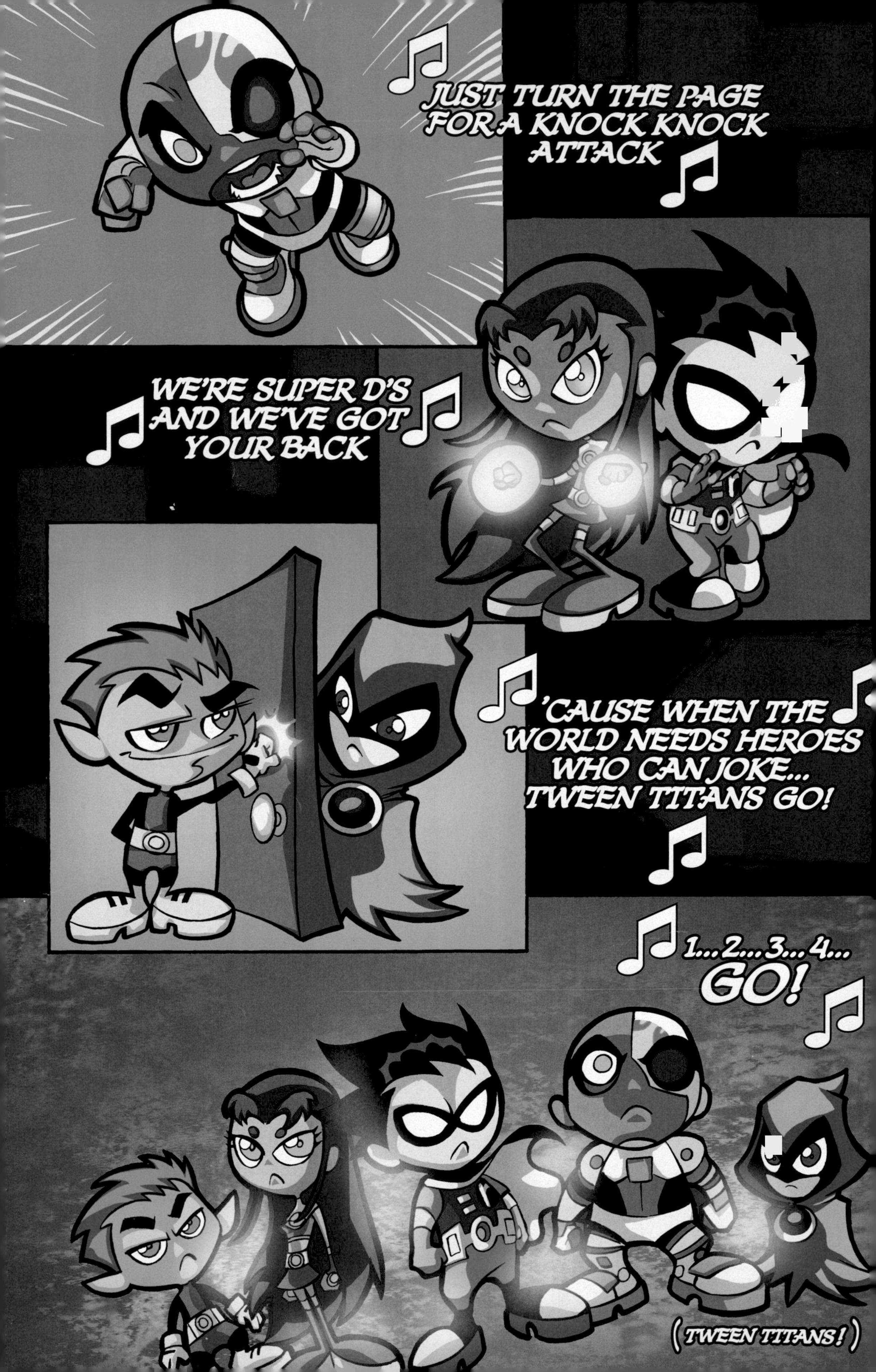
JUST TURN THE PAGE FOR A KNOCK KNOCK ATTACK
WE'RE SUPER D'S AND WE'VE GOT YOUR BACK
'CAUSE WHEN THE WORLD NEEDS HEROES WHO CAN JOKE... TWEEN TITANS GO!
1...2...3...4... GO!
(TWEEN TITANS!)

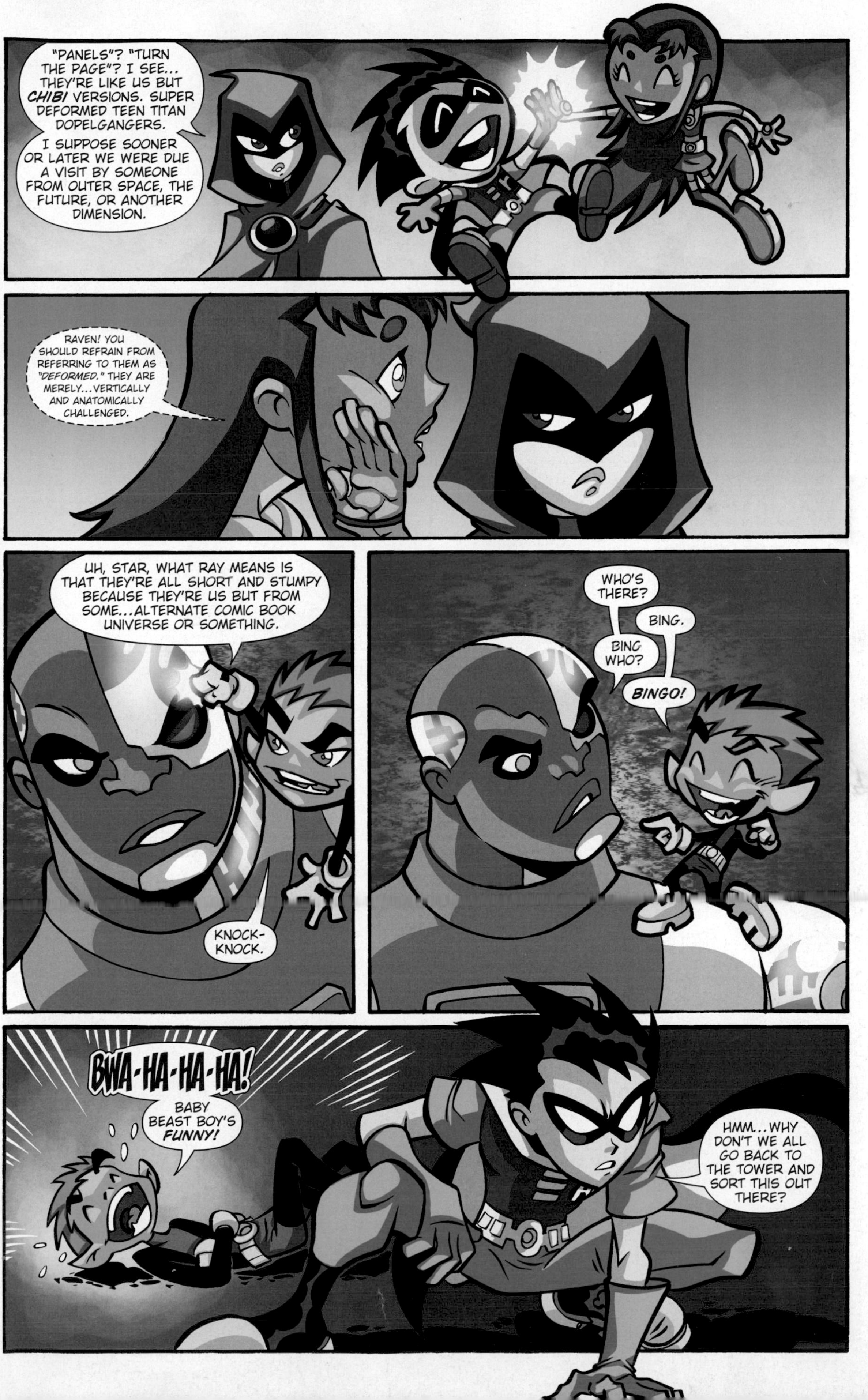
"PANELS"? "TURN THE PAGE"? I SEE... THEY'RE LIKE US BUT CHIBI VERSIONS. SUPER DEFORMED TEEN TITAN DOPELGANGERS.
I SUPPOSE SOONER OR LATER WE WERE DUE A VISIT BY SOMEONE FROM OUTER SPACE, THE FUTURE, OR ANOTHER DIMENSION.
RAVEN! YOU SHOULD REFRAIN FROM REFERRING TO THEM AS "DEFORMED." THEY ARE MERELY...VERTICALLY AND ANATOMICALLY CHALLENGED.
UH, STAR, WHAT RAY MEANS IS THAT THEY'RE ALL SHORT AND STUMPY BECAUSE THEY'RE US BUT FROM SOME...ALTERNATE COMIC BOOK UNIVERSE OR SOMETHING.
KNOCK-KNOCK.
WHO'S THERE?
BING.
BING WHO?
BINGO!
BWA-HA-HA-HA!
BABY BEAST BOY'S FUNNY!
HMM...WHY DON'T WE ALL GO BACK TO THE TOWER AND SORT THIS OUT THERE?

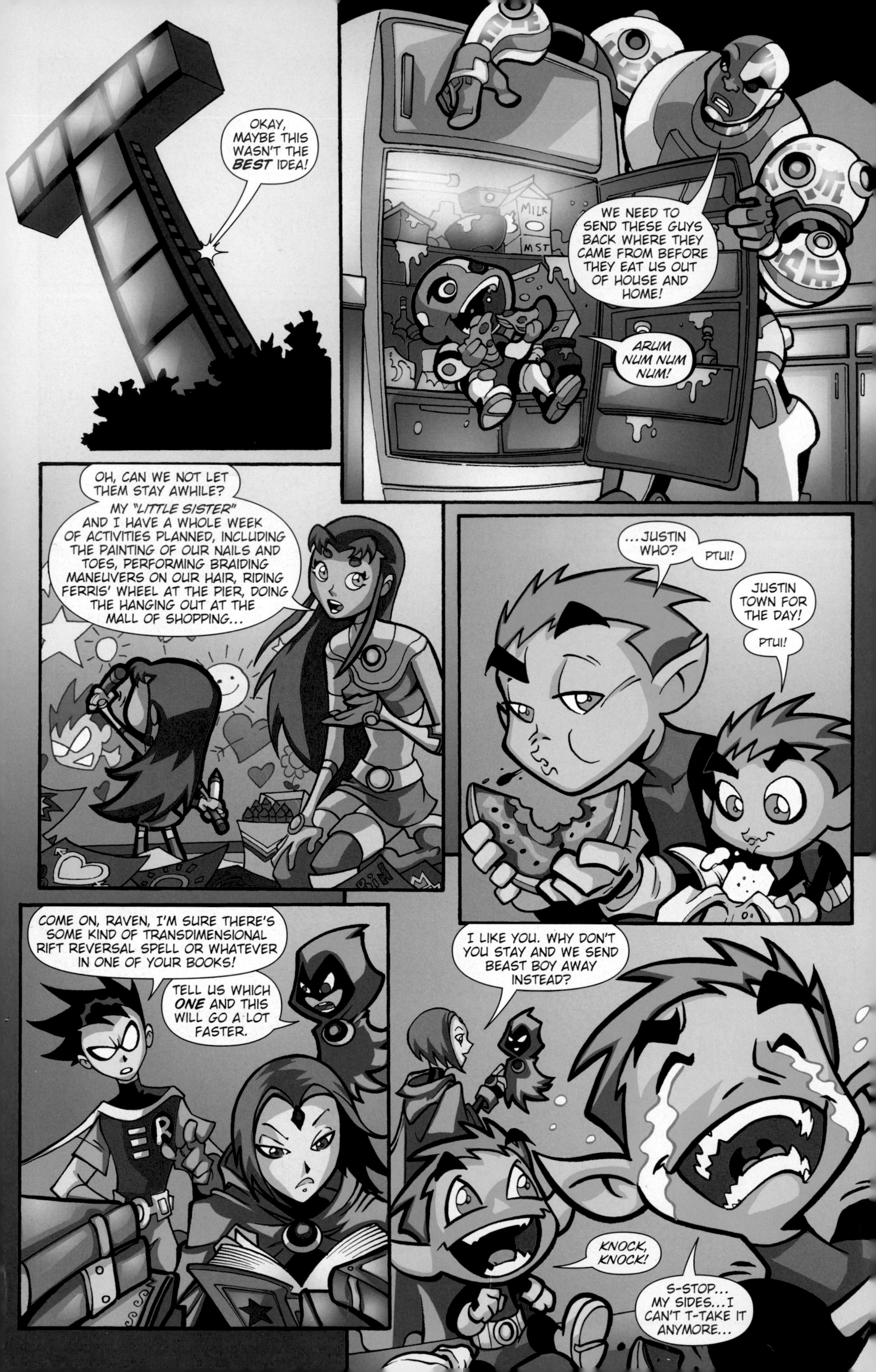
OKAY, MAYBE THIS WASN'T THE BEST IDEA!
WE NEED TO SEND THESE GUYS BACK WHERE THEY CAME FROM BEFORE THEY EAT US OUT OF HOUSE AND HOME!
MILK
MST
ARUM NUM NUM NUM!
OH, CAN WE NOT LET THEM STAY AWHILE? MY "LITTLE SISTER" AND I HAVE A WHOLE WEEK OF ACTIVITIES PLANNED, INCLUDING THE PAINTING OF OUR NAILS AND TOES, PERFORMING BRAIDING MANEUVERS ON OUR HAIR, RIDING FERRIS' WHEEL AT THE PIER, DOING THE HANGING OUT AT THE MALL OF SHOPPING...
...JUSTIN WHO?
PTUI!
JUSTIN TOWN FOR THE DAY!
PTUI!
COME ON, RAVEN, I'M SURE THERE'S SOME KIND OF TRANSDIMENSIONAL RIFT REVERSAL SPELL OR WHATEVER IN ONE OF YOUR BOOKS!
TELL US WHICH ONE AND THIS WILL GO A LOT FASTER.
I LIKE YOU. WHY DON'T YOU STAY AND WE SEND BEAST BOY AWAY INSTEAD?
KNOCK, KNOCK!
S-STOP... MY SIDES... I CAN'T T-TAKE IT ANYMORE...

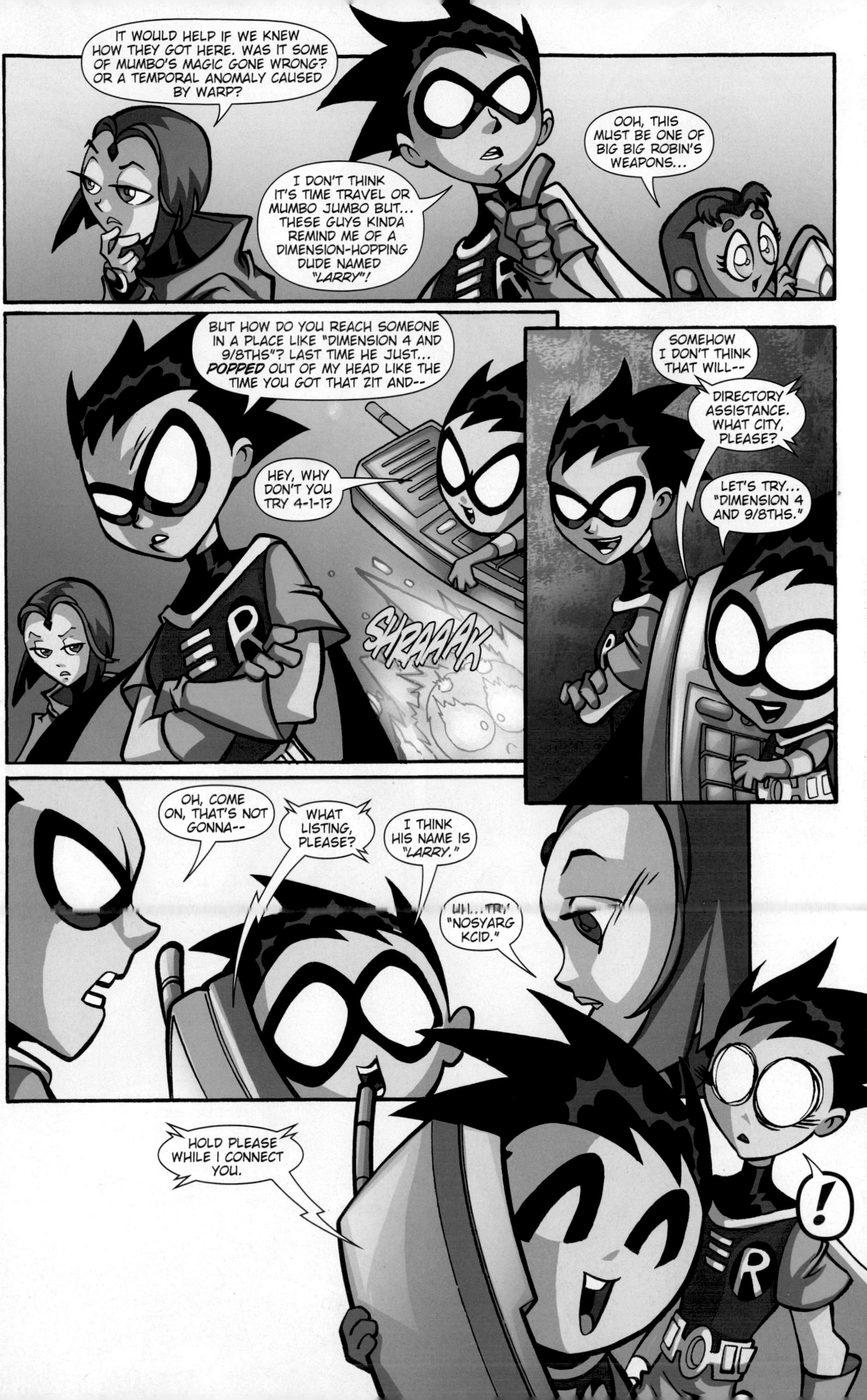
IT WOULD HELP IF WE KNEW HOW THEY GOT HERE. WAS IT SOME OF MUMBO'S MAGIC GONE WRONG? OR A TEMPORAL ANOMALY CAUSED BY WARP?
I DON'T THINK IT'S TIME TRAVEL OR MUMBO JUMBO BUT... THESE GUYS KINDA REMIND ME OF A DIMENSION-HOPPING DUDE NAMED "LARRY"!
OOH, THIS MUST BE ONE OF BIG BIG ROBIN'S WEAPONS...
BUT HOW DO YOU REACH SOMEONE IN A PLACE LIKE "DIMENSION 4 AND 9/8THS"? LAST TIME HE JUST... POPPED OUT OF MY HEAD LIKE THE TIME YOU GOT THAT ZIT AND--
HEY, WHY DON'T YOU TRY 4-1-1?
SHRAAAK
SOMEHOW I DON'T THINK THAT WILL--
DIRECTORY ASSISTANCE. WHAT CITY, PLEASE?
LET'S TRY... "DIMENSION 4 AND 9/8THS."
OH, COME ON, THAT'S NOT GONNA--
WHAT LISTING, PLEASE?
I THINK HIS NAME IS "LARRY."
UH...TRY "NOSYARG KCID."
HOLD PLEASE WHILE I CONNECT YOU.
!

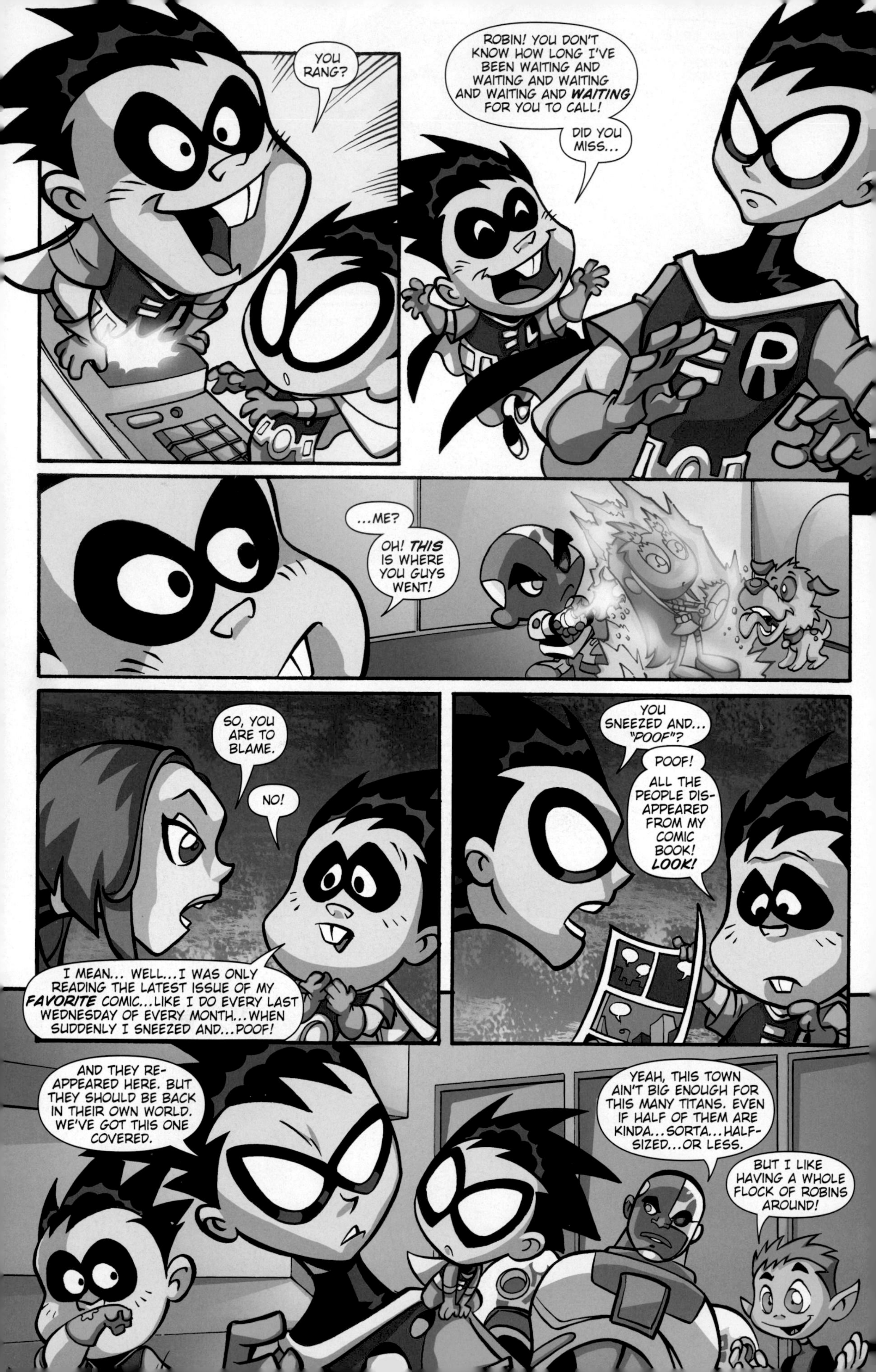

YOU RANG?
ROBIN! YOU DON'T KNOW HOW LONG I'VE BEEN WAITING AND WAITING AND WAITING AND WAITING AND *WAITING* FOR YOU TO CALL!
DID YOU MISS...
...ME?
OH! *THIS* IS WHERE YOU GUYS WENT!
SO, YOU ARE TO BLAME.
NO!
I MEAN... WELL...I WAS ONLY READING THE LATEST ISSUE OF MY *FAVORITE* COMIC...LIKE I DO EVERY LAST WEDNESDAY OF EVERY MONTH...WHEN SUDDENLY I SNEEZED AND...POOF!
YOU SNEEZED AND... *"POOF"*?
POOF!
ALL THE PEOPLE DIS-APPEARED FROM MY COMIC BOOK! *LOOK!*
AND THEY RE-APPEARED HERE. BUT THEY SHOULD BE BACK IN THEIR OWN WORLD. WE'VE GOT THIS ONE COVERED.
YEAH, THIS TOWN AIN'T BIG ENOUGH FOR THIS MANY TITANS. EVEN IF HALF OF THEM ARE KINDA...SORTA...HALF-SIZED...OR LESS.
BUT I LIKE HAVING A WHOLE FLOCK OF ROBINS AROUND!

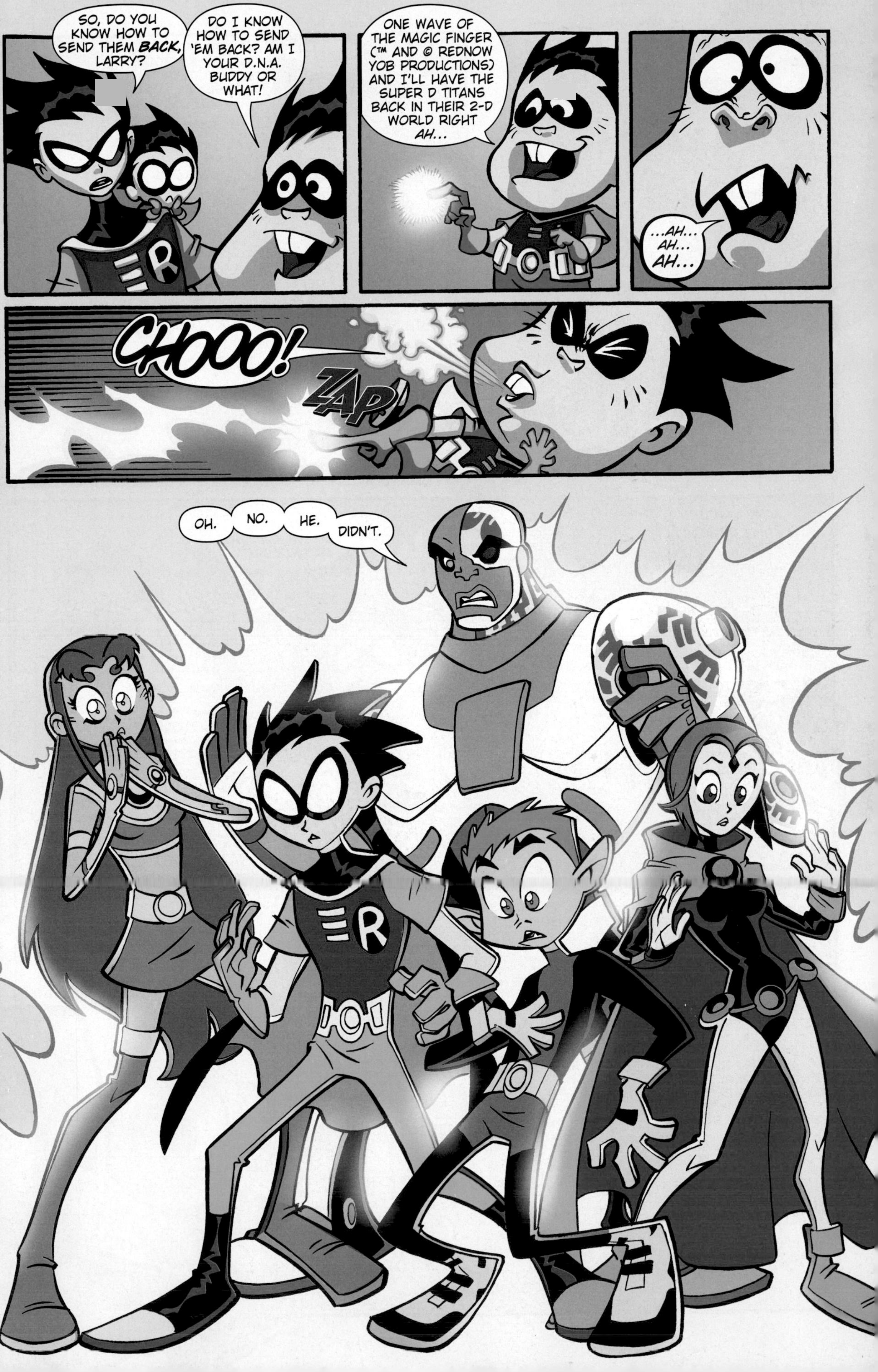
SO, DO YOU KNOW HOW TO SEND THEM BACK, LARRY?
DO I KNOW HOW TO SEND 'EM BACK? AM I YOUR D.N.A. BUDDY OR WHAT!
ONE WAVE OF THE MAGIC FINGER (™ AND © REDNOW YOB PRODUCTIONS) AND I'LL HAVE THE SUPER D TITANS BACK IN THEIR 2-D WORLD RIGHT AH...
...AH... AH... AH...
CHOOO!
ZAP!
OH.
NO.
HE.
DIDN'T.

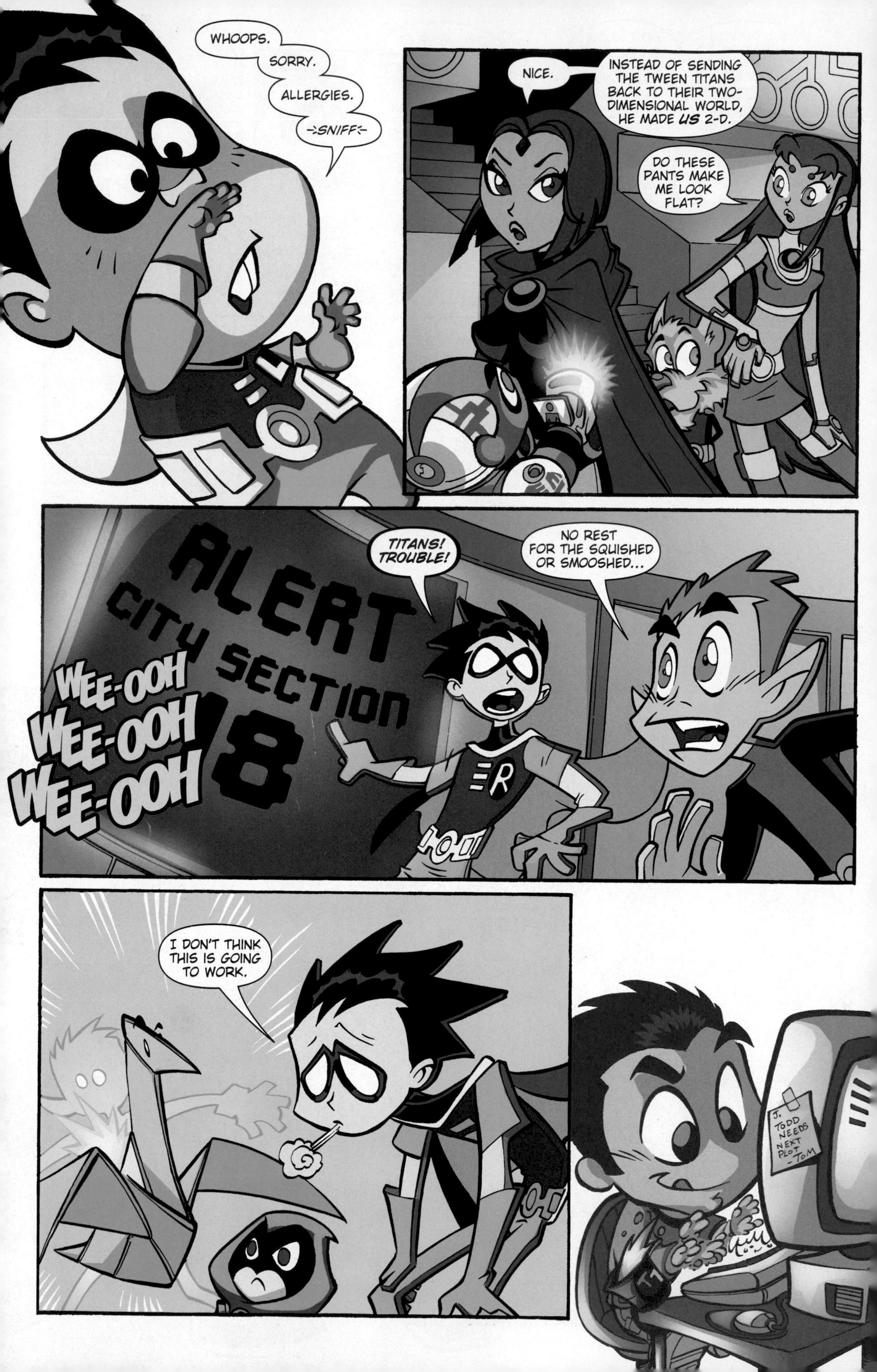

WHOOPS.
SORRY.
ALLERGIES.
-SNIFF-
NICE.
INSTEAD OF SENDING THE TWEEN TITANS BACK TO THEIR TWO-DIMENSIONAL WORLD, HE MADE US 2-D.
DO THESE PANTS MAKE ME LOOK FLAT?
ALERT CITY SECTION 8
WEE-OOH WEE-OOH WEE-OOH
TITANS! TROUBLE!
NO REST FOR THE SQUISHED OR SMOOSHED...
I DON'T THINK THIS IS GOING TO WORK.
J. TODD NEEDS NEXT PLOT -TOM

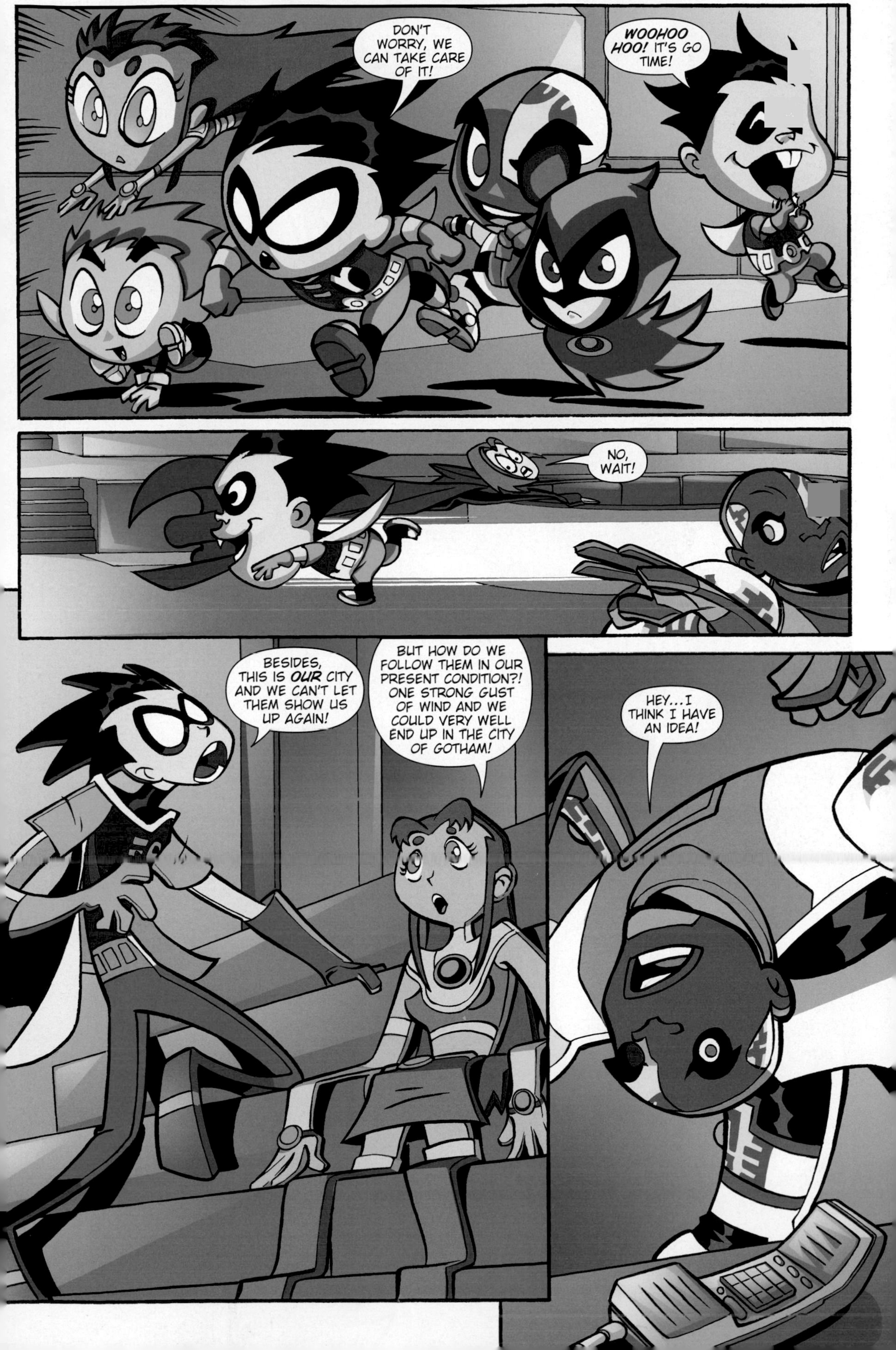
DON'T WORRY, WE CAN TAKE CARE OF IT!
WOOHOO HOO! IT'S GO TIME!
NO, WAIT!
BESIDES, THIS IS OUR CITY AND WE CAN'T LET THEM SHOW US UP AGAIN!
BUT HOW DO WE FOLLOW THEM IN OUR PRESENT CONDITION?! ONE STRONG GUST OF WIND AND WE COULD VERY WELL END UP IN THE CITY OF GOTHAM!
HEY...I THINK I HAVE AN IDEA!

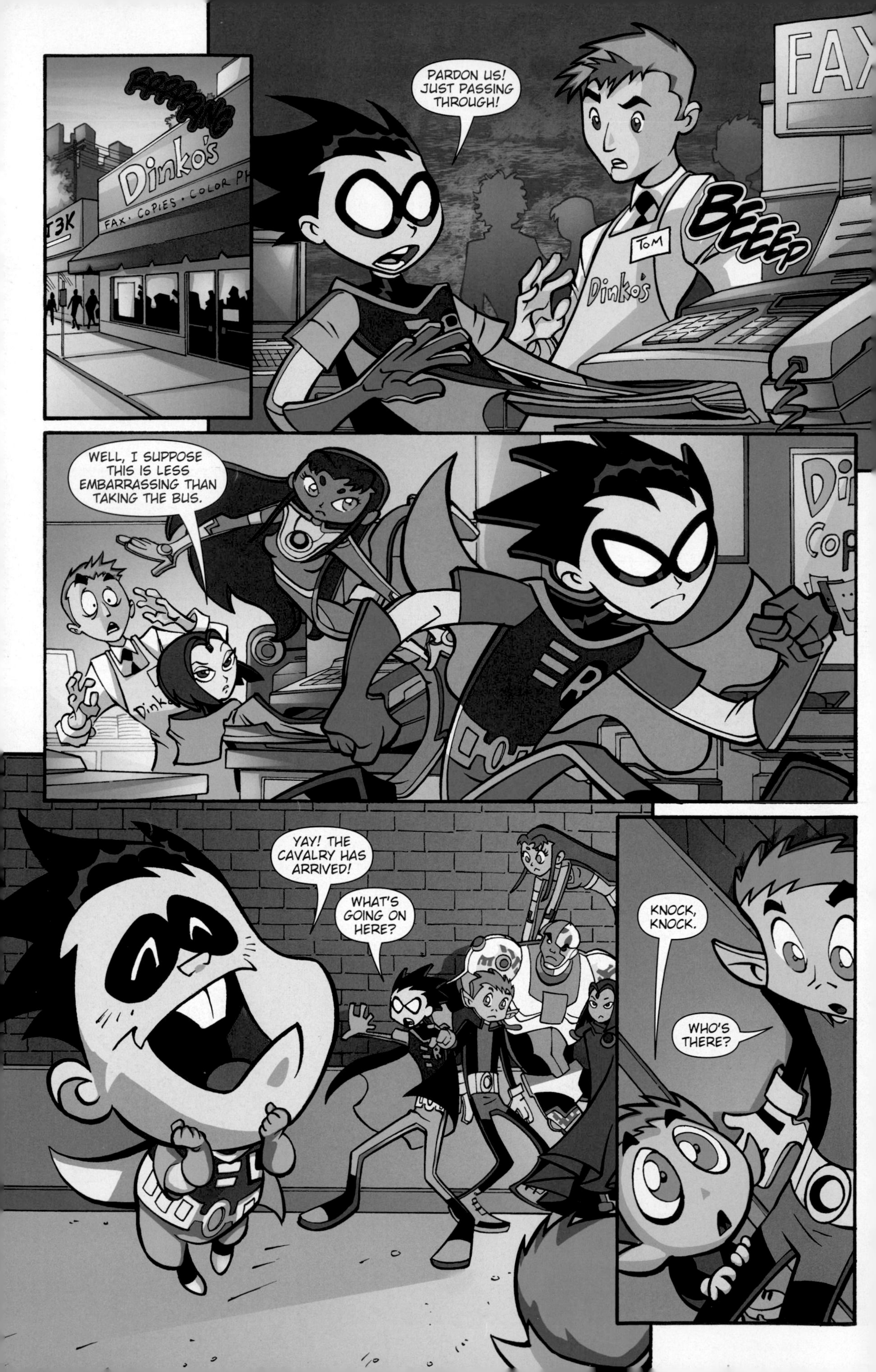

FRRRANG
Dinko's
FAX • COPIES • COLOR PH
T3K
PARDON US! JUST PASSING THROUGH!
FAX
TOM
Dinko's
BEEEEP
WELL, I SUPPOSE THIS IS LESS EMBARRASSING THAN TAKING THE BUS.
Dinko's
YAY! THE CAVALRY HAS ARRIVED!
WHAT'S GOING ON HERE?
KNOCK, KNOCK.
WHO'S THERE?

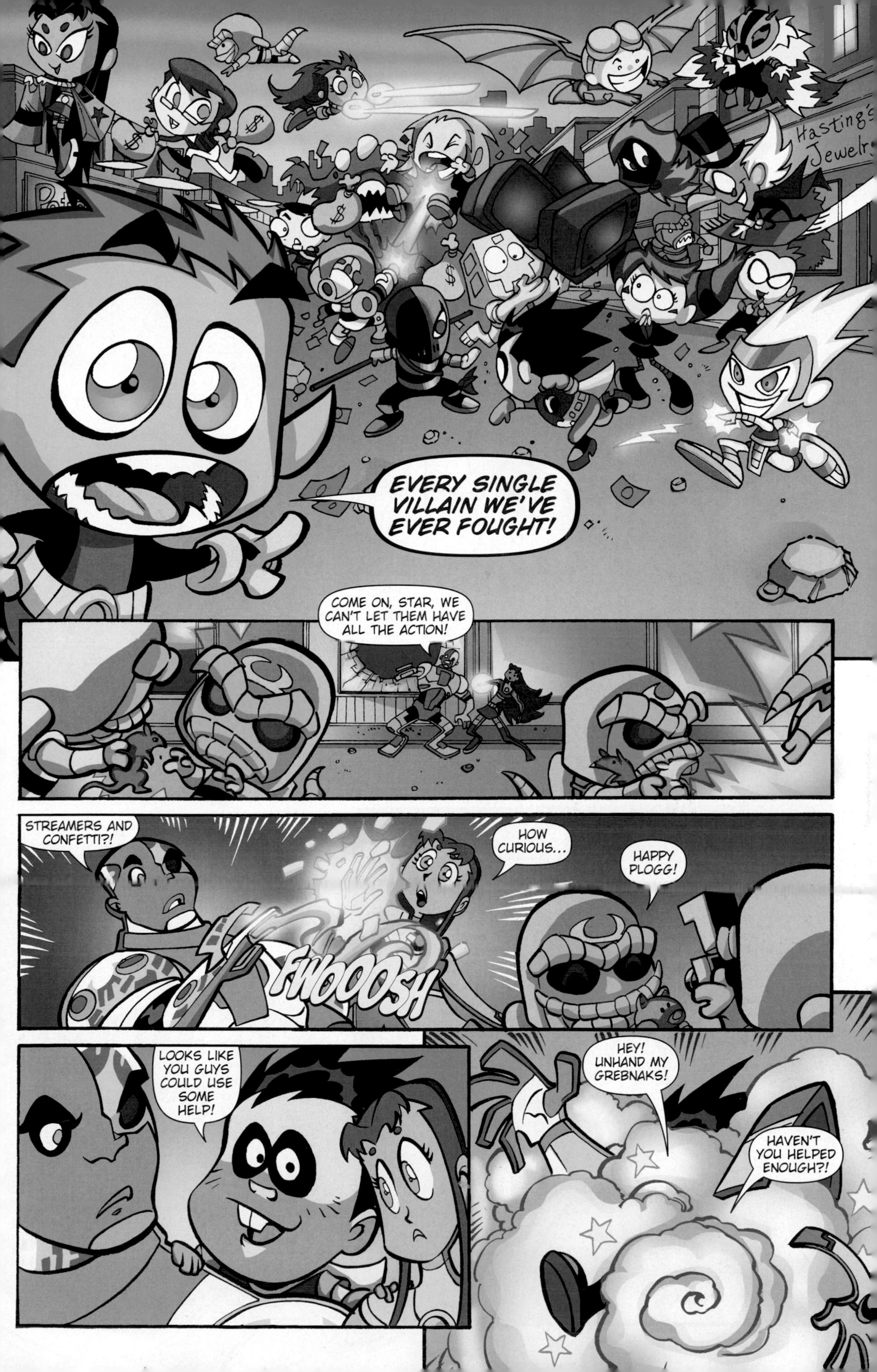
Hasting's Jewelry
EVERY SINGLE VILLAIN WE'VE EVER FOUGHT!
COME ON, STAR, WE CAN'T LET THEM HAVE ALL THE ACTION!
STREAMERS AND CONFETTI?!
HOW CURIOUS...
HAPPY PLOGG!
FWOOOSH
LOOKS LIKE YOU GUYS COULD USE SOME HELP!
HEY! UNHAND MY GREBNAKS!
HAVEN'T YOU HELPED ENOUGH?!

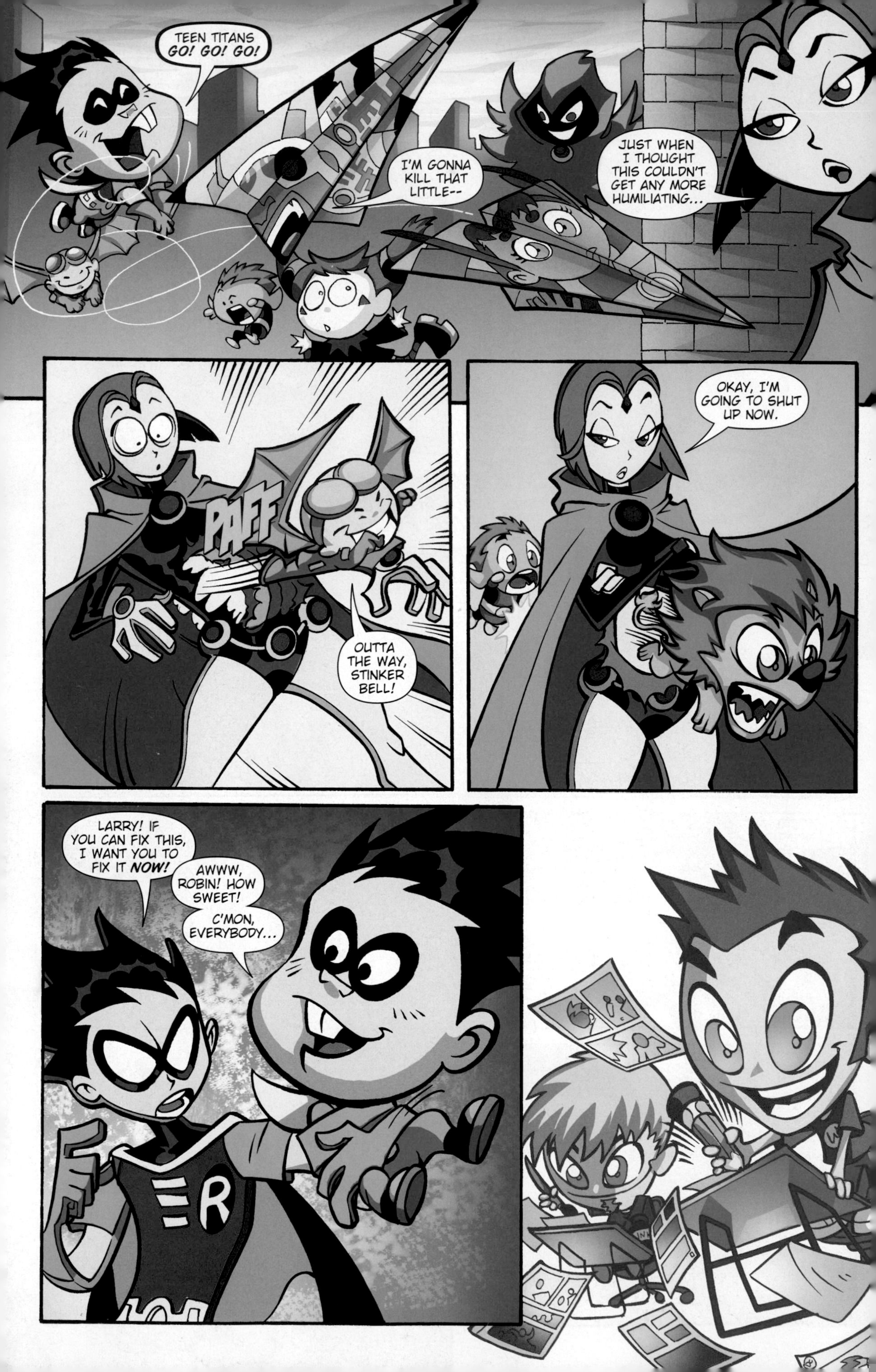

TEEN TITANS GO! GO! GO!
I'M GONNA KILL THAT LITTLE--
JUST WHEN I THOUGHT THIS COULDN'T GET ANY MORE HUMILIATING...
PAFF
OUTTA THE WAY, STINKER BELL!
OKAY, I'M GOING TO SHUT UP NOW.
LARRY! IF YOU CAN FIX THIS, I WANT YOU TO FIX IT NOW!
AWWW, ROBIN! HOW SWEET!
C'MON, EVERYBODY...

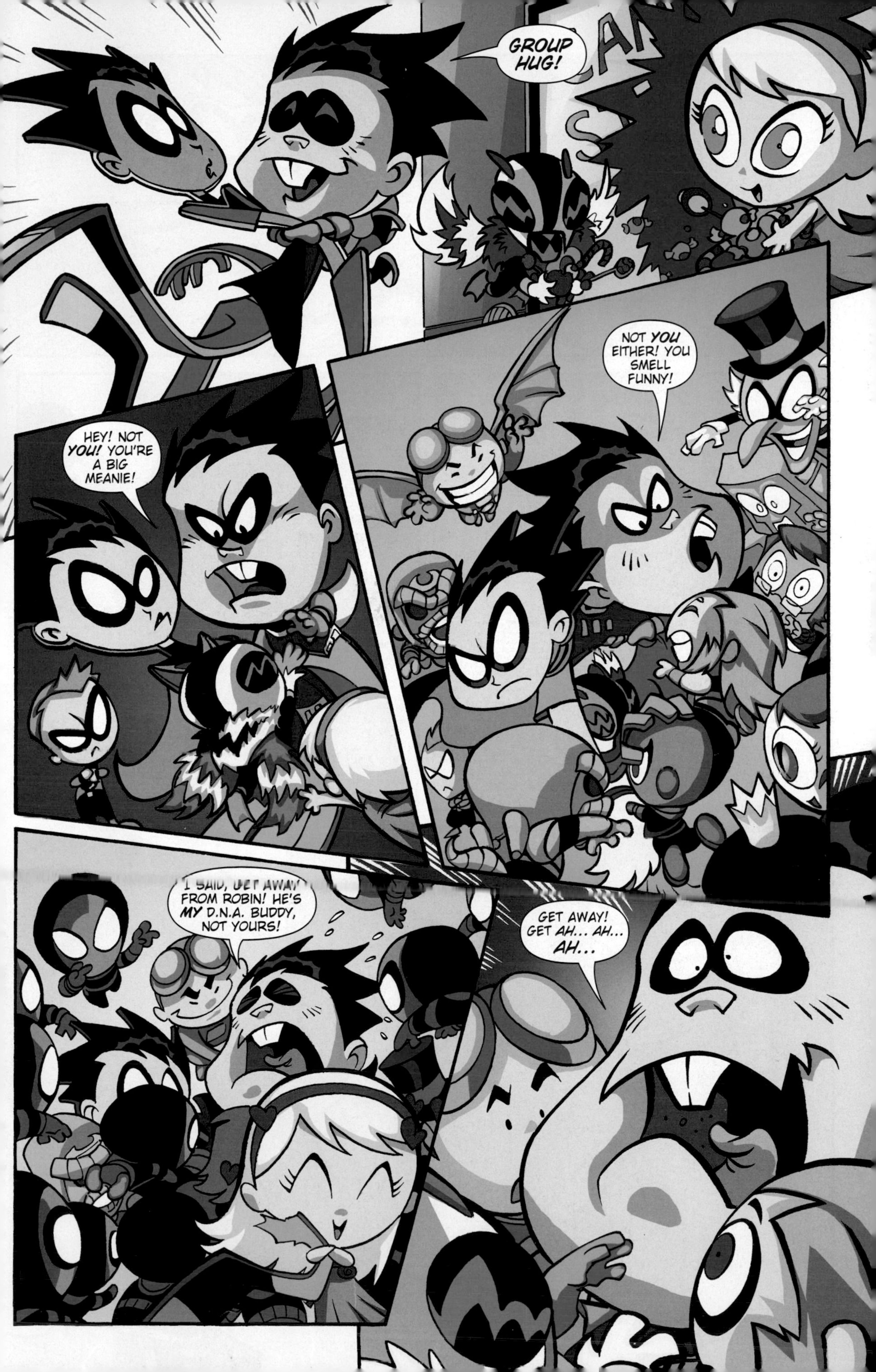
GROUP HUG!
HEY! NOT YOU! YOU'RE A BIG MEANIE!
NOT YOU EITHER! YOU SMELL FUNNY!
I SAID, GET AWAY FROM ROBIN! HE'S MY D.N.A. BUDDY, NOT YOURS!
GET AWAY! GET AH... AH... AH...

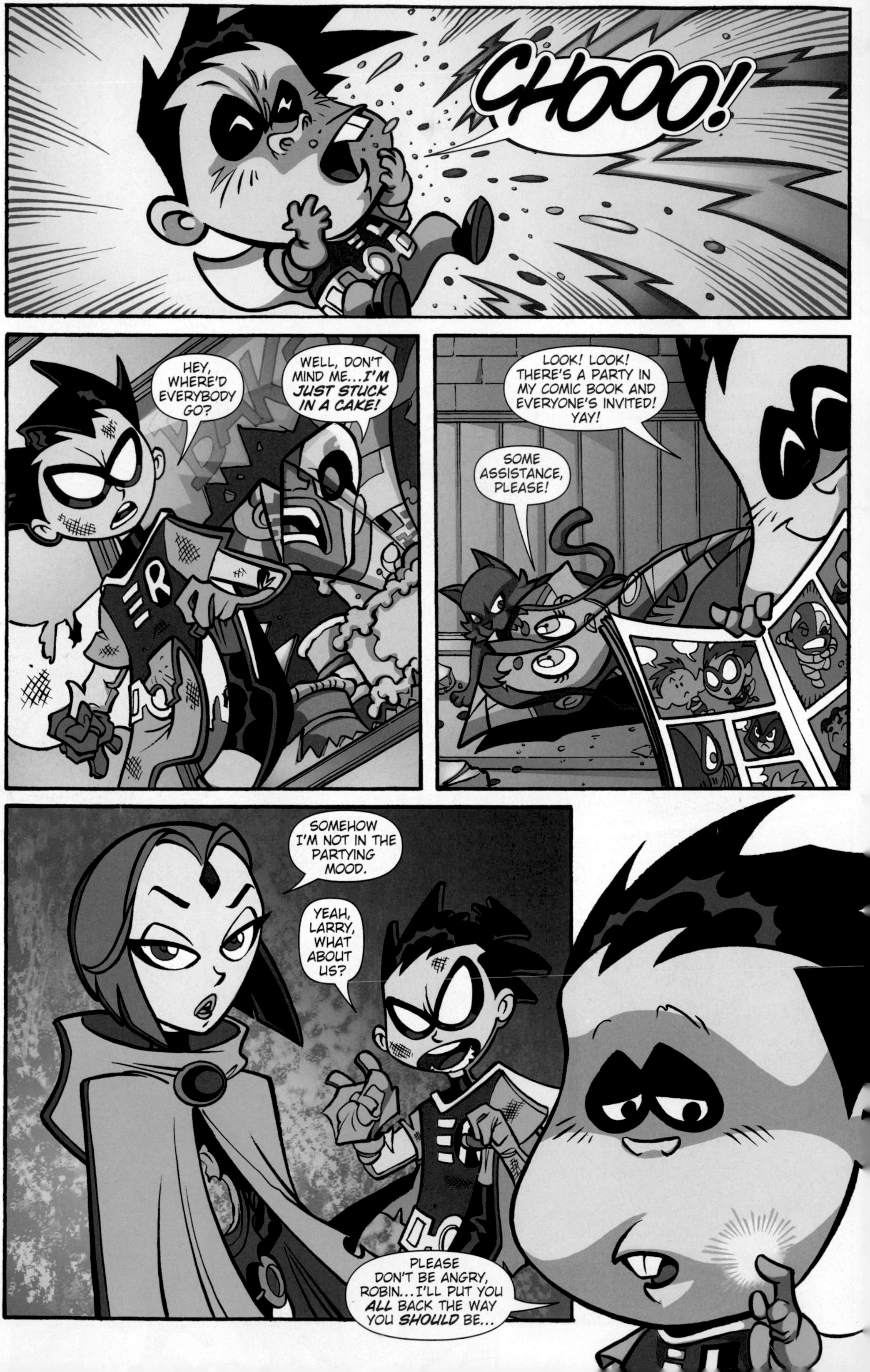
CHOOO!
HEY, WHERE'D EVERYBODY GO?
WELL, DON'T MIND ME...*I'M JUST STUCK IN A CAKE!*
LOOK! LOOK! THERE'S A PARTY IN MY COMIC BOOK AND EVERYONE'S INVITED! YAY!
SOME ASSISTANCE, PLEASE!
SOMEHOW I'M NOT IN THE PARTYING MOOD.
YEAH, LARRY, WHAT ABOUT US?
PLEASE DON'T BE ANGRY, ROBIN...I'LL PUT YOU *ALL* BACK THE WAY YOU *SHOULD* BE...

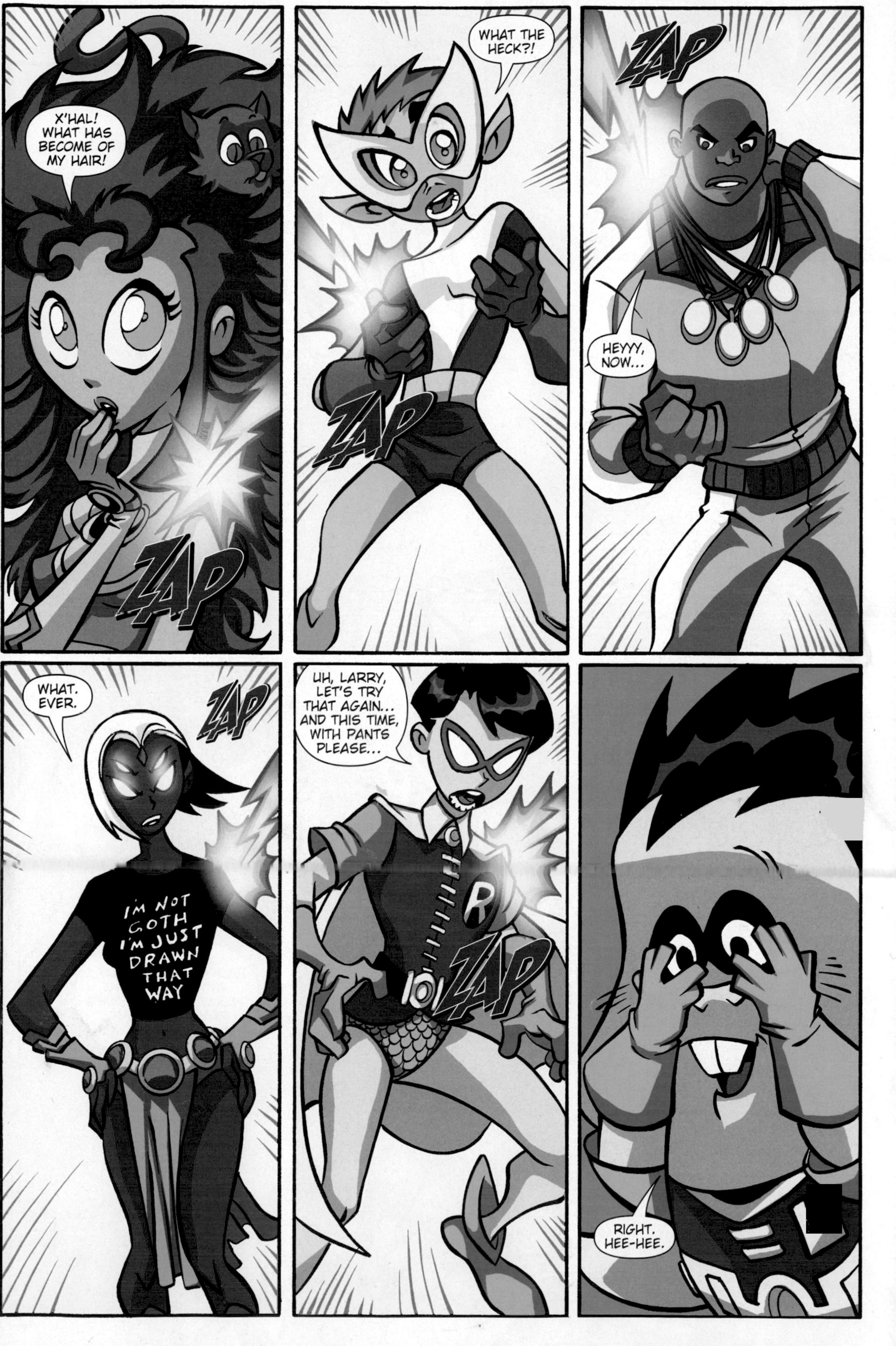
X'HAL! WHAT HAS BECOME OF MY HAIR!
ZAP
WHAT THE HECK?!
ZAP
ZAP
HEYYY, NOW...
WHAT. EVER.
ZAP
I'M NOT GOTH I'M JUST DRAWN THAT WAY
UH, LARRY, LET'S TRY THAT AGAIN... AND THIS TIME, WITH PANTS PLEASE...
ZAP
R
RIGHT. HEE-HEE.

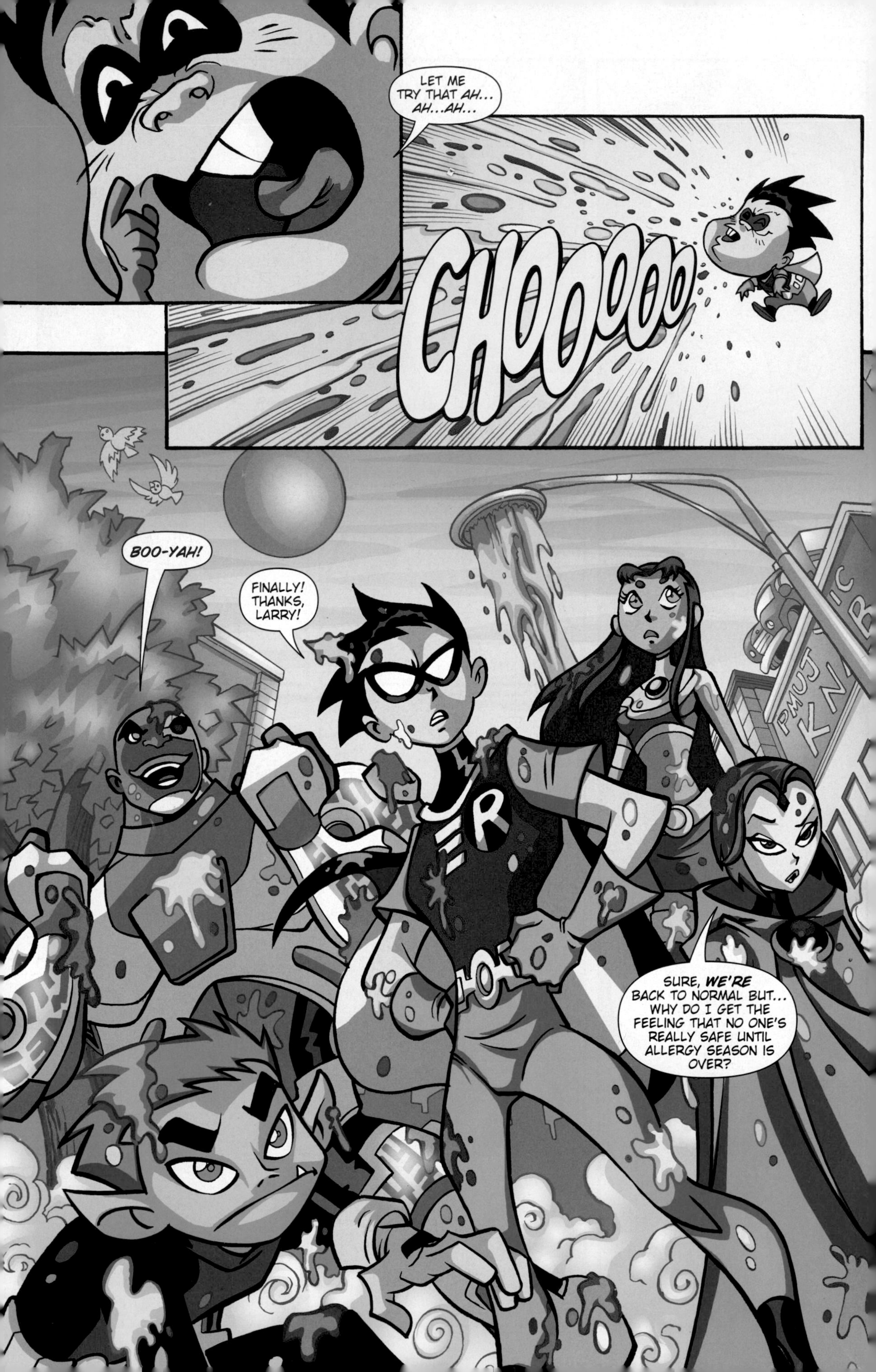
LET ME TRY THAT AH... AH...AH...
CHOOOOOO
BOO-YAH!
FINALLY! THANKS, LARRY!
SURE, WE'RE BACK TO NORMAL BUT... WHY DO I GET THE FEELING THAT NO ONE'S REALLY SAFE UNTIL ALLERGY SEASON IS OVER?

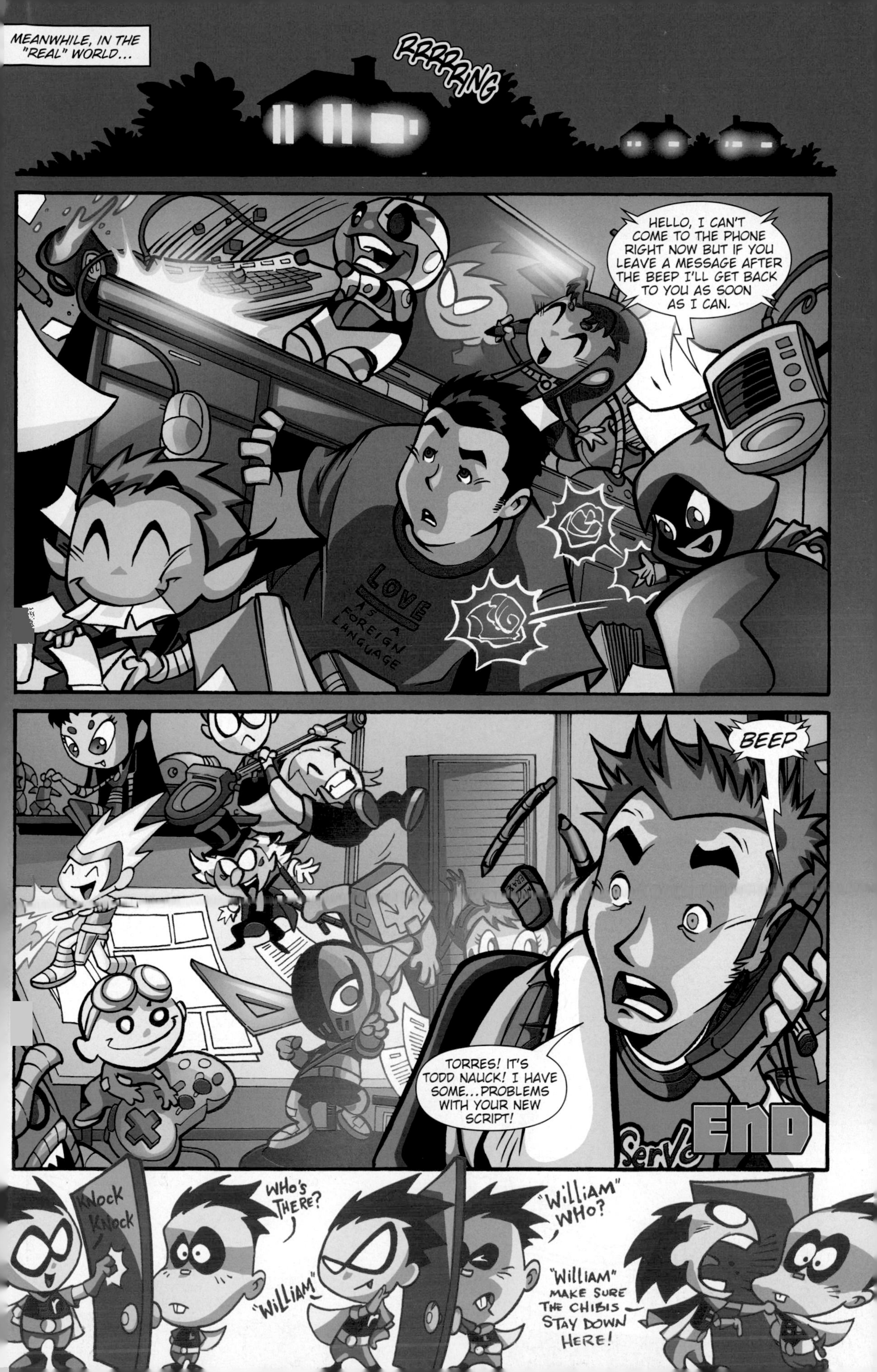
MEANWHILE, IN THE "REAL" WORLD...
RRRRRING
HELLO, I CAN'T COME TO THE PHONE RIGHT NOW BUT IF YOU LEAVE A MESSAGE AFTER THE BEEP I'LL GET BACK TO YOU AS SOON AS I CAN.
LOVE AS A FOREIGN LANGUAGE
BEEP
TORRES! IT'S TODD NAUCK! I HAVE SOME...PROBLEMS WITH YOUR NEW SCRIPT!
END
KNOCK KNOCK
WHO'S THERE?
"WILLIAM"
"WILLIAM" WHO?
"WILLIAM" MAKE SURE THE CHIBIS STAY DOWN HERE!

COLOR TEEN TITANS™

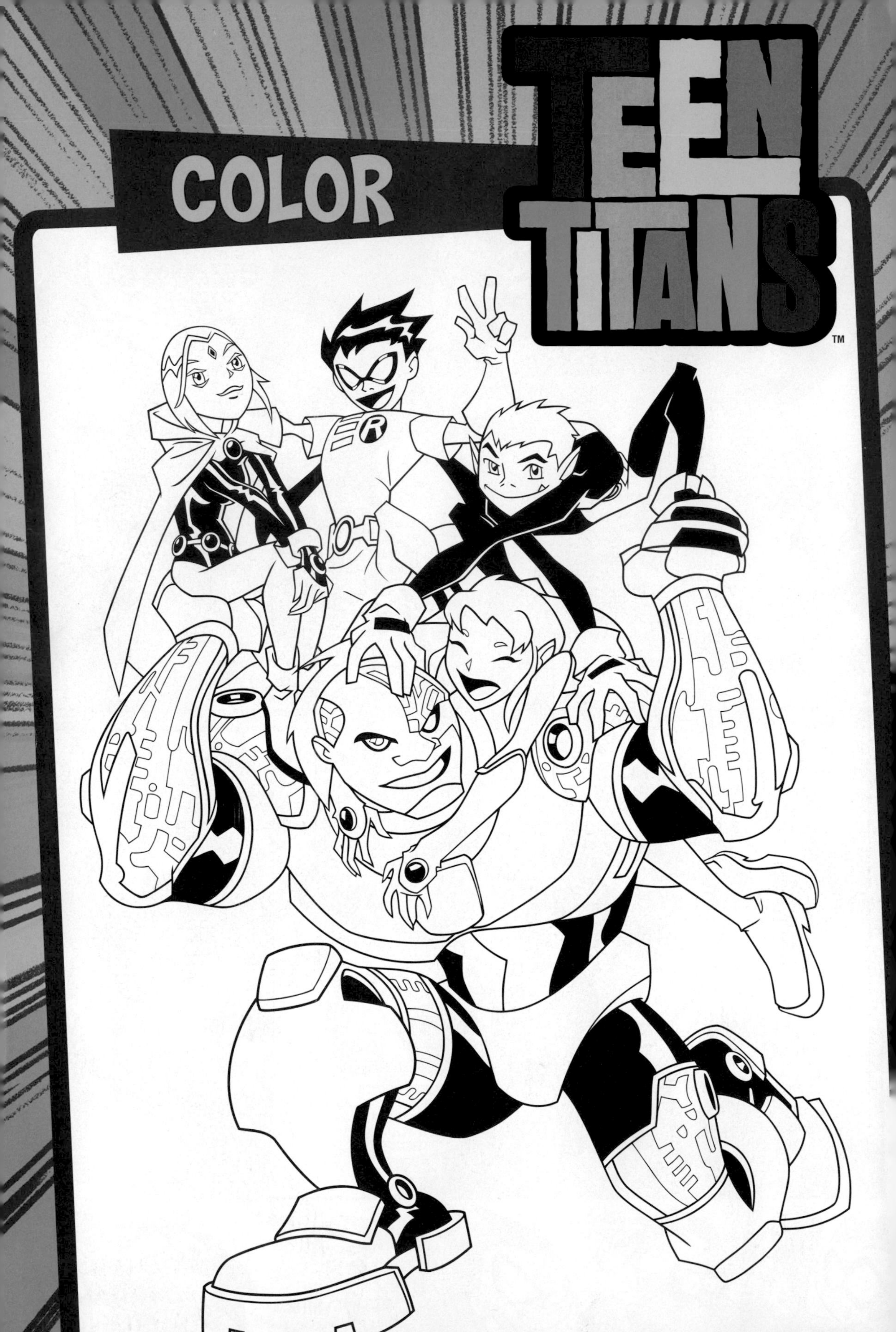

TEEN TITANS™

MATCH

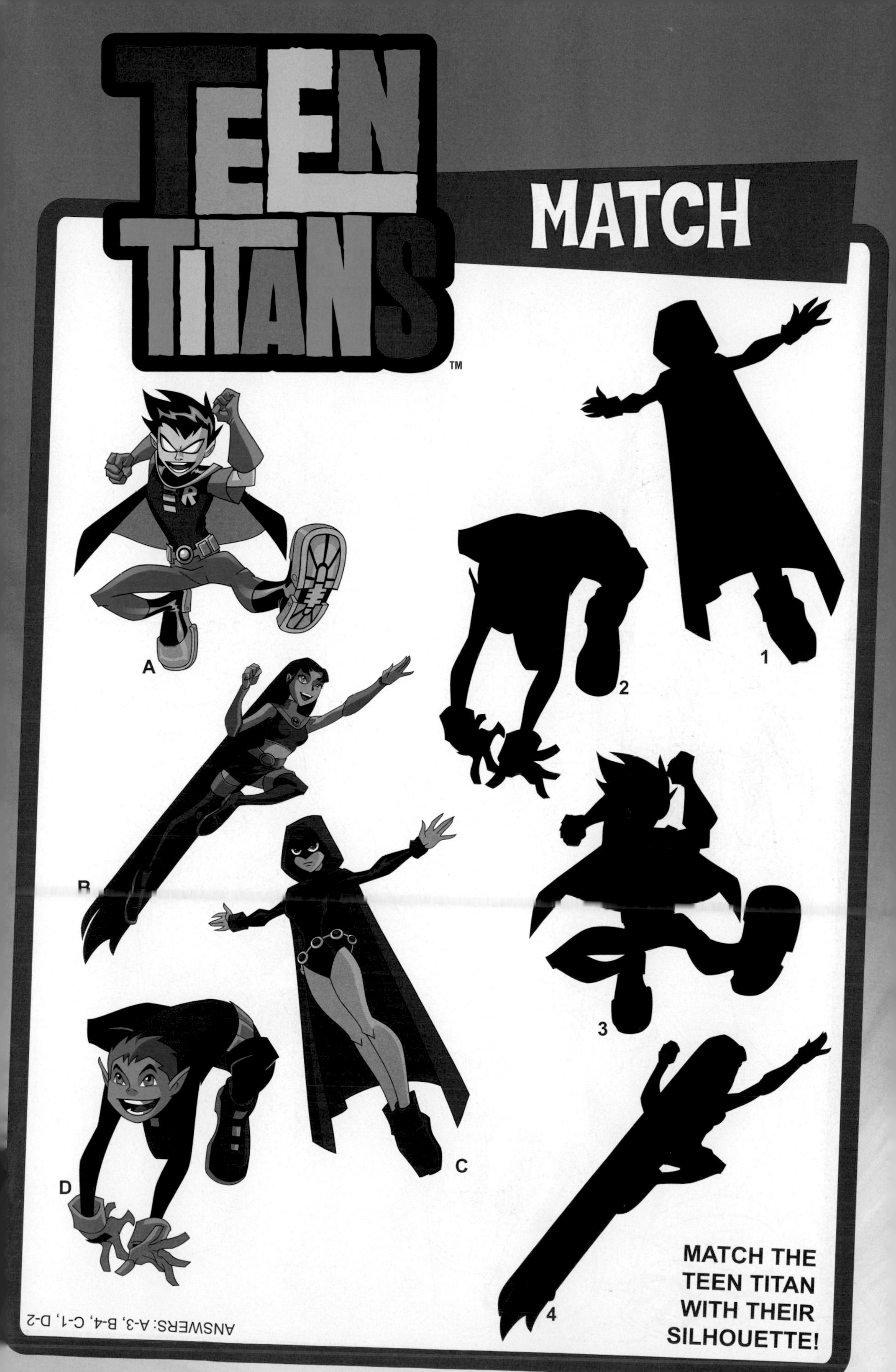

A
B
C
D
1
2
3
4

MATCH THE TEEN TITAN WITH THEIR SILHOUETTE!

ANSWERS: A-3, B-4, C-1, D-2

COLOR TEEN TITANS™

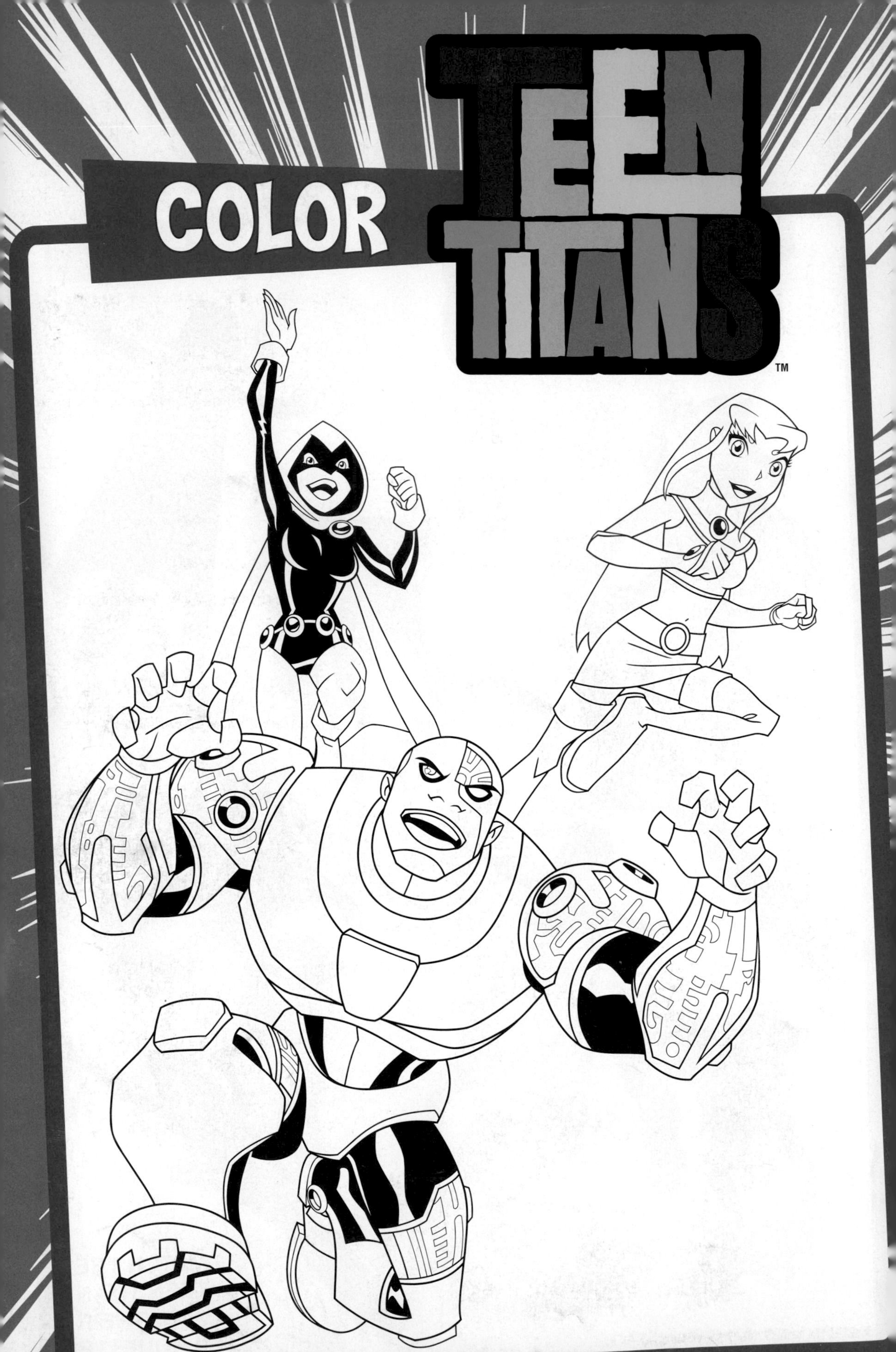

TEEN TITANS™

MATCH

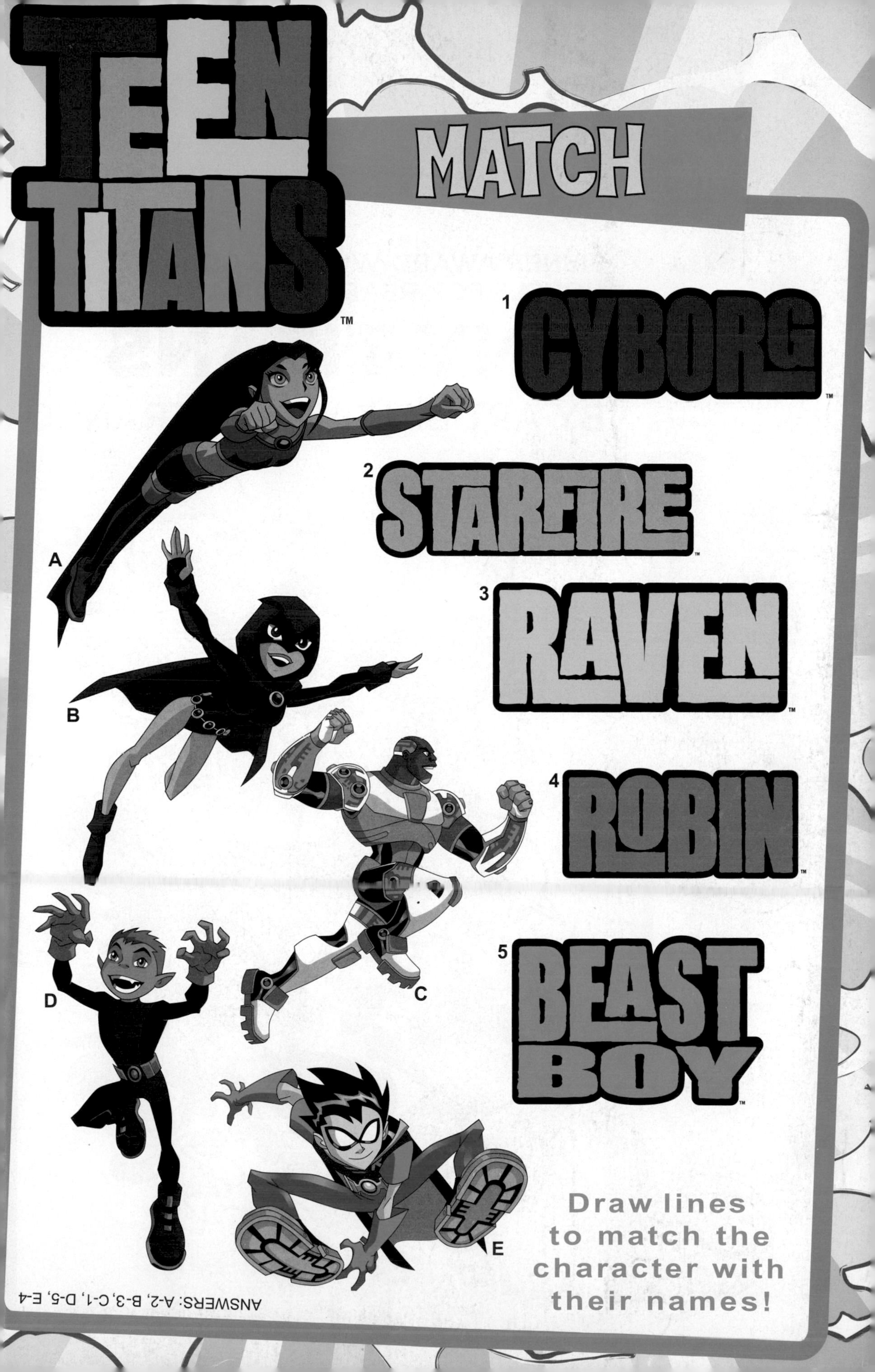
A
B
C
D
E

1 CYBORG™

2 STARFIRE™

3 RAVEN™

4 ROBIN™

5 BEAST BOY™

Draw lines to match the character with their names!

ANSWERS: A-2, B-3, C-1, D-5, E-4